THE
DELTA
SISTERS

ALSO BY KAYLA PERRIN

The Sisters of Theta Phi Kappa

THE
DELTA
SISTERS

Kayla Perrin

St. Martin's Press ❧ New York

ISBN 0-312-30088-3

For mothers and daughters everywhere:
Through ups and downs,
through laughter and tears,
the bond that connects us remains
forever strong.

For my own mother:
Your love has made me a better person.
Thanks for being my biggest supporter!

And finally, for my precious baby girl:
Every day I watch you grow,
I am amazed at the wonder of life.
And when you smile at me—
Ah!
It doesn't get better than that.
I hope to enrich your life
the way my mother did mine.

ACKNOWLEDGMENTS

Writing this book was a labor of love, one I couldn't have achieved without the help of many people. I'd like to acknowledge some of you now. For those I've forgotten, please forgive me!

First, Alisa Kwitney—not only are you a talented author, you are a seventies god! How you have all that great seventies info stored in your brain that you can recite at the drop of a hat, I don't know, and I don't care. The info you gave me helped me color this story, and I thank you for that. Also, thank you for steering me in the right direction regarding voodoo. Any mistakes in this work are my own.

Melinda Jones-McGowan, my dear, dear friend—have I thanked you for falling for a guy in New Orleans? Now that you live there, it came in handy not only to pick your brain regarding the city, but to enlist you to give me a personal tour. Thanks so much! And thanks also for those delicious daiquiris.

Thanks also to Escalante Lundy, a native of New Orleans, for information on the history of the city and its neighborhoods.

I wish to also thank another talented author friend, Deborah (a.k.a. Sabrina Jeffries). I appreciate your patience for all my New Orleans questions! Thanks for steering me onto Marie Goodwin, New Orleans historian and author. Marie, your help regarding the Creole heritage was limitless and extremely helpful to me.

Again, if I've forgotten anyone, forgive me.

THEN

PROLOGUE

Lafayette, Louisiana

Spring 1953

She ran.

She ran as fast as she could, as far as her legs would take her, not daring to stop.

Not daring to look back.

Because if she looked back . . .

Oh, God.

Let it be a dream, she told herself, brushing hot tears from her face. *Please, God. Let it be a dream.*

Not just a dream. A nightmare. One she wished were finally over.

Because what she had done was too horrible to think about. Too horrible to carry with her for years to come.

Don't look back. Keep going. Don't stop.

As she rounded the corner near the water's edge, one leg slid too far forward. She flailed her arms as she lost her balance and barely managed to keep from falling. She'd been running too fast. Not thinking.

She didn't want to think. Didn't want to remember.

Her head whipped around at a sound in the brush. Was someone coming?

She started off again, deciding to hug the perimeter of the water. If they were looking for her, they would expect her to take the most direct route back to her house.

The grass was tall and thick near the water's edge, and she held up her bloodied skirt as she trudged through the underbrush. Her toes sank into mud and slime and other things she couldn't identify. She felt a moment of horror. What other creatures were out here? Would a snake wrap itself around her ankle, inject venom into her bloodstream? Would she die here, alone and unforgiven?

A moan clawed at her throat. If that was her fate, then so be it. She deserved it for what she had done.

"Make me forget, Lord," she whispered in a raspy voice. "Oh, Lord. Forgive me!"

Her throat stung from the effort to speak. She'd gone hoarse from the screaming. Concentrating on the task of breathing, she glanced over her shoulder. She could no longer see Miss Clara's carriage house. Her own backyard was just beyond the thicket of trees.

She moved from the water's edge, picking up her pace as she stepped out of the brush. Her bare feet stomped on the thick, moist grass, and twice she slipped and almost fell.

She heard her name on a whisper of wind. The sound was almost lulling in the quiet night, tempting her to stop.

But she didn't.

Don't stop. Don't stop. Lord forgive me.

Her foot hit a rock. Pain shot through her big toe, continued through her foot and then up her leg. Damn, it felt as if her toe had split in two. She took another step forward, crying out as she did. It hurt to move, but she had to keep going. She started off again, but her knees buckled, and she stumbled. She fell to the ground in a heap.

Tears of frustration poured from her eyes. If only she could stay right there and die.

There was her name again, louder this time.

Don't stop. Keep moving. Lord forgive me.

Digging her fingers into the moist grass and dirt, she heaved herself up and started running.

But where was she going? Back to her house? How could she ever return there?

Helplessly she turned, wondering what direction she should head in, where she should go. The bayou glimmered before her. Beneath the moon's rays, the water looked like liquid gold. It was a sight that had always given her comfort in the past, and it gave her a measure of comfort now.

She stepped forward and gripped the trunk of a sycamore tree. As she paused to rest her body against it, a thought struck her.

And grew.

Could she do it? She stared out at the bayou's vastness, momentarily mesmerized by its tranquility. And in that moment, she didn't think. She only acted on her pain and desperation, on the feeling of emptiness that filled her so completely.

Lifting her skirt, she charged full steam ahead, into the water.

Into a place that would offer peace and solace for what she had done.

CHAPTER ONE

The dirty little whore.

He watched her. Watched the way she moved, swaying her young hips back and forth with purpose as she sashayed through the bar. He watched her stop and chat with man after man, throwing her head back and laughing like she cared about everything they said. He watched her lean in close and whisper in their ears. Watched her hand trail down their arms. Watched her fingers linger on their shoulders or rest on their thighs.

It was a game, he knew. One she played well.

He turned away. Took a swig of his scotch. But as he heard her high-pitched laughter floating on the smoky air, he shifted on his barstool, angling himself to get a better look at her. His stomach clenched when he saw her sitting on the lap of a heavyset man, her arms draped around his neck. The bitch took the miniskirt to a new level, literally—one that barely covered her behind. He could practically see her crotch.

Christ.

He drew in a shaky breath, trying to keep his emotions under control. The fat man's hands were all over her. Their lips were moving, but he couldn't hear what they were saying.

It didn't matter. He knew women like her. Women who thought their looks and their charm would get them everything they wanted. He hated women like her. Loose women who gave their bodies to any man, yet pretended that you were the most special man in the world while they were with you.

He didn't believe for a minute that anything about her was genuine. Not the sexy smile she wore. Not the spark in her eyes. Not those damn eyelashes she was batting like she was the first woman ever to do so.

The bitch was selling a lie, and practically every guy here was buying it.

So why couldn't he take his eyes off her?

His gaze followed her everywhere she went. Disentangling herself from the fat man, she stood and started to make her way around the bar. What was she after? Money? A night of casual sex? He had already seen her get several drinks from various men. Her raucous laughter told him she was well on her way to being drunk.

She didn't stay with any one man long, and he knew she would get to him soon.

How would she play with him? Because he knew she would. This was all a game to her.

He could play the game as well. He would buy her a drink, take her for a spin on the dance floor.

And then . . .

He swallowed, the thought alone giving him an erection.

The erection bothered him. He didn't want to be affected by her. She wasn't worthy of him.

Yet he *was* affected. He was only a man, after all.

And she was a whore. Getting under a man's skin was what she did best.

She turned, and her eyes met his. He was about to look away when she smiled.

He smiled back.

She started toward him, her large breasts jiggling in her tube top. The damn thing looked like it could slip off with the simplest effort. Any guy here might grab at it as she walked by, and in an instant, she would be exposed. That's the way drunk men behaved.

Did she even care?

He didn't think so.

She splayed her fingers across her flat belly, then dragged them lower, toward her crotch. No doubt about it, she thought she was some sort of prize. Her smug expression said she knew it and that he would know it, too.

Throwing his head back, he downed the scotch, getting ready for her. It didn't matter what she wanted. He knew what she deserved . . .

CHAPTER TWO

The summer had been fairly uneventful, until the day Liza Monroe's body surfaced in Bayou St. John.

Liza had been missing for over a week, but everyone in mid-city New Orleans, where Olivia Grayson had been born and raised, hadn't thought much of it. Liza had often talked of leaving town for Los Angeles or New York, so when no one had seen her strutting her stuff in the neighborhood, that's what everyone had assumed she'd done. Cynthia, Liza's mother, had been frantic at Liza's disappearance, but no one had taken her seriously. It didn't surprise anyone that Cynthia knew nothing of Liza's dream to leave town; she and Liza were always fighting, and the rumor was that Cynthia couldn't control her only child—especially without a man around. But those who knew Liza, or had talked with her from time to time, knew of her dream to head to a place where the entertainment business thrived, because the word on the street was that she had a voice like silk and wanted to make something of herself.

That early July morning, however, it became clear that Liza had not left town for New York or Los Angeles. And if she had, she certainly hadn't made it.

Olivia hadn't known Liza personally—not really—but she knew of her. Everyone knew of her. In their mid-city neighborhood, like any other neighborhood, the fact that Liza was so well known was not a good thing. People didn't care about her beautiful voice, and they surely didn't sit around discussing her aspirations for stardom. What they did talk about, what interested them most, was how Liza Monroe spent her time on the streets.

Women whispered when she pranced down the tree-lined sidewalks with her head held high, as if she thought she was better than everyone else. Their mouths twisted in disapproving frowns, women gave Liza a slow once-over, checking her out from head to toe. Liza's hair was always done in the latest style, which, most recently, was a large Afro. Her nails were always neatly manicured, and she wore the type of clothes that models in *Ebony* magazine wore.

But while women talked about her, boys and men vied for her attention.

There was something intriguing about Liza, no matter what you thought about her. Something so intriguing that Olivia and her best friend, Belinda, had once been in awe of her. Liza looked so nice all the time. So classy. She drove around in fancy cars with men who looked sophisticated, and to Olivia and Belinda, it seemed that Liza lived a life right out of a Hollywood movie.

Of course, neither Olivia nor Belinda knew how Liza could afford to look so good all the time, considering Ms. Monroe worked as a waitress—hardly a good enough job to keep her daughter in the latest fashions. However Liza did it, Olivia and Belinda envied her. Not only her classy style but her independence. Liza did what she wanted, when she wanted to.

Olivia and Belinda figured their mothers ought to give them room to grow, let them do things on their own. So, one day, when Olivia's mother had told her that she couldn't go to the Mardi Gras celebration unescorted, Olivia had made the mistake of saying aloud that she wished her life had some excitement, like Liza Monroe's. That she was sure Liza's mother let her go to the parade by herself.

Sylvia Grayson hadn't hesitated before slapping Olivia across the face.

"Don't you ever say you want to be like that girl," her mother had warned, wagging an angry finger at her. "She's not class. She's trash. You hear me?"

"Yes, Mama," Olivia managed softly. The slap hadn't hurt as much as stunned her. Her mama never slapped her.

Sylvia's eyes widened in alarm. "You been hanging with that girl?"

"No, Mama."

"You stay away from her. You hear?"

"Yes, Mama."

"If she tries to get close to you, run the other way. You've got plenty of friends in your Jack and Jill social club. The right kind of friends. You don't need her type in your circle."

Olivia had only been fifteen at the time, the same age as Liza, but as she would soon learn, not nearly as experienced in the ways of the world as Liza was. Olivia hadn't understood all there was to know about the young girl who seemed to have it all. Hours after the slap, as Sylvia held her on the porch, rocking back and forth with her on the swing in the cool of the night, she explained those things.

Surprised at what her mother had told her, Olivia had then shared what she'd learned with Belinda.

"She's fast, and loose," Olivia told Belinda, amazement in her voice. "My mama thinks she's looking for a father figure, since she never had one, and that's why she's always with those older men."

Like Olivia, Belinda had been shocked.

For the next two years, Olivia and Belinda had watched Liza, but with different eyes. So much more made sense now. They realized why she was considered fast and wondered why they hadn't figured it out before. She was always nice to the men in the neighborhood, especially the ones who had some money. It didn't matter if he was a stranger or had lived his whole life in the area. Yet Liza had never forged a real friendship with any of the females.

Oh, she was a social butterfly, flitting around from one club to the next, always on the arm of a man twice her age. No one barred her entrance, even though she was a minor. She may have looked older than twenty-one, but everyone in the area knew she was underage. And while no one could prove it, the rumors said she took money and gifts for sex like a common whore.

"It's a damn shame," Olivia's mother would say on the occasions she saw Liza drive or walk by with some man. "A pretty girl like that allowed to run wild." Under her breath, Sylvia would always add that the apple didn't fall too far from the tree.

While the last comment always piqued Olivia's curiosity, she never asked her mother what she meant by it, and her mother never offered an explanation about Ms. Monroe. But it was clear that Sylvia didn't like Cynthia for some reason; nor did most anyone else in the neighborhood, as far as Olivia knew.

Whatever Ms. Monroe had done, all the adults knew about it, the way they always did in small communities where everyone seemed to know everyone else's business.

Olivia doubted anyone could keep a secret in this neighborhood.

News spread quickly here, like it had this morning. As fast as a flaming wildfire, the word had gotten around that a body had been found in the bayou. Within minutes of the medical examiner's arrival, people had run to the scene. Like so many others from the vicinity, Olivia now stood in the crowd, watching as the team of men pulled Liza from the water. Olivia couldn't see much, certainly not enough to convince her the body was Liza's. But she could hear Ms. Monroe hollering, and she caught glimpses of the distraught woman as she flailed her arms in the air and struggled with those who held her back from running to the body.

That was enough to convince Olivia of the body's identity.

Enough to make a cold chill slide down her back.

Dead. Liza was really dead. Olivia shivered.

There was so much activity at the front of the crowd. Olivia tipped on her toes to get a better look, but she was shoved from both left and right, and her efforts were pretty much futile. The police pushed people back, and as the crowd moved, Olivia saw only flashes of the gurney that carried Liza's now covered body from the scene.

Unable to see much else, Olivia scanned the faces in the crowd. An odd feeling came over her, a strange mix of melancholy and curiosity. How weird that so many people had left their homes to run to the scene, yet no one but Ms. Monroe was crying. Did anyone here care what had happened to Liza? Olivia doubted it. In fact, she'd heard one woman in the crowd say, "That girl had it coming."

Not even the men, who had enjoyed Liza's company in life, seemed to be torn up over her tragic death.

These people weren't here because they cared, but because they considered this the day's entertainment—and they weren't about to miss it. Sadly, Olivia had to agree that this was the biggest event that had happened all summer.

Olivia continued to survey the crowd, checking out those who were chatting in small groups. She knew practically everyone gathered here.

Hugging her torso, she turned in the other direction. Instantly, her eyes met and held someone else's. Her heart spasmed hard. The intense eyes that stared back at her belonged to a man.

He was a young man, maybe a few years older than she. His skin was the color of milk chocolate. He wore his black hair in a medium-sized Afro. She could see the handle of a blue hair pick protruding from the curly mane. The look said he was a bit of a rebel. She liked that.

He was attractive. *Very* attractive, she noted with increasing interest. She had never seen him before. Was this stranger new to the area, or was he simply passing through?

"Oh, Lawd!"

Olivia spun around to see Ms. Monroe throwing herself at the back of the medical examiner's vehicle, and for a moment, she couldn't tear her eyes from the strikingly beautiful woman. Even in her grief, she was stunning.

Her bottom lip quivering, Olivia once again turned, glancing back in the stranger's direction.

But he was gone.

CHAPTER THREE

Murder.

The word made goose bumps pop out on Olivia's skin, despite the humidity of the New Orleans summer day. Stopping before the gate outside her large colonial house, she took a long, wary look around. A few cars drove down the quiet tree-lined street. In the distance, she saw a group of young people walking and laughing.

It was the kind of scene she would expect to see in her neighborhood. Nothing out of the ordinary.

Yet something *was* out of the ordinary. A young woman had been murdered, quite possibly by someone she knew.

Olivia quickly opened the gate and hurried to the front door of her house. Until she'd heard the startled whispers in the crowd, she hadn't realized that Liza had most likely died of unnatural causes.

She shook her head, a little annoyed with herself. She had such an imagination when it came to the stories she created, but she seemed unable to look at the big picture when dealing with real life. Why else would Liza's body be in the bayou if she hadn't been killed?

Murdered. The reality of the situation swept over her, and she once again felt cold.

Olivia placed her hand on the doorknob, but before she could turn it, the door opened. She jumped backward with fright.

Edward Haughton, the houseman, greeted her with a smile and a nod.

"Oh. Hello, Edward." She breathed in deeply, relieved. Who had she expected to see? A man with an axe? She must have been spooked on account of what she'd learned. "You startled me."

"Sorry."

"No problem," Olivia replied, waving off his apology.

"Your mother is in the sunroom. She said she wanted to see you the moment you returned."

"Oh, all right." Olivia could only assume that her mother wanted to see her to get the news regarding Liza.

Edward wiped at the beads of sweat dotting his forehead with a white handkerchief. It didn't matter how hot the day, he always dressed in a uniform that consisted of a long-sleeved white shirt, black pants, and a black bow tie. More often than not, he also wore a matching black blazer. No doubt, Olivia's mother preferred he dress that way.

She watched Edward walk off in the direction of the kitchen. He had been around for as long as she could remember, since before her father had died. Most likely he would be here until he retired, became too ill to work, or passed away. Even if they were ever in a financial bind—which was highly unlikely—Olivia doubted that her mother would let Edward go. Appearances were important to Sylvia Grayson, which meant she would keep Edward, no matter the cost.

But not only that, her mother truly cared for him.

Having met him at a church outreach drive to help the less fortunate, Sylvia had taken a special interest in Edward. He had fallen on hard times emotionally after losing his entire family in a tragic house fire. For two months after the accident, Edward hadn't worked. Instead, he had found solace in hard liquor. With no other family, he hadn't had anyone else to turn to. Having lost everything, he had stayed in shelters for a temporary roof over his head.

All that changed once he met Sylvia. There was something about Edward—perhaps the fact that he had given up on his dream of law to provide for his young family—that had drawn Sylvia to him. She had helped him out with a financial donation as long as he promised to put it to good use. She had been hoping he would go back to school, but he had used the money to get back on his feet. All the while, Sylvia and Edward had stayed in touch; they'd become friends. Right around the time that Edward had been fired from his second menial job, the Graysons' houseman had quit. So, needing a new houseman, Sylvia had offered Edward the position.

Her mother didn't have to say it, but Olivia knew she had a soft spot toward Edward because he resembled Sylvia's late father.

While Sylvia didn't talk much about her family, she had told Olivia on more than one occasion that it was her father she had been closest to. Unlike her mother, her father had made sure to stay in touch with her after she married a man the family had disapproved of. As far as Sylvia's mother had been concerned, Samuel Grayson didn't come from the right social circles, and she would never accept him. The Etiennes were one of the old-money elite black families in Louisiana. The position had been hard-won after slavery, with Joseph Etienne, a freed slave, building a rice farm into a successful enterprise. As far as the family was concerned, their hard work was not only to better themselves, but for the benefit of future generations. As such, they affiliated with those in a similar economic position, through their church and the social clubs they belonged to. They expected the same from their children. Sylvia should have married a doctor or lawyer, not a jazz musician who had grown up in the streets of New Orleans. Hazel Etienne had seen the act as unforgivable and had practically written her off.

But Marcel Etienne had stayed in touch with his daughter, and when he had died, twenty years earlier, he had left Sylvia a small fortune from the rice farm in Lafayette he had sold before retiring. With careful investments, that money had grown into a huge fortune. Olivia's father, the legendary jazz musician Samuel "Silver Touch" Grayson, had left them some money when he died, but that alone wouldn't have been enough to keep them living the life of luxury that Sylvia had been accustomed to.

Heading to the right, Olivia took the shortcut through the large living and dining rooms, which would take her to the sunroom at the back of the house.

The sound of Sylvia's laughter, and another woman's, filled the air as Olivia approached. When she rounded the corner into the brightly lit room, Rosa bounded toward her, startling her. A bichon frise, Rosa was white with a fluffy coat of curly hair. The small dog barked happily at Olivia's feet, and she bent to rub her head and scratch behind her ears. Satisfied, Rosa turned and pranced back into the sunroom and hopped onto Sylvia's lap.

Sylvia sat on the wicker sofa with Miss Della Avery, one of her sorority sisters. Her mother not only had continued to be active in the graduate chapter of her sorority, she was currently that chapter's president.

Two sets of curious eyes met Olivia's. "Hello, Miss Avery," Olivia said, extending a formal greeting, as she'd been raised to do, even though she knew the question that was on their tongues. Olivia bent to kiss her mother on the cheek. "Hello, Mama."

"Hello, baby," Sylvia replied. Then, "Was it her?"

Olivia nodded grimly. "Yeah."

"Oh, my Lord." Sylvia's hand flew to her chest. "Her body in the bayou . . . what on earth happened to that poor girl?"

"They're saying . . ." Olivia drew in a shaky breath. It was so hard to verbalize, much less believe. "They're saying it was murder."

"Murder?" Della's voice was a horrified whisper.

Olivia nodded.

"They're sure?" Della asked.

"It seems so. And I guess it makes sense. Considering where she was found."

"That's a damn shame." Della made a face. Her long, pressed hair swayed as she shook her head. "A girl so young . . ."

"Allowed to run wild," Sylvia contributed, as if that explained everything. "I'm not trying to speak ill of the dead, but I've said it once; I've said it a thousand times. That girl wasn't raised right."

"No matter the circumstance, it's a shame." Della faced Olivia. "Do they have any idea who did it?"

Olivia shook her head. "Not that I heard." She was certain, however, that the rumor mill was already churning. By later today, there would no doubt be many tall tales of how Liza had been killed. Maybe it was a natural thing she had such an imagination, given where she lived.

"I was praying that Liza had run away," Sylvia said. "Or at worst, that this would be a case like what happened with Patty Hearst last year. Being brainwashed by some crazy people. But this?"

"None of us wanted this," Della commented.

"Neighborhood's just not the same as it used to be, Della," Sylvia said, sighing sadly. "All kinds of new people coming in."

"I've told you for years, you ought to move downtown."

What Della didn't explicitly say was that downtown was where the elite blacks lived, and Sylvia ought to live there as well. Among her own kind.

Sylvia waved a dismissive hand. "Moving is such a loathsome task. Besides, I love it here. And so does Rosa." Sylvia stroked the dog's thick fur. "Don't you?"

Rosa barked what seemed to be an agreement.

Olivia had heard the "Why don't you move downtown?" question before, and she knew that her mother felt more comfortable in this neighborhood. Here, people hadn't looked down their noses at her father. Not that all the upper-class blacks did, but there were enough of them who had felt the way Hazel Etienne had. Those people would never accept Samuel Grayson as an equal, no matter how much money he had made.

"And truth be told," Sylvia continued, "anybody could have done this to Liza."

"That's true," Della agreed. "Much as we want to believe no one we know could ever be responsible, sometimes it's those closest to us who commit the worst crimes. Like Douglas Panton. People are still talking about how he butchered his wife, even though that happened nearly ten years ago."

Sylvia visibly shuddered. "I know. Who would have expected such behavior from a well-respected judge? Poor Doreen. I still miss her."

"So do I." *Tsk*ing softly, Della pushed her chair back and stood. "I should be going."

"Oh?" Sylvia stood as well, cradling Rosa as if she were a baby. "You sure I can't tempt you with another glass of lemonade?"

"No, I must be off. Gerald will be home shortly, and you know how much that man appreciates a hot meal." Della turned and gave Olivia a smile. "Olivia, it is always a pleasure to see you." She cupped her cheek. "Every time I look at you, I see your father. The older you get, the more you look like him. Such a shame he passed so young."

A sad sound escaped Sylvia. "I know." She moved toward Olivia and placed a hand around her waist. "We're all each other has."

"Like poor Cynthia. Liza was all she had. It's just so awful."

"True." Sylvia glanced down at Olivia. "The difference is, of course, that I was married. I know who Olivia's father is. Liza never knew her father. I'm sure that's what set her on her negative course in life. Cynthia's to blame for that," Sylvia added sourly.

"It's still sad. No matter what kind of life Cynthia led, it's got to be the worst thing to lose your only child." Della shuddered. "And to murder?"

Sylvia hugged Olivia tighter then, as though she didn't want to let her go, didn't want to contemplate the thought of losing her in such a horrible way. Olivia felt warm in her mother's embrace.

"I didn't want you to go there," Sylvia said to her. "I didn't want you to witness that. That's not the kind of thing you need to see."

"I couldn't really see anything," Olivia explained. "There were so many people."

"Hmm." Sylvia made a sound of distaste. Rosa squirmed, and Sylvia released her. When she landed on the ground, she gave her body a vigorous shake.

"Della," Sylvia said, "I'll make those calls about the charity auction, see where we can have the venue. I should know in a few days."

"Great. I'll get to work on those corporate sponsors for the scholarships."

"If you don't hear from me by Friday, call me."

Olivia quietly observed. As part of the Delta Gamma Psi sorority, her mother was always working on some function or another.

With Rosa at their heels, Sylvia walked Della to the door, both of them continuing to discuss whatever event they were planning. Being president of the sorority's graduate chapter, as well as the president of her own charity, was Sylvia's full-time job. Sylvia often said that because she had been raised with every comfort life had to offer—race aside—she wanted to give back to those who weren't as fortunate. Even racially, she had an advantage. Because of her Creole roots, Sylvia's skin was the lightest shade of brown, as if it had been barely kissed by the sun. High yellow, they called it. And she had good hair— long, brown, and naturally so soft, she didn't need to relax it. Among black folk, that meant she was blessed. That was another reason Sylvia's mother had practically disowned her when she married Samuel Grayson, a man whose skin was so dark it was almost blue-black.

Being the child of a high-yellow mother and a dark-as-midnight father, Olivia's skin was the shade of rich honey. Sometimes Belinda told her she was lucky—lucky that she hadn't been cursed with darker skin like Belinda had been. Olivia always dismissed Belinda's comments. She had never bought into the ideas about skin complexions. The way she saw it, white folks didn't care how black your skin was. If there was black blood flowing in your veins, you were beneath them, plain and simple.

Olivia's mind drifted from the trivial issue of skin color to something much more interesting—Cynthia Monroe. What kind of life had she led? Every time her mother mentioned the woman, she sounded upset. Disgusted, even. What was it that Olivia was too young to know? Would her mother ever tell her?

"So." At the sound of her mother's voice, Olivia whirled around. Sylvia strolled into the room. Her flip hairdo swayed gently as she moved. "There's no talk about who may have killed Liza?"

"No. Nothing. Not yet, anyway. I only know the police are gonna start asking questions."

Sylvia walked to the glass coffee table and reached for the pitcher of lemonade and her tumbler. Rosa followed her. Rosa may have been the family pet, but she favored Sylvia. She loved to sleep with Sylvia, sprawl herself out on Sylvia's lap, cuddle with her practically at all times. The dog fancied herself a baby.

"I certainly hope they catch this person soon. I won't feel safe as long as he's still roaming the streets. Lemonade?"

Olivia shook her head, then asked her mother, "Did Belinda call?" Belinda was the sister Olivia had never had. Their birthdays were exactly a month apart—with Belinda being the month older, as her birthday was in April, and Olivia's in May. They'd known each other since they were in diapers and had been the closest of friends since that time. They attended the same private school and had mostly been in the same classes over the years.

Now they were both excited about their upcoming senior year of high school, and especially excited about their coming-out cotillions. They could hardly wait for the next phase of their lives, which would start after they graduated. Like their mothers had done, they planned to attend Dillard University in neighboring Gentilly and cross over into Delta Gamma Psi sisterhood together.

"No, sweetheart. Belinda didn't call."

Olivia frowned. Why hadn't Belinda called yet? They'd spoken briefly this morning, discussing their trip to the French Quarter tomorrow. But that was it, and that was strange, because they spoke on the phone several times during the day.

Surely Belinda had heard about what had happened today. How come she hadn't called to discuss this major news? In fact, Olivia had been surprised when she hadn't seen Belinda in the crowd.

Still wondering about Belinda, Olivia said, "I'm going upstairs, Mama."

"All right. Be down in an hour for dinner."

"Yes, Mama."

Olivia scurried to the front of the house and the grand staircase. She ran up the stairs two at a time. Once in her bedroom, she picked up the phone and dialed Belinda's number.

No one answered.

CHAPTER FOUR

Gold floated from the sky on the rays of the moon, carried by the tiny droplets of moisture in the humid air. Olivia stood, her face upturned, looking up at the tiny gold specks, enjoying their feel as they landed on her skin.

She stood at the end of the sidewalk, before the small overpass. The trees hid her in the shadows, but she had a good view of Bayou St. John.

Olivia wasn't sure what had lured her back here, back to the spot where Liza's body had been found.

Maybe it was simple curiosity. How could she not be curious about what had happened here?

Olivia often thought that she pondered issues more than the average person, even more than Belinda. All evening, her mind had played out a million scenarios about what had happened to Liza. Finally, she'd known that she had to come back here to this spot. See what her intuition told her.

Olivia closed her eyes and wondered. *When was Liza killed? In the light, or in the darkness? Had she been killed right here, with someone holding her head in the bayou until she drowned? Or had she been murdered somewhere else and dumped here?*

Opening her eyes, Olivia wrapped her arms around her torso. How silly she was being. She wasn't one of those women who were gifted with psychic abilities, though she often fancied she was. She was just a girl with an incredible curiosity, one that often kept her up late at night.

One that had her creating all kinds of stories on paper.

Almost from the time she could hold a pencil, Olivia had been interested in writing stories. Whenever she watched a television show or a movie, she found herself rewriting the ending. If she read a book she didn't like, she did the same thing. She couldn't even share gossip without giving every detail. There was no doubt in her mind that she was born to write. Her overactive imagination was one of the reasons she'd started going for walks at night. Normally, Olivia enjoyed heading out to City Park late in the evening to stroll around and witness the world in a calmer state. That normally helped soothe her mind. And if her mind wasn't buzzing with a million ideas, she could fall asleep easier.

There was another reason for her walks. Something about the night compelled her. There was something magical about the night, something that not even Liza's murder had destroyed for her. Magical and mysterious.

The night was a complex oxymoron. It was a time when the world was calm, yet so much of significance took place. Like whatever had happened to Liza. She was certain it had happened at night. She couldn't imagine anyone having done anything so horrible to Liza during the day.

The night seemed to hold all the secrets of the world.

Olivia Grayson wanted to know those secrets. Again, she thought about Liza. What had happened here? How had Liza spent her last hours? Had she been happy, unaware that she was going to be killed until the last moment? Or had someone abducted her, held her hostage, and made it clear that he planned to kill her—then left her alive for days, torturing her with the knowledge of her impending death?

Olivia began walking. She waited until the traffic on the main street subsided, then hurried across the street and into City Park.

A minute later, she was at the pond. She stood near the water's edge and simply stared out at nature. The aged oak and sycamore trees lined the path around the water and spanned the grounds of the park as far as she could see. White geese glided across the pond's surface.

Before Liza's murder, Olivia had always been curious about what people did in the night, what they did at a time when they thought no one was watching. Perhaps because most people couldn't keep their private lives secret in this neighborhood, she often wondered if anyone was able. Careful enough. What had some of her neighbors done in the darkness right here that they hadn't wanted people to know about? What sins had they hoped to conceal? Had secret lovers met here by the water's edge? Or worse? It was a question that had always intrigued her each time she came here and stared into the darkness.

But more so, Olivia often imagined what *she* would do here. Olivia had never had a boyfriend, mostly because her mother was so overprotective and wouldn't let her have one. Belinda now had one. She was hot on the new guy in town, Bernie. Bernie had moved to New Orleans from Baton Rouge to look for work, but from what Olivia could tell, he didn't do much of anything except hang out. He and Belinda had met one day at the park. Since that time, they'd become friends, and now they were more than that.

Belinda was lucky to meet this new guy. Although Olivia didn't know much about him, she knew that he bought Belinda all kinds of expensive gifts. Like bracelets and charms and even some of the fancy clothes Belinda was now wearing.

Olivia wanted what Belinda had. She wanted a boyfriend more than anything in the world.

On her walks she would pretend that she was out to meet a lover. A man who made her heart race out of control, who set her body on fire with a mere touch. He had to be out there, somewhere. She wanted to stop dreaming about him and meet the real person.

In her mind, she couldn't quite see what he looked like. Yet his presence was so strong, so real . . .

Olivia thought she heard a sound. She spun around, her eyes searching the darkness. Searching, but seeing nothing.

She shook off a sudden chill. This wasn't the first time that she'd felt another's presence on her late-night walks—felt but saw no one. Perhaps she was surrounded by the spirits of many who had crossed over, spirits that now lingered in the shadows.

Olivia shivered, even as she smiled. Her imagination scared her, but it also thrilled her.

She would use all these feelings in a story. She often wrote about the dark side, something that didn't please her mother. Though lately, she had taken to writing about the mystery man she one day hoped to meet.

Inhaling a steady breath, Olivia took a step forward, toward the water. Her mama would be angry with her if she knew where she was, especially since Liza's body had been found earlier today.

Olivia wasn't scared, though. She wasn't that far from home. Still, she threw a quick glance over her shoulder to make sure she could see the lights of her house in the distance. It wasn't hard to see. It was the largest house on the block.

She continued walking, then stopped abruptly when she saw a shadow move. Her mind hadn't been playing tricks on her. Someone *was* out here with her. How long had he been watching her?

Her heart rate quadrupled, and no amount of bravado stopped her from quickly whirling around.

She sucked in a gasp when she turned to find a man standing immediately in her path.

He didn't say a word, and as her heart continued to pound, Olivia stared at him, scared out of her mind and wondering what to do. Her eyes widened in surprise. This was the stranger she had seen earlier, among the crowd gathered at the scene when Liza's body had been pulled from the water.

She'd caught only a glimpse of him, yet he had remained indelibly imprinted on her memory.

She exhaled slowly. Who was he?

And why did he seem somewhat familiar?

Olivia's brain suddenly kicked in, making her remember the day's events and the seriousness of the situation she was now in. Liza had been murdered a rock's throw from here, and so far, the police had no clue who had killed her.

Could it be this man, this stranger, staring at her?

And if it was . . .

"Isn't it late for a young girl like you to be out alone?" the man asked.

His voice was like a jolt of reality, scaring her into action.

Olivia turned and sprinted, not stopping until she reached her house.

She saw his eyes again later that night, in her dreams.
Bright, intense eyes that seemed to bore right into her soul.

Those eyes chilled her, even in sleep. Chilled her, even though they were the most beautiful eyes she'd ever seen on a man.

Yet she wasn't sure it was because she was afraid of him.

Olivia rolled over onto her stomach and hugged her pillow. She'd been tossing and turning ever since she'd climbed into bed. What was wrong with her? Why was it that just remembering the way he looked at her was making it impossible to get any sleep? When she closed her eyes, she saw him. And when she opened her eyes, she saw him as well.

Somehow she knew that as long as she lived, she would never forget this mystery man.

CHAPTER FIVE

Olivia awoke shortly before seven the next morning. She'd hardly slept all night and was still tired, but she could no longer keep her eyes closed.

She decided to get up and write in her journal. It was something she tried to do daily. Yesterday had been so busy, she hadn't gotten around to it. She certainly wanted to get her thoughts out regarding Liza's death.

Pushing aside the mosquito netting from her canopy bed, Olivia got up, stretched, then started for her desk. She smiled at the large-as-life poster of the love of her life that hung on the back of her door: Michael Jackson. Her mother didn't approve of her putting such posters on the wall because the tape would leave marks, so aside from the one on the door, Olivia's pictures of Michael Jackson and the Jackson Five were in a scrapbook.

As she opened her desk drawer to retrieve her journal and pen, Michael smiled up at her from the picture on the cover of her scrapbook.

"Michael, Michael. Why couldn't you be from New Orleans? Or better yet, why couldn't I be from Gary, Indiana? It doesn't matter. We are destined to be together. One day we'll meet." She giggled. "And I sound like some obsessed fan!"

Hands down, Michael Jackson was her favorite singer. And her ideal type of man. If only she could meet him in real life.

Sighing softly at her wishful thinking, Olivia pushed the drawer closed with a hip. Though she had a beautiful mahogany desk, her favorite spot to write was by the large bay window, where she could look out at the beautiful trees.

She settled into her comfy loveseat, curling her legs up beneath her. For the next half hour, her thoughts spilled onto the pages of her journal. She wrote about Liza's body being found, and the shocking reality that she had probably been murdered. Then her heart sped up as she wrote about the stranger she had met, how even though she didn't know him, in a bizarre way he seemed so familiar to her.

Olivia lowered her pen. She wanted to tell Belinda all about this mystery man.

Belinda . . . Olivia felt a stab of guilt for not thinking of her before. She'd forgotten about her dearest friend, all because of the stranger with the mesmerizing eyes.

Worry lines creased Olivia's forehead. Belinda still hadn't called, not even to confirm their plans for today, and no one had answered the phone when Olivia had called her house last night. Olivia had the very distinct sense that something was wrong in Belinda's world.

It was a little early still to call Belinda, so Olivia made her way to the bathroom. She may as well get ready for the day she and Belinda had planned, in the hope that they were still going. She was looking forward to spending this time with her friend, because lately Belinda had been spending a lot of time with Bernie. All three of them had hung out a couple times, but Olivia had felt like a third wheel on those occasions. It would be nice if they both had boyfriends, because then they all could go out on double dates and stuff and Olivia wouldn't feel awkward.

But the way things were looking, Olivia was wondering if she would ever find a boyfriend. All the guys she knew didn't interest her. And with the way her mother didn't like her going out too far from home, how was she going to meet anyone?

Oh, well, Olivia thought, looking at her reflection in the mirror. She wouldn't worry about that now. Today would be a day for just her and Belinda. A fun day of shopping, eating beignets, and checking out the cute men. Most people in the French Quarter would be tourists. Watching tourists was always good for a chuckle.

Olivia set about getting ready. She showered, wrapped a large towel around her body, then padded back to her bedroom and into her large closet. She wanted to wear something casual yet pretty. And comfortable. Comfortable was the definite order of the day, given that it was already muggy.

Olivia settled on her new denim dress. The dress reached her mid-thigh. It certainly wasn't as short as most of the minidresses and miniskirts out there, but her mother had fussed nonetheless before letting her buy it. She wanted to wear her new platform shoes as well, but the last time she had put on high platforms with a skirt above the knee, her mother had marched her back upstairs and made her change.

Back in the bathroom, Olivia applied only lipstick and mascara. The humidity would melt away any foundation. Her hair needed a relaxer touch-up. It was starting to frizz at the ends, and washing it had only made it puffier. At least now it was more of an Afro. While she wanted to wear her hair in this popular style, her mother didn't think the look was becoming on her. She poofed it as best she could, then put a ribbon in it.

Pleased with her appearance, she left the bathroom and went to her bed, where she sat cross-legged. She reached for the phone and dialed Belinda's number. Belinda better not still be sleeping . . .

Again, there was no answer.

Olivia wasn't about to sit around and wait for Belinda to call her. She was going to head to her place and find out what was going on.

When Olivia heard the scream, her body went into action. She charged for the front door of Belinda's house. She didn't bother to knock, instead swinging the door open and running inside.

"Get out of here, you filthy, lying bastard!"

Olivia stopped short, thinking the words were meant for her. But she soon assessed the situation when she saw Belinda and her parents standing in the foyer, Belinda's mother gripping a dinner plate. Olivia barely ducked in time as Mrs. McGowan whipped the plate across the foyer in Dr. McGowan's direction. It slammed against the wall and shattered into hundreds of pieces.

Gasping, Olivia looked around in horror. Mrs. McGowan finally noticed that Olivia was there. She flashed a quick look of contrition, then scowled as she once again faced her husband. "See what you made me do?"

"Hailey, you are acting like a madwoman," he replied, throwing his hands in the air in frustration.

"Mad?" Hailey wagged an angry finger as she took deliberate steps toward her husband. Olivia scooted to the right, out of the line of fire. "You're damn right I'm mad, you—" She balled her hand and raised it.

"Mama, stop!" Belinda cried, throwing herself between her mother's fist and her father's face.

Olivia knew she should leave, but she was transfixed with horror, wondering about the story taking place before her eyes.

"Get out of the way, Belinda!" her mother hollered. "This is between your father and me."

"No, Mama." Tears streamed down Belinda's face.

Her father took Belinda by the shoulders. "You go on. Your mama and I need to talk."

"But you're gonna kill each other!"

"You go on with Olivia." He spoke firmly. "You hear?"

"Yes, Daddy," Belinda said, but it was clear by her tone that she didn't want to leave.

Hailey looked at Olivia, but she didn't meet her eyes. Then she turned to Belinda. "Do what your father says."

Belinda took Olivia by the hand and spun around in one quick motion. She ran out the front door and didn't stop running until she was at the road.

"Belinda," Olivia said, facing her once they stopped, "what's going on?"

Belinda threw her arms around Olivia and squeezed her hard.

"Belinda . . ."

"I think we're really gonna move away this time. My parents—they just can't get along."

"What happened?" Belinda's parents might have argued a lot, but Olivia had never known them to get violent.

"All the rumors about my daddy were true," Belinda said as they pulled apart. "He got Patrice pregnant! And now my mama wants to move to Georgia."

A few weeks ago, Belinda had shared her fear that her father, a well-respected doctor in the area, had been cheating. In fact, her mother had learned

the news one day when she'd gone to see a clairvoyant. Before that, her mother
had had her suspicions, which was why she'd gone to a clairvoyant in the first
place. And Mrs. McGowan had suspected that her husband's lover was none
other than his receptionist, Patrice.

"He really got her pregnant?"

"I don't want to believe it, but it's true. He admitted it!"

"Wow."

"I know my mama's serious about moving this time. Says she's been shamed
and can't show her face around here no more. Says she's gonna leave as soon
as possible."

Olivia felt a moment of panic. She didn't want her best friend to leave.
"What about school? All the plans we made for college?"

"I don't know. I'll probably go to Spelman."

"Spelman?" That was so far away, and Olivia didn't think her mother would
let her go that far. She would miss her too much. They would miss each other.
But how would she survive without Belinda?

"Maybe you can still go to Dillard," Olivia suggested.

"I don't know . . ."

"But our plans—coming out at the debutante ball the Deltas sponsor every
year, then joining the Delta sorority together—what's gonna happen with all
that?"

"I don't know about the cotillion, but I'll still become a Delta."

"But it won't be the same if we're not together," Olivia said with alarm. "I
want to cross over with my very best friend." Olivia's grandmother had been
one of the founders of the Delta sorority, and it was now a part of the family's
history and tradition. Every female had become a Delta. They took membership
seriously. Not only was it a rite of passage into womanhood for the Etiennes
and their offspring, but being a Delta also was a way to give back to the black
community. Being a family of privilege, this was something they firmly believed
in. The more blacks who were educated, the more the race could prosper. That
was one of the main goals of the Delta sorority.

"You know I want to cross over with you, too." Belinda sniffled. "I . . . I
just can't talk about any of this right now. My family's falling apart."

"Of course. Let's walk. Maybe that'll help you feel better."

After walking a few minutes in silence, Belinda asked, "What am I gonna do, Olivia? I don't wanna live with my daddy, but I don't wanna move to Georgia, neither." She paused. "I wish I could move in with you."

"There's nothing I'd love more," Olivia replied, seriously considering the idea. Then she frowned. "But you know your mama won't let you. Neither would mine. She'd send you home, same as she'd expect your mama to send me home."

"Then maybe I ought to run away with Bernie."

The suggestion shocked Olivia. "You'd really do that?"

"Maybe I would. We're getting on real well."

"Where would you go?"

"Somewhere we could be happy. Away from all this craziness."

"Away from me?" Olivia kept her voice steady, even though she felt a stab of pain.

Belinda frowned. "I didn't think about that."

Olivia took her hand. "You still want to go to the French Quarter? It would take your mind off things. Or . . ." Olivia's voice grew with excitement. "I just got a catalog of cotillion dresses. We can go to my place and check it out, see what we could be wearing next spring."

Belinda shook her head, dismissing the idea.

"All right, then. Didn't you say you wanted to see *Jaws* again? Why don't we do that? Just me and you. As long as you promise not to dig your nails into my arm when the scary parts come on."

Olivia chuckled softly at the end of her sentence, hoping Belinda would laugh at how she had behaved when they'd seen the film a few weeks before. No such luck.

Belinda said, "I wanna find Bernie. Who knows how long I'll be around?"

"I guess you're right," Olivia said, not meaning her words. "This isn't a good time to go to the movies." She couldn't help feeling jealous. It seemed Bernie was all Belinda thought of these days.

"We haven't even talked about Liza," Olivia said as they started to walk.

"I know. I can't believe she was murdered. Though I guess it's true what some people said, that she had it coming."

"You really think so?"

"I'm not saying she deserved it, but when you run around so much . . ." Belinda shrugged. "She lived a risky kind of life with all those men. Still, it's a shame. I never thought something like this would happen to her."

Olivia opened her mouth to tell Belinda about the man she'd met yesterday, but she stopped herself. Suddenly the idea seemed silly. He was just a man she'd seen in the crowd, no one special, and she would appear foolish talking about him.

In the last month, since Belinda had been dating Bernie, Olivia's desire for a boyfriend had grown stronger than ever. Maybe that's why she couldn't stop thinking of the stranger she'd met yesterday. Maybe she was so jealous of Belinda's relationship with Bernie that she was desperate to find a connection with *any* man.

"Two nights ago, Bernie told me he loved me."

Olivia snapped out of her thoughts at Belinda's words. "He did?"

"Yep. Said he sees himself spending the rest of his life with me."

"You mean he asked you to—"

"No, he didn't ask me to marry him. But I just know we'll be married one day. Bernie is the one."

The feeling of jealousy grew. Here Belinda was, probably about to move away, yet she couldn't stop talking about Bernie, rather than concentrate on *their* relationship. She and Belinda had known each other all their lives; Bernie had barely been in town six weeks.

Was this what love did to you? Of all the girls Olivia knew, it seemed she was the only one who had never had a boyfriend, the only one who had never felt what it was like to be crazy over a guy.

"And I . . . we did it, Olivia."

Olivia's eyes flew to Belinda's. "Did what?"

Belinda smiled for the first time. "You know."

"You didn't!"

"Yes. Right in the park, the same night he told me he loved me."

Olivia couldn't help wondering how Belinda had managed a night with Bernie when she was seeing him in secret. Like Olivia's mother, Belinda's mother was overprotective and didn't want her to have a boyfriend yet. Especially since his family lived in Baton Rouge and Belinda's parents hadn't yet met them. Would his family meet with their approval?

"I can't leave him, Olivia. I just can't. Nor you, of course," she added as an afterthought.

Olivia squeezed Belinda's hand hard. "Guess all we can do is wait and see. You'll be eighteen next year. You could even move back here then." Olivia could deal with Belinda leaving, as long as she knew she'd be coming back soon.

"Or maybe Bernie can move to Georgia. Same way he moved here from Baton Rouge . . ."

Olivia tuned out as Belinda continued to speak. It was clear nothing she said or did was going to take her friend's mind off Bernie.

"Olivia."

"Huh?"

"I know we're supposed be going out today, but I hope you don't mind that I'm not up for it. I need to find Bernie, tell him what's going on."

Olivia tried to hide her disappointment. " 'Course not."

"I like your hair, by the way."

"Oh." The comment surprised her. Olivia touched her puffy hairdo.

"Yeah, it looks good like that. Better on you than it does on me. I was up for a good hour this morning, making sure my hair was nice and straight."

Belinda always wore her shoulder-length hair straight, even though Olivia had told her that she thought it would look good in an Afro.

"Anyway, Liv, I'll call you later. Okay?"

"Sure."

With that, Belinda ran off. Olivia watched her, a sad feeling gripping her heart. After a good couple minutes, she turned and headed back toward her house.

CHAPTER SIX

What's the matter, Olivia?" her mother asked when she sulked into the kitchen a short while later. Olivia had skipped breakfast so that she could go see Belinda, and now her stomach was grumbling.

"Oh, Mama." Olivia threw her arms around her mother's waist. "It's Belinda. She's moving. She's moving away, and I'm never gonna see her again!"

Sylvia ran a hand down Olivia's back. The delicate floral scent of her perfume wafted into Olivia's nose, a scent that was uniquely her mother's. It reminded her of lilacs.

"Oh, my sweet child. Why don't you tell me what happened?"

Olivia spent the next several minutes telling her mother about her meeting with Belinda, and how she knew, just knew, that if Belinda moved to Georgia, she would never see her again.

"Guess all I'd heard was true."

Olivia pulled back to look at her mother. "You knew?"

"People talk, Olivia. Something like this . . . it's bound to get around. 'Sides, I see Hailey every now and then, and I could tell she wasn't happy."

Olivia supposed her mother was right. All along, she'd been hoping Belinda's suspicions weren't true. But as it turned out, they were. The rumors about Patrice and Dr. McGowan had been based in fact.

"Allen may be a respected doctor, and he may belong to the right social clubs, but there's always been talk . . . oh, never mind."

Olivia wanted to ask her mother what she had been about to say, but she knew there was no point. If her mother didn't want to tell her something, it couldn't be forced out of her.

Instead, Olivia said, "Why do I have to lose my best friend, all because her father wanted to mess around . . ."

"I know it hurts, sweetheart." Sylvia framed her daughter's face. "But don't start thinking all negative. Not until you know for sure. That's only going to bring you down. Hailey's been talking of leaving for some time. She hasn't gone anywhere yet. Families are complex, Olivia. It all may work out yet. You'll see."

Olivia closed her eyes and inhaled a steady breath. Her mother's words made her feel a bit better. She only hoped her mother was right.

"Listen." Sylvia looked down at Olivia. "I know you had your heart set on going shopping today. If you still want to go, the two of us can head into town. Look for a dress for Elizabeth's party. That ought to help you take your mind off your troubles, at least for a little while."

Olivia found herself smiling. She had forgotten all about the party. Like her, Elizabeth would be coming out at the Delta cotillion in the spring. For up to a year before this exciting event, there were parties and dinners for the young debutantes to host and attend. Elizabeth Robichard's was the first such party.

"Yes, Mama. I'd like that."

"Though maybe we ought to head to the hair salon. That mane of yours looks wilder than Rosa's."

"Belinda said she likes it."

Sylvia raised her eyebrows in gentle disapproval. "I'll see if we can get an appointment today. If not, certainly sometime this week, before your next Jack and Jill meeting."

Jack and Jill was a social club for well-to-do black youth, one you could join by invitation only. Olivia had been a member since she was two years old. Her mother wanted her looking her best at all times when she went to the meetings, which meant having perfectly styled hair. Sometimes, Olivia felt the club was a popularity contest to see who was the prettiest, the smartest, the wealthiest.

"You eat your breakfast while I get ready, then we can leave."

"Yes, Mama." The enticing scent of warm corn bread made Olivia's mouth water, and as her mother headed out of the kitchen, Olivia settled down with a plate.

Maybe she shouldn't be worrying about finding a boyfriend. It had been her and her mama for as long as Olivia could remember, and they'd gotten along just fine. There had been only one time when Sylvia had gotten serious about a man other than Olivia's daddy, at least from what Olivia knew. That was back when she was twelve. At that time, Olivia had been horrified by the thought that a man could possibly come between them, and she'd done everything possible to keep her distance from him.

When Sylvia had asked her why she didn't like him, Olivia had answered only with a frown.

Olivia would never know for sure, but when her mother's relationship with Dexter quickly fell apart after that, she was sure it was because of her.

And she'd been glad. Once again, it was her and her mama.

Now that she was much older, Olivia felt a measure of guilt. She hoped her mama hadn't given up her one chance for happiness simply because she had been too spoiled to share her affection.

The doorbell rang, pulling Olivia from her thoughts. As she leaped from her seat, a smile broke out on her face. Maybe Belinda had decided to spend more time with her after all, rather than with Bernie.

"I'll get it," Olivia called, letting Edward know he didn't have to hurry from wherever he was.

Still smiling, she opened the door. But what she saw made her heart slam so hard against her chest that it felt like someone had given her a one-two punch—but in a good way. It was a reaction her body had never experienced before, and the shock of it left her speechless.

Speechless, because the gorgeous man who stood before her was none other than the stranger who'd been in the crowd yesterday. The same man she'd seen last night when she'd been out in the park.

What was he doing here on her doorstep?

As she stood, unable to find a voice to speak to him, the stranger gave her a soft smile. "Hello."

Olivia still didn't say a word.

"I'm hoping this is the right address," he continued. His voice was surprisingly deep.

Does he not recognize me? Olivia wondered, her eyes narrowing on his face.

He gave her an odd look in response to her own. Finally, recognition passed in his eyes. "Ah . . . last night."

"And earlier. At the bayou. When they found Liza's body . . ."

He nodded. "That's right."

"You're not from around here, are you?" Olivia's voice was steady, but her heart was beating overtime.

"No."

"I'm sure you're at the wrong house."

"This is the address I was given." He looked down at the scrap of paper in his hand, then at the number on the house, double-checking. "This is the Grayson residence?"

"Yes," Olivia replied, more confused. She'd figured for sure that he wasn't at the right address.

"I'm looking for the man or the lady of the house."

"There is no man of the house," Olivia said, then wondered if she should have blurted that out. Her mama said she often spoke too quickly, without thinking first.

"Okay, then. The lady of the house?"

"What do you want with her?"

The young stranger paused, clearly caught off guard. "Actually, I'm here because I was told she might have some work for me. You all don't need a carpenter?"

Oh. "Excuse my manners," Olivia said. Her eyes did a quick sweep of his body. His Afro was neat, minus that blue pick in his hair. He wore a clean white T-shirt and brown bell-bottom corduroys. Dressed to impress.

"I wasn't aware that my mama had started looking for someone yet, but you'll have to speak to her, of course. Please step inside, Mr.—"

"Harvey. Call me Harvey."

Olivia stepped back and held the door open wide. "Harvey, then. Do come in."

Harvey crossed the threshold into their home, looking around as he did. His eyes grew wide with wonder. He was clearly impressed.

So was Olivia. She couldn't help eyeing his long, lean body from head to toe. She'd checked out men before, but never one as attractive as this one.

The sound of a jingling bell made both Harvey and Olivia turn. Rosa bounded down the stairs and straight toward Harvey.

Harvey stiffened, taking a step backward.

Olivia couldn't help chuckling at the startled expression on his face, considering Rosa was hardly the picture of a menacing guard dog. "She doesn't bite," Olivia quickly told him. "In fact, she loves just about everyone."

Eyeing the dog, his shoulders relaxed. "Well, you never know. Sometimes the smallest dogs are the fiercest ones."

"I don't even think she knows how to bark."

Harvey lowered himself onto his haunches, offering his hands for Rosa to inspect. She sniffed, then lapped at his fingers.

"She looks like a giant cotton ball," Harvey said. "And feels like one."

Olivia giggled. "She's a bichon frise. Her name is Rosa."

Rosa was excitedly pawing Harvey's legs and licking his hands, then suddenly stopped and turned. So did Olivia and Harvey. Descending the stairs was her mother, a gracious smile on her face. Rosa pranced happily toward her master.

"You must be Harvey," Sylvia said as she glided toward them. "Here about the job."

"Yes, ma'am."

"I spoke with Baxter late yesterday. He told me to expect you."

Olivia looked up at her mother with questioning eyes. Baxter was a friend of the family. He owned a diner a couple blocks away.

"You still need a carpenter?" Harvey asked.

"Yes."

"Mama, I didn't realize that you'd already put out the word for a carpenter."

"Not officially, but I mentioned to Baxter that I'd finally like to get the work done. Next thing I know, he was calling me yesterday, saying he had someone who could do the job."

Olivia nodded her understanding, then looked at Harvey once more. She was unnerved to find he was staring at her, not at her mother.

"Sylvia Grayson." Sylvia offered Harvey her hand.

Harvey shook it. "It's good to meet you, Mrs. Grayson."

"Good to meet you, too. Let's have a seat in the sunroom, where we can talk business."

————

Harvey stared at the elaborately decorated room as he followed Sylvia and the little dog into it. Everything from the tiled floors to the wrought-iron shelving units to the ornate sculpture of lovers embracing spoke of money. He had never known this kind of wealth, and he felt somewhat intimidated.

"So."

At the sound of Sylvia's voice, Harvey stopped gawking and turned to her. She gave him another of her gracious smiles. Was it genuine, or one of those fake sugary smiles rich folks reserved for those they felt were beneath them? "You've worked as a carpenter before, I take it?"

"Yes, ma'am. All kinds of things, really. I've always been good with my hands."

"Wonderful. Sounds like you're just the kind of man I need for this job. I have plenty to be done."

"Did Baxter tell you that I'm only in town for a short time?"

A slight frown marred Sylvia's beautiful features. "No, he didn't."

"Well, how long will you need someone?" Harvey asked. He wasn't planning on staying around indefinitely. Just long enough to achieve what he'd come here to do.

"That depends." Sylvia shrugged. "You're probably the best one to tell me, given the work I need done."

"What do you need done?"

"This is a beautiful house, but it's very old. The wood frames around the windows need to be replaced. The carriage house could use some work on its exterior, too. Some of the wood flooring could be refinished. Other things, as well. I've put it off for so long, but now that my daughter will be hosting a debutante party in the coming months, I'd like the place in tip-top shape. But if you're not available to do all the work, maybe I ought to see a few more applicants."

"My schedule's flexible," Harvey quickly said. He did need the money. And it was obvious from Sylvia's simple yet elegant white dress and the lavish furniture in her home that she had lots of it. "As long as the price is right."

"Of course," she responded easily, making it clear that money was no object for her. "Would you like a drink? Some lemonade?"

"Naw, I'm fine."

"Okay." Sylvia crossed her arms beneath her bosom. "How do you know Baxter?"

"A friend of a friend of a friend."

"Oh." Harvey saw the flash of curiosity in Sylvia's eyes. But she didn't need to know more than what he'd told her; at least not at this point.

She didn't ask him any more questions, which suited him fine. "Do I have the job?" he asked. "Or are you gonna interview other people?"

"Since Baxter is referring you, I know you'll be a good worker. And Rosa seems to like you." Sylvia smiled at her pet, who sat on her hind legs beside Harvey. "And if Rosa likes you, that's a good thing."

"Does that mean you're hiring me?"

"You've got the job."

Harvey smiled. "Thank you, ma'am."

"Are you from New Orleans?"

"No. Well, I was born here, but wasn't raised here."

Sylvia gave him an assessing glance. "What brings you back here, then?"

"Change," Harvey replied simply.

"What kind of change?"

"I was tired of Chicago. Gets too cold in the winter. I needed some warmth."

"Where's your family?"

"Here, there, everywhere." He shifted from one foot to the other, uncomfortable. He wanted to change the subject. "So, how much are you paying?"

"The pay's one-fifty a week, but I'll provide room and board. I think that's fair."

"Sounds fair to me," Harvey agreed.

Sylvia extended her hand. "Let's shake on it."

Harvey took her hand in his and shook it.

Step one in his plan was completed. Now he could worry about step two—the real reason he had come to New Orleans.

CHAPTER SEVEN

It didn't take more than a few days for all sorts of rumors about Liza's demise to start spreading around the neighborhood. Some said that a jealous wife had killed Liza for messing with her husband, but no one had named any names. Of course, the number of men she'd been with meant that practically any wife could be the culprit. Others said that Liza was killed by a crazy sex fiend, a strange-looking man who had been harassing the women in the area. Rumor was the man had now disappeared. Before Liza's murder, no one had mentioned seeing this strange man, so Olivia didn't put much stock in that claim, considering the descriptions of him were different as night and day.

The reality was, a murderer could be lurking among them, not far away from where this had happened. And it didn't have to be some bizarre-looking man who was a misfit in society. It could be someone who smiled and chatted with you every day. Someone who everyone in the neighborhood thought was a model citizen.

It could be . . . anyone.

Yet there was no one Olivia knew who she thought was capable of murder.

It was different seeing stories about crime on the news, when people swore they'd never suspected the person who had been arrested for whatever heinous offense. Olivia had always figured that something about the person must have made it clear he was guilty. Now she knew better. Anyone the police arrested for killing Liza would come as a major shock.

Edward knew about voodoo. Olivia wondered if he could use some potion or spell to figure out who the killer was.

The knock at her bedroom door pulled her from her thoughts. "Yes?"

The door opened a crack and her mother's face appeared. "Belinda's downstairs."

"Oh." Olivia jumped up from her chaise by the window and raced out of the room.

Belinda was smiling like a fool when Olivia went down the stairs to meet her.

"Go on back upstairs and put on something decent," Belinda told her.

Olivia glanced down at her T-shirt and shorts. "What's wrong with this?"

"Nothing . . . if you're hanging around the house."

"I *am* hanging around the house."

"Not anymore you're not. We're going out."

"Where?" Olivia asked.

"Just somewhere. Go change into something nice."

Olivia checked out Belinda's outfit. She wore a denim miniskirt and a crocheted white halter top. Her feet were stylish in thick-heeled sandals. The look was definitely sexy. Very different for Belinda.

"We don't have all day, Miss Olivia," Belinda told her, then giggled. "Hurry up!"

Olivia couldn't help laughing, too. Belinda taking her out to hang somewhere—it was like everything was normal again.

"Yes, ma'am." Olivia saluted Belinda, then turned and charged up to her room. Like Belinda, she decided on a miniskirt made of white denim. Her mother didn't let her wear halters because they showed too much skin, so she opted for a form-fitting T-shirt with multicolored stripes. It showed off her curves. And considering she hadn't developed a decent-sized chest until she was sixteen, she was happy to tastefully show off her curves any chance she got.

"I promise, Mrs. Grayson," Belinda was saying when Olivia returned to the front door. Then she quickly took hold of Olivia's hand.

Olivia barely managed to slip her feet into sandals and mutter a "Bye, Mama," before Belinda whisked her out the door.

"Belinda, where are we going?"

Olivia's excitement about whatever adventure lay before her fizzled when they stepped outside the gate and she saw Bernie standing on the sidewalk to the left.

Belinda released Olivia's hand and threw herself into Bernie's arms. Bernie lifted her high into the air, and Olivia could see Belinda's cotton underwear beneath her skirt.

As Olivia watched, her stomach grew uneasy. Belinda wasn't acting like herself. She'd never been so . . . "loose" was the first word that came to her mind, but she instantly felt bad for it. Her friend wasn't loose. She was in love.

Yes, in love. Olivia could see it clearly, just in the way Belinda let her hands gently linger on Bernie's shoulders. And if Belinda hadn't already told her that she had made love with Bernie, Olivia would have figured it out right now. Belinda's eyes no longer held innocence when she looked at the man of her dreams.

"Hi, Bernie." Olivia smiled sheepishly when they both turned to face her. Their expressions said they'd forgotten she was even there.

"Hi." Bernie barely looked her way as he spoke to her, and Olivia's heart dropped to her knees. He didn't want her hanging out with them. She didn't blame him. She didn't want to be a third wheel.

Bernie slipped an arm around Belinda's waist, like he owned her. "We ready?"

"I guess," Olivia replied. "Considering I don't know what we're doing."

Belinda laughed. "We're gonna find you a man!"

"Excuse me?"

"Oh, don't give me that look. Haven't you been saying you want to meet somebody nice? Well, Bernie has a friend who lives on the other side of the park. What's his name again?"

"Patrick."

"That's right. Anyway, his church's youth group is having a picnic in City Park. Bernie's already told him all about you and he wants to meet you."

"So we could be out for a while. I ought to let my mama know where I'm going . . ."

"I told her when you were upstairs changing."

"Oh."

"Don't look so frightened."

Olivia exhaled slowly and loosened her stance. "I'm not. I'm just . . . nervous. Is this like a blind date?"

"Not unless you want it to be."

At least it was a picnic, so it wouldn't be just the four of them. If she didn't like this guy, she didn't have to spend time exclusively with him.

Bernie took a package of cigarettes out of his pocket and withdrew two. He passed one to Belinda. Olivia watched in horror as he lit the cigarette and Belinda inhaled.

"Belinda, what are you doing?"

"Oh, it's no big deal."

"No big deal? You hate the fact that your daddy smokes. You hate the smell of cigarettes, remember? You always said you'd never start such a disgusting habit."

Belinda inhaled deeply, then blew out a puff of smoke. "Relax, Liv. I was young when I said all that. But I'm grown now, ready to try new things."

"That's right." Bernie winked at Belinda, like they shared some special secret. Then he pulled her close and nuzzled his nose in her neck. Belinda squealed with delight.

Olivia gaped at her friend, wondering what had gotten into her. But Belinda didn't notice her expression. She was too busy hanging on Bernie's arm and giggling.

Olivia felt like she no longer knew her.

The Belinda she knew would have been more cautious about dating, not thrown herself headlong into a relationship with a virtual stranger. Bernie looked the part of a bad boy, from his I-don't-give-a-crap stance to the deep scar along his left cheek. And he was secretive. Olivia had asked him how he got the scar and he'd simply replied, "Wouldn't you like to know?"

But maybe the bad-boy image was part of the attraction?

Olivia had heard girls talk about bad boys as if they were something special.

All Olivia knew was that she was losing her friend bit by bit. She hoped this thing with Bernie wouldn't last very long.

————

Olivia normally felt like a third wheel with Belinda and Bernie, but even more so today. Belinda had seemingly changed overnight, and Olivia didn't like it one bit.

Was Belinda clinging to Bernie like white on rice because she was afraid she'd be moving away and leaving the man she loved?

Maybe I'm just jealous, Olivia thought. *Jealous because I want to feel what Belinda's feeling.*

Laughter and chatter filled the air as the three of them approached the large group of people in the park. Olivia glanced around but didn't recognize anyone.

"Where's Patrick?" Belinda asked Bernie.

Bernie scanned the crowd. "Ah, there he is." He pointed to the right. "The tall one wearing the black T-shirt. Afro bigger than mine."

Which was saying a lot, considering Bernie had one of the biggest Afros Olivia had seen.

"Come on, Liv." Belinda looped her arm through hers. "Let's go meet him."

"Belinda . . ." Olivia protested. "Do we have to run over there, like I'm desperate?"

"He's not gonna think that."

"What if he does?" Olivia was making excuses because she was nervous.

"He's already looking our way."

And he was. Olivia blushed. But she also took a closer look at him, liking what she saw.

He must have liked what he saw too, because he smiled and started walking toward them.

"Patrick," Bernie said a moment later, slapping him on the shoulder.

"Hey, Bernie." His eyes roamed to both Belinda and Olivia. "How you doing, man?"

"Never been better," he replied, but his eyes were on Belinda.

"You must be Olivia." Patrick fully faced her.

He had a smooth voice. Polished. "Yes."

"I'm Patrick." He extended a hand to her.

Olivia slowly freed her arm from Belinda's. She stared at Patrick's hand for a moment, then accepted it. He didn't shake hers. Instead, he simply held it, then caressed the top of it with the pad of his thumb.

"Hi." Olivia practically stumbled over the word.

"You were right, Bernie. She is something."

"Yeah," Bernie agreed. "Why don't you two take some time to get to know each other."

Olivia sent a panicked look in Belinda's direction, but it was pointless. Bernie and Belinda started off, merging into the crowd, leaving her and Patrick alone. Olivia watched them go, her stomach fluttering.

She nearly jumped out of her skin when she felt the hand on her shoulder, then was immediately embarrassed. Goodness, Patrick would think she had never been around a guy before.

"You all right?" he asked.

"Uh-huh. Just thinking."

Patrick moved his hand lower, to the small of her back. "You hungry?"

"Oh, yeah," she answered with enthusiasm.

"There's plenty of food. And don't those ribs smell good?"

"Mmm-hmm." He seemed nice enough. Maybe they would have a good time together.

"Let's get us some food."

Olivia didn't spend much time with Belinda after that, as Belinda seemed to be physically glued to Bernie's arm. So when Belinda ran toward her as the guys went to play a game of tug-of-war, Olivia was happy for some alone time with her friend.

"You like him?" Belinda asked as she plopped herself down on the grass beside Olivia.

"He's all right."

"That's all?"

Olivia shrugged. She hadn't felt any instant sparks, the way Belinda had described her feelings for Bernie. "He seems cool. But I think he's a little old." That was her only concern. Her mother didn't like her dating to begin with, so she definitely wouldn't approve of her dating a significantly older guy.

"A girl needs an older man. 'Cause we mature faster. Bernie's twenty-two, and I think that's perfect for me."

Olivia picked a blade of grass. She began shredding it into thin strips. "What's it like? Making love?"

Belinda glanced away briefly before meeting Olivia's eyes head-on. "Amazing. Just the way it's described in books. Now I want to do it all the time. Only with Bernie, of course," she added, then giggled.

The sound of cheering erupted, and Olivia and Belinda looked up to see that one team had landed on the grass. Patrick cheered while Bernie brushed grass from the knees of his jeans.

"Oh, Bernie." Belinda trotted toward him. She passed Patrick, who was making his way toward Olivia.

Olivia stood to meet him. "Good job."

"Thanks." He reached for her hand, linking their fingers. "Hey, wanna go for a walk?"

"Um . . ."

"To talk," he added.

Of course. How was she gonna get to know him if they didn't talk? "Sure."

Patrick led her away from the crowd and to the shade of a large oak tree. Olivia thought he was going to stop there, but instead he led her farther into the thicket of trees—a much more secluded spot.

Olivia halted, saying, "Patrick . . ."

He slipped an arm around her waist and drew her to him. Grinning down at her, he said, "I like you."

She felt suddenly uneasy. She knew where this could lead, and she didn't want to go down that road. "I . . . maybe we should head back."

"Not until you kiss me first."

She swallowed. "I thought you wanted to talk."

"I do . . . *after* I kiss you."

He may have been cute, but she wasn't ready to kiss him. "A lady d-doesn't . . ." she stuttered. Where was her courage? "A lady doesn't kiss on the first date."

"Ah, don't be so old-fashioned." He tightened his arms around her. Her breasts flattened against his hard chest. "Just a tiny kiss. Then we'll head back."

"But I hardly know—"

"C'mon, gorgeous. I just want to see if your lips are as soft as they look. Is that so wrong?"

Olivia eyed him warily. Was this the way men and women flirted? *Was* she being old-fashioned? Uptight? She had no clue, because she had no experience.

Regardless, she didn't feel comfortable. She felt trapped. But right now, she would do just about anything to get back to the group. "I suppose a small one wouldn't hurt," she finally said.

"You have made my day."

Olivia tipped on her toes to give him a quick peck on the lips, but instead of a peck, she felt Patrick's wet tongue on her mouth.

She gasped in horror. Then she slipped her hands between their bodies and pushed against his chest. But he only held her tighter.

Olivia squirmed. "Stop it."

"Why are you so uptight?" He moved his mouth to her neck.

Was he deaf as well as oblivious to what she wanted? "I don't want to do this." Shoving hard, Olivia finally escaped his grip. She spun around and hurried away from him, back toward the open area of the park and the voices of the crowd.

"Wait, Olivia."

She threw a glance over her shoulder and saw that he was fast on her heels. She whimpered, suddenly afraid. Liza had been murdered, and here she was, off in a secluded area of the park with a guy she'd only just met.

She made it to the open grass just as he caught up to her. His fingers closed around her upper arm. Hard.

"What the hell's the matter with you?" he asked, whirling her around.

"Just leave me alone."

"You're acting like I'm gonna hurt you, when all I want to do is get to know you."

Olivia struggled to free her arm, but he didn't let her go.

Then suddenly she was free, and Patrick was flying backward. Only when he groaned and clutched his nose did Olivia realize that someone had hit him.

She threw her head around. And then she saw *him*.

Harvey.

He didn't seem to notice her, though. His eyes shot daggers at Patrick.

"What's your problem, man?" Patrick got to his feet, his entire body tense.

Harvey balled his hands into fists. "When a lady tells you to let her go, you let her go."

"Mind your own damn business," Patrick snapped.

"This is my business." Only then did he face Olivia. "Olivia, are you okay?"

She massaged her upper arm where Patrick had grabbed her, nodding.

"You know this guy?" Patrick asked her.

"Why don't you get lost?"

Harvey's tone held an edge, and Patrick must have decided that it wasn't worth messing with him.

"The hell with you," Patrick muttered. "You're as crazy as they come."

Patrick's words hurt her, even though they shouldn't have. *He* was the one being crazy.

Olivia watched him stomp away before turning to Harvey. Instead of thanking him, she asked, "Are you following me?"

"No."

She eyed him with caution. "You just happened to be here?"

"I came out for the picnic. Then I saw you and that guy heading off into the wooded area." He shrugged. "At that point, yeah, I guess I was watching you."

His eyes never left hers, and something about his expression made her feel light-headed. She barely knew anything about this man, but something about him made her want to get to know him a whole lot better.

"You make a habit of watching young women?"

"Only the ones I think are worth watching."

She felt a sharp tingling sensation in her private area and instantly flushed. She'd never experienced a feeling like that before, but she knew instinctively that it had to be sexual. The sensation was alarming, yet totally exciting.

She didn't know Harvey much more than she knew Patrick, yet she felt so incredibly alive when around him. She almost wanted him to ask her to go into the woods. And she would, without reservation.

But she quipped, "Did you think Liza was worth watching?"

"Who's Liza? Oh, you mean the girl who was murdered? I didn't know her."

He seemed to be telling the truth, but maybe that's what Olivia wanted to believe.

"Why don't we head back to the rest of the group?"

Not the thing she'd expected him to say. Olivia didn't know much about how men and women related, but she'd swear there was something going on between her and Harvey. Something electric. Something too powerful for her to control it.

But maybe what she was feeling was one-sided, considering he didn't seem interested in spending time alone with her.

Harvey placed his hand on her back, and together they walked back to Belinda and Bernie.

Confusion flashed in Belinda's eyes. "Why did Patrick storm back here like someone had stolen all his candy?"

"I don't want to talk about Patrick. But this is Harvey." She gestured toward him. "Harvey, this is my best friend, Belinda. And this is Bernie."

"Hi."

"Hi," Belinda replied, slipping out of Bernie's arms. "And, excuse us." She took Olivia's hand and led her a few feet away. "Olivia, what's going on?"

"Patrick is a jerk."

"What did he do?"

"It doesn't matter. I don't like him."

Belinda looked over her shoulder. "Who's Harvey?"

"He's . . . he's the new carpenter my mama hired. He hasn't started yet, though."

"Hmm. Not bad. Though he seems a little serious."

"Kind of. Makes me wonder why."

"What else do you want to know about him?" Belinda's eyes grew wide with excitement.

Olivia tried her best, but she couldn't suppress her giggle. Harvey was unlike anyone she'd ever met, and she wanted to know everything about him.

"I saw him that day when Liza's body was found. I noticed him right away."

"Seems he noticed you, too."

"I think so. Well, I hope so."

"You're blushing!"

"No, I'm not." But her face felt warm. "Belinda, you don't mind if I take off, do you? You have Bernie to keep you company, and I probably ought to head home now, anyway."

"Sure. No problem."

Olivia's heart started beating out of control. She was going to be brave and ask Harvey if he wanted to take a walk with her somewhere.

She turned. Then frowned.

Harvey was nowhere in sight.

CHAPTER EIGHT

Of course, you can have your pick of escorts, I'm sure, but Connor Evans is the most coveted." Sylvia's eyes danced with excitement as she spoke about the Delta cotillion next spring. "It won't be too long before he's heading up his father's insurance company, which has already expanded across half the state. Olivia Evans. That has a nice ring to it."

"Mama!" Olivia exclaimed, after swallowing her mouthful of food.

Sylvia sipped her tea. "I know, sweetheart. I'm thinking ahead. Way ahead. But you never know. Connor is such a nice young man. There's no doubt he'd make a proper husband."

"I don't think Connor's my type." Her mother didn't know, but he was pushy and overbearing at the Jack and Jill functions he and Olivia attended together. Many would consider him a great catch, but she did not.

"You're young yet," her mother said by way of agreement. "For the time being, I can hardly wait until May. Even before May. I was thinking you could have your coming-out party in February. All the work on the house will be done by then, and the weather should be perfect. What do you think?"

"Sure. February or March."

"I stopped by the Ritz-Carlton after my Links lunch," Sylvia went on, "and I can't tell you how excited I got just looking around, imagining the cotillion. I just know you'll be the most celebrated debutante. Your uncle Renard will come down from Baltimore to stand in for your father. It's going to be a glorious occasion."

Olivia rarely heard from her uncle. She had seen him briefly last summer when she had gone up north to attend Camp Atwater, and since then she could count the number of times they had spoken on one hand. She didn't feel close to him, and couldn't imagine him taking her late father's place.

"Why not Edward?" Olivia asked.

"Edward," Sylvia repeated, clearly shocked.

"Yeah. He's been with us so long, he's practically family."

Sylvia chuckled softly. "Oh, sweetheart, you know he couldn't."

"Why not?" Olivia challenged. "He's the closest thing I have to a father."

"But he's not your father."

"Neither is Uncle Renard."

"No, but at least he's family."

"I hardly see him. I don't even feel close to him."

"Olivia—"

"Edward would be a great escort for you. And . . . I think he'd like it."

Sylvia's eyebrows shot up at that last statement.

"Don't you think so, Mama?" Olivia saw the way Edward looked at her mother. She was certain he had a crush on her.

"I'm sure Edward has better things to do. Besides, it wouldn't look right. He's the hired help."

Olivia merely shrugged. She didn't much see what that mattered, but she knew it *would* matter to the friends in her mother's social circle. Affluent, they would never date anyone considered beneath them, especially not anyone who worked for them.

Silence settled over the dining room. The only sound was the occasional whimper from Rosa, who sat patiently at Sylvia's side, hoping for scraps of food.

Talk of hired help had turned Olivia's thoughts to Harvey. She had hoped to find him here when she'd returned home.

"Something on your mind?" Sylvia asked after a long while.

Olivia tossed a piece of broccoli around on her plate with her fork. "I was just thinking. That guy you hired. When does he start working?"

"He's moving in in a couple of days and starting Monday."

Olivia nodded absently.

"He'll be staying out in the carriage house, if you're concerned."

"Oh, no. I'm not concerned. Just curious."

"How are things with Belinda?"

"You mean is she moving to Georgia?"

"Mmm-hmm."

"Right now it seems like everything's okay."

"Well, that's good."

"Yeah, I'm happy about that."

"With everything that's going on, I know you must be stressed. And speaking of unpleasant things, Liza's funeral is tomorrow. Noon."

Olivia looked at her mother in shock. "You're going?"

"We're going."

"But why would you go to Liza's funeral? You always said—"

"I know what I've said. And how Liza lived her life has nothing to do with what I wish for her, for her soul. We're Christians, Olivia. We need to pay our respects."

"I guess." But the truth was, Olivia thought it was hypocritical to pay respects to someone in death whom you had never respected in life.

She spiked the broccoli with her fork, then ate it. A moment later, she asked, "Mama, can I be excused?"

"You've hardly touched your food. I guess you ate dinner at the picnic."

"Not that much, but I'm full. And I . . ." Olivia hesitated. "I want to do some writing."

Sylvia shook her head slowly, though she smiled. "You and your stories. I wish you'd start thinking about what you really want to do with your life."

Olivia didn't reply.

"Yes, you can be excused."

"Thank you." Olivia got up from the table and brought her plate into the kitchen, where she dumped her uneaten food into the garbage. Then she charged up the stairs to her room. She could kick herself for mentioning that she wanted to do some writing. Her mother never outright told her not to write, but she always belittled her passion in some indirect way. Olivia hated that. As far as she was concerned, writing *was* what she wanted to do with her life. From the time she was a young child, she had loved creating stories.

It was times like this that Olivia missed her father. He had died eleven years earlier, when Olivia was six, and when he'd been alive he toured much of the time, so she didn't have many memories of him. But the memories she had were special. She distinctly remembered how he had read to her at night. While her mother had also read to her, there had been something magical about that time she had spent with her father, listening to his deep, calming voice. No matter how much time he had exhausted during a given day working on his music, if he was in town, he had made sure to read her a story before she went to sleep. And if he was on the road, he often called to tell her a story at bedtime.

Her love of stories had been born in those cherished times with her father. It was why she wanted to become a writer.

Being a musician, her father was obviously creative, and if he were still alive, Olivia knew that he would support her passion for writing.

Olivia's mother was much better at running committees and organizations than she was at anything creative. In addition to having been the president of her sorority's graduate chapter for four years, she ran a charity organization to benefit New Orleans's poor children.

Her wish for Olivia was for her to become a lawyer or a doctor, or something prestigious like that. The kind of career that not just society said was acceptable, but that well-to-do blacks considered acceptable. But neither law nor medicine interested Olivia. She knew she had what it took to make it as a writer, and she was going to do everything possible to make that happen.

She had already sent a short story off to a magazine publisher in New York. Now she was working on a romance. Belinda had introduced her to those exciting novels, and since that time, Olivia couldn't get enough of them. If she couldn't experience love in real life, she could at least pretend by creating her own. For now. Because one day Olivia hoped to write about love based on her own experience.

Perhaps with Harvey?

Oh, God. Why did that thought come into her mind? It was crazy!

Yet she smiled.

It was crazy in a good kind of way.

She couldn't wait for the next two days to pass. She wanted to see him again, and the sooner the better.

CHAPTER NINE

Hello, Mrs. Grayson," Harvey said when the door opened. She was holding her dog in her arms, much the way one would hold a toddler, its front legs perched on her shoulders. He'd bet his last dollar that this woman treated her pet as if it were an actual child.

"Hello, Harvey." Sylvia's smile was graceful, yet reserved. She stepped backward. "Come in."

Harvey walked into the foyer. Though he'd seen the place already, he was again taken aback by its grandeur. He wondered if the moldings were hand-carved. The work was intricate and exquisite. The chandelier that hung from the high ceiling was magnificent to say the least, and Harvey would bet the metal was real silver.

Must be nice to live so well.

Sylvia looked at his duffel bag. "That's all you have?"

"Yes." It was all he'd had time to take with him before he'd run from Chicago. His entire life in a bag.

"I see."

"I'm low maintenance."

She nodded, but her expression said she would never understand what it was like to live the way he did.

"You'll be staying in the carriage house," she said. She began to walk. "I'll take you there. We can go through the house—"

"It's outside?"

Sylvia stopped and faced him. "Of course." She chuckled softly. "Where else would a carriage house be?"

Harvey felt stupid. "With all due respect, I've never known anyone with a house like this. I just . . . I . . ."

"It's all right, Harvey. And I get the feeling you think you'll be staying in the doghouse. It's far from that. No offense, of course, Rosa."

Sylvia nuzzled her nose with Rosa's, then lowered the dog to the floor.

She started walking again. Actually, her walk was more like a glide, almost like her feet didn't truly touch the ground. She was unlike anyone Harvey had ever met before.

The kind of woman who'd had it easy. Everything had been handed to her on a silver platter, while someone like him had had to struggle all his life.

Outside, they rounded the corner from the side of the house that led to the vast backyard. Rosa sprinted ahead of them. Much of the backyard was shaded by trees, but there was also plenty of sunshine. There was an in-ground pool to the left, but that didn't impress Harvey as much as the carriage house did.

"Hardly a doghouse, now, is it?"

"Hardly, ma'am."

Harvey had imagined something the size of a large shed, but this was a *house*. A small one, probably one or two rooms, but he had known families to live in a house this size.

They crossed the backyard to the carriage house, where Sylvia opened the door. "It's a great guest suite. Not too large, but it has everything you need."

Harvey stepped into the house behind Sylvia. It was like a large bachelor pad. There was a good-sized kitchen at the back. The living area was in the front. It was surprisingly large and well furnished with both a sofa and arm-chair, and even a television.

"That's a sofa bed."

"Uh-huh."

"The bathroom's over there." Sylvia pointed to a door to the left of the living room. "It has a shower and a tub. Towels and linens are in the closet." She turned to him. "Is there anything else you need?"

Harvey looked around slowly. The place was nicer than any he had ever lived in. "Doesn't look like it."

"You can put your bag down."

"Right." Harvey let the heavy bag slide off his shoulder and to the hardwood floor.

"Let me introduce you to my houseman, Edward."

"Okay."

When they stepped outside, Harvey looked up. He saw her instantly. She stood at the window, looking down on him and her mother.

But then she stepped backward, disappearing from view.

". . . for years. He really is the sweetest person."

"Uh-huh," Harvey said absently as he followed Sylvia back to the house. This time, she walked around the perimeter of the pool and up the steps that led to the patio doors. Rosa was occupied at the far end of the backyard and didn't tag along with them.

"Edward," Sylvia said when she opened the door. A man, probably in his early fifties, was at the counter polishing a silver platter. He stopped and looked at them. "Edward, this is Harvey. He's the carpenter I've hired to do some of the work that I've been saying I've wanted to do for so long. Harvey, this is my houseman. He's more like family, really."

Harvey and Edward greeted each other with a handshake.

"If you make a list of the groceries you'll need, Edward can pick them up tomorrow."

"Groceries?"

"I'm providing room and board, so that includes your food."

"Oh. Okay."

"And if you need anything else, please tell Edward. He can help you with most anything."

"Sounds good."

Sylvia clapped her hands together. "I suppose that's it for now. Unless you have any questions for me."

"Not that I can think of," Harvey told her.

"Then you can go ahead and get settled in the guest house. I'd like you to start bright and early tomorrow morning."

"Seven-thirty?"

"Sounds perfect."

"I'll see you then."

CHAPTER TEN

The steady patter of raindrops on the window was interrupted by the loud clash of thunder.

It startled everyone, even the minister. He paused, glanced toward one of the windows, then once again faced the group of mourners.

"So yes, today is a sad day. But even as we mourn, we have a reason to hope. For we have faith in the Lord, and because of that faith, we know we will see Liza again . . ."

Olivia tuned out Pastor Donovan's words as she looked around the room. While practically the entire neighborhood had been at the scene when Liza's body had been recovered, far fewer people attended her funeral right now. In fact, she and her mother were two of only a dozen or so people. Maybe that was why the pastor's voice echoed in the giant room—because it was so empty.

". . . remember the times she brought joy to our lives . . ."

Cynthia Monroe cried out at the front of the church.

Sylvia reached for Olivia's hand, and Olivia glanced at her mother. Wearing all black, her head was lowered with reverence. The brim of her black hat hung over her face, making it difficult for anyone but Olivia to see her eyes.

What Olivia saw perplexed her. Her mother seemed genuinely upset. When Sylvia had told her they were going to the funeral, Olivia had assumed they would simply be paying their respects. After all, her mother had never had anything good to say about Liza or Cynthia Monroe.

But this was death. And death was final. Maybe it brought out sadness in everyone.

When the pallbearers carried Liza's casket past the midsection pew where Olivia and her mother were sitting, Olivia watched with morbid fascination. The glum sounds of the organ music made the mood that much more somber, and Olivia found her eyes misting.

She wiped at her tears as Cynthia made her way up the aisle behind the casket. Again she was struck by the woman's beauty, even in grief. She watched how she walked, poised and with dignity, even as the expression on her face spoke of her immense pain.

Cynthia neared them, her gaze fixed on Olivia and her mother. Sadness morphed into disgust.

"How dare you show your face here?"

Olivia flinched, shocked by the words. It took her only a moment to realize that Cynthia had to be addressing her mother.

Sylvia realized it too and glanced around quickly, clearly looking to see if Cynthia's question had gotten unwanted attention. She gripped Olivia's hand as she softly replied, "Came to pay my respects, Cynthia. I am so sorry—"

"Pay your respects? You mean you came to gloat."

An older woman whom Olivia assumed was Cynthia's mother put her arms around her. "Come on now, Cynthia. This isn't the time."

"This is what you've wanted all these years, isn't it? To see my baby dead. Did you do this to her? Are you the one who took her life?"

"Cynthia," the older woman said sternly, then began to drag her away.

Cynthia's body moved, but her head remained steadfast in Sylvia's direction. Her look could have killed.

Only when Cynthia was out of view did Sylvia release Olivia's hand. Olivia wriggled her fingers to get the circulation going.

Sylvia kept her head high, even as people gave her curious looks. Like Olivia, they all had to be wondering what was going on.

"The poor woman," Sylvia said. Her voice was shaky. "Grief can often make a person lose their mind. So sad."

Olivia and her mother were still standing in their pew when the church had emptied. Olivia looked up at her, but she seemed a million miles away.

"Mama?"

Sylvia snapped out of whatever trance she'd been under. "Let's go."

Sylvia took Olivia's hand in hers and rushed with her out of the church.

CHAPTER ELEVEN

Olivia rounded the corner toward the landing, but abruptly stopped when she heard the soft sound of crying.

"I'm not surprised." That was Edward's voice.

"I tried to put myself in her shoes." That was her mother. "I know she must be dying inside. But still."

Creeping toward the staircase, Olivia peered over the banister. Her mother sat on a bottom step beside Edward. He had his arm draped across her shoulders and was holding her close. Olivia reeled backward, shocked at how intimate they seemed together.

"I'm sorry you had to go through that," Edward said. "I didn't think it was wise, you going."

"I know. I just thought . . . I wanted to pay my respects. But for Cynthia to speak to me that way. To be so hateful."

The sight of her mother distraught was so bizarre, Olivia wondered if she was dreaming. She never saw her mother exhibit this kind of emotion. Even though she knew Ms. Monroe's words had to have hurt, at the funeral her mother had kept any evidence that they had affected her buried inside.

Edward tightened his hold on Sylvia as she loudly blew her nose. With his free hand, he passed her another tissue. "You need to put what she said out of your mind."

"But what if people start to look at me with suspicion? Really believe me capable of murder?"

"That's nonsense. Cynthia said that to hurt you, that's all."

"I ought to get you to make me a voodoo doll of her." Sylvia chortled softly through her tears. "I'm only half joking."

"No need. The woman's already miserable."

"You can take some people out of the ghetto, dress them up in fancy clothes, but never take the ghetto out of them."

"Like me?" Edward's voice held a playful note.

"No, not you." Sylvia shifted, and in one smooth motion she reached for Edward's face. But as she turned, she caught sight of Olivia.

In a flash, Sylvia was on her feet. Edward followed suit. Sylvia wiped at her tears before crossing her arms over her chest.

"Olivia, I didn't hear you."

"Sorry, Mama. I didn't . . . I didn't realize you were talking."

"Your mama's just a little upset is all," Edward said. "I thought it would help for her to talk things out."

"Thank you, Edward." Sylvia's tone was suddenly businesslike.

Edward turned and disappeared toward the left.

"Are you okay, Mama?"

"I'm fine. Funerals always get me down."

But it was more than that, clearly. Her mother hadn't said a word as they left the church and headed home, and Olivia hadn't dared to ask her the question that was on her mind.

Why did Ms. Monroe say that to you, Mama?

She didn't dare ask it now.

She wondered how much Edward knew. Surprising as it was, he clearly knew something.

"I think I'll head on upstairs, take a nap."

Olivia watched her mother walk past her, noticed that her mother wouldn't meet her eyes.

Over the years, Olivia hadn't given much thought to the reason why her mother didn't like Cynthia, but now, having overheard part of her talk with Edward, she couldn't help doing so. All these years, she'd been missing something. The underlying reason for the animosity. And it wasn't simply that her mother didn't agree with Cynthia's lifestyle, because the animosity clearly went both ways.

But as sure as Olivia knew that, she also knew that her mother would never give her any answers.

Belinda's face was just what Olivia needed to see hours later.
A smile broke out on her face. "Belinda."

"Hey."

Olivia hopped off her bed and scurried to her friend. She gave her a big hug and didn't want to let go.

"The funeral was that bad?" Belinda asked.

"Weird is more like it," Olivia replied, breaking the hug.

"How so?"

"First of all, barely anyone was there. Maybe only twelve or thirteen people besides Ms. Monroe. It seemed so sad, to be leaving this world and barely anyone cares to say good-bye."

"And?"

"And . . ." Olivia sat cross-legged on the bed. "Do you think I'm stupid?"

"Huh? What?"

"Do you think I'm stupid?"

"Of course I don't think you're stupid. Why would you ask that?"

"Something's up with my mama and Ms. Monroe. If you saw the way Ms. Monroe looked at my mama when she saw her in the church. She came right out and told her she shouldn't have been there."

"No!"

"Uh-huh. And with so much anger. Made me realize that there's a lot more to why my mama never has anything good to say about her or Liza. A whole lot more. But what?"

It was a rhetorical question, but the look in Belinda's eyes made Olivia's heart flutter. "What is it, Belinda? My God. What do you know?"

Belinda sat beside her. "I never said anything before—"

"What?" Olivia asked desperately.

"It's not that I *know* anything . . ."

"Tell me!"

Belinda shrugged. "It's just . . . one time I heard my mama saying something about yours. Something about how she likes to pretend her life is perfect, but people know she has secrets."

"What kind of secrets?"

"I don't know. That's all I heard."

"Who was your mama talking to?"

"Yours, I think. They were on the phone. Sounded like they were having some kind of disagreement."

Her mother and Hailey usually got along well. "What were they talking about?"

"My daddy, from what I could tell." Belinda scowled. "I think your mama was trying to tell mine she ought to leave him, 'cause my mama said something about not being ready yet. Then she sounded upset and she said your mama was one to talk."

"Talk about what?"

"If I knew, I'd tell you. The whole reason I didn't say anything about this before is because I didn't really hear anything. And when my mama realized I had entered the room, she quickly got off the phone. I don't even know if she was talking to your mama or not. I just got the sense that she was."

More questions. Would Olivia ever get any answers?

She had to put that thought out of her mind or else she would go crazy. "What *is* happening between your parents? You're still here." Her tone was hopeful.

"Things are quiet. They won't tell me a thing. My daddy's acting all sweet, but my mama is being mean to him. Not making him dinner, and I know he's been sleeping downstairs. Nobody's happy, not even Brian. Guess he knows something's wrong, even though he's only three years old."

At least they were still living under the same roof. Maybe that was a sign that things would get back to normal—eventually.

"I don't really like being around there much these days. Everything's so tense."

Olivia nodded her understanding. "How's Bernie?"

Belinda's face exploded in a grin. "Sweet as ever. We've been spending a lot of time together. These days, my mama doesn't even seem to know I'm not around."

"Wow." Like Olivia's mother, Hailey McGowan had not wanted her daughter dating until she went to college, so it was surprising that she had loosened her reins.

"It's not like we're going places to be alone all the time, neither. Bernie wants to be with me because he doesn't want me going anywhere unescorted, on account of what happened to Liza."

"Seems he really does care about you."

"He does." The smile on Belinda's face faltered. "I guess it doesn't matter that we love each other. If we're not living in the same town . . . I didn't have the heart to tell him that I might be moving away."

It was the mountain in the middle of the room, the one they couldn't get around. As much as Olivia hoped today could be just like any other time she spent with Belinda, it wasn't. Sadness gripped her soul at the horrible prospect of what could happen in the next weeks. Still, she said, "I know it's hard, B, but try not to think negatively. Maybe if you think positive, it'll all work out. You said your parents haven't been fighting."

"But they haven't been talking. This time it's different. If there wasn't a baby."

Olivia said, "I've been thinking about it, and even if you do move off to Georgia, you can come back here next year for university. If you tell your mama how important this is to you . . . we can still go to Dillard."

Belinda shook her head. "I want to, but I don't know. You know how my mama is. Always worried about me. She won't want me to leave to go to school." She paused, then her eyes lit up with hope. "Maybe you can make plans to go to Spelman."

"My mama has always wanted me to go to the same school she went to, pledge the same sorority she did. Same as my grandmother did before her. You know how big she is on tradition." Olivia shrugged. "We'll see."

Belinda sighed as she reached for Olivia's hand. "You know what I wish sometimes?"

"What?"

"Sometimes," Belinda began softly, "I wish I could just go away. Go somewhere where I don't have to deal with the fighting. Someplace quiet, where I can just sit on a porch swing and know what peace is." Her voice lowered. "I just want to know what peace is."

"I wish we could go there together," Olivia said.

"I wish that, too. And Bernie. And *Harvey*."

To Olivia's surprise, her breath caught at the mention of Harvey's name.

Belinda giggled, even though there was sadness in her eyes. "Oooh, you've got it bad."

Olivia sighed dreamily. "Maybe I do. I don't know. All I know is, whatever I'm feeling . . ." Her face took on a serious expression. "Whatever happens with him, I want to share it with you."

"I know, Liv."

"But I can't do that if you're not here."

"We'll have to call each other. A lot."

Olivia wiped at a stray tear. "That's just not enough. I need you, B. I need you here."

Tears now spilled from Belinda's eyes.

"I don't want you to leave, B."

Belinda reached for and squeezed Olivia's hand. "I know, Liv. I don't want to leave, either."

CHAPTER TWELVE

But Belinda did leave.

The very next day. There was no time for tears when Hailey had unexpectedly shown up at the door with the children so that Belinda and Olivia could say good-bye to each other.

Olivia had been too shocked to cry. She could only beg Belinda not to forget her, to make sure she called when they got to Georgia.

That was two days ago, and Olivia had been in the dumps ever since.

Harvey had started working at the house, but Olivia could hardly get excited about that. She had pretty much stayed in her room and hadn't seen him. Once, she'd looked out one of her bedroom windows and seen him working in the backyard. He'd spotted her and waved to her, but Olivia had promptly drawn the curtains shut.

Initially, she had been intrigued by Harvey. Ready to see what possibilities the future could hold for them. But nothing was the same anymore, not without Belinda. How could she be excited about anything, even this new mysterious man who had been on her mind more than she had thought possible?

Olivia's stomach growled, reminding her she'd barely picked at her breakfast this morning. She tossed her notebook onto the bed beside her. No words were coming to her anyway, so she may as well go downstairs for food. She hadn't been eating much since Belinda had left.

Olivia was slowly making her way downstairs when Harvey suddenly appeared. She halted, even as her heart started to race.

What was he doing in the house? She thought he'd started work on the exterior part of the house first.

It didn't matter. Olivia hurried down the remaining steps. She mumbled "hi" before continuing on.

She made it several feet away from Harvey before she heard "Tell me." Harvey's deep voice stopped her in her tracks. "Have I done something to offend you?"

Warmth spread over her. She had missed him, no matter how much she had tried to put him out of her mind as she grieved Belinda's moving away.

Slowly, Olivia turned. His light-colored eyes were startling in their intensity. There was something about his eyes, something that made her feel he was always trying to look into her soul.

"No," she said, in brief response to his question. Then she whirled on her heel and started off again.

"I get the feeling you're mad at me."

Again, Olivia stopped, but she didn't turn. She felt like a mouse running from a cat, but this game was exciting. She wanted to be caught. "I'm not mad."

"Not even because of what happened in the park?"

"Nothing happened in the park."

"I didn't feel it was right to stay," Harvey went on. "You were with your friends."

"Oh. I hadn't given that a second thought." *Only a third, a fourth, a fifth . . .*

"Then something else is bothering you."

She shouldn't be excited about spending time with Harvey, not when Belinda was gone from her life. "It has nothing to do with you."

"Can you tell me that to my face?"

Olivia faced him. "It has nothing to do with you."

"You want to talk about it?"

She had the feeling he was going to hound her until she gave him the answers he wanted. "I'm just going through a hard time right now. My best friend moved away a couple days ago. It all happened so fast, before I was ready. Not that I'd ever have been ready."

"Ah." To Olivia's surprise, his tone was genuinely sympathetic. "I know how that can be."

"You do?"

"Sure. It's happened to me a lot over the years. I've lost a lot of friends."

"You have."

"Uh-huh. Though I was the one who usually moved away."

Olivia eyed him, wondering what the mystery was behind him. "My mama said you don't think you'll be in town more than a few months. Sounds like you move pretty often."

"I do."

"Why?"

Harvey shrugged. "I don't know. I guess I never found a place I felt I wanted to stay. Sometimes I didn't have a choice. In the end it doesn't matter. I know what it's like to get close to people, and how much it hurts when they're no longer in your life."

"That's exactly what I'm afraid of. That she won't be in my life anymore. That no matter how much we promise we'll keep in touch, in time, we won't be the best of friends anymore."

"I can't promise that won't happen," Harvey told her truthfully. "But I know that if you both make the effort to stay in touch, you will."

Olivia smiled softly. But though she felt somewhat better, she felt weird talking to a practical stranger about her feelings like this. Especially when she got butterflies in her stomach every time she was around him.

She changed the subject. "What are you . . . are you doing some work in the house?"

"A little. I was checking out the interior window frames to see what shape they're in. Plus, it's so hot out, it was nice to come inside and get a break from the heat."

"Oh, let me get you a cold drink. Edward always makes fresh lemonade. It's really good. Would you like that or something else?"

"Lemonade sounds like just what I need."

"One minute." Olivia gave Harvey a brief smile, then headed to the kitchen. Minutes later, she returned with a tall glass for him.

He accepted the glass, asking, "Where's your glass?"

"Oh . . . I . . ."

"You don't want to join me?"

His eyes sparkled, and Olivia felt a weird sensation wash over her. "I figured . . . you probably need to get back to work."

"A guy needs a break every once in a while. Besides, this juice will be much more pleasant if I have it with some company."

"I doubt that," Olivia replied softly.

"Humor me."

Olivia gave him a bashful smile. "Well, sure. If you insist."

"I insist."

And that's how it started, and how it went from day to day. Each day, Olivia went downstairs to meet Harvey for lunch, lunches spent outside under the shade of the giant oak tree in the backyard.

And each day, she found herself laughing with Harvey, which was a marked change from how she had spent her solitary time in her bedroom recently. Soon, her broken heart was mending, and although she missed Belinda greatly, she was feeling a bit better with each passing hour.

It was good to have someone to talk to, someone to keep her mind off her sadness.

Someone as attractive as Harvey.

What had begun as intrigue where he was concerned had turned to a definite attraction. She liked him, and she found herself wanting to spend more and more time with him.

Which was the case today. Though they'd spent a pleasant half hour together, she found herself missing him only a couple hours later.

"It's such a hot day," she said aloud when she found herself in the kitchen preparing a snack for him. "Harvey must be thirsty again. And a man needs food to keep up his energy."

His smile was all the reward she needed for her efforts.

"You looked hot," Olivia explained. "I thought I'd bring you something cold to drink. And a snack. You must be hungry again with all the work you're doing."

Olivia placed the tray on the picnic table near Harvey's workstation, then held out a glass of lemonade to him.

Harvey took the proffered glass as he slid onto the bench. "Thanks." He winked. "You're always thinking of me."

Olivia blushed.

"You're gonna sit with me?"

"Yes." She sat opposite him on the bench. She sipped her lemonade, then said, "I hope you like fruit."

"This is the best. Watermelon, pineapple, oranges." Harvey perused the fruit plate and chose a slice of apple first. "You're amazing, you know that?"

Olivia's face broke into a grin. "I'm only trying to make sure you're taken care of. That way, you'll do better work."

Silence fell between them, and Olivia watched Harvey eat. Minutes passed before she spoke. "You know, in all the time we've been talking, you haven't told me where you're from. I guess I haven't asked . . . I just know I haven't seen you around here before."

"That's the way I like it. It's not good to be seen too much. Not good when too many people know you."

Like Liza, Olivia thought.

"So you're saying you are from around here? Were you born and raised here?"

"Yeah, I was born in Louisiana. Raised somewhere else."

She wondered why he was giving her such brief answers. "Where were you raised?"

"Illinois. Mostly Chicago."

Olivia sipped. "So what brings you here? Do you have family here?"

"Some. Some cousins."

"Is that why you came? To visit them?"

"Mmm-mmm. I don't even see them."

Olivia wished she had cousins or other family to hang out with besides her mother. "Then why did you come?"

Harvey didn't look at her. "There are some things—things I want to take care of."

"What kind of things?"

Harvey chewed a piece of pineapple before answering. "It would bore you. Why don't you tell me about you? You haven't told me much, either."

"There's nothing interesting to tell."

"Really? A house like this." With his hand, he gestured to the expanse of the backyard. "I'd think you'd have stories."

"Like wild parties or something?"

"No." He leveled his eyes on her. "You don't look like the type."

Olivia wasn't sure if his comment bothered her or pleased her. Was it a compliment or not? She said, "Even if I was the type, my mama wouldn't stand for it."

Harvey raised an eyebrow as he looked at her. "You have a wild side?"

Olivia flushed beneath Harvey's gaze. She shook her head. "No," she admitted. "Believe me, I don't have any interesting stories." *Except the ones I write on paper.* "I've lived here pretty much all my life with my mama."

"No daddy?"

"He died eleven years ago."

"Oh, I'm sorry."

"It wasn't your fault. Besides, it was a long time ago. I almost hate to say this, but I was so young when he died, I hardly remember him. I remember certain things, special times we shared, but much of that even seems like a dream. He was on the road so much of the time . . ."

"On the road . . . what did he do? Businessman?"

Olivia smiled. She was proud of what her father had done, even though it had led to his downfall. "He was a jazz musician."

"Jazz." Harvey shrugged.

"Samuel Grayson." Olivia gave him a moment to let the name sink in. But she didn't see recognition in his eyes. "People knew him as Sammy 'Silver Touch' Grayson. Rumor was, he was born playing the saxophone."

Harvey shook his head. "The name sounds vaguely familiar, but I really can't say I've heard of him."

Olivia pouted. "That's been the worst part of it all. He was so popular in his heyday, but after he died, people quickly forgot him. Even here in New Orleans, where he was born and raised, he's pretty much forgotten. Sure, there are many who do remember him, don't get me wrong. They remember his amazing talent. But no one mentions his name when they talk about the jazz greats. And he'd been playing the saxophone for three of the four decades he'd been alive."

If her father had lived longer, how would he have changed the world of jazz? Olivia felt a pang of sadness over what his life could have been.

"Tell me about him."

"He was born in 1926, and in many ways, his life paralleled Miles Davis's. While Miles played the trumpet, my daddy played the saxophone. My daddy went to Paris, just like Miles did. And he loved it there, too. He didn't experience racism there like he did back here. He felt really appreciated there. And like Miles Davis, my daddy also wanted to move there." Olivia chuckled. "But love won out. My mama didn't want to move to Paris, so we all stayed right here.

"But still, my daddy traveled a lot. He played in New York quite a bit, often replacing Charlie Parker when Charlie was too doped up to perform. He did real well. People loved him."

"Your whole face is lit up. Do you realize that?"

"Oh." Olivia blushed. "No."

"You loved your father a lot."

"Yeah, and I'm proud of him, even though I didn't get as much time with him as I would have wanted." She paused. "He played with most of the greats: Sarah Vaughan, Miles Davis, Dizzy Gillespie. My mama has his albums. I listen to them from time to time."

"I love jazz. Maybe you'll let me listen to them someday."

"You'll have to ask my mama. She's pretty protective of them."

"You said he would replace Charlie Parker sometimes?"

"Yeah. It was a shame what happened to Charlie. Before my uncle Ronnie died—my daddy's brother—he told me that after seeing what had happened to Charlie Parker, my daddy was turned off of drugs." Olivia frowned. "That's why I don't understand how he died."

"What do you mean?"

Olivia lowered her voice to a whisper, as though she were afraid someone might hear her. "It's not something we like to talk about," she confided. "It was real tragic, especially for someone who'd been doing so well. I know Mama feels he brought shame to the family."

"Sounds pretty bad."

"It was. He . . . just like Charlie Parker and some other artists, he got involved with drugs. I guess the pressure of being famous and having to constantly create new music finally got to him. It's still so hard to believe, though, because to hear my uncle Ronnie tell the story, my daddy had been so antidrugs and -alcohol, especially after seeing how some of the men he respected had lost their heads. I mean, Charlie Parker was so talented, but so troubled. I guess the pressure of everything finally got to my daddy, and he turned to heroin. A lot of them did, from what I understand. And he . . ." She whispered. "He overdosed. Right after he left a club. He'd been in the crowd, not playing, just watching some of the men he respected. Maybe that's what depressed him, because he hadn't played for a little while at that time. I don't know. I don't know what was going through his mind. I never will."

Harvey reached across the table and covered her hand. Olivia first felt shock, then warmth. A simple touch, but it had her feeling better.

Her gaze lowered to his lips. They were full. Sexy. She wanted to kiss him.

"That had to be rough, Olivia. I'm sorry you had to lose your father that way."

His comment brought her thoughts back to her father. "Please . . . don't tell anyone. Mama would be upset if she knew I told you. She didn't tell me the truth, not until a couple years ago, when I kept pestering her about it. I guess she figured I'd finally hear the truth from someone else, so she agreed to tell me the story. Before that, I grew up thinking he'd died of a heart attack."

"I don't see why she would lie to you about it. Mrs. Grayson, she shouldn't feel ashamed about how your father died. Stuff . . . it just happens. It's no reflection on her."

Olivia laughed without mirth. "You can't tell Mama that. She has only one picture of Daddy in the house. One. In the living room, on the fireplace mantel. Not even one in her bedroom. I always thought that was weird." Olivia shrugged. "Maybe she misses him too much."

"That could be it. She's never remarried?"

"No. But she's been fine without a man. It's been just me and Mama for years. And Rosa, of course. We've gotten along perfectly fine."

Harvey slipped his hand away, but his eyes lingered on hers, and Olivia got the feeling that he didn't want to stop touching her and only did so because he felt he should. She wanted to tell him that he didn't have to stop, that she wanted more, but she couldn't find the words.

Olivia was suddenly uncomfortable with the silence. Maybe she'd said too much about her father. She stood. "I guess I should let you get back to work."

Harvey rose and stretched. "Yeah, I guess. I'm liable to get too comfortable sitting here. Thanks again."

"No problem." Olivia gathered the tray and started to walk away as Harvey went back to work. Halfway across the concrete area outlining the pool, she paused and looked over her shoulder.

Harvey was watching her, like she knew he would be.

She gave a sheepish smile, then continued to the house.

CHAPTER THIRTEEN

Olivia couldn't stop smiling. She wasn't sure what she felt; she only knew that she was enjoying every moment of it.

And it was all because of Harvey.

Harvey. She really did like him, even though he seemed to have a secretive side. Or maybe that was what intrigued her. All she knew for sure was that Harvey had an easy way about him that made her feel totally comfortable. And he never failed to make her laugh. Just seeing him made her feel giddy. And flushed.

Olivia sighed happily as she lay stretched out on her bed. She thought of Harvey all the time. Was this normal? She doubted she could stop thinking of him any more than she could involuntarily stop breathing.

She rolled onto her side, resting her arm beneath her head. Whatever she was feeling, she didn't think it was one-sided. She was pretty sure that Harvey liked her, too.

Unless he was just being friendly.

Olivia wished Belinda were here. She wanted to talk to her about what she was feeling. Belinda had gone through these emotions with Bernie and could help her figure things out.

Olivia got up and strolled to the window. She hid her body as best she could and peered into the backyard. Her chest filled with heat when she saw Harvey, bent over, sawing a piece of wood.

Sweat glistened on his back, on all his muscles.

He was strong, so strong.

And maybe, one day, he would be hers.

There was a quick rap on her bedroom door before it opened. "Olivia?"

Olivia looked up from her desk. "Hi, Mama. Hey, Rosa." Rosa scurried into the room and jumped onto her lap.

"Are you busy?" Sylvia asked.

"Well, kind of. I was working on a story." She'd had a busy day volunteering at the neighborhood daycare center and was finally getting around to working on her romance novel. Like her mother and grandmother before her, Olivia did a lot of volunteer work. It was a tradition she would continue in a bigger way once she became a Delta. "Why?"

Her mother's eyes lit up. "I was hoping you could help me."

Olivia asked, "Help you what?"

"I have got a ton of applications from the children to sort through, and I admit I'm running behind. For the trip coming up on Labor Day weekend?"

"Yes, I know."

"You remember that I told you the applicants had to write a short piece about why they deserve this trip? Well, since you're so good with writing, why don't you go through the essays? The ones you think are the best, you put in a certain pile."

"Oh." What a surprise that her mother would come to her with this. Olivia's chest swelled with pride.

Besides her charitable work through her sorority and social clubs, her mother had founded her own charity to help less fortunate children. Having been the child of parents who owned a rice farm, Sylvia had never wanted for anything, and never would. So, she'd dedicated her life to helping the less fortunate.

For at least the last few years, her mother's charity, L.G.B. Enterprises—Let's Give Back Enterprises—had been sponsoring this trip for the children. Last year, Olivia had watched her mother going over the entries and had wanted to ask if she could help. But she hadn't.

"You can even choose the winners, if you like. Fifteen children."

"Me?"

"Why not? I trust you." Sylvia gave her a smile. "Besides, I think it would be fun. Take your mind off things, and put your talents to good use."

By "things," Olivia knew her mother was referring to Belinda's leaving.

"And once I'm through with this project, you and I can finally get around to shopping for your cotillion dress."

Olivia's eyes lit up. "I can hardly wait. I saw this beautiful dress in that catalog I sent for. It has the prettiest lace detail."

"So you'll help me with the essays?"

"Sure, Mama."

"You want to head downstairs right now? We can work together in the sunroom."

Maybe her mama was right. Maybe this was exactly what she needed, for more reason than one. Reading these entries could help spark her own creativity. And it would definitely take her mind off her troubles.

And off Harvey.

Olivia lifted Rosa as she stood. "Sure."

Sylvia's heart filled with joy when she saw her daughter's smile. She knew Olivia was having a hard time dealing with Belinda's leaving, and it was good to see her happy again.

Sylvia placed a hand on Olivia's back and led her toward the mouth of the stairs. But as she looked down into the foyer, she froze. Edward was standing there with an attractive, well-dressed black man.

In this humid weather, it was odd to see a man in a suit and tie, and Sylvia immediately knew he had to be a cop.

Rosa squirmed in Olivia's arms and freed herself. She ran down the stairs toward the stranger.

Reaching behind her, Sylvia took Olivia's hand in hers. It was an instinct, a protective one, even though she was sure this man wasn't here to hurt her daughter. Slowly, Sylvia started with Olivia down the stairs.

"Mrs. Grayson," Edward said. "I was just about to call for you. This is Detective Marley. He has some questions for you."

"I see."

Edward quietly disappeared, leaving Sylvia, Olivia, and the detective alone.

Sylvia gave the detective a tentative smile as she extended a hand to him. "Hello, Detective Marley."

"Hello, ma'am." He ignored Rosa, who was pawing at his legs. "Lovely home you have."

"Thank you. Rosa, behave." The dog turned and pranced toward Sylvia. "What brings you by today, Detective?"

"You are aware that a Miss Liza Monroe was murdered two weeks ago?"

She flinched. Had Cynthia sent the detective here? "Yes, of course."

"I'm one of the detectives investigating her murder. We've been trying to follow up some leads. Your daughter Olivia's name came up."

"Olivia?" Sylvia asked with complete alarm.

"Yes," the detective replied calmly. "Her name was mentioned as someone who knew Liza Monroe."

Sylvia put an arm around Olivia and pulled her close. "My daughter did not know that girl."

"Not at all?"

"Well, not in the way you mean."

"With all due respect, you haven't let me explain what I mean. Whether or not Olivia and Liza were close has nothing to do with whether your daughter has information pertinent to this investigation. She may not even know it." When Sylvia didn't respond, the detective continued. "I assure you, this won't take long, and we can clear up any misunderstandings."

He sounded so reasonable, but when didn't they? She still had a bitter taste in her mouth from how the police had handled the investigation into her husband's death, all those years ago. Hmph. What investigation? They'd drawn their conclusions from the beginning and stuck to them, no matter how much she'd pestered them.

Maybe she was partly to blame, but Sylvia had had her family's reputation to consider, so she'd tried to give the police clues in a way that wouldn't have provided gossip for all the nosy people in this town. Despite their asinine conclusions, she had known there was no way in the world that Samuel could have killed himself, even accidentally. But they had ignored her, and that whore Cynthia Monroe had gotten away with murder.

"Ma'am?"

The detective's voice brought Sylvia back to the present. "Oh, you want to speak with her now?"

"Since she's available."

"I-I don't know." Sylvia frowned. "I don't see how Olivia can help you in any way."

"It won't take but a minute," the detective assured her.

And if she didn't agree to it now, the detective would no doubt be back. Sylvia could protest all she wanted, but the police would question her daughter at some point.

"I need to be there," Sylvia said.

"Of course."

"All right. We can do this in the living room. Follow me." Still holding Olivia's hand, Sylvia walked the short distance to the left, leading them into the spacious, brightly lit living room.

They wasted no time sitting on the sofa and getting down to business. Rosa joined them, hopping onto Sylvia's lap.

Detective Marley sat on an angle so that he could see Olivia, since Sylvia sat between them. He said, "Olivia, how did you know Liza Monroe?"

Olivia was silent for a long moment, her eyes downcast. Finally, she glanced at her mother.

Sylvia stroked Olivia's arm. "It's all right, Olivia. Answer the detective's questions."

"Did you know Liza well?"

"I kind of knew her," Olivia replied, her eyes focused on the wood flooring.

"Were you friends?"

"No." She looked at the detective now. "We weren't friends. I just saw her around the neighborhood. Sometimes, we said hi."

"That was the extent of your relationship?"

Again, Olivia paused, and Sylvia looked at her daughter with concern. "There's no need to be nervous, Olivia. You didn't associate with her. Tell the detective that."

Olivia gave Detective Marley a sheepish look.

His eyebrows shot together. "The truth, Olivia."

"I . . . we weren't friends, but there was one time when me and Belinda and

Liza, and a few other girls . . . we were all outside Mr. Johnson's ice cream shop, and we were talking."

Sylvia's eyes widened in utter disbelief. "You told me you had nothing to do with that girl."

"I . . . I didn't. She was just there that afternoon. There was nothing to it."

"Were there boys there?" Sylvia asked. "Or knowing Liza, men?"

"No!" Olivia replied, adamant. "It was just girls, about five of us, and Liza wasn't there long, anyway."

"Olivia." The detective's stern voice brought her attention back to him. "Did Liza ever talk to you about any enemies?"

"No."

"Did you know anyone who didn't like her?"

"Most everyone. She wasn't very popular," Olivia quickly explained. "Usually, she didn't talk to the other girls in the neighborhood. We didn't really like her because of that."

"But that's not a motive for murder," Sylvia interjected.

"I didn't say it was, Mrs. Grayson," Detective Marley said. The look he gave her told her to keep her mouth closed.

The detective turned his attention back to Olivia. "You said she didn't talk much to the women. What about men? Do you know who she was dating?"

"She didn't have a steady boyfriend, if that's what you mean. Everybody saw her with a lot of men. Seems she was with a different one every time I saw her."

The detective nodded, as though he'd heard this before. "Do you know any of the men?"

She shrugged. "Not really . . ."

"Olivia, this is very important."

Olivia threw her mother a quick glance before answering the question in a hushed voice. "Sometimes, I saw her with Mr. Johnson."

"Mr. Johnson!" Sylvia exclaimed. "But he's married."

"Mrs. Grayson, please," Detective Marley said. He scribbled some notes. "I understand that your daughter's a minor, and you want to be present while I question her, but please, let her speak."

Sylvia cut her eyes at the detective. She didn't appreciate being told to keep her mouth shut, not in her own home.

"Mr. Johnson?" the detective asked. "Who is that?"

"Mr. Alvin Johnson. He owns the ice cream shop, Johnson's Ice Cream. That's who I saw her with," Olivia stressed. "There were other men, too. Some I didn't know. A lot of them I've seen around, and I know they're married. They're older. Much older than Liza was."

The detective made some more notes.

"Did you know of anyone who wanted to hurt Liza?"

"No," Olivia replied. "I just know that a lot of the girls didn't talk to her much, which is why it was strange that day when we were outside of Johnson's Ice Cream." She paused, then suddenly said, "Wait. I remember something. Liza didn't really say anything to us that day, but we heard her arguing with someone inside the shop. Then, when she came out, she seemed upset. She looked like she'd been crying."

The detective's eyes lit up at this news. "Who was she arguing with?"

"I don't know. I guess it could have been Mr. Johnson. He's always there. But I don't know that for sure. Anyway, when she came out and saw us, she acted as if everything was cool. That's when she stopped and talked to us for a while."

"What did she say?"

"Normal stuff. Hi. How you all doing. Sure is hot. That kind of stuff. It didn't last more than a couple minutes, then she hurried off."

"And how long ago was this?"

"About a week before she disappeared."

Detective Marley scribbled more notes. "Did you ever see her in an altercation with Mr. Johnson?"

"No."

"Okay." Detective Marley blew out a sigh, then tapped his pen against his police notepad.

"Clearly, she doesn't know anything that can help you," Sylvia said.

"Actually, she's already helped me. Given me a new direction to pursue." He withdrew a card from his inside jacket pocket and passed it to Sylvia. "Here's my card. Olivia, if you think of anything else, anything at all, please let your mother know, and she can call me, or you can call me."

"All right," Olivia told him.

Rosa jumped onto the floor as Detective Marley stood. Again, he ignored her. "Thank you for your time. Wait, I almost forgot." He reached into his jacket pocket and pulled out a photograph. "This ring was missing from Liza's body. Have you possibly seen anybody with it?"

Olivia shook her head. "No."

"Mrs. Grayson?"

The detective's voice sounded hopeful, and Olivia glanced at her mother. She looked like she had seen a ghost.

"Mrs. Grayson, have you seen this ring before?"

She hugged her torso and briskly shook her head. "No."

Olivia's eyes narrowed on her mother. Something seemed off about her. Had she just lied?

"Okay, then." The detective replaced the photo in his pocket. "Thanks again."

Sylvia stood. "You're welcome. Let me see you out."

Sylvia led the way to the door, and the detective followed her. Olivia lagged behind, watching Rosa dance around their steps. She heard her mother say, "I'm sorry she couldn't be more help."

Olivia drew in a breath and held it. She felt stressed from all the questions, but mostly from the fear that her mother would be disappointed in her because she'd spent some time with Liza.

She watched her mother close the door behind the detective. Slowly, Sylvia turned and faced her again. As she started toward her, Olivia swallowed.

"Olivia. You didn't tell me that you'd talked to Liza."

"But I didn't. Not really. She just spoke to the group of us. Only a few words."

She stroked her hair. "I guess you didn't think you could talk to me about this, but I want you to know, you can talk to me about anything."

"What about you, Mama? Can I ask you anything?"

Sylvia hesitated. "Yes. Yes, of course you can."

Olivia thought of how best to pose her question. "That day, at Liza's funeral . . . why did Ms. Monroe say those things to you?"

Sylvia's already pale skin grew paler. She bent to pick up Rosa, as if she were stalling. "Like I told you, grief. It can cloud a person's mind. Cynthia wasn't thinking straight."

"You're sure?" Olivia added timidly.

"Of course I'm sure," her mother snapped. Then she softened her tone. "I'm sorry, Olivia. It's just that the memory isn't pleasant. I went there to pay my respects and she humiliated me in front of everyone. Of course, that's not your fault." Sylvia inhaled a deep breath and blew it out slowly. "Mr. Johnson, hmm?"

"Uh-huh."

"Brother."

Olivia got the impression her mother had deliberately changed the subject to take the focus off herself.

She couldn't help wondering why.

CHAPTER FOURTEEN

Harvey crouched out of view at the side of the house, behind one of the large, flowery bushes. He had seen the well-dressed man when he approached the house and knew right away that the guy was a cop. A detective. He'd been inside with the Graysons for a fair bit of time, and Harvey was anxious as all hell.

His calves hurt from resting on his haunches for so long, but he didn't dare move. He felt only a small sense of relief when the door opened and the detective stepped outside. He wanted to know what was going on, even if that meant the worst possible scenario.

As he watched the detective look around, his heart pounded hard against his chest. Maybe he had made the wrong decision by sticking around. Damn. What should he do now? Flee? Surely if he ran he would never get away.

No, it was best he stay hidden. If the cop started looking for him, he had a better chance of avoiding him if he stayed right where he was.

The detective withdrew a cigarette from his inside jacket pocket, then made a cup around his mouth as he lit it. He skipped down the front steps and headed to the front gate. Sure enough, he was leaving. Harvey stayed in the bushes until he heard the man's car drive away.

With the detective finally gone, Harvey allowed himself to breathe in a deep, easy breath. If the cop had been here for him, certainly he wouldn't have left.

Still, Harvey wasn't sure he could relax yet. Not until he knew for sure.

Slowly, he headed through the backyard to his worktable. Thoughts ran through his mind a mile a minute. He kept glancing at the patio doors, expecting to see Mrs. Grayson charging out to look for him, yet hoping he would see Olivia. This was one time he hoped she'd pay him a surprise visit with a snack or just to talk. If she came out, he would ask her what the cop had wanted.

But Olivia didn't come out.

Harvey continued to work, but hours later his thoughts were still on his past, on what he'd run from in Chicago. Who knew how long he could stay here? And yet he wasn't any closer to accomplishing his goal here in New Orleans.

Yes, he needed to make money, which is why he'd accepted this job. He had left Chicago with less than two hundred dollars in his pocket. But he had a mother to find, the mother he'd never known. And he had to find her before he'd be forced to leave again.

He had been taking his time, building up his courage to contact her. He didn't want to be rejected.

But if she would have him—if she would love him—he could use her support right now. He needed someone in his corner.

Harvey tried to block out his problems as he gathered the scraps of wood and carried them to the back of the carriage house. The place was getting to be a mess, but he'd clean it up later.

On his way back to the worktable, he sensed her. Looking up, he saw Olivia standing at her bedroom window. She was staring at him, as she'd done so many times before.

He stared back, trying to sense if something was wrong. After a moment, she smiled and waved.

Everything seemed fine. He waved back.

Back at the worktable, he lifted another piece of wood and locked it in place in the vise. But his thoughts stayed on Olivia. She liked him, he knew. And he was falling for her. She was pretty and sweet, and she made him wish for things with a woman that he'd never wished for before.

A life. A happy one.

A painful knot formed in his stomach, and he dropped the saw in frustration. He had no right to wish for anything with her.

Because if she found out the real reason he was in town—what he was running from—Harvey knew she would want nothing to do with him.

CHAPTER FIFTEEN

Sylvia?"

All the blood drained from Sylvia's head as she held the receiver to her ear. Oh, God. It was her mother. After the amount of time they hadn't been in touch, Sylvia had thought that Hazel Etienne no longer had the power to affect her one way or another. But she realized now that she was wrong.

It had been well over two years since Sylvia and her mother had last spoken. Before that, they'd had the obligatory Christmas and birthday conversations—until they'd both decided not to continue with the facade. Their relationship had virtually died when Sylvia had gone against her mother's wishes and married Samuel Grayson.

Things had gone sour before that, actually, during that awful, awful time . . .

But the relationship had taken a final turn for the worse during Samuel's tragic and public demise. Sylvia had hoped for some support from her mother, for a shoulder to cry on. All she'd gotten were smug I-told-you-sos.

After that, Sylvia had given up hopes of salvaging a genuine relationship with her mother, and she was certain her mother felt the same way. In fact, when they had stopped talking altogether, Sylvia had been relieved.

So why was the great Hazel Etienne calling her now? A surprise call could mean only one thing: bad news.

"Sylvia?" Hazel repeated.

"What is it, Mother?" Sylvia asked without preamble. "What's wrong?"

"Hello to you too, Olivia."

Sylvia rolled her eyes, even as a long, familiar pain gripped her heart. Her mother had always made her feel two inches tall, ever since she'd hit puberty. It was something Sylvia hated. Something she hadn't overcome in the twenty years since she'd officially been an adult.

"Hello, Mother." Sylvia didn't bother to point out that she'd be less surprised to win the Publishers Clearing House Sweepstakes than she was to receive this call from her mother. "How are you?"

"I'm keeping well."

"To what do I owe this honor?"

"I'm not sure you'll think it's an honor when you hear what I have to say." Instinct made alarm spread through her. She was right. Her mother *was* calling with bad news.

Sylvia tried to keep her voice calm. "Why don't you just say it?"

"Clinton Morrison."

Sylvia's knees gave way, and she was thankful that her bed was immediately behind her. She sank into the softness of the mattress.

She opened her mouth to speak, to repeat the name she had tried to burn from her memory so long ago, but nothing more than a whisper of breath escaped her.

"Yes, Sylvia. You heard me correctly."

"Clinton?" she finally managed. "Why on earth are you calling about Clinton?"

Hazel paused, then replied, "I got off the phone with him not more than five minutes ago."

"What?" Sylvia felt her airwaves constricting. "He . . . he called you? I don't understand."

"I was as surprised as anybody could be."

"But how did he find you? You don't even live where we used to live . . ."

"I don't know, Sylvia. Somehow, he tracked me down."

This was the worst news. The worst possible news. So long she had kept the past buried. But now?

"Why?" Sylvia asked.

"Says he was looking for you."

Sylvia's heart spasmed. "W-what did you tell him?"

"What do you think I said? I told him that he had no business calling."

"And he said?"

"He said he needs to talk to you. That it's important. And that if you didn't call him, he would find you."

"You didn't tell him my married name, did you?"

"No. No, of course not. I'm just as happy keeping that chapter closed forever."

"Well, that's good news." Sylvia felt a little better. Without her married name, Clinton wouldn't know how to track her down.

Or would he?

One day, when you least expect it, he will come into your life. The clairvoyant's words sounded in Sylvia's mind like a whisper in her ear.

A chill swept over her. Was this what the clairvoyant had been referring to?

"I'm not sure it matters if he knows your married name, Sylvia," Hazel was saying when Sylvia tuned in to her mother's words. "Investigators are smart. They know how to find people if they have to. That's their job."

"Are you trying to scare me?"

"I'm just telling you the truth. A quick marriage search at city hall . . . oh, God. Think about it, Sylvia. This could be disastrous. At first, I wasn't sure what you should do. If you should talk to him or ignore him."

"I think I'm capable of making my own decisions." Sylvia would not let her mother bully her into a specific action, not this time.

"Please, hear me out. I know you want nothing to do with him. Believe me, I want the same thing. However, I've thought this through, and I think you need to call him, Sylvia. Find out what he wants. Then deal with him before he becomes a problem."

"I have nothing to say to him."

"Have you been listening to me? Do you want him to track you down?"

"Of course not."

"Then you have to contact him first. Because if he's calling after all these years, I'm sure he's desperate enough to hire someone to find you."

Sylvia conceded the fact that perhaps her mother was right. "He gave you the number? Obviously. That was a dumb question." Frazzled nerves had her not thinking straight.

"Yes."

"All right." This was not something she wanted to do, but right now it seemed she had no choice. "Give me a second to grab a pen and paper."

Sylvia placed the receiver on the night table, then opened her drawer in search of something to write on. She scooped up a notepad and pencil. Moments later, she brought the receiver to her ear. "Okay. What's the number?"

Hazel recited the number and Sylvia scribbled it down.

"That's Texas."

"Houston."

Sylvia blew out a quick breath. "Okay, I'll call him."

"Please," Hazel quickly said, perhaps fearing Sylvia would hang up. Her voice held an uncharacteristic note of desperation. "When you find out what he wants, will you let me know?"

Sylvia hesitated a moment, then replied, "Sure. Talk to you later."

Minutes after ending the call, Sylvia sat on her bed, her back iron-board stiff. For the life of her, she couldn't figure out what was going on.

Why on earth would Clinton be trying to reach her now, so many years after they'd last spoken? And the way they'd parted . . . it didn't make sense.

Sylvia glanced at the piece of paper in her hand, at the number written on it. And she knew there was no way she could take that walk down memory lane.

Rising, she shredded the paper.

She didn't care what Clinton wanted. She would *not* call him.

If by any chance he tracked her down, she would deal with him then.

For now, she was happy enough to take her chances that he wouldn't be able to find her.

CHAPTER SIXTEEN

S he was running.

Running as fast as she could, as far as her legs could take her.

Tears burned her eyes, making it harder to see in the darkness. But she didn't slow her pace. She kept up her sprint, running toward the water she knew was in the distance.

The water.

The water would wash away her sins . . .

A s the water splashed onto her face, Sylvia cried out from fear. She didn't dare open her eyes. She didn't want to see her watery grave.

As she held her breath and prepared to die, she realized there was something strange about this wetness. She felt only spots of moisture on her face, yet she was submerged.

Her eyes flew open. She saw the puffy white hair just as she realized Rosa's tongue was flicking across her face.

Rosa. She'd been dreaming.

"Rosa," Sylvia said, partially relieved. Sitting up, she reached for her dog, pulling Rosa onto her lap. Though she knew she was safe in her bed, her heart beat out of control.

The dream had seemed so real.

It had been real. Once.

"Forget that time," Sylvia whispered. "Forget it all."

Rosa gave a soft bark in reply to her comment.

"No, Rosa. Not you."

Drawing in a steady breath, Sylvia looked around her bedroom, at this familiar space of hers, and reassured herself that all was well. She was in the present, in the here and now, not back in the past.

She had to remember that, hold on to that.

She lay back in her warm bed. She clung to Rosa as if the dog were a line of defense against the past.

The nightmare had returned after all these years, and it was just as disturbing as it had always been. And there was only one reason why she was being haunted again—the call she'd received from her mother.

Restless, she sat up a second time. She held Rosa tightly against her chest. The dog whimpered, concerned. Could Rosa hear her erratically beating heart, or simply sense her fear?

Sylvia's pulse continued to race out of control. Would it ever return to its normal pace? Maybe not. Maybe nothing would ever be normal again. There was a hole in her stomach, a hole that had once healed, but with one phone call, the old wound had been ripped open.

And with the raw wound had come the dream again.

Even now, Sylvia second-guessed herself. Had she made the right decision? Should she contact Clinton? Would the dream stop if she did? Or would she learn something that would plunge her world into a place she didn't want to go?

She had considered all her options earlier, and there were no easy answers. Right now, she could deal with the status quo, because the status quo was safer. But calling Clinton could change everything.

"It's over, Clinton. I'll never go back there. You won't drag me back to that awful, awful place."

But despite her firm words, her body began to shake.

Olivia wanted to die.

Now she knew why some people became totally depressed after the breakup of a relationship. She and Harvey hadn't even been dating, yet his rejection of her earlier had made her even more sad than when Belinda had left for Georgia.

Earlier today, she'd gotten up the courage to suggest to Harvey that maybe they could go out sometime. She'd suggested *One Flew over the Cuckoo's Nest*, a movie she really wanted to see. Either that, or a restaurant for some dinner. Somewhere they could get to know each other better.

"Not like a date or anything," she had quickly lied when his face registered no reaction to her suggestion. "Just something to do."

For several agonizing seconds she had waited for a reply from him.

"I don't think that's a good idea," he had finally said.

And just like that, he had crushed her heart.

Hurt and embarrassed, Olivia had quickly gathered up the tray with their lunch plates and scurried into the house, all the while hoping Harvey would call out to her, tell her to stop, give her a logical reason for the words that had come out of his mouth.

But he hadn't.

And Olivia had felt like a fool.

How could she have been so wrong about him?

It was hours later, and Olivia still felt like a fool. She wanted to erase today from her memory.

She got out of her bed and slipped into jeans and a T-shirt. Considering it was after ten P.M., her mother should be in her room reading her Bible, as she did every night at this hour. It was during these times that Olivia snuck out of the house to go for her walks at City Park.

Quietly, Olivia opened her bedroom door and listened for a sound. She heard nothing. So far so good. She closed the door behind her and paused again. Still no sound. Hopefully Rosa was sleeping and wouldn't be alerted by her footsteps.

Tiptoeing, she made her way to the top of the stairs, then quietly descended to the first level. She always went out the side door when she went for her walks.

That path took her past Edward's private room. She saw flickering lights beneath his door. Candles. He had a ton of them on some sort of voodoo shrine near his window. Voodoo was Edward's religion of choice, but Sylvia forbade him to talk about it, even to Olivia, who had tons of questions. It was devil worship as far as Sylvia was concerned, and more than once she had tried to save Edward by converting him to the Christian faith. It hadn't worked, and Sylvia had given up, agreeing finally that everyone had a right to his or her own religious choice. And while Sylvia didn't want him talking about voodoo in her home, she didn't mind that he did his ancestor worship and other voodoo practices in the privacy of his own room.

Olivia paused for several seconds outside Edward's door, and hearing nothing but quiet, she continued down the few steps that led to the side door and stepped outside.

The warm evening air held the sweet scent of magnolias. Instantly, Olivia realized how much she had missed her late-night walks. It felt good to be outside.

She hurried from the side of the house toward the main road. But she came up short when she saw the taxi pull up in front of her house.

Slinking backward, Olivia peered out at the car. Edward! She dove behind the bushes, praying he hadn't seen or heard her.

Edward paused outside the gate and glanced around. Had he heard her? Or was he checking out something else? And what was he doing out this time of night? Where was he coming from?

It seemed to take forever for Edward to open the gate and enter the yard, and Olivia held her breath the entire time. She didn't move for several minutes after he'd entered the house through the side door.

Pain shot through her thighs as she rose from her crouched position. Wasting no time, Olivia rushed to the gate, opened it, and stepped out onto the sidewalk.

She part walked, part jogged until she felt she was far enough from her home. Glancing over her shoulder, she didn't see Edward behind her. Thank the Lord.

The tension ebbed from her shoulders, and she allowed herself to enjoy the walk. She hadn't taken a night stroll in a week or so, because she hadn't felt like going out. Besides, she'd been on a roll with her writing, and had been busily creating chapter after wonderful chapter about a teenage girl falling in love for the first time.

Now she wanted to burn it.

She didn't care about romance anymore, and it was all Harvey's fault.

Olivia walked slowly, crossing her arms over her chest. Lights were on in the neighboring houses, and a few streetlights cast soft glows in the night. But the street was quiet, and she didn't see anyone else around.

Just the way she liked it.

She continued on at her casual pace, absorbed in the magical quiet of the night. Now at the main road, she stopped, waiting for traffic to pass before she attempted to cross the street.

Suddenly, there was a hand on her arm.

She managed a short scream before a hand covered her mouth and silenced her.

CHAPTER SEVENTEEN

Shh." The whisper in Olivia's ear was low, seductive.

And even though her heart beat erratically, she instantly relaxed.

The hand slowly slipped from her mouth and Olivia whirled around. Harvey looked down at her with those intense, sexy eyes of his.

"Harvey!" she exclaimed as if surprised, but she'd recognized the deep timbre of his voice the moment she'd heard it. She pounded him on the chest. "What were you thinking? You scared me half out of my mind!"

"I'm sorry, baby. I didn't mean to."

The word "baby" caught her off guard, but she was determined not to let him see he had affected her. So after a beat, she went on, "You should never, never sneak up on a person, much less in the middle of the night."

Harvey merely stared at her, the corners of his lips curling in a smile. And suddenly, Olivia's protests died in her throat. She couldn't lie to herself. She was relieved to see Harvey here, rather than some stranger.

She was happy, even, yet she fought a smile.

When Harvey remained silent, Olivia asked him, "What are you doing out here?"

"I was out," he replied. When Olivia continued to look at him as if she expected a further explanation, he continued, "I uh, I got a bite to eat. And I saw you walking down the street as I was heading back to the house." He paused. "What about you? Why aren't you tucked comfortably in that fancy bed of yours?"

Had Harvey secretly been spying on her, going through her room, searching through her things? "How do you know what my bed looks like?"

"A girl like you . . . it's easy to imagine."

His eyebrows rose with that remark, and Olivia's body instantly grew hot. Had he been imagining her naked? Had he thought of making love to her?

"Are you gonna answer me?" he asked. "What are you doing out here?"

Olivia glanced down the street. Then she stepped to the right, moving beneath the cover of a large oak tree.

"I left the house to take a walk. I often do, as you already know."

"And like I told you the first time I saw you out late, it's not safe for a young lady to be out here all alone this time of night."

"I'm not alone. Not anymore." Her stomach fluttered with nervous anticipation. Why did seeing Harvey give her butterflies? He was the same man who had rejected her proposal earlier today.

The memory of that made her say, "But if you don't mind, I actually would like to be alone."

"Really?" He sounded doubtful.

"Yes, really."

"I'm surprised. I thought you'd like my company."

"You thought wrong," Olivia answered as casually as possible.

"Just this afternoon, you said we needed to spend some time together outside of your backyard."

"And you told me you didn't think that was a good idea. You didn't even think about it."

"I . . ."

Harvey's voice trailed off, and Olivia stared at him, trying to figure him out. She saw conflicted emotions on his face, and once again, her stomach got that warm and woozy feeling.

"What, Harvey?"

"Yeah, I said that, but not for the reason you think."

His admission set her heart pounding wildly. "Then why?"

Harvey debated telling her that he was all wrong for her, confessing all the reasons that they couldn't be together. But in that moment, as she looked up at him with those beautiful eyes of hers, he simply couldn't form the words.

So he changed the subject. "What's with Edward?"

"Edward?" Confusion flashed in Olivia's eyes. "What does he have to do with anything?"

"Is he dating your mother?"

"What?" Olivia exclaimed. "No! Why would you even say that?"

"I've seen him come in late a few times. I know you saw him tonight, too. Guess I was worried that he might have been out with another woman. But if he and your mother aren't involved—"

"Where is this coming from, Harvey? You're making no sense."

He looked away, then back at her. "I was out a few nights ago . . . and I saw him."

"And? You make it sound like he was doing something illegal."

"No, but . . . I have to admit, I was a little surprised to see him. First, because I kinda figured that he and your mother might have a thing going. That's why I was shocked to see him having a good ole time on the dance floor with some young thing. Couldn't have been more than twenty-five."

"Edward?" He had turned fifty earlier this year. "Are you sure?"

"Yeah, I'm sure. He didn't see me, though."

How bizarre. Edward at a bar? She would have sworn he spent every night at the house, in his room. She would bet her mother believed that, too.

After a moment, Olivia shrugged. "I suppose he's allowed to have a good time." Then, "Wait a minute. You were at a bar a few nights ago?"

"I'd had a long day. I went for a drink."

Olivia's stomach plummeted. He wouldn't have told her, except that he'd mentioned Edward. "I see. And were you . . . were you with someone?"

"You mean a girl?"

Her eyes grew as wide as saucers. "You were out with a girl?"

Harvey chuckled. "Sounds like you care."

"Stop teasing me and answer the question."

Harvey answered her by slipping his arms around her waist. He whispered in her ear, "Anyone ever tell you you ask too many questions?"

Oh, goodness. His lips were brushing against her ear, and the feeling was completely delicious! What would it feel like if they did more?

"Hmm?" He kissed the side of her neck.

"Harvey." Olivia was breathless. "What are you doing?"

"Isn't this what you want?"

She wanted him to touch every part of her body. She wanted him to take her clothes off and make love to her beneath the Spanish moss hanging from the tree branches.

But she replied, "Not if you have some girlfriend. Some girlfriend at that *bar*."

"Are you jealous?"

With all her might, she pulled away from him. She didn't like him playing with her. "Fine, you keep your secrets."

"Now you're mad at me."

"You won't tell me anything."

"Hey, a guy's gotta have some secrets. Keeps things interesting."

Olivia sighed, as if to say she knew she had to accept him the way he was. "You want to walk with me?" she asked.

"I'm not leaving you alone. There's still a killer on the streets."

"Then come on." Olivia took Harvey's hand. She tugged on it, urging him to run, and he did. She didn't stop running until she reached City Park across the street. There, she slowed to a walk.

She inhaled some harried breaths before her breathing returned to normal. Still, she held Harvey's hand. She wondered if he would kiss her neck again.

Looking up at the stars, she said, "I love coming here at night."

"Tell me why."

"It's so peaceful at night. So beautiful. Look at the water. See how the moonlight sparkles on the ripples?"

"Uh-huh."

"Don't you think it looks like liquid gold?"

"Liquid gold?"

"Mmm-hmm."

"Those are a writer's words."

"Maybe. It's the way I see it. Tell me I'm wrong."

Harvey stared at the water, noting how the moonlight shone on the gentle waves. He couldn't argue with Olivia's description. It did look like liquid gold.

After a while, Olivia pointed to one end of the lake. "See the geese?"

"Yeah."

"I love to watch them swim at night."

"Why at night?"

"I don't know." She shrugged. "The night fascinates me. The whole world seems like a different place."

"Are you into werewolves and ghosts and stuff? All those creatures of the night?"

"I like to learn about everything." Olivia released Harvey's hand then. She started toward the water's edge. Harvey followed her.

"I guess . . . I guess I like to think here. I told you I like to write stories, and when I come here, my imagination comes alive. I think about secrets, things people do in the night." She giggled softly. "I know that must sound silly to you."

"No," Harvey said from behind her. "It doesn't."

"I'm sure it must."

"No, really. It sounds . . . intriguing. To think I'm here with you now, where you get inspired." He paused. "When do I get to read some of your work?"

Olivia giggled, the very thought making her nervous. If she let Harvey read her work and he didn't like it, she would be heartbroken.

"Hmm?" Harvey prompted.

"Maybe never."

"Never?" Harvey took hold of her arm, whirling her around to him. She landed against his strong chest, and the simple movement left her breathless.

He stared down at her. She stared up at him. Even in the night, his eyes looked electrified.

"Why never?"

"I . . ." She looked down. "I don't want you to be disappointed."

"I wouldn't be."

"It's just a hobby. Something I like to do."

"So?"

"So, I got my first rejection a few days ago. It was for a short story. No big deal."

"And you're discouraged?"

"No. Not really. Well, I *was* disappointed, but I know it was only one story. Only one publisher. There are others I can try."

"That's the way to look at it."

Olivia paused, realizing that Harvey was actually encouraging her. Her mother would have told her not to waste time on a silly dream, that the rejection was proof that it would be too hard to pursue it. But Harvey was doing what she knew her father would, supporting her goal unconditionally.

She said softly, "I'm not as good as you might think."

"I'm sure you are."

"You're much too kind."

"Besides, I like to read. I love the classics. I know I'd enjoy what you write."

"The classics! My work is far from that."

"I don't expect it to be like the classics. But your work . . . it will give me insight into your soul. I want to know all about you, Olivia. Everything."

Slowly, she raised her gaze to his once again. "And I want to know everything about you."

The implied meaning of their statements hung in the air, and they both stopped talking. Just stared. Olivia wondered if he might kiss her then. But he didn't.

Instead, he broke the silence and asked, "Does your mother know that you come here at night?"

Olivia smiled sheepishly. "No."

"I don't like you walking out here alone, Olivia. It's not safe."

"I don't see why it should matter to you." But she was testing him, testing his feelings for her.

"Of course it matters to me. Do you think I wouldn't be hurt if something bad happened to you?"

Olivia merely shrugged, then turned back to the pond. Two white geese glided across the water's surface noiselessly. The peacefulness was completely contrary to how her insides felt.

She didn't know much about courting, but she knew you couldn't appear too anxious. You had to make the guy sweat a little. At least that's what people had told her. She was sure he was making her sweat.

Harvey slipped his arms around her waist. "I really like you." His voice was as deep as the night was dark.

Her eyes fluttered shut, and she placed her hands on his arms. "I like you, too."

"Whenever you come back to this spot, or go walking anywhere at night, I want to be with you, Olivia. I don't want you to be alone."

"I'd like that," she said quietly. And she would. Maybe she'd do the things she imagined others did here, in the quiet cover of darkness, with the first man who'd stolen her heart.

It was a wonderful thought, one that made her warm all over.

She turned in his arms. "Do you want—?"

Seeing the alarm in his eyes, she stopped. "Harvey?"

He didn't answer right away. "Do you hear that?"

Olivia hadn't heard much beyond the pounding of her heart. She strained to hear. There was another pounding. Drums?

"I hear a drumbeat. Don't you?"

"I think so."

Gripping her tighter, Harvey quickly pulled Olivia to the right, behind a large tree. Alarm shot through her as he forced her onto the grass. Oh, God. What was he doing?

This wasn't how she imagined their first time would be.

"Harvey—"

He pressed a hand over her mouth. "Quiet!"

Her heart beating at a frenzied pace, Olivia looked up at him. But he wasn't looking at her. His head was cocked to the side. At that moment, she heard the drum beat louder and realized that's what had his attention.

"There's something weird going on. A bunch of people . . . some are holding flaming sticks. And they're dancing."

Olivia struggled to sit up. Harvey released his hold on her. Moving beside him, she peered around the tree trunk. A group of about ten people were moving together, some beating drums, others holding flames to light the way, all of them shaking their bodies in some weird sort of dance. It looked like a ritual.

"Shit. Isn't that a chicken?" Harvey asked.

As one person moved in a circular motion, Olivia saw that indeed it *was* a chicken. The person swung the chicken around his head. The bird clucked frantically with fright.

"Looks like some kind of voodoo ritual," Harvey whispered.

"This *is* New Orleans. Voodoo's really big with some people down here."

"I wonder if that's what happened to Liza—that she was killed for some type of voodoo sacrifice."

"Oh, God. You think so?" Edward always said that people exaggerated the negative side of voodoo, that it was a religion like any other. She couldn't see Edward hurting a fly.

But these people . . . she was certain they would kill that chicken.

"I don't think it's safe to be here."

He started to get up, but Olivia put a hand on his arm to stop him.

"What?" he asked.

"I don't know . . ." Her voice trailed off. Surely her eyes were fooling her. "The guy with the machete . . . he looks a bit like Edward."

The man in question turned then, marching in step to the ritualistic moves, obscuring his face from view in the process.

"I can't tell," Harvey said.

Could it be Edward? Olivia had seen him heading into the house. Had he merely gone in to change before heading out again?

"Whoever he is, I don't like the look of that knife. Let's get out of here." Harvey rose to his feet. He reached for Olivia and pulled her up as well, sheltering her body with his as they stood together behind the tree. "I say we run through those trees and get out the park another way. Okay?"

Olivia didn't answer right away. She merely stared at him.

"What?" he asked.

"I guess this has pretty much ruined . . ." She shook her head. "Never mind."

"You mean this?" Harvey lowered his face toward hers and planted his lips on her lips.

Heat spread through Olivia's body, right down to her toes.

He broke the kiss with a groan and looked over his shoulder. "We really ought to go."

Olivia took his hand. "Okay."

And even though there was drumbeating and chanting and who knew what kind of danger, Olivia felt excitement. Because she knew in her soul that she'd finally found what she'd always been searching for.

That special man. The one she would love for the rest of her life.

CHAPTER EIGHTEEN

You seem a million miles away, Olivia."

Olivia looked up from her plate of fresh fruit and faced her mother. "Guess I'm still tired, Mama." Her gaze drifted, moving to the large dining room window. She was looking for any sign of Harvey, even though she knew it was unlikely that he'd pass by at that moment.

Of course, he didn't.

"Are you sure that's all?" Sylvia asked. Her tone was stilted, like she knew something but wasn't saying.

"No . . . I . . ." She couldn't stop thinking about the time she'd spent with Harvey last night. His body pressed against hers when she'd been on the ground, the simple intimacy of holding his hand as they'd run from the park.

"This is about that boy, isn't it?"

Olivia was surprised at her mother's accurate summation. "Harvey, you mean?"

Sylvia laughed softly. "Is there another boy?"

"No. Oh, no." Olivia rested her chin on her palm. Since her mother had brought it up, Olivia would tell her how she felt. "He's nice, Mama. Really nice. I like him."

"Do take your elbow off the table, Olivia."

Olivia quickly did as her mother instructed, realizing she'd messed up with her table manners. She knew better, of course, having learned proper etiquette at charm school, but she couldn't think straight, not when the only thing on her mind was Harvey.

Olivia's smile disappeared as she looked at her mother. Sylvia's back was rigid, her lips pulled in a tight line. Clearly, she wasn't happy about what Olivia had just told her.

Olivia's stomach bottomed out. Because her mother had mentioned Harvey, she'd assumed that her mother wouldn't mind hearing the truth about how she felt about him. But she was obviously wrong, and Olivia instantly realized that Harvey wasn't a topic she could discuss with her mother.

"How serious is this?" Sylvia asked.

"Oh, not serious at all, Mama," Olivia quickly replied, her palms sweating with the lie she was telling. The truth was, it was very serious. At least for her. She was in love with Harvey.

"That's good to hear, Olivia. Because he's a man, and you're still a girl."

"I'm not a girl, Mama. I'm almost eight—"

Sylvia's cold eyes silenced Olivia's protest.

"I'm just saying . . . there's nothing to worry about. I like talking to him. He seems nice enough. There's no harm in talking to him, is there?"

Sylvia ate a morsel of pineapple, then replied, "As long as you keep things in perspective. He's the hired help, Olivia. What would people say?"

Olivia felt a flash of annoyance. Her mama and her damn concern about everybody else. And this whole issue of Harvey being the hired help. For a woman who liked to give back to those less fortunate, Olivia couldn't understand how her mother could be such a snob at times.

But she didn't say any of those things. Instead, she said, "I *am* keeping things in perspective, Mama. Like I told you, we're only talking. He must be bored out there all day, with no one to talk to. I'm just trying to be nice. I wouldn't think you'd have a problem with me being nice."

"Olivia, that tone is not necessary."

"I'm sorry, Mama. I'm a little tired still. I don't mean to be cranky."

When Sylvia merely looked at her, Olivia pushed her plate away and stood. "I . . . I'm not hungry."

"Olivia," her mother called as she headed out of the dining room.

Olivia paused and looked over her shoulder. "I'll eat later, Mama." Her tone was once again respectful. "After I've had some more sleep. Okay?"

Sylvia gave her a baffled look, but then said, "Okay."

Olivia took the stairs to her room two at a time.

When Olivia dialed Belinda's new number, her friend answered the phone on the first ring. Olivia squealed with delight, and Belinda joined her.

A moment later, they settled down, giggling. Olivia said, "Finally I've reached you! Oh, Belinda. I've missed you so much. I need you here."

"Liv, I've missed you, too. And believe me, I want to be there with you. I hate Macon."

"I have so much to tell you," Olivia said. "All the kids miss you at the daycare."

"I miss them, too. So much."

"I haven't seen Bernie around. Did he go to Macon, too?"

"No. You haven't seen him at all?"

"Not since you left."

Belinda was silent a moment. "He did say he might move back to Baton Rouge if I wasn't there anymore. Oh, God. Will I ever see him again?"

Olivia hadn't meant to put her friend in a down mood by making her remember Bernie and the fact that he was no longer in her life. "Of course you will," she replied, hoping to make Belinda feel better. "If you love each other, you'll work it out."

"Yeah, maybe when I'm eighteen . . ."

"Eighteen schmeighteen. As if we're not old enough now. Yet our mothers treat us like we're still babies." Olivia groaned.

"Uh-oh," Belinda said. "Sounds like something's going on in your world?"

"I'm falling in love," Olivia blurted.

Belinda drew in a sharp breath. "Love? With that guy working at your house?"

"Yes, with Harvey."

"My God, Liv. It's that serious?"

"Yes, and I have no one to talk to about it. My mama asked me about him today, and when I told her I liked him, she said I needed to be careful, because he's a man and I'm a girl. Then she said I need to know my place with him.

Like he can't be good enough for me because he does manual labor. I don't care about any of that. He makes me laugh." She paused. "Belinda, I get butterflies every time I see him, every time I *think* of him."

"You do have it bad, Liv."

"Last night, we walked to City Park, and it was so nice being with him. He put his arms around me, and then . . . then he kissed me."

"Oooh!" Belinda exclaimed.

"I've never felt like this before, never known I could feel this way."

"I told you."

"And you also said I would have to experience it for myself to know what it was like, and you're right. Is this how you feel about Bernie?"

"Yeah." Belinda's voice was soft and sad.

"I'm sorry. I don't mean to make you miss him more."

"I think about him all the time, anyway." She paused. "So, what are you gonna do if your mama says you can't see Harvey anymore?"

Olivia had given this much thought since her chat with her mother earlier. "I'll see him secretly if I have to, then when I'm eighteen, I can do what I want. My mama's just gonna have to deal with it." Tough words, but Olivia knew her mother wouldn't stop meddling in her life the moment she officially became an adult. She'd probably always see her as her baby.

"I miss you so much, Belinda. Why'd you have to move away just when I was about to fall in love?" It was a rhetorical question, and Belinda didn't answer. "I know, it's not your fault. I just miss you, that's all."

"I miss you, too."

"How's your father? Have you spoken to him?"

"No, and I don't want to. I'll never forgive him for what he's done to our family. If it wasn't for him, I'd still be in New Orleans. Still with you. And with Bernie."

"I know."

"And from what my mama says, my daddy has lied to her before. He's been involved with other women."

"I'm so sorry about all of this. I know how hard this is on you. And your mama and your brother."

"My mama's trying to keep herself together, but she's been pretty depressed."

"She's strong. She'll get through it. It's like when my daddy died, me and my mama got through those dark days."

"I guess you're right."

Olivia sighed. "Well, I should probably let you get off the phone. Since it's long distance and all. I just wanted to update you with what's going on in my life. Plus, I needed to hear your voice."

"Me, too. We'll talk soon, okay?"

Seconds later, Olivia replaced the receiver, the sting of melancholy jabbing at her heart. When would she ever feel better about her friend's moving away?

Soon school would start, and they'd both be busy. Would she miss Belinda less then? Would Belinda miss her less? Would she soon find a new best friend and forget Olivia forever?

At least Olivia had Harvey. She didn't want to lose him, too. But New Orleans wasn't his home. What did the future hold for them?

"You never know what tomorrow holds," she suddenly remembered her daddy saying. "You have to live for the moment. Live for today."

Had he sensed his impending demise? Regardless, his words were true for any time.

She would adhere to them now. Harvey was still here, still in her life. And she would cherish every moment with him.

CHAPTER NINETEEN

Is there something I can get for you, Olivia?"

The sound of Edward's voice nearly scared Olivia out of her skin. Instantly, she released the side door's knob and whirled around, feeling as though Edward had caught her sneaking extra cookies past her bedtime.

Edward looked at her with a weird expression. Suspicion?

A chill slithered down her spine. She remembered the voodoo worshippers in the park, and Harvey's suggestion that Liza could have been killed as part of some bizarre voodoo sacrifice. How deeply involved was Edward in voodoo? Had he slit a chicken's neck?

"Edward, hi." It was important that she not act afraid. Predators smelled fear.

Why was she thinking of Edward as a predator?

"Are you okay, Olivia?"

"Yes. Of course. You just startled me." It was late, and she was planning on heading out to the carriage house to meet Harvey and see if he wanted to go for a walk with her to City Park.

But she certainly couldn't tell Edward that.

"Can I get you something?"

She glanced at the side door, then back at Edward. "Um, no."

"It's late." Edward's tone said he was surprised she wasn't in bed.

"I know." Why did he have to show up now? Olivia desperately wanted to head outside and check on Harvey. She had noticed that the lights in the carriage house hadn't been on for hours, and that had left her wondering what was going on. It certainly seemed like he wasn't there, unless he'd been sleeping this entire time. But if he wasn't home, she wanted to know why. Where had he gone?

To meet another woman, perhaps?

She hated this insecurity she was feeling, and she wondered if that was always a part of caring for someone.

Really, she just wanted to see him and know that he was okay.

To Edward she said, "I guess I just . . . I was gonna get a quick breath of fresh air, then grab a snack."

"It is a beautiful night. Why don't you stick your head out for a minute, get that fresh air you want, then meet me in the kitchen. I'll make you your snack. Will a sandwich do?"

Olivia tried to hide her disappointment. What was Edward doing out here, anyway? She never saw him out of his room past nine in the evening. Had he just come in from a night out at some bar?

Or worse?

There was no doubt that he wouldn't let her head outside at this hour, so she gave in. "Sure. But I'd rather some fruit as opposed to a sandwich."

"Wise choice," Edward said, then headed in the direction of the kitchen.

Though Olivia tried to get rid of him, Edward insisted on watching her as she ate the plate of kiwi and watermelon. Oh, he didn't sit at the table and play chaperone, but he busied himself in the kitchen, as if he had a million things to do while she ate.

It was almost as if he knew she was planning on disappearing if he gave her the chance.

Olivia popped a piece of kiwi into her mouth, but her mind was too preoccupied to taste the sweet fruit. What could she do?

Nothing. Reluctantly, she gave up on the idea of meeting Harvey tonight. It was too risky.

Every day, she was more and more intrigued about the mystery man working at her house. What business had brought him to New Orleans, and where was he right now?

She wanted to see him. Desperately. So much so that her stomach was in knots. She wasn't used to feeling this way.

But as much as she wanted to see him, she would just have to wait. Tomorrow would come soon enough. She would see him then.

CHAPTER TWENTY

She was almost there. Almost home free. Soon, her sins would be washed away.

But as she plunged into the water, hands grabbed both her arms and pulled her back. She fought, trying to get away. She had to get into the water . . .

"Let me be!" she cried. She continued to struggle, but they wouldn't let her go. "Let me be! Let me—"

Sylvia's eyes flew open, her own voice waking her. She found herself tangled in the sheets.

The sheets.

She'd been dreaming again.

A long breath oozed out of her. Thank God it was only a dream. She slowly moved around, untangling herself, the feeling of relief bittersweet. It wasn't so much that she was only dreaming, but the fact that the dream was continuing to haunt her, making the past part of her present once more.

Frustrated, Sylvia threw off the sheets. She dragged a hand over her face before getting out of the bed. Last night she had slept fitfully, which is why she'd gone back to bed midmorning for a nap.

Yet she didn't feel more rested. How could she, if she continued to be haunted by the nightmare?

She groaned softly, then strolled to her bedroom window. From this view, she could see the side of the house and part of the backyard.

Rosa was lying in the shade near the fence. Sylvia's gaze moved closer to the house. Her eyes bulged and her heart lurched. Then her throat began to close, making it extremely difficult to breathe.

Lord have mercy.

Olivia was lying on a lounge chair by the pool, wearing the bikini Sylvia had allowed her to purchase a couple months earlier.

And Harvey, instead of working, was perched on the edge of the lounge chair beside Olivia's, his elbows resting on his knees as he leaned close to her.

But the worst thing was Olivia's expression . . . Sylvia saw on her daughter's face all the emotions she had once felt when she'd first been falling in love, all those years ago.

Transfixed with horror, Sylvia could only stand and watch them for several minutes, the hole in her stomach growing larger all the while.

This had to stop.

Dragging herself away from the window, she went downstairs to speak with Edward.

When Sylvia found Edward cleaning the windows in the kitchen, she asked him to meet her in the sunroom immediately. Though Olivia was probably too absorbed in conversation with Harvey to overhear what she and Edward would say, Sylvia didn't want to take any chances.

Sylvia whirled around and looked at Edward expectantly when she heard him enter the room. "Well?"

"She was planning to head out again last night," Edward told her, confirming Sylvia's fears. "But when she saw me, she changed her mind. I saw her up to bed, then told her I would be reading in the living room."

Sylvia nodded slowly. At least Olivia hadn't gotten to leave the house again. But Edward certainly couldn't stay up every night waiting for her, and neither could she. Right now, Sylvia was interested in seeing how serious this relationship of Olivia's and Harvey's was. And to do that, she had to pretend she didn't know of her late-night excursions.

Sylvia glanced outside. It was such a beautiful day, but she knew she wouldn't enjoy it. She turned back to Edward. Though she knew the answer, she had to ask the question. "And the night before, you're sure they were kissing?"

"Yes, Mrs. Grayson. There is no doubt they were kissing, but like I told you, nothing more."

She should be relieved that nothing more had happened, but instead, Sylvia's stomach cringed. If they were kissing, how long would it be before they took that next step? And if they continued to rendezvous in the park . . . She knew what teenagers did at night, in the dark, if they thought no one was watching.

Sylvia blew out a sharp breath. "Thank you, Edward. I appreciate you watching out for her."

"You're welcome, Mrs. Grayson."

When Edward was gone, Sylvia sat on the wicker armchair, a feeling of panic sweeping over her.

This had to stop.

Olivia didn't know that Sylvia knew of her late-night walks to the park, but she did. She had known for quite some time. And Edward followed her every time she left the premises, lingering in the distance, watching to make sure she was okay.

She knew her daughter wasn't a baby anymore, that she deserved more freedom. But Sylvia's number-one priority was to keep her safe.

When she'd first learned that Olivia was sneaking out at night, Sylvia had been worried that her daughter was heading out to meet a boy. She'd quickly enlisted Edward to follow her. After following her a few times, Edward had told Sylvia that Olivia simply walked to the park, stood by the pond's edge for ten or so minutes, then returned home.

Sylvia had naturally been relieved.

Now Harvey was accompanying Olivia to the park at night. And they were kissing. How long before things escalated?

Her daughter had told her that she liked him, found him nice. But he was a man, and Sylvia knew how easily a young woman could get caught up in the emotions of falling in love with a man who was no good for you.

One day, when you least expect it . . .

Sylvia heard the clairvoyant's words as a piece of the nightmare flashed in her mind. She clenched her fist so tightly, her nails broke the skin of her palms.

She couldn't help thinking of Clinton. Why had he been desperate to reach her?

And with that thought came a slow chill that spread through her body, freezing the blood in her veins.

"Dear God, no," she said.

It couldn't be.

Lord help her, it couldn't be.

CHAPTER TWENTY-ONE

Olivia," Sylvia called. "I need to speak with you for a moment."

Olivia was startled to hear her mother's voice and looked up to see her standing on the back porch. She quickly sat up, slipping her arms into her beach robe as she did.

Giving Harvey a sheepish smile, she said, "Uh, give me a minute."

"Sure."

They both stood. Harvey headed back to his workstation, while Olivia started for the back porch. She walked slowly, apprehensive. What did her mother want to talk to her about? She couldn't tell by looking at her face.

Olivia steeled her shoulders as she reached the foot of the patio steps. "Yes, Mama?"

Now she definitely knew something was wrong. Anger flashed in her mother's pretty eyes, and her lips curled in a slight scowl. "Come inside."

Olivia climbed the stairs and entered the kitchen. "What is it?"

Sylvia spoke while walking toward the kitchen table. "How on earth do you expect Harvey to get any work done when you're distracting him with all your chatter?"

"He was taking a break. I brought him something to drink."

"Again?"

"Pardon me?"

Sylvia waved a hand dismissively. "Seems you did more than bring him a drink."

"You know I like to swim, Mama. It's a hot day. Perfect weather for a cool dip."

"Hmm."

Olivia studied her mother. She seemed . . . jittery. Almost like she was doing all she could to keep herself together.

"I know you miss Belinda, but Harvey is here to work, Olivia. Not be your companion. I told you before, you need to keep things in perspective." Sylvia met Olivia's eyes as she sat at the kitchen table. "And I don't think it's proper for you to be out there dressed like that."

"You don't want me swimming?"

Sylvia's mouth pulled in a tight line. "No. I guess I don't. Not while Harvey is working here."

"Why not?" Olivia challenged. "It's the summer. When else am I supposed to swim?"

"I'm not really concerned about that. You, dressed like that in front of Harvey—it's not proper. When it's just you and me, that's fine."

"And Edward."

"I trust Edward," Sylvia snapped.

"I'm just saying that he's a man, too." One who, according to Harvey, liked much younger women. "So if you're conc—"

"Edward isn't the issue. Harvey is. Like I told you before, you keep Harvey from working when you're always around him."

"That's not true." Olivia sat in a chair opposite her mother. Maybe she could reason with her. "I haven't been keeping him from getting his work done."

"I want you to spend less time with him," Sylvia said. "You need to cool things down."

"But there isn't anything to cool down," Olivia protested. "I just help him pass the time, since he's putting in so many long hours."

"That's how it starts, Olivia. You're young, and not as experienced as I'm sure he is."

"I'm not that inexperienced."

Sylvia's eyes bulged.

"I don't mean it the way you think," Olivia quickly said. "But I know about men and women, Mama. And Harvey and I—we're just talking. We haven't done anything out of line, and we're not about to."

Except for sneaking off in the middle of the night! "You heard me," Sylvia said, her tone stern. "Besides, we don't truly know this man. He's doing some nice work for us, but I've been thinking. He appeared in town at the time Liza died. The police still haven't found Liza's killer. Is that a coincidence?"

Olivia abruptly stood. "Are you trying to say you think he's a *murderer?*"

Sylvia gave her another stern gaze, and Olivia slinked back into her chair. "The point is," Sylvia continued calmly when Olivia was seated, "we don't know."

"Ms. Monroe seemed to think the same thing about you."

"Olivia!"

"I'm sorry, Mama."

"My God. What's happening to you? You're changing right before my very eyes."

"I'm only trying to say—"

"This is because of Harvey. He's already turning you against me."

"No, Mama." What was wrong with her? "He's not doing that."

"You heard me. You are much too involved with him. There are so many other things you need to be thinking about at this point in your life, like Elizabeth's upcoming party. Your party that we'll have to start planning. Before we know it, February will be here. And don't you have to make preparations for the Jack and Jill junior picnic? You said you were in charge of planning the artistic activities."

"I was waiting to hear back from Tiffany."

"Why don't you call her right now? Take it from me, you can't wait until the last minute to do this, Olivia."

"All right, Mama. But Harvey and I were in the middle of a conversation. I should at least tell him I have something to do. It would be rude of me not to," she added, appealing to her mother's sense of good manners.

"I'll speak with him," Sylvia said. "You go on upstairs and put some clothes on."

With that, Sylvia headed to the patio door.

Through the glass, Olivia watched her mother walk that always poised walk of hers across the concrete patio and onto the grass where Harvey was working.

She saw Harvey look up, then brush his hands off on his overalls. He would no doubt be confused as to why Olivia wasn't coming back out to be with him.

Olivia frowned. What was wrong with her mother? Why was she getting so upset about her talking to Harvey? She ought to be happy. She was openly spending time with Harvey right here at home, under her mother's and Edward's watchful eyes.

Olivia watched her mother for a moment longer. Then she turned and ran from the kitchen, not stopping until she reached her bedroom.

Olivia breathed a sigh of relief when her mother left the house to run some errands a couple hours later. Normally, she wouldn't mind tagging along with her mother for something to do, but today she wasn't interested.

Her mother had suggested she join her so that Olivia could pick up items for the picnic, but Olivia had declined, claiming she had to confirm things with Tiffany.

The truth was, with her mother gone, Olivia was hoping to steal a few moments with Harvey.

She dropped the checklist for the picnic and strolled to the den's window. She didn't see him at his workstation. Maybe he was at the side of the house, or even inside.

Leaving the den, Olivia noted that the place seemed eerily quiet. She searched around, but Harvey wasn't anywhere inside.

Olivia made her way to the kitchen and opened the patio door. When she didn't see Harvey, she called his name.

No answer. "Harvey!" she called again. Still, she got no response.

Olivia frowned. Harvey wasn't anywhere. Maybe he was out running some errands. Picking up more materials for the work he was doing on the house.

Figuring that had to be it, Olivia went up to her room.

She opened her bedroom door. And screamed.

Harvey!

"What are you doing here?" she asked. She hurried inside and closed the door behind her.

Harvey slowly turned to face her. It was then that Olivia noticed he had her notebook in his hands.

She marched angrily toward him.

"This is good," Harvey told her.

Olivia reached for her notebook, snatching it from his fingers. "You had no right."

"This is about the murder, right? Liza? It's so vivid. I felt as if I was right there when I was reading this. It was so real, I wonder if that's what happened to her."

Olivia thought of the other stories in her notebook, like the X-rated fantasy she'd come up with in the last couple days. Her face grew warm as she wondered if Harvey had read that story.

"It's not . . . it's not about anything."

"Whatever it's about, it's great."

"Is that . . . is that all you read?" Olivia managed.

Harvey gave her a sly grin. "Wouldn't you like to know?"

"Harvey!" Olivia exclaimed. "I told you I wasn't ready for you to read my stories. Why couldn't you respect that?"

"I'm sorry."

"Yeah, you seem it."

"What can I say? If that one story about the carpenter has anything to do with me—I'm flattered."

"Oh, God." Olivia threw a hand to her face. She thought she would die of the embarrassment.

"Hey, no need to be embarrassed."

"I feel so stupid."

Harvey reached for her hand and urged it from her face. When she looked at him, she saw contrition in his eyes. "Look, I didn't realize you were so sensitive about your writing. You're right. I should have respected you. I *am* sorry."

"Did you read it all?"

"I read the story about Liza. Well, about whomever. That one really captivated me. I'd just started reading the one about the carpenter when you walked through the door."

Maybe he hadn't read all her X-rated thoughts.

"It really is good. I like your style."

"Really?" Olivia asked, her voice holding a hopeful note.

"Yeah," Harvey said, and Olivia could tell he meant it.

"You truly like it?"

"I love it. Seems to me you have a real shot at being a writer."

Olivia's heart pounded at Harvey's compliment.

"You really think so?"

"Yeah, I do."

Harvey's support and encouragement meant the world to her. Still, she tried to play it cool. "Listen, Harvey. I don't like anyone reading my work. Not before I'm happy with it. You might think it's silly, but it's important to me."

"Believe me, I am sorry. It's just that I wanted to know more about you."

"All you have to do is ask."

He was silent as he stared at her, and his expression instantly changed from curious to something that made Olivia's stomach jump.

It was the way he looked at her . . . like he was stripping her naked with his eyes.

She wanted him to do it in reality.

Goodness, this was crazy. She couldn't get all hot and bothered with him in her room! Her mother would strangle her if she came home and found Harvey in here.

"Harvey." Olivia giggled nervously. "You can't be in here. My mama . . . she would tan my behind if she found you in here. You have to go."

Harvey's lips curled in a playful smile. "What if I refuse?"

"You can't!" Olivia laughed. "Really, Harvey. You have to go. Before she comes back."

"Tell me why you didn't come back to the pool."

"Why don't you tell me where you were for the last hour? I know you weren't in my room the entire time. And what about last night? The lights weren't on in the carriage house."

"Checking up on me?"

"Curious, that's all."

"I was taking care of some business last night. And today I was out getting some supplies. Satisfied?"

"What kind of business?"

"Personal business."

"You don't want to tell me?"

"It has to do with my family."

"Something bad happened?" Olivia asked, picking up on his slight frown.

"You could say that. Maybe I'll tell you about it later."

She didn't want to push him. "Okay."

"Now tell me why you had your mother come out to let me know that you were too busy to spend any more time with me."

"I will tell you." Thinking about her talk with her mother brought her down. "Later."

"When?"

Olivia put a hand on Harvey's shoulder and gave him a gentle shove toward the door. "Later. We can go for another walk."

"What time?"

"I'll come by the carriage house later. Maybe around ten tonight. Will you be around?"

"Sure."

"So we can go for another walk?"

"All right." Harvey flashed her a charming smile, and she almost melted on the spot.

Olivia drew in a deep breath and got herself together. She couldn't get all weak in the knees right now. If her mother came upstairs at this very moment . . .

Olivia opened the door a notch and peered into the hallway. After a second, she turned to Harvey and said, "The way's clear. Hurry."

"Later?" he asked.

"Later," she promised.

CHAPTER TWENTY-TWO

The hours until Olivia saw Harvey again seemed to pass by in slow motion.

And when ten o'clock came, even though she'd been waiting all day to see him, she decided it was best to wait a little longer before heading out of the house. Just to be on the safe side, to make sure Edward was asleep.

As she'd hoped, when she went downstairs around ten-thirty, Edward wasn't around. That left her free and clear to head out to see Harvey.

Even though the grass wouldn't give her away, she crept quietly across it nonetheless. A minute later, she was at the carriage house.

Olivia's stomach fluttered with nerves as she stopped outside Harvey's door. She blew out a deep breath, then knocked.

"Harvey," she said in a hushed voice.

Harvey opened the door just as she knocked again. Olivia's face erupted in a smile. "Harvey."

He slipped his arms around her waist and drew her to him, closing the door with a shove from his foot. Olivia giggled for exactly a second before he covered her mouth with his.

The kiss was as incredible as the first time, leaving her heart beating so quickly, she thought it might explode. Her private area pulsed even faster than her heart.

Harvey pulled away first. Surprised, Olivia looked up at him.

"You should see your face," he teased. "The disappointment that my lips aren't on yours anymore." He raised an eyebrow. "I think you like me."

"You know I like you."

Harvey gave her nose a soft kiss. "So do I."

"Oh, Harvey. I have to tell you. I've never felt this way before."

His eyes filled with warmth, the kind of warmth Olivia felt right down to the tips of her toes. There was something about Harvey that made her lose all control of her senses. She wanted to kiss him again. Who was she kidding? She wanted to do much more than kiss him.

"How do you feel?" he asked softly.

"What do you mean?" Goodness, had he read her thoughts just by looking in her eyes?

"I mean." His gaze locked with hers, he trailed a finger from the base of her neck to the top of her cleavage. "Is it as good as what you described in your story?"

"Harvey!"

"Is it?"

She blew out an unsteady breath. "It's better."

"Forgive me," Harvey said. He brought his hands to her shoulders. "I know I should take things slowly."

"I . . . maybe I don't want you to." But she couldn't look in his eyes.

"No, I don't think so. Not yet."

"No, Harvey—"

"Shh." He kissed her forehead. "It's okay."

"No, hear me out. I really like you. But I guess I just feel paranoid, wondering if my mama or Edward is watching me."

"Huh?"

"The reason I didn't come back out to see you earlier is because of my mama. She thinks . . . she thinks we're spending too much time together. I told her that nothing was going on, that she didn't have to worry, but she's acting all worried. I don't know why."

"She doesn't like me." It was a statement, not a question.

"I wouldn't say she doesn't like you," Olivia said. But she heard her mother's admonishments, her concerns that Harvey was not only the hired help but a possible murderer. She began to pace. "She's just worried about me. She thinks I'm young. I've never had a boyfriend."

"Never?"

Looking at him, Olivia shook her head. Was it her imagination, or did she actually detect the hint of a smile on his lips?

"Well, you are her baby. She's gonna be concerned." He shrugged. "I understand where she's coming from."

Olivia felt a moment of alarm. "What are you saying? You think . . . you want to slow things down?"

Harvey strolled toward her. "No. That's not what I'm saying. I feel things for you, Olivia. Things that make me want to be closer to you."

Olivia's breath caught in her chest as Harvey gently caressed her face. "What kind of things?"

He looked deeply into her eyes. "You've *never* had a boyfriend?"

"Never. Well, not really."

"Then some of the things I'm feeling . . . you might not understand them."

"I may not have had a real boyfriend, but I'm not a child. I . . . I know—"

"You know about making love?"

"Yes," she said boldly.

"That's what I want to do with you."

"You do?"

Harvey didn't respond with words. His mouth covered hers softly, gently nipping at her lips with his teeth. Then he slipped his tongue into her mouth and let it mingle over hers. All very slowly. Every one of his actions made heat pool between her legs.

"Has anyone ever kissed you like this?"

"No," Olivia managed in a husky voice. "Never."

Harvey trailed his hands upward, then forward, touching the outline of her breasts. "Has anyone ever touched you like this?"

Olivia actually whimpered, his touch was making her so weak. "Never."

Harvey wanted to touch her everywhere, get naked with her and make her his. And he almost did just that. But something stopped him.

She was a virgin. Emotions could get complicated with a virgin.

Especially if he wasn't sticking around forever.

With all the strength he possessed, he stepped away from her. The confusion on her face tugged at his heart. He wanted her, but not yet. Not before he knew what was going to happen next in his life. Because he cared about her enough that he didn't want to hurt her.

"No," Olivia protested softly. "Don't walk away."

"This isn't right."

"It feels right."

"The timing. There's no need to rush." Harvey could hardly believe the words coming from his mouth.

"Is it because I'm a virgin? You're disappointed?"

Her look was so innocent, it touched him in a way he didn't expect. She was so beautiful, so sweet. "No, no. Not at all. Believe me, no guy is gonna be unhappy about that."

"Then what?"

"Maybe we have to wait a while. Till your mama stops worrying about us."

Boldly, Olivia put her arms around his neck. "I don't care about what my mama thinks."

"Not right now . . ."

She pecked his lips. "Not tomorrow, not any time. I'm not a baby anymore."

"Maybe not, but I'm sure that wouldn't stop her from coming after me. Let's face it, Olivia. If we . . . if we don't stop, your mama will know. She'll look at you tomorrow and know what we did."

Olivia let her hands fall to her sides. That much she didn't doubt. Her mama had radar that way.

"You better go."

Olivia frowned. "I don't want to." These sensations she was feeling, it was like a fire was burning between her legs, one that would only be put out if he touched her there. "I'm ready, Harvey. I am."

Harvey groaned. "Don't tempt me."

"Why not?"

"Because I want you to be sure."

"But I am sure." She put her arms around him again, resting her head against his chest.

Harvey was silent a long while. Olivia could hear the rapid beat of his heart and knew this wasn't easy for him.

As she snuggled closer to him, Olivia felt something strange and hard press against her belly. She pulled her head back and looked up at Harvey. "W-what's that?"

Harvey chuckled softly. "Baby, that is what you're doing to me. That is how much I want you."

"Oh."

He whispered in her ear, "Believe me, I want you to stay with me tonight. But we'll have to do it another time. When we don't have to sneak."

Olivia tipped on her toes and gave him another kiss, brief but hot.

Then she pulled away from him and hurried to the door, afraid that if she didn't right now, she never would.

As she opened the door, she glanced over her shoulder. "Guess we forgot all about that walk."

"We sure did."

She smiled softly. "I'll see you tomorrow, Harvey."

"Tomorrow."

Olivia slipped through the door, closing it behind her. She ran across the grass, giggling as she did. These feelings inside her made her feel like she could fly. Giddy, she swirled around, spreading her arms as she did. If this was what love did to you, made you feel so high like you were floating, she wanted to stay this way forever.

And she would.

She didn't care what her mama said. She was in love with Harvey, and her mama had no right to interfere in her life. Not about something as important as this.

No way, no how.

Her mother didn't think he was good enough, just because he was a carpenter.

But Olivia thought he was perfect.

Absolutely perfect.

CHAPTER TWENTY-THREE

For the next week, Olivia kept a low profile where Harvey was concerned. She snuck out to see him every once in a while, on the occasions when her mother left the house, but that hadn't been often. It was almost like her mother was sticking around just to keep an eye on her.

And her ploy was working. Her mother had gotten off her case about Harvey. That was a plus.

It was a greater struggle than she'd imagined staying away from him. To occupy her time, Olivia spent her days working on her novel, often getting her inspiration from watching Harvey work outside. Her writing was going very well, with ideas and words coming to her easily.

He touched her knee, Olivia wrote. *But he wanted to do more. He wanted to rip her shirt off and kiss her breasts.*

She put down her pen and giggled. How was she ever going to send this story off to a publisher if she couldn't stop blushing as she wrote it?

She picked up her pen and thought about how she would write the love scene. But something got her attention. What was that? She listened closely. It sounded like hollering and screaming outside.

Jumping up, Olivia sprinted from her room and down the stairs. The commotion was louder as she got downstairs. Something serious was definitely going on.

Olivia threw open the front door. There was a crowd on the road outside her house. There was a mix of frantic sounds and cheers.

A fight.

She ran to the road. A tangle of legs and arms flashed around on the ground.

"Harvey!" Olivia screamed when she realized he was one of the two men engaged in the brawl. She forced her way through the group of people in front of her and ran toward him. She threw herself to the ground. A foot landed in her stomach. Groaning, she fell backward.

"Son of a bitch!"

That was Harvey's voice. He was on his feet now. He glanced at her, started toward her.

"Harvey, watch out!"

The other man tackled Harvey before he could turn. Olivia screamed again and this time threw herself on the stranger's back. She wrapped her hands around his face and dug her fingers into his eyes.

"Damn you, bitch. Get off me!"

The guy wobbled as he got up. Olivia held on. "Run, Harvey," she told him.

The sound of a siren pierced the air, and the crowd immediately started to disburse. The guy fighting Harvey grabbed Olivia's hands and wrenched them off his face. Her hands in his arms, he threw her off his back.

Olivia cried out as she landed hard on the asphalt. The police car skidded to a stop beside her as Harvey scooped her into his arms.

"Harvey, are you okay?"

"I'm fine. Damn, what were you thinking?"

A police officer interrupted them. "What's going on here?" he asked.

"Nothing," Harvey replied.

"Harvey," Olivia protested. She looked at the cop. "The guy you want took off running."

"It was just a disagreement," Harvey quickly said.

"You look pretty banged up," the cop noted.

"I'll live," Harvey told him.

The officer hesitated before saying, "You want to press charges?"

"There's no reason. Everything's fine now."

"Okay." The police officer looked frustrated, but he walked back to his cruiser nonetheless.

Harvey quickly led Olivia through the gate that led onto her property. He didn't stop walking with her until he was at the side of the house.

"How stupid could you be?" he asked her. "And not only do you try to get yourself hurt, you practically beg that cop to stay around! Couldn't you see I wanted him to go?"

Instantly, tears filled Olivia's eyes. "I was trying to help."

"You could have been hurt." His tone now soft, he no longer seemed angry. His eyes swept over her. "Damn, you *were* hurt."

He ran a hand over her arm, gently fingering the bloody scrape.

"I'm fine, Harvey. Who was that guy? And why on earth were you fighting?"

"Just someone."

Olivia pounded a fist against his chest. "Damn you, Harvey. Why won't you tell me anything?"

"Because there are things you shouldn't know!"

He was back to being angry, and Olivia flinched from the tone of Harvey's voice. He had never talked to her this way before.

"I'm sorry," he said after a moment.

"Are you?"

"Yes."

"Then tell me what's going on. You said you wanted that cop to leave? Why?"

Harvey turned. Groaned. His back was still to her when he said, "Because there's a warrant out for my arrest."

"A . . . a what?" Olivia wasn't sure she had heard correctly.

He faced her. "I almost killed a man. Are you happy now?"

Olivia was too shocked to speak.

"See, that's what I didn't want. You looking at me like that. With such . . . disappointment."

Had her mother been right on the mark where Harvey was concerned? Could he be the one who had murdered Liza?

Good Lord, did she know him at all?

"It was self-defense."

"That was him?"

"No, that was his cousin. My second cousin."

"Your own family?"

"They never liked me. My father and his cousin barely got along. They only took me in because I was desperate."

"Why were you desperate?"

"Because my father got messed up with some stupid people. Robbed a bank and ended up in jail. I didn't have anyone else to turn to after losing my last job."

Olivia nodded. She could get more specific details another time. "So what happened with your cousin?"

"I got into a fight with Dennis over something stupid. I don't know if he's been smoking too much weed, but his brain is fried. He's so damn paranoid all the time. Thought I was after his wife."

"And you weren't?"

"No."

"Okay." Olivia believed him. "Go on."

"I was out one night. This was about a month ago. I was just hanging with some guys, and Dennis's wife, Charlene, was walking by. It was late, so I decided to walk her home to make sure she was safe. The south side of Chicago isn't the safest area. There's a lot of gang violence these days. Anyway, Dennis saw me walking her up to the door and he flipped. He started beating on Charlene, so I jumped on him, trying to stop him. He backed off, and I thought that was it. Then he grabbed an empty beer bottle and broke it over my head."

Harvey took Olivia's hand and brought it to his head. He rubbed one of her fingers over a long ridge hidden by his hair. "Feel that?"

"Yes. That's where he cut you?"

"Uh-huh. I was bleeding pretty badly, but I got angry. I started fighting back, hitting on Dennis as hard as I could. Next thing I know, he was out cold. Charlene was screaming for me to stop. She ran to the phone and called the cops."

"After how you helped her?"

"I know. All I could do was grab my stuff and run."

"But if it was self-defense—"

"I wasn't about to take any chances, not with Dennis out cold and Charlene taking his side. Hell, I thought I'd killed him."

"And you headed to New Orleans?"

"Yeah."

"So how did they find you here?"

"This is where my family's from."

"You contacted your father's family? Why? You said it was his cousin—"

"I know. But I didn't have much choice. I was hoping my aunt would be willing to hear my side of the story. She told me there was a warrant out for my arrest and that if I ever came back, I'd be taken to jail."

"Why not go to your mama?"

Harvey paused. "Because I don't know who she is. She never raised me."

"What?"

"I guess she didn't want me."

"Your own mother?"

"I know, Olivia. I've lived my whole life wondering why."

His tone made it clear this wasn't a happy topic for him. Naturally. She had so many questions about him. "So that was your cousin fighting with you now?"

"Yeah. Dennis's brother. Clayton."

"But I don't understand. If your family's angry with you, why did you go back to your aunt's today?"

Harvey hesitated. "Clayton . . . he saw me when I was out."

"Where were you, anyway? I thought you were supposed to be working?"

"I was working." But Harvey sounded annoyed. "Picking up supplies. Clayton must have spotted me, because he followed me back here and jumped me."

"He knows this is where you're staying?" Olivia asked with alarm.

"I don't think so. He was following me, but I wasn't at your door yet. Unless he figured it out because of you."

"He wouldn't have seen where I came from, if that's what you're saying."

"I hope not."

"You think he'll be back?"

"Not if he's smart. I don't think so, but I can't be sure."

They were silent for a long while. Olivia took a good, long look at Harvey. He had scrapes on his face and arms, and his T-shirt was dirtied and torn in some places. Olivia reached for his face, gently touching a bloody spot on his mouth.

Harvey winced. "Ouch."

"You're really hurt. Maybe you should see a doctor."

"No. No doctors."

Olivia didn't protest. "Well, you at least need to get cleaned up. Let me help you."

Olivia offered Harvey her hand, and he accepted it. Together they walked to the carriage house.

CHAPTER TWENTY-FOUR

S on of a bitch!"

"Sorry." Olivia lifted the damp cotton ball from Harvey's shoulder and blew cool breath onto the cut. "But it's gotta hurt. That's the only way it's gonna get better."

"I know."

Harvey braced himself for the next swipe of antiseptic. His body jerked, but he didn't make a sound.

"Just a few more," Olivia told him. She looked at the wide breadth of his back. She had never been this close to a half-naked man before.

The words she had used to describe him in her story were hardly adequate. There were no words good enough. Everything about him was so beautiful.

He mesmerized her. His topless body was strong and rippled with muscles. She couldn't help admiring it.

"What are you thinking?"

Harvey turned around on the stool, facing her. Olivia's face instantly grew warm.

"Huh?" he prompted. "What's going through your mind right now?"

Olivia dabbed a fresh cotton ball with antiseptic. "Nothing."

"Really?" His tone said he didn't believe her.

"Just that . . . you're banged up pretty good. You probably ought to take a warm bath so you don't end up with aches and pains."

"You want to give me a bath?"

Olivia's eyes bulged. "No, that's not what I meant!"

"You wouldn't want to?"

"Harvey . . ."

"You don't want to see me naked?"

Olivia's heart was beating in a frantic pattern. If what she saw was already turning her on, she couldn't imagine how she'd react to seeing all of him. "Why are you saying these things?"

"I don't know why, Olivia. Something about you makes me want to get wild with you."

Wild . . . Olivia had never been wild in her entire life. But she wanted to. With Harvey, she wanted to do everything.

He placed his hands on her waist. Olivia started to get hot all over. "What about you, Olivia? You want to get wild with me?"

"You mean . . . right now?"

Harvey laughed. "No. Not right now." He paused, letting out a sound of frustration. "In fact, you probably ought to head back to the house before your mama misses you."

Olivia placed her hands on his shoulders. "She's out at some meeting."

"Still, we can't take the chance. Yet."

"When?" Olivia found herself asking.

"Soon, Olivia. When it's right."

Every part of her body ached to touch him. But he was leading this game; she followed his lead. As much as she wanted to throw herself into his arms, there was a part of her that was too shy to do so.

Yet as he stared at her, she wondered, *Should I kiss him?*

The sound of furious pounding on the door made Olivia and Harvey jump apart. They barely got away from each other before the door opened.

The look of horror on Sylvia's face made Olivia's blood turn to ice.

"Olivia!" Sylvia marched toward her. She grabbed her by an ear. "What the hell are you doing in here?"

"It's not what you think, Mama."

Sylvia released Olivia and scowled at Harvey. "And you," she said to him. "What were you thinking?"

"He was hurt," Olivia explained. "I was helping him with his cuts, that's all."

Sylvia gave Harvey a closer look then. "So Edward was right. It *was* you in a brawl outside of my home. Just what kind of trouble are you in?"

"It was . . . a stupid misunderstanding. It won't happen again," was all Harvey said.

"It better not." Sylvia turned back to Olivia and took hold of her arm. "You're coming with me."

"Mama," Olivia protested, but her mother dragged her out of the carriage house. Her face flamed from the embarrassment. "Mama, will you stop?"

Sylvia jerked to a stop several feet away from the carriage house. Her fingers dug into the skin on Olivia's arm.

"You're hurting me, Mama."

"Are you sleeping with him?"

"What?" Olivia asked, shocked.

Sylvia wagged a finger in front of Olivia's face. "Are you having sex with Harvey?"

"No, Mama!"

"Don't you lie to me."

"I'm not!"

"Then why are you still seeing him? Waiting until I leave the house? Yes, Edward has told me. He's seen a change in you too, so you can't accuse me of being paranoid."

"But you can accuse me of lying?"

"So this is how you treat me now. You think you're grown, that you can talk back to me?"

"You can't treat me like a child forever."

"You have no idea what you're getting yourself into," Sylvia told Olivia. "Sex . . . it's a huge step, one you are too young to be taking."

"I haven't."

"The first man you spend any real time with, and you're suddenly acting like you can do what you want. You still live under my roof."

Olivia stared at her mother, hardly recognizing her. "You're not even listening to me."

"It wasn't right, you and him alone in his place. What were you thinking?"

Olivia did her best not to raise her voice. "Nothing happened."

"I know what you say, Olivia. But I also know this is how it starts. All the talking, the laughing. Spending time together. The first kiss ... before you know it—" Sylvia stopped abruptly.

"I don't see how you would know anything," Olivia snapped. "When was the last time you were even on a date?"

Sylvia gawked at Olivia. "I can't believe..." She brought a hand to her chest. "I put you first, Olivia, and you dare to throw that in my face? It was me and you. After Dexter, I knew you wouldn't adjust well to another father. I sacrificed for you. And now you have the lip to stand there and tell me I know nothing about love?"

"I'm sorry, Mama." Olivia felt bad. She shouldn't have spoken to her mother this way. She knew what her mother had sacrificed. "I ... I shouldn't have said that."

"You've changed. You're not even the girl I knew last month."

"I haven't changed, Mama. You've changed. You don't talk to me anymore, don't ask me any questions. You open my bedroom door without knocking. You make all sorts of accusations."

"This is my house."

"Why are you fighting with me, Mama? Believe me, I haven't done anything wrong. Harvey got into a fight—"

"I'm trying to protect you."

"Protect me from what? If you only knew what Harvey says to me, you wouldn't even worry."

"Oh, I'll just bet. He's probably as smooth-talking as Clinton was."

"Who's Clinton?"

Sylvia looked suddenly flustered. "Nobody. You get on in the house. Go to your room. I don't want to see you until dinner."

"See, Mama? You won't even listen to me."

"You aren't saying anything I don't know. Believe me, Olivia, I am trying to protect you—from men. Men like Harvey. They look good, and they say all the right things. Lies, Olivia. You don't know."

Olivia gave her an odd look. What wasn't her mother telling her?

She must have sensed the question on her mind, because she said, "I was your age once, Olivia. And I know many young women who got their hearts broken over some pretty boy. I ... I saw a lot of my good friends devastated by men. I don't want to see you hurt."

"I won't get hurt."

"No one ever thinks they'll get hurt, sweetheart." Sylvia smiled and spoke in a sweet voice. "Besides, what do we know about Harvey? I asked him about his family more than once and he refuses to tell me a thing. I don't even believe the last name he gave me. Harvey Smith? It doesn't sound right. He's secretive, Olivia. And I can't help but wonder why."

"Mama, is there something else going on?"

With the question, Sylvia steeled her shoulders. The smile vanished, replaced by a scowl. "Stay away from him, Olivia. You haven't been a Jack and Jiller all these years to end up with someone like Harvey. You should be thinking about the Delta cotillion. I have it on good authority that Connor wants to escort you."

"I don't even like Connor."

Sylvia's eyes widened in surprise. "All these changes. Don't you see? This can't continue. Whatever is going on between you and Harvey stops now. This is the last time I'm going to tell you. That man will hurt you. Mark my words. Now go to your room."

"Bu—"

"And I don't want to hear one word of protest or I'll ground you for two weeks."

Olivia bit down on her bottom lip, fighting the tears and the anger. Her mother had said she had changed, but the truth was her mother was the one who had changed. She seemed high-strung and paranoid, and Olivia wished she knew why.

Sylvia's eyes narrowed on her. "I'll count to five."

Olivia turned and started running to the house.

CHAPTER TWENTY-FIVE

One day, when you least expect it, when you're least prepared for it, he will come back into your life...

Sylvia closed the door behind her and shook her head, trying to toss the memory.

But how could she forget?

Clinton's unexpected call was weighing more and more on her mind. That plus the words the clairvoyant had told her twenty years ago.

Could her worst fear be true?

Lord help her.

Sylvia sucked in a sharp breath and walked to the pantry. This was so uncharacteristic of her, but she wanted a drink. A couple shots of scotch and maybe she could sleep off this headache.

It will still be there when you wake up.

Sylvia filled a tumbler with scotch, then carried it with her to her bed.

"Damn you, Clinton," she said as she sat.

She looked at the glass in her hand, then at the phone. The scotch wouldn't solve her problems. But one phone call and there would be no more question.

She placed the tumbler on her night table. If her suspicion was right, she had to know.

There was only one way to confirm this awful suspicion, or to rule it out forever.

Sylvia had to call Clinton.

The dreams wouldn't stop until she did, until she knew if what she now suspected was truth or fiction.

She had hardly been able to think of much else these past days, so much so that it was starting to affect her work. She was forgetting to make calls, forgetting to return calls. How was she to run the charity in this state of mind?

She needed an answer, one way or another.

Clinton was the only one who could give that to her.

His call to her mother had been so out of the blue, but maybe it made sense. And maybe, just maybe, he was looking out for her.

Which was hard to believe, considering how he'd abandoned her so many years ago.

Sylvia pushed that thought from her mind. That was the distant past, and she was over his betrayal. It was the present she was concerned about.

She picked up the phone.

Minutes later, Sylvia had her mother on the line.

"Hello, Mother," Sylvia said.

"Sylvia?"

"Yes, it's me."

"Are you okay?"

"Oh yeah. Everything's fine. Just fine."

"You're sure?"

"No, I'm not sure," she snapped.

Hazel sighed loudly. "Have you spoken to Clinton?"

"That's the reason I'm calling. I know I said I would call him after I spoke with you, but I simply couldn't do it. But now . . ." She bit back a sob. "Now I wonder if he didn't have a good reason for trying to track me down."

"What sort of reason?"

Sylvia took a deep breath, hoping to keep herself together. "I want to talk to Clinton before I jump to any conclusions." *And before I tell you a damn thing.* "I'm hoping you still have his number."

"I know I have it around here somewhere."

Sylvia waited while her mother searched for it. Minutes later, she came back on the line. "Here it is."

Sylvia scribbled down the number her mother recited. "Thanks."

"If you need me . . ."

"I'll let you know what he wants, if there's a problem."

"Fine."

Sylvia disconnected. Immediately she dialed Clinton's number. She had to do it now, while she still had the nerve.

A woman answered on the third ring.

"Hello." Sylvia swallowed, nervous as hell. "I'm looking for Clinton."

There was a brief pause. "What did you say?"

"Clinton Morrison. I'm an old friend of his. He called and left a message for me, actually. I'm returning his call."

"Oh, my God."

"What?"

"You don't know . . . I thought we'd contacted all his friends."

A chill made its way down Sylvia's spine. "W-why?"

"I am so sorry to tell you this. But Clinton died a couple days ago."

"*Died?*"

"Yes." The woman's voice became hoarse with emotion. "A car accident."

"Oh, God."

"It was horrible. The only blessing is that he died instantly. If you want, I can give you the information about the funeral."

"No." Sylvia's head was spinning. "No, that won't be necessary."

She hung up without saying good-bye.

Then she grabbed her empty glass and hurled it across the room.

It shattered into a million pieces.

Just like her life had.

CHAPTER TWENTY-SIX

oon, Olivia. When it's right.

Olivia rolled onto her side, sighing happily. She had spent the entire evening in her room because of her mother, even having her supper in there, but she hadn't let that spoil her mood. She didn't care about what her mother said. She and Harvey were getting closer. It was the one thing that felt right in her life.

Her mother was wrong. He wouldn't hurt her.

In fact, he totally respected her. She hadn't considered Harvey the old-fashioned sort, but after thinking about the meaning of his words for hours, she had realized that they could mean only one thing. He didn't want to sleep with her without a commitment.

She knew he thought she was a good girl—which she was—and she loved him for not wanting to take advantage of her.

But if they were married . . . marriage would change everything. They could be intimate, and it would be right in the eyes of the world and in the eyes of the Lord.

The very thought of marriage made her stomach flutter, like a million butterflies were going crazy inside her.

She was crazy. Thinking of marriage at her age!

A smile on her lips, Olivia glanced at the clock radio. It was a little after four in the morning. Her eyes wandered from the clock radio to the window. Moonlight spilled into her room. Out in the carriage house, was Harvey also unable to sleep? Was he thinking of her the way she was thinking of him?

Olivia rolled onto her stomach, her thoughts taking another turn. If the idea had crossed her mind, had it crossed his? Did he want to make an honest woman of her?

Not that they'd done anything out of line, but maybe he cared about her enough that he wanted the blessing of marriage before crossing the line to an intimate relationship.

"You're nuts, Liv," Olivia said aloud, even as she giggled. Goodness, the thought really was ridiculous.

Wasn't it?

"You have been spending way too much time in la-la land." How else could she explain the fact that she was lying here thinking of getting married?

But the more she thought about it, the less ridiculous the idea seemed. She already felt for Harvey more than she could imagine ever feeling for another man. And if she felt like this now . . . why not get married?

Of course, Harvey would have to agree with that idea. But she could picture it now. Maybe a wedding in November, right here at the house.

Olivia dragged a pillow over her face. Had she lost her mind? Belinda would definitely say so!

But it was true. She wanted to be with Harvey. She wasn't too young to know that. She loved him.

In her heart she knew there would never be another man like him.

She closed her eyes and continued to fantasize about what it would be like to be Harvey's wife.

CHAPTER TWENTY-SEVEN

She had taken a risk, and given the lethal expression on her mother's face, she was now going to pay for it.

"I told you to stay away from Harvey," Sylvia began as Olivia slowly made her way up the stairs toward her, "but you won't listen. And since you refuse to listen, you are going to lose some of your privileges."

Though Olivia had tried to keep her dealings with Harvey to a minimum in the days following her mother's strange outburst, today she had given in to temptation. She'd seen her mother leave with her briefcase and had expected her to be gone for a couple of hours. Apparently she hadn't even been gone forty minutes. Barely enough time for Olivia and Harvey to get through the lunch she had prepared for them.

Olivia slowed when she got to the top of the steps. She contemplated scooting past her mother but thought better of the idea.

"You're grounded. Starting right now."

"Grounded?"

"No spending time in the backyard with Harvey. No spending time outside your room. You hear me?"

"That's ridiculous!"

"And if you give me any more lip, you can forget about Elizabeth's party."

"I don't care about Elizabeth's party. She's a snot who thinks she's better than me because her daddy is a judge."

"Then you will miss all the parties of the season!" Sylvia countered. "I don't care what people will say."

That got Olivia's attention. "You're gonna treat me like a prisoner?"

"You deliberately disobeyed me. I won't tolerate it."

"You can't stop me from seeing him."

Sylvia's eyes flashed fire. "What did you say?"

"I'm in love with him. He's the man I want to be with forever. You can't stop me from becoming his wife."

"His *wife*? Did that fool ask you to marry him?"

"He's not a fool, Mama. And if you only gave him a chance, you would see how decent he is. He respects me. You have no idea. In fact, if you'll just talk to him—"

"Marriage?" Sylvia guffawed. "Do you hear yourself, child? You're a baby, and you're talking about being a wife?"

"I'm not a baby, Mama. I'm almost eighteen. And if I want to marry Harvey, if I want to have sex with him, I will."

Sylvia drew her hand back and slapped her daughter across the face.

Olivia flinched, but she didn't show any other emotion. Except perhaps defiance. Her mother could slap her, but she could not make her obey her. Not anymore.

"Stay away from him, Olivia. That is an order. This isn't up for debate."

"You don't care, do you?" Olivia looked at her mother, disillusion swirling within her. "You don't care if you push me away."

"I'm trying to protect you." But Sylvia's voice was cool and calm, as if she weren't moved by Olivia's emotion.

"Protect me from what?"

A tendril of Sylvia's hair fell from her chignon. "Don't you question me," she replied, her voice raised.

"Why not? Because you're the only one in this house who has brains? The only one with any feelings? Is this what you did to Daddy? Pushed him away until he lost himself in heroin just to escape you?"

Sylvia's eyes bulged, and once again she drew her hand back.

"Do it. Push me away, too."

Her mother didn't strike her.

"In less than a year, I'll officially be an adult. Pretty soon, I won't have to listen to a word you say. And . . . and I won't have to put up with you slapping me."

Sylvia drew in a controlled breath. "I'm not your enemy, Olivia. Liza's killer still hasn't been found. What if it's Harvey?"

"If you believed that, you never would have hired him. Or you would let him go."

"Believe me, I've considered it. He is doing a good job, however, and it's not right to fire a man based only on speculation."

"Well, it's nice to hear you say that."

"I'm not an ogre. I'm simply saying you need to be cautious. The man was in a street fight outside our house. What does that say of his character? What else could he be capable of?"

"It was a stupid fight."

"People are talking."

"They don't know him," Olivia protested.

"Neither do you. All you know is that this man strolled into town, and he's the first man you got all hot and bothered for. Now you think you know everything."

"I know I love him."

Mother and daughter stared each other down, but neither said a word for several seconds.

"How well did you know Edward before you hired him?" Olivia asked. "Not that long, but you trusted him. If you think I could be wrong about Harvey, don't you think you could be wrong about Edward? He's into voodoo, he goes out with young girls . . ."

"Oh, stop your foolishness. You live under this roof, you'll do what I say. That's the bottom line."

"Then maybe it's time I move."

"Pardon me?"

Instead of answering, Olivia ran past her mother and toward her room.

"Olivia!"

Olivia didn't stop. She ran into her room and locked the door behind her.

———

Hours later, Olivia looked up as she heard her bedroom door open. Her mother poked her head into the room.

"May I come in?"

Like her mother would listen to her if she said no. "Whatever," Olivia replied, then once again looked down at the book she was reading.

Sylvia walked toward her slowly, her delicate scent floating on the air. Normally, the smell of her mother's perfume brought her comfort. Made her think of hugs and being tucked into bed.

Not tonight.

"Is that a good book?" her mother asked.

"Mmm-hmm."

Sylvia lowered herself onto the windowsill in front of Olivia. Olivia kept reading.

"If you want, we can sit outside on the porch swing like we used to. Haven't done that in a while."

"You told me I had to stay in my room, remember?"

"Yes, but I can make an exception for tonight."

Olivia glanced at her mother. Her mother's smile was shaky. Was this how it would be between them from now on? It seemed like overnight a gap as wide as Lake Pontchartrain had grown between them.

"I'm all right."

Sylvia nodded. "Before we know it, the summer will be over."

"I guess."

A minute of silence passed before Sylvia said, "I'm sorry I was harsh with you earlier. I shouldn't have slapped you. Please try to understand, I'm only concerned about you."

Olivia didn't respond.

"Please say something."

"I heard you."

Sylvia sighed. "All right. I'll change the subject. I was wondering if you wanted to go along with the group of children for their four-day end-of-summer camp trip."

Olivia looked at her mother then. "Me?"

"I know I've never asked you to go before, but it seems to me you played such a role in choosing which ones were the best candidates . . . the board agreed, the essays you selected were astounding."

Sylvia chuckled softly and leaned forward to place a hand on Olivia's leg. Olivia shifted uncomfortably. Sylvia removed her hand, her soft laughter dying.

After a moment she said, "It only makes sense that you go."

"Oh." But Olivia really wanted to ask, Why now? Was her mother going to any lengths to keep her away from Harvey?

"Besides, Elizabeth has been very visible lately with community events. If she's not at the nursing home working with the elderly, she's volunteering at the soup kitchen. She's working very hard to boost her image as a caring young girl, which we know is false, but I wouldn't want to see her last-minute efforts rob you of what you're due. Connor Evans will want to escort the most popular debutante. That's you, of course. And everything you do is sincere. When you work with children, you do it because you truly care. I'm rambling, sorry. It's just that I'm so proud of you."

Really? was the thought that popped into Olivia's mind, but she didn't vocalize it. Her mother had done a complete one-eighty since earlier today.

"Well, what do you say? As you know, being on the board, I only select the children who will go, but I never travel with them. Though I do hear it's a lot of fun."

"Four days with a bunch of kids?" Olivia asked skeptically. Normally, she would relish the idea. But not today.

"There'll be other teenagers there. The counselors. Think about it—four days away from me." Sylvia's smile was sugar-sweet.

"I don't think I'd like it."

"Why not, Olivia?"

"Because . . . because I don't think so. I'd rather stay here. Work on my novel."

Sylvia's eyes registered surprise. "It's only four days."

"I'll think about it."

"Last year you wanted to go."

"Belinda and I would have gone then. It's just not the same now."

"Hmm."

Olivia knew there was something else her mother wanted to say, something that had to do with Harvey, but she must have thought better of it. She stood suddenly.

"All right. You think about it and let me know."

"Sure."

Olive went back to reading as her mother left her room. But the words blurred. She couldn't see a thing.

CHAPTER TWENTY-EIGHT

The bar was a dive, the kind of place people went to escape their problems in a bottle of booze. It was dark, and a heavy layer of cigarette smoke hung in the air. Yet he didn't want to be anywhere else. The seductive sounds of Billie Holiday were washing away his troubles. Making him forget that void in his heart, the one only his mother could fill.

"But when the Lord up above you, sends someone to love you," Billie crooned in "The Blues Are Brewin'."

"Sing it, Billie." He raised a hand in the air. Swayed it.

He lowered his arm as his senses came alert. He smelled her before he saw her. The light, sweet fragrance made him turn. He just knew she'd be something special.

The lady took his arm, holding him tight. But there was so much smoke, he couldn't see her face.

"Harvey."

He didn't see her lips moving. And why did she sound angry?

"Harvey."

Harvey's eyes flew open. He shot upright when he saw Sylvia Grayson standing over him.

"M-Mrs. Grayson." Aw, hell. He'd been dreaming.

"I knocked. You didn't answer." Her arms were crossed over her chest in a defensive stance. It was obvious she wasn't here on a social call.

The fog clearing from his mind, Harvey reached for a T-shirt and slipped it over his head.

"Exactly what are your intentions with my daughter?"

He didn't reply right away, making sure he had heard her correctly. He got to his feet, saying, "I have nothing but honorable intentions where Olivia is concerned."

"Honorable? Is that what you call it?"

"Mrs. Grayson, I know you're worried, but we haven't done anything wrong. Anything you would disapprove of."

"Like your late-night walks to the park?"

Harvey saw satisfaction in her eyes that she'd shocked him.

"You thought I didn't know?"

"I like Olivia. I would never disrespect her."

"I wonder what the definition of disrespect is where you come from, Harvey. Where is that, by the way? I'm not sure you've told me."

"I did tell you. Chicago."

"And what are you doing here again?"

"I came for the weather," Harvey replied, suddenly unable to tell Mrs. Grayson what he'd told Olivia about his family. He had no doubt that she would call the cops to have him taken to jail if he told her of his situation.

"The real reason," Sylvia snapped.

Did she know? Harvey wondered, feeling a moment of panic. But if she knew, wouldn't she have called the police already? And he would be on his way back to Chicago.

She paced back and forth, then stopped. "What do you want from me? Money? Is that why you showed up here?"

"What do you mean? Other than the money you're paying me for the job I'm doing?"

"Don't be cute."

Harvey stared at her in confusion.

"Do you know Clinton?"

Did she mean Clayton? "I don't know any Clinton."

Sylvia was silent a moment. She narrowed her eyes on him, like she was trying to decide if she could believe him. And there was something else she was searching for in his face, but he didn't know what.

"You have no idea what I'm talking about?"

"None," Harvey replied.

"Of course, you wouldn't tell me if you did. That would ruin your plan."

Harvey threw his hands up in frustration. He wondered if Mrs. Grayson was normally this suspicious of people, or if she was making an exception where he was concerned.

"I liked you, Harvey. Like you. I don't have any problems with you as a person. But if you have ulterior motives, another reason for being here—and I suspect you might—I will be very unhappy.

"Though you're doing a good job, maybe I was hasty in hiring you. You came to town just when Liza was murdered."

"And you think I had something to do with that?"

"I don't know what to think."

"You know good and well that I had nothing to do with that girl's death." Sylvia's eyes grew wide. Alarm? Harvey wondered.

"What does that mean?" she asked.

He had heard the word on the street. He knew what Cynthia Monroe had accused Sylvia of at Liza's funeral. But he replied, "Mr. Johnson was taken in for questioning more than once. He's the prime suspect."

"Make no mistake about it," Sylvia went on. "If you hurt Olivia, or try to hurt her—"

Harvey felt a spurt of anger. She was jumping from one topic to another without any logic. "Mrs. Grayson, I mean no disrespect, but you are out of line. I would never hurt Olivia."

"And," she said loudly, cutting him off. "If I find out that your reasons for being here are anything other than honorable, I will make sure a detailed background check is run on you. If you're the one . . ." She paused. "If you did indeed kill . . . kill Liza . . . you will be punished."

After she finished tripping over her words, Sylvia gave Harvey one last look of distaste, but he saw fear deep in her eyes. What the hell was she so afraid of?

She stalked out of the carriage house, leaving him to wonder what the hell had just happened.

Sylvia rapped on Edward's door a moment before opening it. His eyes flew to hers in surprise.

"Oh, my!" she exclaimed, seeing a topless Edward sitting on the sofa. Embarrassed, she whirled around. "I'm sorry."

"Mrs. Grayson? What is it?"

"I-I shouldn't have barged in on you."

"It's okay."

There was the sound of shuffling, then Sylvia could hear footsteps as Edward approached her.

"You can turn around," he said.

Swallowing a deep breath, Sylvia did just that. Edward had slipped on a black satin robe. The one she had bought for him two Christmases ago.

"Has something happened?" he asked. There was concern in his eyes.

"You could say that, yes."

"Come in. Take a seat."

"I . . ." She felt oddly flustered. She had spoken with Edward in his room many a time, but never when he was partially dressed. She felt like she was invading his privacy.

Edward took her hand. A tingle of warmth shot through her arm.

He led her to the sofa where he had been sitting moments ago, practically naked. He forced her to sit, then said, "Tell me what's going on."

"I need your help." Sylvia clenched her hands. "And I know this is going to sound weird, considering for years I've always questioned why your religion of choice is voodoo—"

"I've told you many times. I grew up in the Voudon faith. It's a mystical religion that originated in Africa as a form of ancestor worship—"

"I know, I know," Sylvia said, interrupting him. "And . . ." She took a deep breath. "And that's why I think you can help me."

"Help you what?"

"Make Harvey go away."

Edward's eyes grew wide with her comment. "I'm certain I did not hear you correctly."

"I need him gone, Edward. I realize that—"

"Mrs. Grayson, you know I don't believe in using voodoo for ill."

"Please, Edward. It's just you and me. You know you can call me Sylvia when no one's around." It seemed ridiculous, given what she was asking him, for him to address her formally. "And I'm not asking you to do him any harm. I simply want him out of our lives."

Sylvia looked at the small table near the window. Several white candles were lit and flickering. It was a voodoo shrine of some sort, but she had paid no attention to it before. Funny how things could change.

Wrenching her hands, she turned back to Edward. "I see you with Olivia. I know you love her as much as any father could love a daughter. Do you want this man to stay here, hurt her? Because that's exactly what's going to happen if he does stay here. He's got her wrapped around his finger. I know his type, Edward. You yourself have expressed concerns. Taking her out to the park . . . how long before he takes her virtue?"

Edward sauntered to the window and looked outside. For a long while, he didn't speak. Finally he turned back to Sylvia and said, "Let me consult with a voodoo priestess. See what she suggests."

"How long will that take?"

"I'm sure she'll get back to me in the morning."

"The morning? I was hoping we could . . . if it was possible, perhaps now?"

"Right now? But it's late."

"I understand that, but . . ." To her own ears, she sounded desperate. But this was her daughter. She *was* desperate. "Isn't there *somebody* you can contact? Didn't you say that the voodoo priestesses are on call for emergencies?"

"This isn't exactly an em—"

"Not life and death, no. But I need this taken care of as soon as possible. I can barely sleep, barely eat. I'm hardly myself anymore."

"I do know you've been stressed." Edward dragged a hand over his face. "Let me call High Priestess Geneviève."

"Thank you, Edward. I'll wait for you in the sunroom."

Sylvia left Edward's room and headed for the sunroom. Hearing the jingling bell on Rosa's collar, she looked around. Rosa had appeared from nowhere.

"Rosa, darling." Sylvia sat on the wicker sofa and Rosa jumped onto her lap.

Perhaps sensing Sylvia's weird mood, Rosa snuggled close, whimpering softly.

"Don't you worry, Rosa. I'll be okay. As soon as Harvey's gone, I'll be just fine."

Sylvia?"

She stood at the sound of Edward's voice. "What's the word?"

"She'll meet with us."

Sylvia's stomach fluttered with nervous anticipation. "Now?"

"Yes. At her home. Near Vieux Carré. She said to bring something of Harvey's."

"Like what?"

"Anything that belongs to him."

"Oh." Sylvia frowned. How was she supposed to accomplish that? She had already seen Harvey once this evening. She didn't want to disturb him again.

Stroking Rosa, she gave thought to her quandary. "All right," she said slowly. "Let me see what I can find."

"Then we'll head off. Priestess Geneviève would like to see us as soon as possible. The fee is two hundred dollars."

Sylvia nodded. She would pay much more than that if it meant Harvey would leave forever.

"And you will need to bring an offering for the loa."

"The what?"

"The spirits. Our ancestors."

"Something more than the two hundred?"

"The offering needs to be something of sentimental value to you."

"Okay. Let me get something from Harvey first."

Sylvia released Rosa and made her way to the side door. She slipped outside and quickly closed the door behind her before Rosa could follow her out. Creeping like a criminal staking out a place to rob, she made her way across the vast backyard to the carriage house.

Her heart pounded as she contemplated what she would say to Harvey. The last thing she wanted to do was speak to him again for fear he would intuitively know what she was up to.

She raised her hand to knock on the door, but stopped when her gaze went to the right. Lying only a few feet away were Harvey's discarded dirty clothes.

Expelling a sigh of relief, she rushed over to the pile and scooped up the first item. It was a T-shirt. Smeared with paint, it smelled of his perspiration. This would do.

T-shirt in hand, she hurried back to the house.

CHAPTER TWENTY-NINE

Sylvia was sitting in the passenger seat of her Mercedes while Edward was driving. She was far too nervous to control a vehicle.

She clutched Rosa on her lap. She hadn't planned on taking her pet, but Rosa had jumped ecstatically when Sylvia had picked up the car keys. At that moment, Sylvia had known that her four-legged family member would not be happy staying home alone while she went on a trip in the car.

Besides, Sylvia felt somewhat better with Rosa accompanying them, although Rosa would be much more suitable as a powder puff, as opposed to a guard dog. Rosa didn't even like to bark . . . unless she was left alone and wanted attention.

They drove in silence for several minutes. Sylvia finally took a moment to focus on the view. The pale moonlight filtered through the leaves of the oak trees, casting an eerie glow on the moss that hung low from their branches. It made her think of evil things. Voodoo curses. Black magic.

The very things she would be calling on tonight.

Lord forgive me. But I have to do this. I have to protect my daughter.

Edward turned left, taking them in a direction she had never been before. Sylvia glanced around, concerned. With each passing mile, the scenery grew more rural. Fewer businesses, more greenery. Hefty bushes, trees with branches that stretched over the entire road. And far fewer streetlights than where they had been traveling minutes before. Ahead of them seemed to be endless darkness.

"Are you sure this is the right way?" Sylvia asked. "This doesn't look like we're heading to the French Quarter."

"I said her home is near the Vieux Carré."

"We're heading to her home? Not that voodoo temple in the Quarter?"

"Priestess Geneviève has a temple in her home. She is not commercialized, like some of the other priestesses in the city."

"Oh."

"Her temple is small, but she invokes the loas just the same. Believe me, you do not want dime-store voodoo."

The words alone made Sylvia shiver. What was she getting herself into?

Edward reached across the seat and squeezed her hand. "Don't worry."

Edward's warm hand offered her unspoken comfort, yet the feeling was awkward. She pulled her hand away. "I just want this done already, is all."

Moments later, Edward turned onto a gravel path. At first Sylvia thought it was another street, but she soon realized that it was a driveway. He pulled up in front of a house almost entirely obscured by shrubs and brush. Sylvia had never seen such a mess pass for a yard. Unkempt was the only way to describe it.

"This is it?" Sylvia asked, shocked. "I thought you said it was a temple?"

"It is not a temple in the traditional sense," Edward explained. "This is Priestess Geneviève's home as well."

Some home. Looks more like a dungeon.

As Edward killed the engine and got out of the Mercedes, Sylvia sat silently, staring out the car at the house. Flames flickered in the first-floor window, providing the only light. It was a peculiar sight, making the place seem alive with entities.

Her door opened, and Sylvia's fingers tightened on poor Rosa as she drew up short. Seeing Edward, she sighed with relief.

"You don't need to be afraid." Edward held out a hand to her.

"This is a little . . . creepier than I expected." The place looked like the definition of a haunted house. "I hope this wasn't a mistake. I've never been to a voodoo temple."

"It is Hollywood that gives voodoo a bad name. Would you be afraid if you were outside your minister's home right now?"

"No. But this is hardly a normal-looking house."

"What you see, what you feel—it's an experience. That's what voodoo is. It's a religion rich in African mysticism." When Sylvia didn't reply, Edward went on. "You've known me for ages. Do you think that when the lights go out, I cast evil spells?"

"Of course not."

"Priestess Geneviève is very kind. You'll like her."

"Rosa, you're going to have to stay here." The dog moaned her displeasure. "None of that, you hear? I'll be back shortly."

She closed the car door, leaving Rosa inside. The window was rolled down a fraction to let in fresh air.

This time, Sylvia reached for Edward. Together, they walked through the brush up to the front door. The staccato beating of drums was the only sound in the darkness. That and a chorus of crickets.

Edward knocked.

Sylvia bit back a gasp when the older woman opened the door, and she would swear her heart stopped beating for a good few seconds. When it started again, it took off racing, faster than the steady drumbeat, which was even louder now with the door ajar.

Sylvia looked at the woman. Despite the woman's smooth, dark skin, her piercing eyes said she was much older than she looked. It was disconcerting to think that this woman could physically look fifty, yet perhaps be eighty. Sylvia couldn't help remembering the stories of New Orleans's legendary voodoo priestess, Marie Laveau, and how it was rumored that while she was close to one hundred years old, she hardly looked it.

Wearing a flowing white skirt and cotton white top, the only color on the woman's outfit came from the several rows of beads around her neck. She also wore a white head wrap.

"Good evening, Priestess Geneviève," Edward said. "Thank you for agreeing to see us on such short notice."

The woman nodded and stepped backward, inviting them in. Sylvia followed Edward, gripping his arm. Behind her, she could hear Rosa barking. Rosa, who very rarely barked.

Was this a bad omen?

"Follow me." The silver and gold bracelets on Geneviève's arm clinked as she motioned for them to follow. Then she turned and seemed to float across the wooden floor. Sylvia wouldn't be surprised if she indeed *was* floating—she couldn't see the woman's feet beneath her long skirt.

As they walked further into the house, the drums grew louder still. The rhythm was strangely intoxicating. Sylvia could feel the beat inside her, feel it more than she could feel her own heart. That's how powerful it was.

Powerful enough to ensnare one's soul?

Priestess Geneviève glanced over her shoulder at them. "Houn'gan Lucien is finishing a late wedding ceremony."

Sylvia peered inside the living room as they reached it. A man, also dressed in white, held a white dove in each hand and circled them over the heads of a man and a woman, who were kneeling on the floor. Three men pounded an exotic rhythm on bongos.

Priestess Geneviève paused only briefly outside the entrance to the living room, smiled in the direction of the ceremony, then turned to the left and walked up a wooden staircase that was beginning to warp. Upstairs, candles lit the path they took into a bedroom.

"Wait here."

Priestess Geneviève disappeared. Sylvia looked around the large space. This room wasn't truly a bedroom. It seemed like a second temple. There was a table against one wall, clearly some type of altar. Draped in silk, the table was covered with black and white candles, various trinkets, and ornaments of the crucifix. There were also mason jars filled with what appeared to be spices.

The candles provided the room's only lighting. What was it with voodoo and physical darkness?

At the foot of the altar lay a bed of leaves. It was hard to tell in the dim lighting, but some of the leaves appeared to be stained with a dark substance. Blood? No doubt some chicken or pig had met its fate at the priestess's hands.

There were also a few jars on the floor. One was filled with a clear liquid and looked like something one would find in a science class. Sylvia's eyes narrowed on it, then bulged. Good Lord. Was that an umbilical cord?

"You wish to make someone go away?"

Sylvia started at the sound of the woman's voice and nearly screamed. She hadn't heard her return to the room.

"Yes," Sylvia answered, barely getting the word out.

"Why?"

"Because." Sylvia swallowed. "This man . . . I fear he will hurt my daughter. She's started to change because of him. It's worrying me."

"Please sit."

Edward lowered himself onto his knees. Sylvia followed his example.

"Give me your hands."

Sylvia hesitated.

"I will not hurt you," Priestess Geneviève assured her.

Inhaling a steadying breath, Sylvia surrendered to the woman and extended her hands. The priestess took Sylvia's hands in her bony ones. Several moments of silence ensued, punctuated by the disjointed beating of the drums downstairs.

"Are you a follower of the Voudon faith?"

Sylvia shook her head. "No."

"You think badly of voodoo? You fear it?"

"I wouldn't say that." But Sylvia was suddenly wondering if this woman was able to read minds. Were voodoo priestesses capable of that as well? "No," she went on, "I don't fear it. If I feared voodoo, I wouldn't associate with Edward."

"So you are here with an open mind, an open heart?"

"Yes. I am." And high expectations. Even though she knew she would have to pray for hours for daring to dabble in devil worship.

Priestess Geneviève closed her eyes. "I sense your fear," she said.

Sylvia was about to object when the woman continued: "You are afraid of this man, aren't you?"

"Yes," Sylvia answered without hesitation.

"What is this man's name?"

"Harvey."

"And you wish to make him simply go away? You do not wish him harm?"

"No, no harm."

"Good. Because while some people can cast spells for ill, the loa do not look kindly on this." Geneviève released Sylvia's hands and picked up something from the floor beside her. A rattle. She shook it to Sylvia's right, then to her left, as if she were spraying some invisible substance onto her.

"Have you an offering for the loa?"

Sylvia reached into her change purse. "It's not much." She produced a gold coin that her father had given her. It was unique; Sylvia had never seen another one like it and didn't even know where her father had obtained it. She had planned to give it to Olivia one day, but now she could not.

"It doesn't matter what the offering is, as long as it means something to you."

Priestess Geneviève brought the coin to the table and placed it there before one of the many candles. From the foot of the table, she lifted a bottle and a small glass vial.

She returned to Sylvia, sitting.

"This is graveyard sand," she said of the medium-sized bottle. She opened the bottle and poured some of its contents into the vial. "On its own it is powerful, but for it to be effective for this spell, it must be mixed with fresh dirt from a grave."

"You mean—"

"Yes." Priestess Geneviève's voice was as serious as her eyes. "You must go to a graveyard and scoop up fresh dirt."

"But a graveyard? I don't want—"

"It does not mean death. But it is necessary for the spell. You have the item of the man's clothing?"

Sylvia dug into her tote and produced Harvey's shirt. "Here."

Priestess Geneviève took the shirt. She placed it on the floor and shook the rattle over it. Then she passed it back to Sylvia.

"Take this shirt and put it into a plastic bag. Sprinkle this graveyard dirt into the bag, along with the fresh dirt. Shake it well. Take the bag to the river and throw it in. The bag will float away, the same way Harvey will float out of your life."

"That's everything?"

"Yes."

"When will he be gone?"

"He will be gone within three days."

Three days. She hoped against hope that this would work. "Thank you."

Sylvia slowly started to stand, but Priestess Geneviève extended a hand, urging her to sit down with a gentle touch.

The woman met Sylvia's confused gaze with one of prudence. "You are troubled, are you not?"

Sylvia shot a quick glance at Edward. He gave the slightest of nods, letting her know she should answer. "Yes," Sylvia finally said.

Geneviève stood and walked back to the altar. When she returned to Sylvia, she was carrying a small sac. "This is a gris-gris bag," she explained. "It is for good luck. It will help to keep the evil spirits away."

She pressed it into Sylvia's hand.

"How much?" Sylvia asked, knowing it couldn't be free.

"Pay me something. That's all."

Pay her something. What was that supposed to mean? Sylvia again glanced at Edward for help. She had the two hundred he'd instructed her she would need to pay Geneviève, plus a bit extra.

"I think it's a good idea," Edward told her, misreading her question. "I wish I'd had mine before I lost Charlene and the kids. I'm certain someone put a hex on my family. The gris-gris bag could have protected us."

Sylvia opened her wallet and withdrew a fifty. "Here."

Geneviève smiled. "Thank you."

"And this is for . . . for your help." Sylvia passed the woman two crisp hundred-dollar bills.

Priestess Geneviève accepted the money without looking at it. "I wish you luck."

"Mam'bo Geneviève, are we finished?" Edward asked.

"Yes."

"Thank you," Edward said to her.

"Anytime, my friend."

When she rose to her feet, Sylvia followed her lead.

As Sylvia and Edward left the house, Sylvia hoped this woman wasn't a hack. The type who exploited people's fears for a quick buck.

Yes, everything had seemed real, from the atmosphere to the electric charge Sylvia had experienced when the woman had touched her. But was it real, or imagined?

It *had* to be real. Because if this didn't work to get rid of Harvey, she wasn't sure what she was going to do.

CHAPTER THIRTY

Olivia awoke with the premonition that something was wrong.

She glanced at the clock. It was after eight. Bright sunlight bathed the room with light and warmth. Outside, she could hear birds chirping.

By all appearances, everything was normal. So what was it that bothered her?

Olivia threw off the sheets, then pushed aside the netting. Instinctively she went to the window, fearing the worst.

Her shoulders drooped with relief. Harvey was there. He was carrying a can of paint toward the carriage house.

Smiling, Olivia went back to bed. Clearly, she had had a bad dream. The kind you didn't remember, but that left you with a feeling of foreboding nonetheless.

Yes, she decided. That had to be it.

A little while later, Olivia was surprised to find she was eating breakfast alone.

"Where's my mama?" she asked Edward.

"Your mother isn't feeling very well this morning," he told her.

"The flu?"

"I'm not sure. She hasn't seemed quite herself over the last few days."

That was definitely true. Until this moment, Olivia had assumed her mother was running herself ragged with paranoia. But maybe there was another reason for her out-of-character behavior.

Goodness, could she be sick?

As Olivia ate her breakfast of fried eggs and grits, she gave that idea more thought. All this time, she'd been getting angrier and angrier at her mother for getting on her case about Harvey. But maybe her mother was simply trying to tell her that she needed her now more than she ever had before.

Olivia pushed aside the plate of half-eaten food and shot to her feet. If something was wrong with her mother, she needed to know.

She hurried upstairs.

After knocking twice on her mother's door and getting no answer, Olivia turned the knob and walked into the room.

She walked quietly to the bed and looked down at her mother. She debated turning around and leaving, but she had to know. Had to know if her mother was okay.

"Mama?"

Her mother stirred, and after a moment she opened her eyes. Olivia moved the netting aside and sat on the edge of the bed.

"Olivia?"

"Mama, are you sick?"

"I'm not feeling too well this morning."

"But that's it? You're not dying or anything?"

"Heavens no."

"You wouldn't lie to me, would you?"

"Mmm-mmm."

"All right." Olivia placed a hand on her mother's arm. It felt awkward there. "I'll let you sleep."

Olivia was at the door when her mother called her name. She turned. "Yes, Mama?"

"Don't be mad at me. Everything I'm doing—I'm doing it for you."

"What, Mama?"

But her mother didn't answer.

———————

Harvey steeled his jaw when there was a knock on his door after ten P.M. He'd made sure to lock it today after how Sylvia had barged in on him last night. He didn't need another surprise visit.

Slowly he made his way across the room and opened the door. He was hoping to see Olivia, but instead Sylvia greeted him with a smile.

Maybe the woman was insane.

"It's late, Mrs. Grayson," he said.

"I know, and I'm sorry. I feel bad about how I dealt with you yesterday. Believe it or not, it is out of character for me, and I thought I should explain myself. You see, Olivia is my only child. It's just me and her, and I'm worried about her. She's had enough heartache this summer, and as much as she feels strongly for you now, it's only natural that she's going to get her heart broken. First loves rarely last. You know that."

Harvey steeled his jaw.

"This isn't about you," Sylvia quickly said. "It's about her. Maybe I am being overprotective, but I have my child's best interests in mind."

Sylvia paused, then continued. "I'm prepared to make you an offer." She pulled an envelope from inside her cardigan. "A very generous offer."

She passed Harvey the envelope. He hesitated a moment before taking it.

"I suppose this is what I think it is."

"Ten thousand dollars. It was all I had in the family safe. I'm hoping it's enough for you to leave town." She paused. "And not come back."

Ten thousand dollars. A serious price to pay for a woman who claimed simply to be trying to protect her daughter from heartache.

Exactly what was she afraid of?

"You can count it if you like—"

"Why are you doing this?"

"If you truly don't know, then I'm sorry." Genuine regret flashed in her eyes. "But if you do know, then I hope this will satisfy you. I've made a good life for myself now, for me and my daughter, and I cannot allow anyone to destroy it."

Harvey looked at her carefully, trying to read what was in her eyes. But she wouldn't meet his gaze directly.

"What are you hiding, Mrs. Grayson?"

"Like I said, if you don't know, then I'm sorry. But I suspect you do." She sighed. "You don't have to leave tonight. But in the next couple days. That'll give you time to finish the work on the exterior of the carriage house. It really is coming along nicely."

The woman was out of her mind.

"But in the meantime, you need to stay away from Olivia."

Harvey merely shook his head.

Sylvia turned for the door. "I am sorry," she said as she opened it. "I really am."

Then she rushed out, disappearing into the night.

The next morning, Olivia's premonition of trouble was even stronger than it had been the day before. She remembered her mother's words the previous day, that she was doing what was best for her. Olivia still had no idea what her mother was alluding to.

But something told her she had to see Harvey.

She went to the backyard via the side door. Harvey was at the far end of the yard, painting a portion of the carriage house.

Seeing him made her smile. Her anxiety ebbed away.

Because he didn't see her, Olivia crept toward the carriage house. With every step closer to him she took, he still didn't turn. Directly behind him now, she lurched forward, slipping her arms around his waist and yelling, "Boo!"

"Son of a—" Harvey jerked forward and to the side, his body colliding with the wall. With her arms wrapped around him, Olivia also stumbled against the side of the house. She felt the wet paint graze her arm.

She laughed and jumped apart from him, preparing for his playful wrath.

"Olivia." His tone was serious as he glanced around. "What are you doing?"

The uneasy feeling returned.

"You shouldn't be down here," he said.

"I needed to see you."

"That's not a good idea."

Her stomach dropped. "It's my mama. She's gotten to you, hasn't she?"

Harvey looked at the wall he'd been painting. "Damn. That spot's gonna have to be repainted."

"Don't ignore me."

Again Harvey looked beyond her, glancing around the yard. Then he took Olivia's hand and whizzed her into the carriage house.

"Tell me, Harvey," Olivia implored the moment he closed the door.

"You have to go back to the house. If your mother finds you here—"

"Just tell me."

"All right. Your mother came to talk to me last night."

"She did?"

"Yes. And the night before that as well. But last night she was even more serious about what she wants. She told me in no uncertain terms that she doesn't want us seeing each other anymore." He paused. "She's a woman on a mission. I don't know what exactly her issue is, but she . . ." Harvey's voice trailed off. "I won't be working here much longer."

"She fired you?"

Harvey blew out a ragged breath. "She wants me to leave town. She paid me, even."

"My God."

"She wants me out of your life, and I'm not sure why. Seems to me your mama has some secrets, secrets she's afraid I'll stumble across."

"I don't believe this. I thought for sure—"

"Nothing you or I say is gonna help. She wants me gone by tomorrow night."

"No!" Olivia threw herself into Harvey's arms. She couldn't stop the tears. The thought of Harvey leaving made her feel despair beyond anything she had ever known. "You can't leave. I can't lose you, Harvey."

"I can't stay here. When I say she paid me, I mean she really paid me. She gave me enough money to make a new start somewhere else."

"No."

"Ten thousand dollars."

Olivia looked at Harvey in horror. "Oh, my God. You took it?"

"She didn't give me a choice."

Olivia's heart went into overdrive. "You're really gonna leave me?"

"Your mother didn't give me much choice. She must know I'm in some kind of trouble, 'cause she said she's gonna go to the cops if I stay around."

Olivia moaned. "Where will you go?"

"I don't know."

"I want to go with you."

"You know your mama won't allow it."

"I'm not gonna ask her. I'm just gonna leave with you. Wherever you are, I want to be there." Olivia paused as she looked into Harvey's eyes. "Harvey, I love you."

Harvey's lips slowly curled in a smile, and he stared down at her with tenderness. "God, Olivia. You have no idea how much I love you."

Olivia's whole body grew warm, and if they were anywhere else but this carriage house on her mama's property, she would take off her clothes, then take off his. She knew she was ready to make love to him.

"I . . . I want to marry you, Harvey. I want to be your wife."

Harvey held her tightly, and in his embrace she heard all the things he didn't say. That he wanted her too, that he wanted a life with her.

Olivia knew they had to make a plan.

"You said my mama wants you gone by tomorrow?"

"Uh-huh."

"Then let's leave tonight."

"Are you serious?"

"Of course I'm serious. Harvey, you can't leave me. Together, we can have a good life. I know that. I just want to be with you. Tell me you want the same thing."

Harvey framed her face. "Of course." He kissed her briefly, but with a passion that stole her breath. "Of course, baby."

Olivia felt the sting of happy tears. This wasn't something she wanted, but her mother was giving her no choice. Olivia didn't understand her anymore. At one time, she would have bet money that she could talk to her mother about anything.

Of course her mother would be concerned about her dating. That was only natural. But the caring approach would have been to talk to her—not bark out commands as if she were the hired help.

If her mother loved her, she should talk to her about her concerns. And if she loved her, she would realize that she had to trust her to make her own decisions at this stage of her life.

Why didn't her mother believe she had raised her right? She wasn't loose, or careless. So why was her mother acting like she had gone and lost her mind?

It didn't matter, Olivia thought sadly. She didn't want to leave, but the great Sylvia Grayson would get over it. Maybe in a month or so, she could call her and her mother would be so happy to hear from her that she'd forgive her for what she was about to do.

And hopefully, by then she would accept the fact that she was married to Harvey.

"I'll meet you tonight," Olivia told Harvey. "By the pond in City Park. Let's say around eleven. Maybe a little later, just to be sure. I won't need much, just some clothes to last me till we get wherever we're going. I'll try to go to the bank today and withdraw the money I have."

"Olivia—"

She placed a finger on Harvey's lips. "Shh. I want to do this. If you leave me, I'll have nothing to live for."

The reality of her words hit her full force, but she knew they were true. She'd already lost Belinda. She couldn't lose Harvey. Not like this.

Harvey was speechless as he looked down at her. Olivia slowly smiled, heat spreading throughout her veins. She knew she was doing the right thing.

"You really want to do this?" Harvey asked.

"I've never wanted anything more."

Harvey chuckled. "Olivia, you sure are crazy." Pause. "But I love you anyway."

Olivia looked over Harvey's shoulder to the window. "My mama's sick in bed this morning, but I'd better head out of here in case she's up and is looking for me."

She gave Harvey another kiss on his lips and squeezed both his hands. "I love you. And I'll see you tonight."

CHAPTER THIRTY-ONE

Olivia's heart was beating frantically. Every sound in the house made her jump. She half expected her mother to barge into her room any minute, telling her that she knew what she was up to and she wouldn't get away with it.

Just in case, Olivia lay still and quiet in the dark, tucked securely beneath the covers. If her mother checked on her, she would find her in bed. But under the sheets, she was dressed and ready to leave the moment she felt it was safe.

A shaky breath escaped her. She was afraid, yet determined. She wanted to do this.

Needed to.

And she was ready. She had two bags packed with necessary items, and she had withdrawn almost all the money from her bank account.

Now all she had to do was wait. And it was the waiting that was getting to her.

She was certain that someone was still up in the house, even though it was nearly eleven P.M. Was it Edward? And if so, was he heading to some weird voodoo ritual or had he just come in? Olivia had crept to her door and peered into the hallway, but she hadn't seen anything. Not even Rosa. It was possible that her mother was still up at this hour, considering she'd stayed in bed most of the day.

Olivia groaned her frustration. All she could do was wait.

Harvey stood beneath the cover of a large oak tree in City Park. He paced back and forth near the pond, waiting for Olivia.

He flicked his wrist forward, angling his watch so that the moonlight caught it. He read the time. It was after eleven-thirty. He'd been out here for over twenty minutes.

Where was Olivia?

Placing his hands on his hips, he turned and faced the water. Geese were gliding across the tranquil pond the way they had been when he was here with Olivia. The sight made him miss her all the more.

Hearing a sound, he whirled around. A figure moved toward him. This person had curves. Clearly a woman.

"Olivia?"

She didn't answer, and Harvey narrowed his eyes to see better. "Olivia?" It had to be her. Who else would be heading straight for him? "Where have you been?"

She removed her baseball hat.

Harvey's stomach hit the ground.

Sylvia's eyes were cold as she said, "Olivia couldn't make it."

A chill crept over his skin.

"You really thought she would go through with this?" When he didn't respond, Sylvia chuckled sarcastically. "Oh, my. You did."

She could be lying, Harvey thought. "I don't know what you're talking about."

"Of course you do."

"I'm simply out taking a walk."

"Olivia's decided not to run off with you."

Okay, so she knew. No, it wasn't okay. *Damn.* He steeled his jaw. "Why wouldn't Olivia tell me that herself?"

Sylvia folded her arms over her chest. "I think she was ashamed. She really does care for you, Harvey. And she feels bad for leading you on. She came to me, Harvey. Broke down and cried when she told me what you two were planning. She said she realized she just couldn't do it, and she didn't know how to tell you. That's why she came to me, hoping I could tell you her decision. She didn't want to hurt you, at least not intentionally. Don't take it personally. She just came to her senses and realized that running off with you wasn't what she wanted for her life."

Harvey swallowed hard. "I . . . I told her she needed to think this through."

"Well, it's nice to know you had a moment of sanity." Sylvia paused. "Look, I understand this is hard for you to accept, and I'm not trying to rub salt in your wound. But you know it wouldn't have worked, don't you? Even if she left with you, she probably would have come home after a little while. She's got a whole life here, one you'll never understand. Social clubs, volunteer work . . . things that are very important to her. She'd miss it all if she left. Olivia is practically a baby. How's she to know what she really wants at this stage?"

Harvey turned toward the water. It felt like Sylvia had dug her hands inside his body and was twisting his guts. He was a fool. He'd gotten his hopes up, but he should have known better. When had anything in his life ever gone the way he'd wanted it?

"For what it's worth, I am sorry."

Harvey whirled around. "I bet you are."

She took a step toward him, extending another envelope. "I do feel bad. This is another five thousand. To make things a bit . . . easier."

Harvey snatched the envelope from her.

"You need to disappear tonight, Harvey. As soon as I leave. I never want to see you in these parts again. That's the deal."

His life was one big disaster after another. Where the hell was he supposed to go now?

Screw it, he thought. Things hadn't gone the way he had hoped they would here, and he may as well cut his losses. Start over somewhere where he didn't know anybody, and use this money to get the education he'd always wanted. He would never find his mother. She was lost to him forever. What did it matter if he never returned?

"Fine," he agreed.

"Please don't call her. Don't write. This is hard enough."

"I won't."

"There are plenty of hotels around, in case you can't leave the city tonight. But I expect you gone by tomorrow. Catch a bus, take a plane. It doesn't matter. As long as you start a new life for yourself somewhere far from here."

"No problem."

"And I hope the fifteen thousand is enough so that I'll never hear from you again."

Believe me, if I never see you again, it will be too soon. "I understood you the first time."

Sylvia nodded. "Good-bye, Harvey. Good luck."

Harvey didn't say a word. He couldn't.

He could only watch Sylvia turn and walk away, his heart splitting in two.

When Olivia heard the floorboards outside her bedroom door creak, she sat up. Before her mother knocked, she knew that she would.

Olivia called, "Come in."

The door opened, and Sylvia stepped inside. "You've been in bed a long time this morning."

"I had trouble sleeping." She hadn't been able to make it to the park until nearly one A.M. To her horror, Harvey hadn't been there. Olivia had run all the way back to the carriage house, just in case he'd gone back there to wait for her. She had pounded on the door, tried the knob—all to no avail. Either he'd been sleeping or he hadn't been around.

For half the night, Olivia had intermittently tossed and turned and looked out her window, hoping to see Harvey. Would he have left without her?

No, that was impossible. He wouldn't do that to her. He wanted to be with her as much as she wanted to be with him.

But something about her mother's visit had Olivia on guard. There was something wrong. Something terribly wrong.

Sylvia made her way to the bed. She sat down beside her daughter. Olivia shuddered when her mother ran her hand over her hair.

"What is it?" Olivia asked. She was unable to keep the alarm from her voice.

"Oh, sweetheart. I'm not sure how to tell you this."

"Something happened to Harvey?"

"Yes, sweetheart. Something's happened."

"Whatever it is, just tell me." Her heart was beating rapidly, her stomach sick with tension.

Sylvia sighed sadly, but the sound wasn't genuine. And Olivia knew right then that whatever had happened, her mother was secretly happy about it.

"Harvey . . ."

"He's gone, isn't he? That's what you're here to tell me. But I know, Mama. I know you sent him away!"

"Olivia, please. This is not the time to get angry with me. There's more I have to tell you."

Alarm shot through Olivia. "What? Has something happened to him? Oh my God. Mama?"

"He's . . . oh, Olivia . . ."

"Tell me!"

"He's dead."

"Dead?" Olivia couldn't help shouting the word. She jumped out of bed and onto the floor. "No."

"I'm so sorry, sweetheart."

"No!" Someone may as well have taken a sledgehammer to her midsection, the pain was so intense, the struggle to breathe overwhelming.

Tears spilled out of her eyes. "Mama, please tell me you're lying."

"Oh, sweetheart. I wish I were."

This was a lie. It had to be a lie. Just yesterday, Harvey was painting the carriage house. How could he be dead? They were going to spend their lives together.

Olivia rushed to the window and looked outside. All she saw was Rosa lying on the grass.

She spun around. "Where is he?"

"Olivia, there was a car accident."

A ray of hope. "But Harvey doesn't have a car."

"Apparently he stole one," Sylvia replied. "He wrecked it on I-10 about forty miles from here."

Olivia started shaking. An awful wheezing sound escaped with each breath.

"I just want to say—"

"How would you know about any accident?" Olivia challenged.

"I have friends on the police force," Sylvia said softly. "Originally, I had asked one of them to check on Harvey's background. But he called me this morning with the news of the accident." Sylvia walked toward Olivia, placed a hand on her shoulder. "I suppose had it not been for the car Harvey stole, I might never have learned this news."

Olivia shrugged away from her mother's touch and ran to her bed. Plopping herself down, she scooped a pillow onto her lap and gripped it until her fingers hurt.

"I'm sorry, Olivia."

Olivia wanted to throw the pillow in her mother's face. Sure, she wore a slightly sad expression, but behind it Olivia saw relief. And something else.

Smugness? Happiness?

Oh, God. Olivia's eyes widened in horror. "You did this," she said slowly. "You're responsible for this."

"Sweetheart, it was an accident."

"You wanted him out of my life. But he didn't want to leave. So you made him." Olivia's head was spinning. Her words made a sick kind of sense. *Had* her mother resorted to murder?

Cynthia Monroe had practically accused her of it. Good Lord, did she know her mother at all?

"I know you don't—"

"You were willing to do whatever it took to get rid of him, weren't you, Mama?"

"That's not true."

"Yes it is." Olivia knew it in her soul.

Her voice cracking, she barely got the next words out: "One way or another, you caused this to happen."

"You can't believe that. I would never—"

"Get out."

"I won't leave you. Not at a time like this."

"I said get out!" Olivia threw her pillow across the room. It knocked a crystal ornament of an elephant onto the floor, splintering it.

Sylvia started, a look of shock crossing her face. But then she said, "That's your grief talking. You need me, Olivia. Now more than ever."

Olivia burst into tears.

Her mother rushed to her and gathered her into her arms. If Olivia had the strength she would have wrenched herself free. But her despair was all-consuming, and she didn't have the strength to do anything but cry. She wished she were dead.

"Hush, sweetheart. I know it's hard now, but it's going to be okay. Things will return to normal. You'll see."

Olivia saw no such thing. There would never be normal again. Not when her life had died in a car crash on I-40.

"We still have each other, Olivia." Sylvia held her against her bosom, the way she used to when Olivia was a small girl. "You'll always have me."

But Olivia didn't want her mother. She wanted Harvey.

Her body shook with her sobs. She dribbled mucus onto her mother's chest. But nothing would change the reality that had crashed down on her shoulders.

Without Harvey, what was she going to do? She absolutely knew that her life would be a mess. Her biggest dream had been smashed to smithereens. And she had her mother to blame for that.

Her mother had taken away the man she loved.

Olivia would never forgive her.

NOW

CHAPTER THIRTY-TWO

Someone knows.

Someone knows that you're a whore.

The hairs on Sylvia's nape stood on end as she finished reading the note. She stared at the plain white paper and typewritten words until everything blurred.

Someone knows.

Sylvia tossed the letter beside her on the bed and scooped up the envelope it had come in. Nothing was written on it other than her first and last name, and that was also typed.

Where had this come from? She had found it in the stack of mail and folders that she had retrieved from the den last night. Then, she had been too tired to bother going through the mail and had saved the task for this morning.

But had this note even come in the mail? Obviously not, since it didn't have an address on it. So had someone put it in her mailbox?

Or had someone slipped it into her belongings at her recent graduate sorority meeting?

That was certainly a possibility. For the most part she was well liked, but there were at least a couple women who envied her position on the regional board. Put a group of women together, no matter how civilized, and there were bound to be some problems.

She blew out a sigh. She was too old for this. Much too old for silly games.

Sylvia grabbed the note and crumpled it. She would put it out of her mind.

There was no way she would let an unknown person rile her with this foolishness. If someone had a problem with her, then she would have to make herself known.

Sylvia climbed out of bed. She needed to get dressed and head downstairs for breakfast.

Rachelle Harding watched her mother waltz into the dining room, her red silk robe billowing about her legs, and couldn't help rolling her eyes. No, she didn't miss a step. No, she didn't fall flat on her face. She didn't even stagger in the least.

But the dark Versace sunglasses gave her secret away.

They were hardly appropriate at the table for a family breakfast, but if her mother were wearing them because the bright sun bothered her eyes, that would be one thing. The truth was, Olivia Grayson-Harding played out this pathetic routine nearly every morning: sweeping into the dining room like some all-important diva, wearing dark glasses that didn't fool anyone.

She was hungover.

Her eyes were no doubt red and swollen from excessive drinking and lack of sleep. The stale scent of alcohol wafted across the table as she pulled out a chair and sat.

"Morning, morning," Olivia said in an overly cheery voice. She brushed long strands of her uncombed hair off her face.

Rachelle's grandmother, Sylvia Grayson, gave Olivia a look of distaste. It wasn't the first time she had clearly expressed her displeasure with Olivia, but it was a wasted effort. Either Olivia didn't notice her mother's disapproving looks or she simply didn't care. Rachelle tended to believe the latter.

They were the antithesis of a Norman Rockwell painting. Her grandmother poised and stoic, dressed in a crisp cotton Kate Spade robe, her dyed black hair pulled tightly off her face in a neat bun. Her mother the epitome of a self-proclaimed diva, hiding behind dark sunglasses, her dark hair unkempt but her lips covered in a bold shade of red. And Rachelle herself dressed in jeans and an oversized T-shirt, wearing no makeup at all, her shoulder-length black hair captured with a purple scrunchie.

They were the picture of dysfunction.

Why her grandmother even insisted that they all gather for a family break-fast was beyond Rachelle. There was nothing "family" about it. There was no feeling of warmth. In fact, everything felt fake. Forced. Her mother acted like she was some prima donna, and except for an uptight expression here and there, her grandmother pretended everything was okay.

After her grandmother's heart attack seven years earlier, Rachelle and her mother had moved in with her. It had seemed like a good idea at the time, a way to be close to her in case her health took a drastic turn for the worse.

It had been the family relationship that had taken a drastic turn for the worse instead. The way Rachelle saw it, they'd be better off in separate homes.

And Rachelle . . . she would be better off far away from here.

It wasn't her grandmother she didn't care to see. She got along well with her. But the sad fact was that most of the time her own mother didn't even notice her, and that was extremely hard to deal with.

Oh, there were times her mother would pretend to care deeply for her, but Rachelle knew that was a lie. Like last year when Rachelle had been applying to colleges out of state. Her mother had surprisingly made a big stink about her wanting to head out of town. Suddenly, it mattered so much to her that Rachelle go to Dillard University, the same university she had attended. She'd talked of tradition as if she hadn't shunned it every time her own mother had mentioned the word.

In the end, the only college she had been accepted to was Dillard, and Rachelle had reluctantly resigned herself to her fate of having to go to a school so close to home. When she had suggested living on campus, both her mother and grandmother had strongly objected.

Now Rachelle watched her mother get seated. Olivia's lips formed a sugary smile. "Sorry I'm late. I was up most of the night, working to meet my dead-line."

Olivia was a published author. Rachelle's friends were fascinated by her mother's career. But if the topic came up with those who didn't know her well, Rachelle would lie and say that her mother wrote family dramas. She was too embarrassed to admit the truth. Her mother's stories were twisted. Werewolves and graphic sex and brutal murders. Rachelle couldn't relate to them. The books sold very well, though, so clearly many people had a taste for the bizarre.

"The food's getting cold," Sylvia told Olivia.

"I'll live." Olivia reached for the teapot that Edward always put out specifically for her, and she filled her mug. "At least the coffee's hot." She took a sip. "Mmm. This is exactly what I need."

"Too much caffeine isn't good for you," Sylvia commented. But Rachelle knew she was really saying, *If you'd go to bed at a decent hour, you wouldn't need three cups of coffee to start your day.*

Olivia ignored her mother and faced Rachelle. "How're your classes going, sweetheart?"

It was more than odd to stare at your mother and never really see her. And not simply because of her ridiculous sunglasses. Rachelle felt like there was a barrier between them, one that had prevented her from getting to truly know Olivia over the years.

So many times she had wished that she and her mother could sit on the porch on a warm evening and talk. Or spend time together in the sunroom, or in the park, or even at a mall. Just do something together that normal mothers and daughters did, where they could talk about everything and nothing.

All her life she had dreamed of this closeness, prayed for it, even, but in the last few years she had come to accept that it would never be. The only thing her mother was close to was her computer. She spent countless hours in her office working on her novels.

It was sad to say, but Rachelle almost preferred it when her mother was out of town on a book tour. She and her grandmother had much less stress at those times.

"My classes are going well," Rachelle said in reply to her mother's question. "Thanks for asking."

"I knew you'd enjoy Dillard. It's a great school. And at least you're close to home."

Rachelle added butter to her grits. "Yes," she muttered, but didn't really mean it. She had desperately wanted to go to a college out of state. "I know we talked about this already, but I was thinking..." She paused, cleared her throat. "Thinking that um..." *Just spit it out!* "Now that I've started my classes and I've been driving back and forth to school, it just seems to me... well, I was wondering if I wouldn't have a better college experience if I lived on campus. You know, really immersed myself in everything."

Olivia nursed her coffee. "I lived at home and went to Dillard. I had a fine experience."

"Yes, but—"

"But what sense does it make to spend money living on campus when you can live here for free?" her grandmother asked.

As if money had ever been an issue with them. Rachelle wasn't sure how much they had in family assets, but she knew they were loaded. "I know, but being right on campus means spending less time getting ready for classes. And as for the cost, I wouldn't expect you to pay for it. I can get a job."

"And risk your grades?" Sylvia asked. "I wouldn't allow it."

"I don't think—"

"Remember," her grandmother continued, "you need a decent grade point average to get accepted in the Delta sorority. How will you accomplish that if you're working in addition to volunteering? Besides, the sad truth is that kids these days just aren't behaving the way they ought to. A sweet young girl like you living on campus . . . you know I want to protect you from the negative influences you'll find there."

Rachelle bit back her disappointment. She should have known that once again, this conversation would get her nowhere. They'd shot her down the first time, before she could put all her cards on the table.

"I have to agree with your grandmother there."

Sylvia gave Olivia a look of mild surprise, then turned back to Rachelle, saying, "Believe me, darling, once you're involved in the sorority, your college experience will be rich beyond anything you can ever imagine."

Like yours? Rachelle didn't ask the sarcastic question that instantly popped into her mind. Her grandmother was still active in the graduate chapter of the sorority, and it seemed to be one of her reasons for living. Yet Rachelle wasn't sure what she really got out of it, except an escape from her life at home.

Her grandmother's heart attack had barely slowed her down. She ran from one meeting to the next, planned one charity event after the other. Everyone in the community respected her. Given how well she performed every task under her belt, no one would believe that Sylvia Grayson's home life was anything less than ideal.

"I can hardly wait until you cross over," Sylvia said, clasping her hands beneath her chin. "I know there's a reason God has blessed this family with daughters. So that we can carry on the tradition your great-grandmother began when she helped found the Delta sorority."

Yada yada yada. Rachelle had heard the story so many times, she knew it by memory. And nothing about it impressed her. Who cared about sisterhood and tradition when their family, at its core, was dysfunctional?

Maybe she would see things differently if they all got along. Instead, it seemed there were walls up between all of them.

Things had been different when Rachelle's father had been alive. Better. His affection had made up for the lack of her mother's. With her father around, she hadn't felt the sting of her mother's rejection so badly, because she knew her father had suffered it as well. He had hidden his pain, or at least he'd tried to, but Rachelle knew he'd been hurt by how emotionally unresponsive her mother had been to him. It wasn't that her mother had been outright distant with her father; rather, it seemed like she was holding something back. Something vital. Even when Rachelle's father had been sick with cancer, she hadn't seen her mother break down and grieve. Rachelle, on the other hand, had cried practically nonstop during that awful time.

Perhaps her mother was simply incapable of loving anything other than alcohol and her sordid stories.

"Gosh, look at the time." Rachelle glanced at her Gucci wristwatch, then pushed her chair back. She didn't like thinking about her relationship with her mother. It always brought her down. "I'm late."

"I thought your first class is at ten."

"Yes, Grandma, but I . . . I have a test, and I'm meeting with some other people to study before we take it." The truth was, she wanted to get out of there.

"All right." Sylvia smiled at her. "Good luck, even though I know you're so smart you don't need it."

Rachelle got up, kissed her grandmother, then made her way around the table and kissed her mother.

"Good luck, sweetheart," Olivia said. She reached for a biscuit. "See you later."

Was her mother even looking at her from behind those dark glasses? Rachelle wanted to grab them off her face and scream at her. Would that get a reaction from her?

Rachelle doubted it.

So instead she said, "Yes, see you later."

Then she headed out of the dining room, wondering what she'd ever done to make her mother not love her.

CHAPTER THIRTY-THREE

don't care, Marnie," Olivia told her agent. "I have no interest in continuing the series. I'm ready to move on."

"I'm not sure you heard me," Marnie said. "*Twice* your last advance."

"Yes, I heard you, and I admit, I'm tempted."

"Good."

"But not tempted enough." Twice her previous advance was definitely significant, but Olivia wasn't concerned about the money. "You know I want to write something more mainstream."

"Of course. And I agree with you. But your last books had a nice showing on the *Essence* bestseller list. You have a great following for this series, and my feeling is the one you're about to turn in will hit *USA Today*. Things are progressing as they should, Olivia. You have to think of the big picture."

"I am thinking of the big picture. I have a limited audience."

"But a growing one. The more success you have with this series, the more people will know your name, and the more they know your name, the more they'll buy your work when you cross over to mainstream fiction."

"Marnie . . ."

"Personally, I'd love to see Darius's story. He was such a complex secondary character, he'd be great for a spin-off."

Olivia loved her agent, but she had tunnel vision. She saw only sales figures and advances.

"I'll think about Darius," Olivia grudgingly agreed. But she didn't want to.

Writing this last book in the series hadn't been much fun. In fact, it had been grueling. She was more than ready to be done with it.

Though the reviewers wouldn't believe it, she had a lot more in her than erotic werewolf stories. She wanted to try her hand at a literary novel, one that had been burning in her imagination for years. About a jazz musician, it was loosely based on the life of her father. It dealt with genius and demise. It didn't have a happy ending, but one that was realistic and hopeful. And she was sure the reviewers would love it.

And if not that story, then she was ready to write mainstream mysteries. People loved the erotic element of her work, and she loved writing it. Her mother, of course, hated it. The fact that it riled her mother so much often led her to push the limit of erotica. The result was successful, though, and she would definitely keep that component in her stories. But werewolves—they hadn't gotten her any literary respectability.

"I know you want the reviewers to like your work."

"Damn, how do you always know what I'm thinking?"

"You don't think that after ten-plus years of representing you that I know you by now?" Marnie didn't wait for a reply. "That's why I know what's best for you."

"I think my readers will follow me if I write mysteries. As long as I keep the level of eroticism the same."

"Maybe. But—"

"I'm not saying no to another werewolf book. Just . . . give me some time to think about it. See if another idea comes to me."

"Fair enough. Let's touch base in a couple days."

"Sounds good, Marnie."

They ended the call, and Olivia replaced the receiver. She felt the beginnings of a killer headache, the last thing she needed, considering she had to get through the last couple chapters of this book.

Maybe another glass of scotch . . .

The bottle of scotch on her desk was nearly finished. When had she drunk it all? Maybe Edward could make the trip to the liquor store and buy her some more.

Olivia reached for the bottle and poured out the last bit into her glass. She took a liberal sip before placing her hands on the keyboard.

"I can do this," she whispered.

Scotch had gotten her through the many unhappy days of her life the last several years. Certainly it could get her through the rest of this day.

You're right, Belinda," Olivia said hours later. "This is exactly what I needed." Despite her headache, she had plugged away at her novel, and yes, the scotch had given her enough creative inspiration to get through the last forty pages. She wasn't entirely happy with it, but she would send it to her editor for feedback.

"I told you."

"Yeah, I do feel more alive. This is so much better than hanging in your living room with a pitcher of daiquiris. Not that I mind that, but a change of pace never hurt anybody. Besides, it's good to get out and move my body. Feel the music."

"*Hear* the music. Liv, will you hush?"

"Sorry." She'd been so involved in finishing her book over the last weeks that she hadn't spent time with friends. Now she realized how starved for human interaction she was.

"Oh!" Belinda perked up as the first notes of the next song filled the air. "Girl, this is my song!"

Olivia recognized it immediately. "Shining Star" by Earth Wind and Fire. And she would never forget the year she'd first heard it, even if she wanted to.

1975.

It had been a year of hope and great promise, and also a year of utter despair. The year she and Belinda had met the loves of their lives. Then Olivia had lost hers forever.

A knot of jealousy formed in her stomach as she watched Belinda sing, watched her snap her fingers in beat to the rhythm. Of the two of them, Belinda was the one whose dreams came true. Although Belinda had moved to Georgia and left Bernie behind all those years ago, they ended up together. Unable to live without her, Bernie had moved to Macon to be with her shortly after she had, and they married only months after she graduated from Spelman. Now they had the perfect family—a thirteen-year-old son and nineteen-year-old daughter.

People were always shocked to learn that Belinda had a daughter in college, because Belinda looked so young. She had a baby face to match her slim, youthful body. Her finely braided hair, a style popular with younger women, only helped cement the illusion that Belinda was years younger than her actual age.

As the song finished, Olivia forced a smile. "Girl, how many songs do you and Bernie have?"

"Bernie?" Belinda asked. Her eyes registered surprise. "I said it was *my* song, not *our* song."

"The way you were crooning to that tune? It had to be Bernie you were thinking of. Besides, I remember the year that song was released. Same year you two met."

"That doesn't mean anything."

"Uh-huh."

Belinda took a swig of her beer, straight from the bottle. "Not everything is about Bernie."

"Yeah, and I've got some swamp land to sell you right here in the fine state of Louisiana." Who was Belinda trying to fool? For her, life *was* Bernie—Bernie and their two children.

Olivia reached for her own drink, knowing she needed something to make her stop talking. If she kept blabbing on, she would surely let her jealousy show. And Belinda didn't need that. After all, it wasn't Belinda's fault that Harvey had died. It was her mother's.

She sipped her martini, though what she really wanted to do was throw her head back and down the whole thing. Something to help erase Harvey from her memory. Because there was no point thinking about him. Thinking about him wouldn't change a thing. It wouldn't erase the miserable years she'd endured. It wouldn't make things better for her now.

Some would find it hard to believe, but after all these years she still needed to find a way to forget him.

She glanced at Belinda. The expression on her face said she was still off in la-la land, thinking of Bernie.

A sigh escaped her. At least one of them was happy. Olivia had had hopes of happily ever after with Harvey that long-ago summer, but they had died with his death, and her life had never been the same.

Observing Belinda all dreamy-eyed made it so much more difficult to put Harvey out of her mind. Every time she saw Belinda and Bernie together it was tangible proof of what she had lost with Harvey. Belinda and Bernie, the perfect couple.

"Nineteen seventy-five," Belinda suddenly said. "What a summer that was."

"Wasn't it, though?" Olivia agreed. "Liza's unsolved murder. You meeting Bernie. Me meeting Harvey. You moving away." *Harvey's mysterious death.*

"It seems like forever and yesterday."

"It sure does." Olivia scooped the olive out of her drink and popped it into her mouth. She didn't want to take this trip down memory lane. She wasn't sure she could keep it together if she did.

"Sometimes I wonder—" Belinda stopped short, her eyes bulging as she looked over Olivia's shoulder. "Oh my God."

"What?" Olivia whipped her head around.

"Bernie."

"Oh." Olivia relaxed. Belinda's surprised tone had worried her. "Bernie's here?"

"Not more than twenty feet away from us. He was supposed to be out with his boys while I was out with you."

Olivia spotted him making his way through the crowd. It was hard not to notice him in a room. Towering over six feet tall, he was striking. Not pretty-boy handsome, but there was something about him that drew women to him. The scar across his cheek only added character.

As he got closer to their table, Olivia said, "The poor love-struck fool probably couldn't bear a moment away from you."

Belinda's mouth broke into a smile as Bernie reached the table. *Strange,* Olivia thought, noticing that the smile seemed forced.

"Sweetheart." Bernie bent to kiss her cheek. "I didn't know you were gonna be here."

"Really? I'm pretty sure I mentioned I was heading here with Olivia."

Bernie shrugged. "Guess I missed that. I'm here with Cameron and Stan. Evening, Olivia."

"Evening, Bernie."

"You taking care of my wife?"

"You know it."

"Good. See to it she doesn't step out of line." Bernie softened the words with a smile.

"I always do." Olivia chuckled.

"When will you be home?" Bernie asked Belinda.

"By midnight, I'm sure."

"Me too." He paused as he stroked Belinda's cheek. "I'll see you then."

"Okay, darling."

Bernie's hand lingered on Belinda's shoulder before he walked off.

Belinda watched him disappear among the crowd of patrons at the bar, then turned to Olivia, saying, "I'm sorry, Liv. I didn't know he was going to be here."

"Don't be silly. There's no need to apologize."

"Well, it *is* a girl's night out. I don't want you getting the wrong idea."

"What kind of idea?"

"I don't know . . . that Bernie doesn't trust me, or something. That he showed up here just to check on me."

Olivia waved a dismissive hand. "Of course I wouldn't think that. But even if he did stop by to visit because he knew you were going to be here, so what? That man loves you to death. It must be nice having a man who wants to be with you all the time."

Her words made Olivia think of the love she would never have again. The love she had lost forever before she'd even turned eighteen.

"Even a good thing gets tiring after a while."

"Are you serious?" Olivia was unable to hide her surprise.

Belinda looked in Bernie's direction. Smiled and wiggled her fingers. "In a way I am serious. All these years, we've always been together. The only time we were apart was when I went back to Macon to bury my mother."

"Do you know how lucky that makes you?"

"I know. I am lucky. I don't take anything for granted. All I'm trying to say is that I wouldn't mind a vacation. Time away just for me. Away from Bernie and the kids. Time to rejuvenate."

"Ah," Olivia said, understanding. "I hear you. The kind of thing Dr. Phil talks about. Taking care of yourself so that you can better take care of everyone else in your life."

"Exactly."

"Why don't we plan a weekend away, then? I'm finished with my latest book and believe me, I'm due for a break."

Belinda's eyes lit up. "Me and you? Girl, you know that could spell trouble."

"Just tell me where you want to go, and we'll work it out."

"I was thinking maybe South Beach."

"South Beach for relaxation?"

"I don't care if I relax or not. What I want is a little me time. I want to remember what it was like before I had a husband and kids."

"Uh-oh." Olivia grinned. "You weren't kidding about trouble, were you?"

"A little partying never hurt anybody."

"So you're gonna get buck wild."

"Then relax at a spa after a night of partying."

"Sounds like a plan."

"Don't get me all excited, not if you don't think you'll go."

"Me?" Olivia pointed to herself. "I'm not the one with a man to worry about."

"What about George?"

"I got tired of him."

"He was cute."

"Boy toy. It was good while it lasted." George, a young bartender at a downtown hotel, had satisfied her a few times when she'd desperately needed male companionship. But Olivia had known from the start that they would never have a future.

It's not that she didn't want a steady relationship. She was lonely, that was certain. Yet her heart wasn't into serious dating. She spent a night here or there with a man when she needed to, but that was it. There were plenty she could call, plenty who wanted more from her. But none she felt comfortable waking up with in the morning.

Olivia had felt that way about Arthur, her late husband. She had been comfortable with him, happy even. He was a man her mother heartily approved of—right down to his proper lineage. Their thirteen-year marriage had been a good one. Yet something had been missing in the relationship. She wrote about that something in her books, drawing on the memory of the one time she had truly felt it.

Her relationship with Arthur had been missing a spark. Yes, she'd felt close to him. Yes, she'd cherished his warm body in their bed as they snuggled together. But their sex had simply been pleasant, not wild and exciting the way she always imagined it should be.

Arthur had been thirty years Olivia's senior, and she'd reasoned that his age had made the kind of intimacy she craved impossible. She didn't realize until after his death that she hadn't wanted that kind of intimacy. Something had died in her when Harvey died, and while she'd had to go on, she hadn't wanted to share with any man what she should have shared with the only man who'd ever have her heart.

Still, she did enjoy sex, even if it was emotionless. Like it or not, her body needed it. During the last years of Arthur's life, she'd gone without. First, because various medical problems had made it difficult for him to sustain an erection. Then, once he'd gotten cancer, sex had been impossible. She had stayed true to Arthur during that time. But no one, least of all her mother, had understood why she'd barely waited for Arthur's body to turn cold before she'd gone out and quenched her sexual thirst.

With each new man, there was always hope. The hope was consistently followed by disappointment. Because as much as she prayed she'd make that special connection with someone, she never did.

No one could replace Harvey in her heart.

Olivia reached for her drink and downed a huge sip. In all these years, she hadn't found anything to take away the pain of losing Harvey, but alcohol did a good job of numbing it.

At least for a while.

Some would tell her to get over it. Or at least to get on with her life.

Harvey was dead.

Logically, she knew she couldn't have Harvey, and she didn't expect the man to rise from his grave. But she had hoped to find someone who made her feel as alive as Harvey had made her feel that long-ago summer.

With a sigh, Olivia had to acknowledge that that wasn't going to happen. Yet that didn't make it any easier. It was over twenty-five years since she'd last seen him, and she still felt the same passion for him she had back then. She still got teary-eyed when she thought of what kind of life they could have had together if he hadn't died.

Twenty-five years had passed and she was still in love with Harvey.

CHAPTER THIRTY-FOUR

Honestly, Rachelle. I've never seen you so shy."

Allette took a firm hold of Rachelle's hand and led her up the stairs to the door of the sorority's dormitory. For a girl barely five feet in height, she had a lot of strength.

"Wait," Rachelle protested. "I'm not . . . I'm dressed like a bum. I at least want to make a good impression."

"Your T-shirt and jeans hardly make you look like a bum. Besides, you don't need to do anything special to make a good impression. When I told my big sisters that I know you, they nearly dropped dead from excitement."

Of course they had. Her reputation preceded her. "That's my point. They're gonna expect someone much more . . . I don't know. Sophisticated?"

Allette's short bob bounced around as she threw her head back and laughed. "Oh, you really are being shy. They'll love you. Why wouldn't they?"

Rachelle sighed heavily as Allette opened the door. In her second year at Dillard, Allette was currently a pledge with the Delta Gamma Psi sorority. She and Rachelle had been friends for most of their lives, ever since Allette's parents, Belinda and Bernie Rousseaux, had moved back to New Orleans some twelve years earlier.

Like Rachelle's mother and grandmother, Allette was excited about sorority life. She had worked her butt off during high school, volunteering for a number of associations, all so that the sorority would consider her. Her dream had been to come out at the Delta cotillion, but that was not to be. While her grandparents had had great social ties in the community, her own parents did not. Bernie was a shrimp fisherman who seemed to be out of work more times than not. Belinda had steady work as a hairstylist, but that wasn't a career that got your child into any of society's elite social clubs.

So Allette had lived vicariously through Rachelle. In fact, she had been much more excited about Rachelle's coming-out ball than Rachelle had been. Allette had helped her choose a dress, advised her on whom to accept as an escort. The irony was, Allette would have looked much better in the dress than Rachelle did because she had a killer body. Petite, her small frame was enhanced by naturally large breasts. The kind men lost their heads over. If Rachelle could have, she would have let Allette go in her place.

Not that Rachelle didn't look good. But at five feet nine, she was a little tall for her liking, and a little too thick.

But you didn't need a great body if your name was Grayson-Harding.

Everything Rachelle had done in her life—being a member of the Jack and Jill club, volunteering to help the elderly and less fortunate, coming out at the Delta cotillion—had all been part of preparing her for this new phase of her life: sorority sisterhood. For her family, being a member of a sorority wasn't simply something to do; it was a rite of passage. Not only that, but her grandmother had often expressed her wish for Rachelle to head up the organization one day as its president, which she had once been. According to her grandmother, it was the ultimate way to honor their place in history with the Delta Gamma Psi sorority.

And since Rachelle's mother had failed to achieve that title, thereby greatly disappointing Rachelle's grandmother, the responsibility fell to Rachelle.

But first she had to cross over into Delta sisterhood. She was expected to. There had never been any question. She'd never had any choice in the matter.

Rachelle gripped Allette's hand and whispered, "I don't want anyone thinking I expect to be handed sisterhood on a silver platter just because of my family."

"Of course they wouldn't think that. But they are excited to meet you."

The sorority's colors, purple and white, were everywhere. A handful of people milled around the common area, most of them wearing some combination of white and purple.

Allette made a sort of whooping sound that grew into a high-pitched squeal.

The others in the room replied with the same sound. Rachelle knew it was the sorority's call.

"Big Sister Heavy D," Allette said, walking toward an attractive, robust woman. "This is Rachelle Harding, great-granddaughter of Hazel Etienne, granddaughter of Sylvia Grayson."

The woman's eyes grew as wide as saucers. "Hello." She took one of Rachelle's hands in both of hers, almost reverently. "Oh, my. It is *so* nice to meet you."

If her enthusiastic greeting was indicative of everyone's interest in meeting her, Rachelle seriously doubted she would ever be denied entry to this sorority next year, regardless of her grade point average. Her grandmother was not only still active in the graduate chapter, she was currently on the regional board. For years she had been the chapter's president and she'd had a stint as the national president. It would be hard for any of these Deltas to ignore that.

And while Rachelle's mother had never held any office—probably because she couldn't be counted on to be sober, Rachelle thought sourly—she did go to charitable events and mentoring drives put on by the graduate chapter.

More in Rachelle's favor.

And she didn't want any favors.

"My real name is Diane."

Rachelle realized she had drifted off when the woman spoke again. She smiled at her. "It's nice to meet you, Diane."

"Believe me, it's an honor to meet you. Your family has played such a great part in this sorority's history. Wow. I still can't believe we'll be undergrad sorors at the same time."

"Thanks." What else could she say?

"Big Sister Heavy D, I was thinking that Rachelle could head out with us to some of our charity drives. I know she's not pledging yet, but we could always use the help. Especially from someone who will no doubt be a great asset to our sorority once she crosses over."

"Of course," Diane said.

More expectations of her. Would it ever end?

"All the charity work you do only makes your application stronger," Diane went on. "Not that I have to tell you that. And I'm sure you volunteer for a lot of great causes. After all, your grandmother still does so much with her own charity, not to mention sorority events."

"Yes, I do a lot of volunteering," Rachelle said. Even though it had been expected of her, she actually enjoyed volunteering. It was the one thing that made her feel like something good had come from the dysfunction of her family. "I especially love working with kids."

Diane smiled from ear to ear. "Not just the great-granddaughter of one of our founding sorors, but a true sweetheart. Good people, as they say."

"I told you," Allette said.

"Nadine, Esther, Margaret." Diane motioned to the other women in the room. "Come meet Hazel's great-granddaughter."

"That's really not—"

"Sarah!" Diane called to a woman heading down the stairs. "Let everyone upstairs know that Hazel's great-granddaughter is in the house."

Rachelle shifted from one foot to the other uncomfortably. She didn't want this attention.

"I told you they would love you," Allette whispered in her ear.

"Yeah." Rachelle feigned enthusiasm, but the truth was, she wasn't in the least happy about this. How could she be, when she had made up her mind not to join *any* sorority?

CHAPTER THIRTY-FIVE

That sums it up for the minutes from the last session," the graduate chapter's secretary announced. "I'll hand it over now to our regional board member, Sylvia Grayson."

As Olivia watched her mother get up and stroll to the front of the room, she couldn't help thinking that her mother was born for this stuff. There was a pep in her step. A confidence she exuded without saying a word. From her neat hair and designer jacket to her notebook and designer mules, she looked the part of successful socialite. She truly did thrive on running groups and committees.

Maybe because she had failed to effectively run her household . . .

Okay, that was mean, Olivia acknowledged. And for the first time in a long time, she felt a measure of sadness. Because looking at the woman at the front of the room, she didn't see her mother. She saw a poised woman. A generous one. But not the woman she saw in the privacy of their home. Alone with her mother, Olivia faced a woman who was aloof. A woman she would never please, no matter how hard she tried.

It had been so long since there'd been genuine happiness between them that Olivia couldn't be sure if the memories she had of more pleasant times were real or a dream.

Was there a chance they could recapture the happiness they'd once shared?

"As you know," Sylvia began, "on November third, every chapter across the nation will be participating in Outreach Day. The community is very excited about this, and I think we'll get some good press. We now have ten schools where we'll be hosting a career day as part of this outreach program. *Ten* schools." Someone began to clap, and everyone in the room followed suit. "Because of the tenth school, I'll need one other person to head up a subcommittee for this project. Can I get a volunteer?"

Olivia's hand went up with several others. Her mother picked someone else.

"Thank you, Lorna," Sylvia said. "After the meeting, I'd like to meet with all the leaders of the subcommittees so we can confirm the agendas. Now, regarding the art auction . . ."

Olivia tuned out her mother's voice. Her earlier nostalgia dissipated, and now she was seething. Damn her mother. To choose someone other than her own daughter!

And to think that Sylvia was always so damn concerned with appearances.

Olivia glanced around the room, certain that her sorors were staring at her, quietly wondering why her own mother hadn't picked her for the subcommittee. But she didn't see any curious looks. Still, Olivia was angry with her mother. She did this crap all the time. The last time Olivia had asked her why she hadn't chosen her to head up one of her subcommittees, her mother had calmly told her that an alcoholic couldn't be relied on.

An alcoholic! The memory still stung. Just because Olivia enjoyed a martini or a glass of bourbon didn't make her an alcoholic.

Why had Olivia even bothered to reminisce over what had clearly been a false memory of happiness?

The meeting came to an end, and the women mingled, chatted, and drank juice and coffee. Olivia avoided her mother until they reached the car, when she could no longer hold her thoughts in check.

"Mother," she said. She had long since stopped calling her "Mama"—a much more intimate name. "I'm just gonna lay this on the table. I'm your daughter—your own flesh and blood—and when you time and time again choose someone else over me—"

"Lorna is much more qualified. You haven't run a committee in years."

"Because I have a limited amount of time. I can't be as involved in the grad chapter as you are. But when I am ready to offer assistance, you always strike me down."

Sylvia was silent, her eyes fixed on the road ahead of her.

"You're trying to piss me off so I don't attend Career Day."

"Don't use that language with me."

"That's why I haven't heard from anyone, isn't it?" Olivia stared at the side of her mother's face. "You probably have everyone thinking you've got me on *your* list."

"I wasn't sure what your schedule would be like. You're always so busy with your deadlines."

"Oh, that's bullshit."

"Olivia—"

"This is not a Jack and Jill career day. These parents won't expect only doctors, lawyers, and businessmen to speak to their children." Olivia paused briefly. "You may not like it, but writing *is* a career—one many people strive to do. I know those kids would want to hear me speak."

Sylvia finally faced her. "And what are you going to do? Talk to children about that filth you write?"

Olivia recoiled as if she had been struck. Damn, that hurt. It hurt even though she had long ago told herself she didn't care.

"Have you read any of my novels?" she said in the best nonchalant voice she could muster.

"I know what you write."

"But have you read my work?" When Sylvia didn't respond, Olivia said, "That's what I thought."

The air in the Lexus was suddenly thick and hard to inhale. Olivia dropped her head backward against the headrest in frustration. She was forty-five years old and her mother insisted on treating her like a child.

Concern for her mother's health had led her to move in with her once again after her husband's death. She had had a heart attack at fifty-nine, and Olivia had felt real fear that she would lose her. Deep in her heart, she had hoped they could repair their relationship before her mother passed away.

Sylvia had recovered, and in the last seven years she had been okay. Okay enough to remain stubborn and remote. Now Olivia regretted the decision to move back into her mother's home. The rift between them was still as wide as Lake Pontchartrain.

"Before you judge me and try to write me off for Career Day, why don't you read some of my work? It's not like you'd have to go to a bookstore and buy it. I always give you an autographed copy."

"I didn't say I was writing you off."

"Great, so you're going to avoid the issue altogether."

"Olivia, you are blowing this way out of proportion."

"Still no answer."

"We'll discuss this later."

"When?"

"When you've calmed down."

"Of course." Olivia threw her hands in the air. "It's always me."

Silence followed. Olivia glanced at Sylvia, but her mother wouldn't meet her eyes.

Fine, Olivia thought. She knew it would do no good to press the issue. Her argument would fall on deaf ears.

So she let her mother have her way. She let the matter drop.

CHAPTER THIRTY-SIX

As Sylvia listened to Pastor Greene preach, a foul taste filled her mouth. The minister was going on and on about how wonderful his family was, how blessed they were. His two daughters were now nurses, and his son was studying to be an engineer. According to him, he had no complaints in life, nothing at all to be down about. Only reasons to be singing praises to the Lord.

Lies, all of it. Well, maybe not now, but not too long ago, Pastor Greene's family had had many burdens to bear. One of his daughters had been caught with marijuana, but somehow she'd escaped all charges. His son, until recently, hadn't been talking to him. He'd been living in sin with a white girl in Metairie.

"I tell you, brothers and sisters, the Lord is good. Can I get an amen?"

"Amen," the congregation replied in unison.

Sylvia glanced to her right, to the empty spot where Olivia should have been sitting. Her daughter had promised she would be at church this morning. The sad truth was, she was probably still in bed, hung over.

Sylvia gritted her teeth. Olivia expected her to give her more responsibility on the various projects she headed, yet time and time again, she proved how irresponsible she was. How could you trust someone who couldn't even be counted on to show up at church?

Sighing, Sylvia's gaze went back to the minister. She felt a flash of annoyance and immediately understood why. It was hard to listen to Pastor Greene speak about how blessed he was when she had so much to be ashamed of. She went to church every week, paid her tithes without fail. Why was her daughter causing her so much grief?

There was a time when she had been proud of Olivia, but that was eons ago. Now, her only daughter butted heads with her at every turn, like a spoiled teenager.

And those horrible books she wrote! Sylvia had skimmed them and been disgusted by all that smut that no self-respecting woman should write. Not simply sex, like what Sylvia had read from time to time in romance novels, but perverted sex—the kind one would expect only some raunchy whore to know about. It didn't matter that the stories were supposed to be fiction. Everyone Sylvia knew thought Olivia wrote about her own sexual escapades. Sylvia had never had the courage to ask.

Read it, Mama, Olivia had said after getting her first novel published. *All the things you wanted to protect me from with Harvey. I bet you'll wonder where I learned them.*

Sylvia shook off the wretched memory, but the pain in her heart didn't dissipate. Her heart was heavy, while the others at her church seemed so blessed.

She didn't covet anyone's blessings; she simply wanted a piece of happiness for herself. Was that so wrong to hope for?

With that thought, Sylvia turned to her left. She smiled. Rachelle—dear, sweet Rachelle—was there beside her.

She could count on her granddaughter. Rachelle was a wonderful child, with a great sense of purpose and decency. Selfishly, Sylvia was happy that her granddaughter was still in New Orleans. Surely it was a miracle from above that she had only been accepted at Dillard.

Sylvia reached for Rachelle's hand, took it in hers. When Rachelle looked at her, Sylvia squeezed it gently.

She may have lost Olivia, but she would not lose her granddaughter.

"Hey. Hey, wait up."

Rachelle turned, wondering for the first time if the voice she'd heard calling in the distance was trying to attract her. Indeed it was. A woman smiled and waved at her from several feet away.

It took Rachelle a moment to recognize her. She was one of the Deltas she had met at the sorority's dorm.

The girl ran to catch up with her. "Hi."

"Sorry," Rachelle said. "I heard someone calling but didn't realize it was for me."

"No problem." She breathed in and out heavily, even as she continued to smile. "It's my fault. I couldn't remember your name."

"Rachelle."

"Hi, Rachelle. I'm Nadine."

Rachelle shook Nadine's proffered hand.

"Where are you heading?" Nadine asked.

"To the library. To do some studying."

"I'm going in that direction." Nadine beamed. "Mind if I walk with you?"

Rachelle's guard went up. What did Nadine want from her? But despite her wariness, she shrugged and said, "Sure."

Rachelle started to walk, and Nadine fell into step beside her. "I have to tell you, I was pretty excited to meet you."

"Me? Why? Oh, because of my great-grandmother?"

"Well, yeah. I've wanted to be a Delta forever. It's kind of neat to meet someone related to one of the founders of this sorority."

"It's not like I can help you cross over," Rachelle blurted out, speaking her mind. But as soon as the words left her mouth, she regretted them.

"Oh, gosh. I hope that's not what you think. That's not why I wanted to talk to you."

"I'm sorry. I shouldn't have said that."

"I guess I can understand. You must get that a lot. The truth is, when I saw you . . . I don't know. I just hoped we could be friends. I have the feeling you and I have a lot in common."

"Oh?"

"You remind me of me last year. I was pretty shy. It took me a while to come out of my shell, but it really helped to have some people reach out to me."

Rachelle gave Nadine a smile. "You're not psychic, are you?"

Nadine laughed. "No, but like I said, I've been there. Let me give you my number. We can hang out sometime, if you'd like. Once I officially cross over," she added, with a wry grin.

"Honestly, I didn't mean what I said—"

"Not because of what you said," Nadine quickly clarified. "The pledging process is keeping me extremely busy. But I can't complain, not even about some of the stuff the big sisters make us do. I know what the reward is in the end."

"Hmm."

Nadine scribbled her number on a sheet of paper and handed it to Rachelle. "Call me anytime."

"Thanks," Rachelle said. She looked at the number, then met Nadine's eyes. She seemed sincere. "I will."

At her desk in the library, Rachelle grinned as she entered Nadine's phone number into her Palm Pilot. Maybe attending Dillard wouldn't be so bad after all. She didn't know why she'd had the feeling she would be an outcast. Probably because she was upset at not having gotten into another school, so she subconsciously felt her whole experience at Dillard would be negative. But thanks to Nadine and the other women she had met at the sorority house, she realized that she had been selling herself short. She was here. She may as well make the best of it.

"Uh, excuse me?"

Rachelle jerked from fright, then looked up to see the most beautiful eyes on a man she had ever seen. She quickly sat up straight.

"Sorry." His lips curled in a slight smile.

"Yes?" She managed to sound calm, despite her pounding heart.

"You'll probably think this is a dumb question, but I noticed you with your gadget. Is that one of those Palm Pilots?"

Rachelle was disappointed, even though she shouldn't have gotten her hopes up. Guys as hot as this one didn't hit on her. He looked like a jock, and she was hardly a jock-type girlfriend. She was too big-boned and introverted for that role.

"Yeah, it's a Palm Pilot," she responded.

"You, uh, you like it?"

"Uh-huh. It's great for organization."

"Hmm."

"You want me to show you how you use it?"

The guy hesitated, then said, "Actually, I was wondering what your name is."

Rachelle swallowed her shock. "My name?"

"Yeah. You got one, don't you?"

"Of course. It's Rachelle."

He chuckled softly. "I know. That was pretty lame. You must think I'm some kind of moron."

"I . . . I'm not sure what to think."

"I was hitting on you. Well, trying to."

Rachelle eyed him skeptically. "You were?"

He withdrew a Palm Pilot from the back pocket on his jeans. "Yeah."

Rachelle let out a loud laugh, then clamped a hand over her mouth. She glanced around to see if she had disturbed any of the other patrons in the library. No one seemed disturbed by her outburst.

"At least I made you laugh."

This was turning into a very good day. "So, do *you* have a name?" she asked, adding a touch of sass.

"Grant. But people call me G."

"All right, G. Is that all you wanted?"

He went down on his haunches beside her chair. "Oh, no. You're not gonna do me like that, are you?" He placed a hand over his heart, as if he were crushed.

"I don't know what you mean."

"You're gonna make me beg. Okay. Rachelle, I like what I see." He gave her body a quick perusal. The kind that made her feel appreciated, not dirty. "And I'd like to get to know you better."

Rachelle didn't know what to say. Not because she wasn't interested, but because she felt entirely out of her element.

"You're not interested—"

"No," Rachelle quickly interjected. "I mean yes. I was just surprised. I don't normally meet . . ." Her voice trailed off. She didn't want to say anything stupid.

"Maybe I can join you here?"

"Are we gonna work?"

"A little."

Rachelle grinned. She liked him. "Sure. I was ready for a break, anyway."

CHAPTER THIRTY-SEVEN

Evenin', Sylvia."

Sylvia whipped her head around at the sound of Edward's voice. He stood at the entrance of the sunroom, holding a bunch of white roses.

She slipped off her reading glasses. "Edward."

A smile lifted his lips. There was something especially handsome about him when he smiled. Like he brought a piece of sunshine into the room.

The way her father once had.

"The rosebushes near Rosa's grave are so pretty, I figured I'd pick some and put them in here for you. Hope you don't mind."

"No, of course not."

Though years had passed, Edward's face was surprisingly smooth and almost free of wrinkles. He hardly looked sixty, much less his true age of seventy-eight. Still, there was something frail about him. His face was drawn because he'd lost a good twenty pounds, a result of the diabetes he'd developed ten years earlier. He had looked much healthier when his visage had been fuller.

While his features didn't give away his age, his hair did. His low-cropped Afro was entirely white.

As Sylvia watched Edward move into the room, she couldn't help remembering days gone by. Days when he had been energetic and quick. Now he moved slowly, favoring his right leg. Her once strong houseman seemed only a shell of the person he had once been.

The years had taken their toll on him. Not only did he have diabetes, he also suffered from arthritis. He was a trooper, though, never complaining even when he was obviously in pain.

Sylvia had told him he could retire but continue to live with her. He was, at this point, family. But Edward had refused to stay on with her and do nothing. So he did small things, like make tea or breakfast, and dust. "Helps keep me young," he had insisted. A gardener came twice a week to do the work Edward could no longer do. A housekeeper also came once a week to do the heavier work inside.

"What happened to your leg?"

"My knee's bothering me, is all." Edward placed the roses in a vase. They were in full bloom and smelled heavenly.

"You shouldn't have been out there picking roses," Sylvia said. "I don't want you hurting yourself."

"Oh, don't you worry 'bout me. My hands are fine today."

He was nothing if not stubborn. He would send himself to an early grave just because he didn't know his limitations. "The roses are lovely."

"I knew you'd like them." Edward withdrew one from the vase and handed it to her.

Accepting it, she passed the flower under her nose and sniffed its sweet scent. "Mmm."

"Let me get some water for them."

"I can do that, Edward."

"There's no reason I can't."

"Yes, there is. Your leg. You need to rest it before you make it worse."

"All right," he said, sounding relieved. "If you insist."

"I do."

Edward turned and started to walk away, but Sylvia called his name, and he halted. "You can rest right in here if you want. Keep me company."

His face brightened. "Okay, then." He hobbled to the wicker sofa and took a seat beside her. As he sat, he said, "There's something I've been meaning to ask you, Sylvia. Is this a good time to talk?"

"Of course."

Edward glanced toward the larger window, then back at her. Something about his expression made Sylvia's heart pound with fear. "What is it, Edward? Is it your health? Are you sick?"

"Oh, no. Nothing like that. You know I'm too stubborn to let any illness get the better of me."

She was relieved but didn't let it show. "Then what?"

"Well," Edward began. His Adam's apple bobbed up and down as he swallowed. "I was wondering if we might do something. Perhaps this evening."

"Do something?"

His eyes were hopeful. "It's a nice evening. We could head into town and have dinner in the French Quarter. Maybe even take a walk along the riverfront."

Sylvia didn't answer. She merely stared at him, shocked at his proposal.

Well, not entirely shocked. Edward had suggested this sort of thing before. The last time had been more than a year and a half ago. She had always turned him down, or settled on having dinner together in the backyard.

"I don't think you should be walking on that leg."

"I'll bring that cane you gave me for my birthday. Come on," he pleaded, flashing a charming grin. "I'm not getting any younger."

"I really don't know what to say," Sylvia replied. "I'm much too busy to head into town." Although she told herself that his suggestion was strictly friendly, she didn't want to hurt his feelings. She would be lying if she said she didn't think that Edward was at least moderately attracted to her.

"We could make a date for another day. I really wouldn't mind taking in part of that jazz festival."

"I've got my hands full with a couple projects, Edward. I really won't be able to. But if you want to take an afternoon—"

Sylvia bit her tongue as an unmistakable look of disappointment crossed his face.

"I see," he said.

"It's just that I have so much to do," Sylvia explained. "If I had some time—"

"Not even then, I don't think."

Edward got to his feet. There was a cracking sound from his knees as his legs extended. He started to walk away, then stopped. "I just thought that for once we might do something together," he said, not facing her. "In public."

"You're angry."

"At myself," he replied. "I should have known better. Should have known my place."

"Edward . . ."

"I'll have dinner ready at six P.M. sharp, Mrs. Grayson."

Sylvia didn't utter a word as he made his way out of the sunroom.

CHAPTER THIRTY-EIGHT

This first paper is worth twenty-five percent of your mark," Professor Jackson said. "And let me remind you. This isn't high school. I won't forgive things like bad grammar and spelling mistakes. If you're sitting in this class, then you ought to know how to string sentences together coherently. You ought to know how to express an argument on paper. It's pretty sad that I have to say this, but the truth is I'm seeing more work these days that is far below standards for anyone in a university." The professor surveyed the crowd, clearly letting his words sink in. Then he grinned widely. "That said, if you have any questions, don't hesitate to talk to me. Believe it or not, I don't bite." There were widespread chuckles. "That's all for now. See you Friday."

Rachelle gathered up her belongings, mentally narrowing down the great leaders in black history she could write about. There was always Martin Luther King Jr. He was a natural choice, but one many would probably choose. Maybe she ought to choose Frederick Douglass. Or even Rosa Parks, a woman who had accidentally become a leader by taking a firm stand against injustice.

Rachelle merged into the thinning crowd of students, then began the slow walk toward the exit. But she stopped suddenly. Was that her name?

She turned.

"Rachelle."

Professor Jackson started toward her.

Rachelle slipped back into one of the rows of desks, allowing other students to pass her. When the last of the stragglers strolled by, she once again stepped into the aisle.

"Rachelle Harding, right?" Professor Jackson asked as he neared her.

"Yes." Rachelle felt a moment of panic, immediately fearing the worst. "Did I do something wrong?"

"No." He gave a nervous smile. "Not at all."

Rachelle waited for him to say something else, but he didn't. The professor simply stared at her as if studying her intently.

Good grief, she hoped he wasn't going to make a pass at her.

"Have you been enjoying the class?" he finally asked.

Brother, Rachelle thought. He *was* going to hit on her. At least it was early enough in the semester that she could switch to another African studies class, if necessary.

She replied timidly, "Yes, so far."

When he continued to stare, Rachelle shifted uncomfortably beneath his gaze.

"Did you need to talk to me about something?" she asked, breaking the silence. "Because I'm supposed to meet someone in a few minutes." Only Grant, but she didn't want to keep him waiting.

"I'm sorry. I don't mean to stare at you. It's just that you . . . you remind me of someone."

Of all the lame lines, Rachelle thought.

"I know this is going to sound weird," Professor Jackson continued. "And please don't be offended at my question."

Somehow, Rachelle controlled herself from rolling her eyes.

"I'm wondering if you're possibly related to someone, someone I used to know. You look so much like her. Her name is, or at least was, Olivia Grayson."

Rachelle's stomach fluttered at the sound of her mother's name. Professor Jackson knew her mother?

"It was worth a shot," the professor said, misunderstanding her silence.

"Actually, Olivia is my mother."

The professor's mouth exploded in a wide grin. "Your mother," he said, amazement in his voice. "The resemblance. I knew it. I knew you had to be related."

"You know my mother?"

"I did. A long time ago." He paused. Rachelle couldn't read his expression. "A very long time . . ."

He smiled softly, and it was clear his thoughts had taken him to a place in the past.

What was the nature of her mother's relationship with this man?

"What's she doing now?" the professor asked.

"Writing."

His eyes lit up. "Ah, she is. Published?"

"Eight novels."

"No kidding. Good for her."

"She's happy."

Professor Jackson nodded as he crossed his arms over his chest. "So, she's Olivia Harding now?"

"Yes."

"I see." A frown marred the professor's attractive features. "She's married," he said, as though trying to accept that fact.

Rachelle wasn't sure how much she should say, but she told him, "Not anymore. My mother is a widow. My father died several years ago."

The spark flamed in his eyes once again, a spark that made a lie of his words, "I'm sorry to hear that."

"It was a long time ago. Now it's just me, my mother, and my grandmother."

"You still live at the same place? You know, forget I asked. You probably find this entire conversation quite strange."

Rachelle didn't know what to say. "Do you want me to give my mother a message or something?"

"Um, no. That's okay."

He would do one better. He would check Rachelle's address and see where she lived.

Then he'd make a surprise visit.

Olivia didn't touch a drop of alcohol for the next several days. And to her surprise, she felt much better than she had expected.

She didn't need any stimulant. She didn't need anything to numb her negative thoughts. For the first time in as long as she could remember, she felt the burning desire to write. That inspiration alone had her in a good mood.

"Forgive me, Marnie, but I have to tell this story."

It wasn't so much a story as it was a collection of thoughts and memories of her father. Initially, she had figured she would tell his story as a fictional drama, but now she wondered if it wouldn't be better as a biography. The true-life story of his accomplishments and his failures, told to the world by his own flesh and blood. What better way to immortalize him, to make sure his place in jazz history would never be forgotten?

"Yes, that's it," she said aloud. Forget fiction. Nonfiction was the best way to let the world know about the man behind the jazz artist.

Olivia got up from the window's ledge. Excitement surged through her. She wanted to write this story already. But to tell it and do it justice, she needed more information.

She all but ran out of her bedroom and went downstairs in search of her mother. She found her in the sunroom. "Mother."

Sylvia looked up from her seat on the sofa, resting the planner she'd been perusing on her lap. Her reading glasses were perched on her nose. "Yes?"

"Are you busy?"

"Not really. I was just going over my schedule of meetings. Why?"

Olivia strolled into the room. "I was wondering if I could talk to you for a few minutes."

"Oh?"

"I was hoping we can talk about Daddy."

"Your father?"

"Yes. I . . ." Olivia considered how best to broach this subject. "I decided I'm going to write a book about him. Not fiction," Olivia clarified when Sylvia's eyes flashed utter shock. "I want to do a kind of biography of his life. A tribute of sorts."

"A book about your father."

Olivia sat on the sofa. Her heart hadn't pounded with so much excitement since she'd gotten the news that her first book would be published twelve years ago. "What can you tell me about him?"

"You already know everything."

"No, I don't. I was only six when he died, and since that time, it's almost like he never existed."

"There's really not much more I can tell you that you don't already know. Unfortunately."

"At the very least, your memory of him will be better than mine."

"I wish I could help you, but I can't."

Anger began to bubble inside Olivia. Her mother was dismissing her idea without a second thought. "Can't or won't?"

"Your father's been dead a long time, Olivia."

"What does that mean? That you've forgotten who he was?"

"That's not what I said."

"Good. Because I need you to do this. I need you to tell me stories about my father. Something that will make him real, rather than a vague memory. The kind of thing readers want to know. How did you meet, for example? Did you fall in love at first sight? Or did he woo you until you finally gave him your heart?"

"Oh, Olivia." Sylvia waved a dismissive hand. "I don't want people knowing my private business."

"I'm not asking for personal details. Just . . . something. Something to make him a human being who had a family as well as a career. A real man who had hopes and dreams, not just a drug addiction. I want people to know the positive, not all the bad stuff. Hell, I want people to remember him. He was such a great artist, yet he's pretty much forgotten in the world of jazz."

"Your book won't change anything. Those who remember him do, and those who don't, won't."

"I think you're wrong. With the right kind of exposure, he can be immortalized."

Sylvia sighed. "I don't know why you want to bother with any of this."

"I don't know, either. It's just something I feel compelled to do."

"Honestly, I can't help you. All that was so long ago. I hardly remember anything."

Olivia gritted her teeth to contain her anger. "How could you not remember? He was your husband. The only one you had."

"He spent a lot of time on the road."

"*I* remember things, Mother. I remember him reading to me at night. I remember him calling to tell me he loved me when he was on the road, then making up a story for me because he knew I would sleep better once he'd told me one. If I can remember that and I was only a young child, surely you must remember *something*."

Sylvia glanced away. She muttered something that sounded like, "You don't want to know what I remember."

"What did you say?"

"Nothing."

Her mother's response made it clear that Olivia had not misheard her. "What did you mean by that?"

"I didn't mean anything."

Olivia shot to her feet. "Damn it, Mother. Why do you do this?"

"I know. Your father was perfect. I'm just someone . . . someone you loathe."

Where was this coming from? "What's this about—jealousy? Of course." Olivia slapped her forehead. "This is about you doing anything you can to thwart my dream, all because I became a writer and you didn't want that. At least I married a lawyer. Wasn't that good enough for you?"

"Think what you want."

"Because you could care less."

Sylvia didn't reply.

Olivia groaned. "I don't know why I bother." She started out of the room, then spun around to face her mother. "I know how concerned you are about appearances. I wouldn't think you'd want me getting information about Daddy from someone other than you. But I'm sure there are other people who can answer my questions. I *will* write this book."

"Don't go asking questions you don't want the answers to."

Sylvia picked up her planner, effectively ending the conversation. Olivia stalked out of the room, not bothering to ask the next logical question.

CHAPTER THIRTY-NINE

Sylvia opened the front door and stepped outside. *What a beautiful morning,* she thought, inhaling deeply. She loved the scent that hung in the air as the sun started to rise, a mix of damp earth and sweet jasmine.

It was exactly what she needed today.

"Edward," she called into the house. "I'll have my tea out on the porch this morning."

He had been acting weird in the last few days, ever since she had rejected his offer to go out for dinner. Not so much weird as distant. And he constantly addressed her as "Mrs.," something she knew he did when he was upset with her.

Pushing thoughts of Edward aside, she bent to pick up the *Times-Picayune.* She unfolded the newspaper and shook her head with disgust. The large headline declared that a nine-year-old boy had been killed in a drive-by shooting in the projects. When would all the senseless killings end?

As she turned and made her way to the porch swing, she noticed what looked like a bottle standing between the swing and the house. She narrowed her eyes. Were they playing tricks on her? She slipped on her reading glasses. No, she wasn't mistaken. It *was* a bottle.

Securing the newspaper under her arm, Sylvia walked across the porch and bent to retrieve it. Turning the container, she saw that it had an odd label. A homemade one, she realized on closer inspection. That meant it was home-brewed wine.

The words BOTTLED IN 1953 were typed in large letters across the top of the plain white paper.

Her stomach fluttering, Sylvia's eyes went lower.

Enjoy this wine, she read.

And as you do, remember the year it was bottled.

1953.

That was a good year, wasn't it?

Sylvia's heart rammed hard against her rib cage as her breath snagged in her throat. 1953.

Good Lord in heaven.

Half a decade ago, it was a year she would never forget. But how on earth—who would have sent this? Who could *possibly* know?

There was a sound of shuffling feet and Sylvia whipped her head around, her stomach lurching. "Who's there?" she called.

She saw nothing to the left or right but the bushes that lined her property.

A sudden movement overhead. Alarm gripping her, Sylvia looked up. A black crow took flight from a branch of the magnolia tree.

"Sylvia."

She screamed. The wine bottle slipped from her fingers and smashed against the porch's concrete floor.

"Sylvia!"

Jumping backward, her body slammed hard against the side of the house. She looked down. "I'm bleeding." Her breath came in gasps. "Oh, God."

Edward was suddenly on his knees before her. His fingers probed her feet and her legs.

"Edward," she cried. Her entire body was trembling.

"It's okay," he told her. "It's the wine, not blood."

"The wine," she repeated in a shaky voice. *Of course.*

"Careful," Edward said. "There's glass everywhere." He stood and extended his arm to her. "Here. Hold on to me."

Sylvia gripped Edward's arm with both hands, as if her life depended on it. He led her past the shards of glass and pool of red wine. Only when she was at her front door did she feel some of her anxiety ebb away.

"Forgive me, Sylvia," Edward said. "I didn't mean to frighten you. I came to ask if you wanted some fresh-brewed mint tea as opposed to Darjeeling."

"Oh, Edward." She placed a hand over her heart. "It's not your fault. I just . . ." Her voice trailed off.

He looked past her. "I'll clean up the mess."

"How did that get there?"

"Hmm?" Edward's eyes flashed confusion.

Of course he didn't understand. She breathed in deeply before continuing. "I found that bottle of wine on the porch this morning. Do you know where it came from?"

"I have no idea."

Sylvia trembled. Could Olivia have put it there? Her daughter was no doubt angry with her. Just yesterday evening Olivia had stormed out of the sunroom, upset that Sylvia wouldn't answer her questions. Sylvia hadn't seen her since, and knew she hadn't spent the night here.

Had she returned at some point and slipped the bottle of wine on the porch? But how would she know about 1953?

How would anyone know?

"Are you okay?" Edward asked.

"Yes." She swallowed. "Yes, of course."

"I don't suppose you still want to have your tea outside this morning."

Sylvia shook her head in reply. "I think I'd prefer it in the sunroom."

"All right."

Edward started to turn, but Sylvia reached for him, stopping him.

"Yes, ma'am?"

"I'll clean up the glass." No, that wasn't what she'd wanted to say. "But first . . . I was wondering if you'd like to have tea with me?"

He smiled, and in that moment he looked so much like her late father that her eyes actually misted.

"I'd be happy to join you."

"The fresh mint you suggested sounds wonderful."

"Give me ten minutes to brew it."

"I'll go to the kitchen with you," Sylvia said. She didn't want to be alone.

She didn't want to think about the one thing she had spent her life trying to forget.

don't care, Belinda."

Belinda eyed Olivia with skepticism. "That's why it's a new day and you're still talking about it? Not to mention that you stayed here last night like a runaway teenager."

"I'm a grown woman. I can do what I want."

"But you know your mama's gonna fret, thinking you were off with some man you picked up after a night out at some bar. And that's exactly what you want her to think, because at least when she's fussing you know that she cares."

"I didn't ask you to be my shrink."

"Oh, no?"

"Okay, so maybe it comes with the territory." They'd been friends so long, they would offer advice and commentary whenever they felt it was appropriate and felt secure doing so.

"Why don't you try talking to your mother again? Convince her that this story is really important to you."

"As if that will matter to her."

"It can't hurt."

"I don't think you've heard me. She didn't even want to discuss the idea with me. She's playing like she's got amnesia where my father is concerned. Which is a huge load of bullshit. I just don't know why she won't talk about him. Because he embarrassed her by dying of a drug overdose? When will she get over that? She likes to act like she hasn't made her share of mistakes, but I know that's a lie."

"I don't know what to say." Belinda leaned forward and reached for the pitcher of iced tea on the glass coffee table. She refilled her tumbler.

"Maybe I should move out."

"You've been saying that for as long as I can remember. But you know you're not gonna do that, because of her health. And because you love her more than you're willing to admit."

"Of course I love her. It's just that we can't get along."

"At least she's still alive, Liv. I miss my mama more than I ever dreamed possible."

Belinda's words silenced her. Though Olivia and her mother didn't get along, the truth was she couldn't imagine her life without her. Even if it meant another fifty years of bickering.

"But," Belinda went on, "I don't want to think about my mama right now. The day is much too beautiful to spend it depressed. So let me tell you about the call I made before you woke your lazy ass up."

Olivia cut her eyes at her friend. "What call?"

"You probably didn't think I was serious when I said I wanted to go away somewhere. But I am. So with you here, I decided to call a travel agency. The woman I spoke to was very nice, great with suggestions. She planned out a package for us. Air, car, a few nights in Miami, then a few nights in the Florida Keys. Or if you want, instead of Key West, we could head to Freeport on a cruise and spend a few days there."

"Girl, you really were serious."

Belinda's eyes danced with anticipation. "I'm gonna pick up the brochures later today. If you give me an idea of what you'd prefer, the agent can give me some prices."

"I say Freeport. We can always drive to the Keys on our own."

"That's what I was thinking."

Olivia clapped her hands together. "Ooh, I'm excited."

"Me, too. Now I just have to run it by Bernie."

"He'll be fine with it. A man who loves you as much as Bernie does would never deny you a vacation. Even with a wild, single woman like me. Ha!"

Belinda grinned at Olivia's comment. "That's what I'm hoping. He's been working so much anyway, he won't have time to miss me. Oh, and I mentioned to Allette that I was thinking of going away on a vacation just for me, and you know what she said? She told me it was about time. Even said I should do something really crazy—like go to a strip club and have myself a lap dance!"

A jolt of pain stabbed at Olivia's heart. Not only did Belinda have a perfect husband, she had a perfect daughter. She and Allette were extremely close and could talk about anything—unlike Olivia and Rachelle.

Olivia said, "Wow."

"Shocked the heck out of me. I don't even want to know what she did when she went to Daytona for spring break this year." Her tone was light, despite the look of reproof on her face.

"She'd probably tell you. You and Allette have that kind of relationship. Rachelle, on the other hand . . . hmm."

"You don't think she'd tell you?"

"I know she wouldn't, not even if she went on a trip like that and was on her best behavior. I wish we had the kind of relationship you and Allette have, but we don't. And it seems even worse now."

"Now why?"

"Rachelle's always been pretty reserved. I'm used to that. But lately . . ." Olivia sighed. "Maybe I'm being paranoid, but I've felt her slipping away. I feel like something's going on with her that she doesn't want to tell me."

"Starting college can be daunting, especially for someone as quiet as Rachelle. I'm sure that's all it is."

Olivia's mouth twisted with doubt. "Sometimes I look at her and she seems so unhappy. More so since she started school last month." She paused. "I know I should have let her go, but I just couldn't do it."

"Let her go?" Belinda raised an eyebrow. "What are you doing? Walking her to school every morning?"

"Not hardly." Olivia couldn't even muster a smile at Belinda's playful tone. "I did something, something I'm not proud of, and I can't help wondering if that's why she's so sad."

"Olivia, what are you talking about?"

She had already opened this can of milk. She may as well spill it. "You know how much she was looking forward to going away to school?"

"Yes."

"I couldn't bear it, Belinda. The very thought of losing her had me depressed. One of the colleges she applied to was all the way in Washington state, for goodness sake. How could I live with her being so far? And do any black folks even live up there? Talk about culture shock. I did her a favor. She'll have a wonderful time at Dillard. It's where she needs to be."

"Exactly what are you saying?"

Olivia bit down hard on her bottom lip. She trusted Belinda, but still she said, "You can never breathe a word of this."

"You know I won't."

"She *did* get accepted to the other colleges she applied to. But I got her mail . . . and I . . . I threw out the acceptance letters."

"You didn't!"

Shame washed over Olivia in waves. "How could I let her go away?"

"Oh, boy." Belinda shook her head.

"Don't give me that look. I know it wasn't right. I just couldn't deal with her leaving."

"I'm not judging you."

Olivia heard something and glanced over her shoulder. "What was that?"

"What?"

"I thought I heard something."

"Probably just Bernie coming out of the shower. He'll be heading to work soon."

Satisfied with that answer, Olivia continued in a hushed tone. "It was the only thing I could do, Belinda. Rachelle will enjoy her time here. It's not like Dillard isn't a good school. I went there and was perfectly happy."

"You did what you had to do."

"Now Rachelle and Allette are going to college together, the way you and I had once hoped to do."

Belinda reached for the pack of cigarettes on the table. She withdrew one and lit it.

"You think I'm pathetic, don't you?"

"No." Belinda blew out smoke through her nose and mouth. "I could never think you're pathetic."

"Well, thank you." Olivia smiled sadly. At least Belinda wasn't giving her grief over what she had done. Because she *had* done the only thing she could.

Still, Rachelle would hardly see it that way. If she ever found out, she'd never forgive her.

CHAPTER FORTY

Rachelle wasn't impressed.

She sat on a loveseat in one corner of the room, watching the flurry of activity around her. People laughed, danced, flirted, and chatted in small groups. They moved by her without even glancing her way, as if she were merely part of the furniture. And she literally felt that way, considering how many of them had bumped into her when she had been standing.

This wasn't her. She didn't do the party scene.

It wouldn't be so bad if Grant hadn't left her twenty minutes ago and not returned. She didn't even know where he'd gone off to. He was nowhere on this dorm floor at the moment.

"Syvon, stop." An attractive girl giggled as she stepped backward. Male arms wrapped around her, but they didn't stop the girl before she fell backward against Rachelle.

Rachelle jumped to her feet. She gaped at the couple, but they didn't even look her way.

Forget this! Rachelle made her way through the group of people near her. And just at that moment, she saw Grant weaving through the room.

"Thank God," she muttered.

Then she saw the woman who lingered behind him.

"Hey, baby."

Grant opened his arms wide to embrace her, but Rachelle stepped away from him.

"Jus' had ta get somethin'."

Great. He couldn't speak without slurring his words. He clutched a beer like it would kill him to let it go. And he smelled like a damn brewery.

"Get what?"

"Jus' somethin'."

He wrapped his arms around her, and Rachelle didn't fight him. "Who's that girl?" When Rachelle looked over Grant's shoulder in the woman's direction, the woman was smiling smugly at her.

"Wa gurl?"

Oh, no. Rachelle wasn't going to allow him to play dumb. She pulled away from him and nodded toward the woman. "That one."

Grant followed Rachelle's line of sight. "Her?"

"Yeah, *her*."

Rachelle studied him as he chuckled. "That's Evoni."

"I don't care about her name," Rachelle snapped, surprised at herself. "Are you involved with her, too?"

"No!" He sounded completely shocked at the suggestion, but was that an act? "C'mon. Ya know I wouldn't do that."

"I don't know anything."

"C'mere." Grant draped an arm around her waist. He led her to a sofa along one wall that was unoccupied. Rachelle didn't bother to fight him.

They sat, and Rachelle said, "You left me here all alone, and I don't know your friends. Then I see you with that . . ." *That woman who is so much more beautiful than me.*

"Evoni's a friend. Thassall."

Was he telling the truth? "I'm not having fun. I want to leave."

"That's cuz you're sittin'ere so uptight. But don' worry." He gave her a conspiratorial smile. "I got somethin' ta loosen ya up."

"What?"

"Here." He passed Rachelle the drink and reached into his jacket pocket. He produced some little white pills.

"What are those?" Rachelle asked.

"You ain't tried ecstasy, baby? Oh, man. You hafta try it. Once you're high, all ya can think 'bout is your partner. And the sex . . ."

"I'm not trying ecstasy."

"C'mon."

"No."

He sucked his teeth. "Damn, you're a priss."

"I don't do drugs, Grant."

"You wan' weed?"

Rachelle abruptly stood. "I don't do drugs," she repeated slowly and clearly. And she sure as hell wasn't about to start.

Grant grabbed her arm and yanked her back down onto the sofa with him. "Don' you fuckin' geddup when I'm talkin' to ya. What're ya tryin' to do? 'Barrass me in fronta my friends?"

For a moment, Rachelle was afraid. Grant was so unlike how he'd been before. In this state, what was he capable of?

But she looked around the room, saw all the people, and realized that Grant would be a fool to do anything to her here with all these witnesses.

Or would he?

"I'm leaving," Rachelle told him. This time, when she stood, she started walking. As she feared, Grant was on his feet with lightning speed, following her.

"Ya know what? Forget you."

Rachelle kept walking, trying to pretend he wasn't beside her, looming over her in a way that scared her.

"Ya think I can't get anotha pussy? I can. Girls prettier'n you."

Rachelle had been trying to simply avoid him, but now she spun to face him and yelled, "Then why don't you go to them?"

Grant stared down at her. His face was contorted with anger; he almost looked like a different person.

"Yo, Grant."

Both Grant and Rachelle turned at the sound of the voice. A pretty woman placed her hand on his arm and smiled at Rachelle. "I think you had a little too much to drink, hon."

Rachelle's eyes narrowed on the woman.

"I'm Claudia," she said, extending a hand to Rachelle. "Grant's cousin."

"Oh."

"I hope everything's okay here." Her eyes flitted between Grant and Rachelle. "It looked like there was a bit of trouble going on, so I decided to come over."

Grant took a swig of beer. "Naw, man."

Claudia gave Grant a doubtful look. Then she grinned at Rachelle. "Grant truly is a sweetheart, even if he's right now acting like an idiot."

"Hey," Grant protested.

"I'm trying to smooth things over for you," Claudia said, giving him a pointed look. "Why don't you take a seat and start to sober up?"

Grant stared ahead dumbly. Then he said, "A'ight. Rachelle, later."

He walked away, and Rachelle chuckled mirthlessly. Clearly, he forgot he'd been arguing with her.

Alcohol. She hated the stuff.

Claudia faced her again. "Rachelle, right?"

"Yes."

"My cousin was right. You are very pretty."

"Me?" Rachelle asked, then regretted her words. Everything she said made her sound like some kind of fool.

Claudia giggled. "Who else? You could do something different with your hair, though. And your clothes are a bit conservative. But other than that, yeah, you got it going on."

"Well. Thanks."

"My cousin really likes you. It's just that he tends to drink too much with his fraternity brothers. Other than that, he's a nice guy."

Rachelle didn't know what to say. Alcohol or not, she wasn't impressed with how he had treated her tonight.

"I was just on my way out," Rachelle said.

"No." Claudia took her hand. "Don't go yet. The party's barely started."

"I know, but . . . but I wasn't planning to stay too long anyway. I have to get started on a paper."

Claudia threw her head back as she laughed. "Girl, it's a Saturday night."

"I know, but—"

"No buts. While Grant sobers up, why don't I introduce you to some people?"

Rachelle had a feeling Claudia wouldn't let her leave now even if she tried.

"All right."

CHAPTER FORTY-ONE

Olivia groaned and dragged a pillow over her head. Little good the pillow did. There was clearly no way to ignore the incessant pounding on the front door. But she had a headache this morning, courtesy of too much bourbon, and the last thing she needed was all this noise.

"For the love of God," she uttered when the knocking started again. Where was her mother? Edward?

"Fine," she muttered, crawling out of bed. She couldn't very well ignore the door forever. After all, it could be a courier with a package from her publisher.

Olivia slipped on a robe. "All right. I'm coming."

Her head throbbed from her sudden movements, and she let out a long string of curses as she made her way downstairs.

Scowling, Olivia drew in a deep breath, then opened the door.

And greeted a ghost.

For a full twenty seconds, all Olivia could do was stare.

He did the same, his eyes wide as they roamed over her from head to toe, as if he didn't believe his eyes were telling him the truth.

"Oh my God," Olivia said breathlessly. Could it be? Surely she was imagining this.

"Olivia."

Her body trembled. That voice. It sounded the same, except deeper, richer.

Yet how could this be?

"When I found out you were still living here—"

"Harvey?" His name escaped her lips in a whisper, the fear in her heart keeping her from screaming out in joy. If he was a ghost, or someone else altogether . . .

"Yes, Olivia. It's me."

Her heart thundered in her chest. *Harvey.* She had dreamed of this moment for so many years, all the while knowing the dream could never come true.

"I don't understand. I thought you were . . ." Her voice cracked with emotion as it always did when she reflected on what had happened to him. "Thought you had . . ."

He stepped toward her. Reflexively, Olivia stepped backward. Maybe this was someone else. Someone pretending to be Harvey.

Yet something in his eyes told her he was the man she had never stopped loving.

"I'm not going to hurt you."

His words made her realize that her face was so skewed with confusion, she must have looked scared. "I just don't . . ." Her eyes narrowed on him. "How can this be?"

"I know you have a lot of questions. Maybe we can sit down and talk."

"You're really not dead."

"Dead?" His eyes widened in shock. "Hell, no."

For twenty-eight years, she had believed him dead. Prayed it wasn't so but knew that it was. But still, she had dreamed of him often. Dreamed that he had simply gone away, that he would come back to her one day. In those dreams, when he came to her door—came back to her—she reached out and gathered him in her arms without hesitation, then led him to her bedroom, where they made love for days. Their bodies answered all their unspoken questions.

But this was real life. A life she had spent mourning him. And all this time, he had been alive.

"Considering you're not dead, where have you been for the last twenty-eight years?" She was surprised at the trace of bitterness in her voice.

"In Chicago, mostly. Now I'm back here, teaching at Dillard."

In Chicago, while she had been here, crying over him like a heartbroken fool! If only she had long gotten over him. If only she had been able to truly give her heart to Arthur or even another man. Her life would have been so much easier. And it would be easier to now deal with the truth that he had obviously rejected her. Because if he was alive and had cared about her, he would have gotten in touch with her eons ago.

"I'm not sure I even want to know why you're here at my door now, considering you didn't even have the courtesy to tell me you were leaving town without me."

"Whoa." Harvey held up both hands. "You actually think I'd come back here after all these years if I walked away from you? Let's sit down and talk, Olivia. Clearly there's a lot we need to iron out."

Exhilaration and anger fought for control of her heart. His words made sense. Why would he be here if he had left her in 1975? Then again, maybe everything else in his life had fallen apart and he'd gotten the weird idea in his head that he could have a second chance with her.

Or worse, maybe he had simply come to offer an apology. The way all those black men had offered apologies to the sisters in their lives during the Million Man March.

"Please, Olivia."

"All right," she said. "You can come in."

She turned and headed toward the living room on the immediate right. Her mother wasn't here, which was a good thing. And she suddenly remembered that Edward had a doctor's appointment, which was why he was out of the house.

In the living room, she faced Harvey. Her stomach fluttered as she took in the sight of him again. He was really standing here before her.

"You can take a seat if you like," she told him. As for herself, she was going to stand. At least standing she would not feel as vulnerable.

"You thought I was dead?"

"That's what my mother told me."

"Ah. I should have known." He ran a hand over his low-cropped hair and emitted a groan. "Now you realize I've been alive all along and you question why I'm here. I know it's out of the blue. And I wouldn't be here if I had learned that you were happily married. But I never left you that day, Olivia. I thought you were the one who wanted nothing to do with me."

"How can you say that? We made plans. It may have been twenty-eight years ago, but I remember it as if it were yesterday."

"That's right, we did make plans. But you never showed up. Instead, your mother did. She said you'd broken down and talked to her, told her that you were planning something stupid with me but had changed your mind. She said you didn't know how to end things, so you asked her to do it."

"That's a lie!"

"I didn't know what to believe at the time. I'd been waiting for you in the park for so long."

"Edward was up," Olivia told him. "I couldn't leave."

"Well, when I didn't see you, I started to worry. I wondered if you'd changed your mind. Then, out of the darkness, your mother appeared. And she told me you had sent her. It didn't make sense, even at the time, but I knew you were young. I knew running off with me was going to be a big step for you, and I figured . . . I figured that maybe you did change your mind. And I could see where if you *had* changed your mind, you wouldn't be able to face me."

"I may have been young but I knew what I wanted. I never changed my mind, and I surely didn't send my mother to talk to you. I went to the park the moment I could, and you weren't there. I must have waited for a good two hours before I realized you wouldn't be meeting me. And when I didn't see you at the carriage house, I thought you'd left without me. The very next morning, my mother told me you had died." It had been the worst day of her life. "Oh, God."

Silence filled the room. After a good thirty seconds, Harvey said, "Your mother was willing to do whatever it took to keep us apart. And it worked."

Olivia paced the living room floor. At the window, she stared outside. The large magnolia shaded most of the front yard, but sunlight still streaked through the branches, like little rays of hope.

She felt a ray of hope now.

"I met your daughter, Olivia. I saw her and I knew she had to be your child. She told me you're a widow. And God help me, I knew I had to see you."

Love was a strange thing. It didn't play by any rules and it couldn't be controlled. It swept you up to the heavens and brought you to the depths of hell.

Right now, Olivia was soaring to the heavens.

"I don't know what I expected. I guess I just wanted to see you. To know that you were okay. And maybe . . ."

She didn't even flinch when she felt his hands on her shoulders. "Maybe what?"

Harvey's lips brushed the back of her head. "Rachelle . . ." He sighed. "She should have been ours."

A lightning bolt of desire shot through her body. She knew if he touched her she would be wet.

Somehow she managed to keep her voice even as she asked, "You never had any of your own?"

"No."

"Did you marry?"

"Never."

Olivia's eyelids fluttered shut. Had he waited for her?

She turned in Harvey's arms and looked up at him. She saw the answer in his eyes. He *had* waited for her.

Emotion overwhelmed her, made her stomach clench with pain. All these years spent without him, because of her mother. "Twenty-eight years."

"And I don't want to waste another minute."

He swept her into his arms. The past twenty-eight years melted away the moment his lips went down on hers.

It wasn't a sweet kiss, but the hungry kiss of two starved lovers meeting after time spent apart.

His body molded to hers the same way it had before. His lips tasted as sweet.

"Harvey," she said in wonder, accepting that he was really here, that this moment was indeed true.

He deepened the kiss, his tongue delving into her mouth, twisting with hers. And his hands never left her body, not even for a second. They roamed over her back and body with a sense of desperation, as if he possessed her.

Which he did. He had always possessed her heart.

Olivia didn't realize she was crying until Harvey pulled his head back and kissed her tears before wiping them away.

"Oh, Harvey." Olivia framed his face.

He clamped his mouth down on hers once more, and an inferno of heat engulfed them. Olivia threw her arms around him and held him tight, savoring everything about him. His scent, the softness of his skin, the perfect fit of his body against hers.

Then her hands were on his shirt, pulling it from his khaki pants. He followed her lead, nudging her robe off her shoulders.

As his teeth came down on her skin, sanity intruded on the moment. Although she knew they were alone, Olivia glanced around as if she expected someone to walk in on them. Which could easily happen if the front door opened.

"Not here," she said. She took Harvey's hand and ran with him out of the living room and up the stairs to her bedroom, where she closed and locked the door behind them.

Safe from interruptions, she and Harvey immediately continued where they had left off. Olivia grabbed Harvey's T-shirt and tugged it over his head, then tossed it onto the floor. He reached for the tie on her robe but in his haste to loosen it he only made it tighter.

"Pull it off," Olivia whispered in his ear when he was having difficulty.

She raised her hands high above her head and Harvey dragged the robe and nightgown upward. There was a quick tearing sound when the knotted tie went past her shoulders. Something on the silk robe had ripped, but Olivia didn't care.

Harvey dropped her clothes to the floor, then stepped toward her. He reached for her breasts, covering the soft mounds in his palms. He caressed, squeezed, tweaked.

"My breasts aren't what they used to be," Olivia said, suddenly self-conscious. She wished they were as high and perky as they had once been, the way Harvey would have found them had they left town together in 1975. "Rachelle nursed for eighteen months."

Clearly, he hadn't heard her, or he simply didn't care. Because he said in a gruff voice, "So long I've waited for this. Dreamed about this."

"You have no idea how many times I've dreamed of this." So many nights she had cried herself to sleep after wondering what it would feel like to lie in his arms.

Harvey took a nipple into his mouth. Olivia gripped his shoulders and moaned.

"You're perfect," Harvey said. His hands and lips went everywhere. Down her stomach, over her behind. Lower, to the very essence of her.

He pushed aside her panties and explored. Teased.

Olivia arched her back and bit down on one of her fingers. This was right. She'd always known it was.

"So much lost time . . ."

"We'll make up for it," Harvey said, his words sounding like a promise.

He kissed his way up her body and brought his lips back to hers. Olivia reached for the button on the front of his pants. Harvey stepped back, allowing her to strip him. She dragged his pants and briefs off at the same time.

Harvey took off her lacy panties.

He reached for her, but Olivia simply took his hand and linked her fingers with his. She didn't move toward him. She wanted to savor this. Savor every inch of him.

Naturally, his body had changed in the years they had been apart. He still exuded strength, but his muscles weren't as solid. His stomach was noticeably softer where it had once been firm. And it wasn't as washboard-flat anymore. He had a little pouch.

Her gaze went higher, to his face. It was the same, but more mature. There were soft lines around his eyes, but otherwise his skin was still firm. The biggest difference was his hair. Not only was his Afro dramatically shorter, it was speckled with gray.

Not the man she remembered in her dreams, but still the man she loved. The man she had always loved.

She moved toward him and planted her mouth against his. With their lips locked, Harvey lifted her, and Olivia wrapped her legs around his waist. If he had planned to carry her to the bed, he suddenly decided against it. Instead he lowered her slightly, then reached between their bodies and guided his penis inside her.

Olivia cried out from the mix of pleasure and pain. Harvey filled her completely, in a way she had never before experienced. Because before this, it had always been about sex, never about love.

With each tender stroke, she felt the hole in her heart healing. At long last, she was where she had always wanted to be.

She was home.

CHAPTER FORTY-TWO

Dean Escoto will see you now."

"Thank you." Sylvia rose, securing her beige hobo purse under her arm as she did.

She walked across the wood floor toward the dean's office, unsure of what to expect. The dean's message that he needed to see her, as relayed to her by Edward, had her worried. Although Dean Escoto hadn't said this meeting was urgent, her stomach had still been in knots this morning as she'd driven Edward to his doctor. In fact, she had left Edward at the doctor's office and promised to pick him up later, all so that she could hear what Dean Escoto wanted to tell her as soon as possible.

The middle-aged man smiled at her as she stepped into the room. *The calm before the storm?* Sylvia wondered, hoping that everything was fine with Rachelle.

"Dean Escoto, hello." She accepted his extended hand in both of hers.

"Always a pleasure, Mrs. Grayson."

"Likewise." Sylvia liked him. He was of black and Hispanic descent, but had greater ties with the black community.

"Please have a seat."

Sylvia sat down on the large leather chair opposite the dean's desk. She crossed her feet at the ankles and folded her hands in her lap. She was concerned, but it would be improper to show it.

"I must admit," Sylvia began as the dean pulled out his chair, "I was rather surprised to get your message."

He narrowed his eyes quizzically as he sat. "My message?"

"The one you left this morning."

Confusion marred the man's face. "I didn't leave you a message this morning."

"But that's why I'm here." And when she had spoken to his secretary about meeting him, she had gotten the impression that they were expecting her.

But then, she gave so much money to the university that they would likely fit her in, no matter the occasion.

"Perhaps your secretary called about something?" Sylvia said.

"If she had, I would know about it. The first I heard of your coming here was twenty minutes ago when you arrived and asked to see me."

Sylvia bit her bottom lip. What was going on?

"So everything is okay with my granddaughter?"

"As far as I know."

Edward had distinctly told her that Dean Escoto had called, that it wasn't urgent, but he wanted her to come by his office as soon as she could. Could the man have so much on his plate that he had forgotten?

Sylvia decided not to press the issue. She stood. "I'm terribly sorry to have bothered you, then. My houseman must have been mistaken."

"Oh, don't worry about it. I was happy to see you, even if it's such a short visit."

"I'll see you again soon. The alumni dinner is only two months away."

"I'm looking forward to it."

Sylvia gave a polite smile before heading out of the office. She had a strange feeling that something weird was going on. Something she would not like.

She got even more of a shock when she headed into town to pick Edward up from his doctor's office.

The young secretary looked at her with a confused expression. "I'm sorry, Mrs. Grayson. Edward left at least fifteen minutes ago."

"What do you mean he left? I was coming back here to pick him up."

"I wish I could help you. As far as I knew, you *had* returned. He looked outside and said something about seeing his ride."

Seeing his ride? Sylvia didn't know whether to fume or be concerned. Edward had never done anything like this before. Had he seen a car he thought was hers and stepped outside? And if he had, would he not have returned to the sitting area when he learned it wasn't her?

"He didn't say anything else?" Sylvia asked.

"No. I wish I could be of more assistance."

Sylvia backed away from the reception desk. Her head began to swim as a myriad of terrifying ideas came to her.

Dear Lord, what if Edward's become disoriented? What if he's hurt somewhere?

Spinning around, she ran out of the office.

Later, their bodies spent from marathon lovemaking, Olivia and Harvey lay in bed together. They lay spoon-fashion, their fingers linked over Olivia's abdomen.

There was an aura of peace surrounding them. Olivia wished they could stay like this for days and days.

She said softly, "Harvey?"

"Hmm?"

While she knew in her heart how he felt about her, she was suddenly nervous about what she was going to tell him. The last thing she wanted was to be a fool for any man.

He kissed her ear. "What is it, baby?"

She blurted, "I never stopped loving you. Not in all these years. Not even when I got married. You were always the man in my heart."

"Ah, baby. It feels so good to hear you say that. Because I couldn't stop thinking about you. Not even when I figured you'd fallen in love with someone else and moved on. I wondered about whom you were with, whether or not you were happy. Sometimes I thought I would go mad because I couldn't get you out of my system."

"Why didn't you come back sooner?" Olivia asked. "I know we can't change the past, and I know your answer may hurt me—"

"I was afraid of your mother."

"Afraid?"

"She told me to make sure I left town and never came back."

Olivia turned in his arms, facing him. "Are you saying she threatened you with physical harm?"

"Not that, no. But she pretty much threatened to have me arrested and thrown in jail. Remember that girl who had been murdered?"

"Yes. Liza Monroe."

"Your mother said something about knowing I was responsible for that girl's death, and how she'd make sure the police arrested me if I didn't disappear. I wasn't, of course, but I took that to mean she'd have evidence made up to prove I *had* killed her. She was dead set on getting rid of me. I realized she would stop at nothing to have me out of your life. I told you she had given me ten thousand dollars?"

"Uh-huh."

"Well, when she met me in the park, she gave me another five grand to sweeten the deal. The only condition was that I had to leave right away."

Damn her mother. She had told her so many lies. "My mother told me you stole a car and that you'd wrecked it leaving town."

"Stole a car?" Harvey huffed his disgust. "What the hell is up with that woman? Fine, she wanted to get rid of me, but did she have to vilify me?"

"I think she wanted to make sure I'd never look for you. Because she knew I would have, had I thought you were still alive. She was smart."

"She was wicked. Evil. She had no goddamn right to mess with my life."

Olivia shook from the intensity of Harvey's wrath. He squeezed her fingers so hard, it hurt.

"Harvey." She tugged at her hands, trying to pull them from his.

"Sorry." He loosened his grip. "And listen to me, taking the Lord's name in vain. I never do that. I'm just so pissed off when I think of everything your mother's done."

"I know exactly how you feel. Believe me."

"I could have bought a car with the money she gave me. But she had me so scared I didn't even want to stick around until the next morning. I caught a cab to the bus station, then stayed there the whole night, wondering what to do. Where to go."

Harvey released a long, weary breath. Olivia brought their joined hands to her mouth, kissing his, letting him know that he could go on, no matter how difficult.

"You said you went back to Chicago. After what had happened with your cousin, why would you head back there?" She remembered every detail of the story, and she felt angry on Harvey's behalf that he had been forced back into that awful situation.

"I decided I couldn't go on always watching my back. Your mother's threat to have me arrested made me realize how vulnerable I was. It was part of the reason she'd been able to coerce me into leaving you. And losing you . . . it was too great a cost."

"What happened with your cousin?"

"I was charged, had to get a lawyer. Your mother's money came in handy for that. Still, I couldn't afford anyone high profile, and I thought I was going to do hard time. But the DA ultimately dropped the charges. Clayton's wife admitted that I'd beaten him in self-defense." Harvey paused for a long while, and Olivia could see he was reliving the entire incident.

He finally kissed her forehead. "After that I used the rest of your mother's money to get an education. That was the one thing I'd wanted to do most in the world, get a degree so I could teach."

"I didn't know that."

"I figured there was no point in telling you. It seemed like an impossible dream because I had no clue how I'd be able to afford it. As manipulating as she was, at least I can thank your mother for that."

"I should have been with you. We should have been together."

"You're damn right we should have been."

"Why did she hate you so much?" Olivia said aloud, more to herself than to Harvey. "Why would she go to such lengths to get you out of my life?" Emotion clogged her throat. "How could she do this to me? It was one thing to try and force you out of my life, but to make me believe you had died? She knew that would devastate me, yet she didn't care. I thought she loved me, but no mother who loves you would do something like that."

"I know she's your mother, and I shouldn't bad-mouth her, but she doesn't sound capable of love."

"She doesn't, does she?"

Harvey glanced away at Olivia's question. There was more he clearly wanted to say, but he wasn't voicing what was on his mind.

What could anyone say? Her mother's behavior was inexcusable.

So much made sense now. When Liza Monroe had died, the entire neighborhood had known. There'd been talk about it for weeks. When Harvey had disappeared, Olivia hadn't heard a word. She'd trusted that her mother's story had been true, but it had all been a calculated lie. Sylvia had wanted Harvey out of Olivia's life, and she had stopped at nothing to see that happen.

Olivia opened her mouth to speak, but a beeping sound caught her attention and her head flew up.

Harvey looked at her with curiosity. "What?"

"I think that was the door."

"Your mother?"

She whispered, "I think so."

They both lay still, listening. The distinctive sound of footsteps got closer as someone climbed the stairs.

"Edward?" Sylvia called.

Olivia clutched Harvey, hardly daring to breathe.

"Edward, where are you?"

"What do you—?"

"Shh!" Olivia clamped a hand over Harvey's mouth.

Several seconds passed. "I hope I locked the door," Olivia murmured.

No sooner had the thought left her mouth than there was a loud rapping on her door. Scared witless, Olivia threw the covers over Harvey. If her mother barged in, she would know there was a man in her bed, but she wouldn't know who it was.

"Don't open the door," Olivia snapped. "I'm not decent."

"I wasn't planning to," her mother replied. "I was wondering if you've seen Edward."

"Not since breakfast."

"You've been up?"

"Yes, I've been up. And he hasn't been here."

There was a long pause. "If you see him, will you please tell him to call me on my cell phone? I have to head back out, but I'm a little concerned about him."

"Sure, Mother." If Harvey weren't here, she would have asked her mother why she was concerned. But she couldn't take the chance of her mother finding Harvey.

Silence ensued. Olivia and Harvey listened. They heard Sylvia's footsteps growing fainter.

"Is she gone?" Harvey asked.

Olivia shook her head.

The alarm beeped faintly, indicating that the door had been opened. It beeped again, and Olivia knew the door was now closed.

"Now she's gone."

Harvey rolled onto his back. "Shit."

"If she found you in here, so be it. But I wasn't in the mood for a confrontation with her just yet."

Wrapping his arms around her, Harvey turned onto his side. Her breasts brushed against his chest as he settled close to her.

"What are you thinking?"

Olivia realized then that she'd closed her eyes. She opened them and looked at the face she had dreamed of seeing more times than she could count.

"I wanted to go with you that night, Harvey. So badly. My life since then has been a mess—"

"Shhh." He placed a gentle hand on her face.

"I don't know if I can forgive my mother for this."

"You don't need to think about that right now. People like her will get what's coming to them."

"All this makes me realize I don't know her at all. I have no clue anymore what she's capable of."

"Are you going to tell her about me?"

Olivia's lips curled in a mischievous grin. "As soon as we've made up for lost time, I'll take great pleasure in it."

"Maybe we could start with this." Harvey slipped a hand between her legs. He ran his thumb over her nub.

"Great minds think alike."

"Climb on top of me."

Olivia did. She took Harvey's erection in her palm and held it steady as she sat on it.

"This time when you ride me, don't hold back. I don't give a shit if your mother comes back in."

Olivia didn't care, either. Her mother had taken enough from her. She wouldn't take another thing.

CHAPTER FORTY-THREE

Sylvia jumped up from her seat in the living room when she heard the alarm system beep. Relief flooded her when she realized it wasn't the front door that had opened. If it was the side door, that meant it had to be Edward.

She rushed toward the back of the house. "My God, Edward," she cried, seeing him. "Are you okay?"

Confusion flashed in his eyes. "Of course I'm okay."

Sylvia checked him out from head to toe. He looked okay. There were no scratches, no visible signs of distress. His eyes seemed clear.

"Where have you been? I spent more than half the day going crazy with worry. You just left the doctor's office—"

"You didn't get my message?"

"What message?"

"I left word that I was leaving with a friend."

"No, that nitwit of a receptionist did not tell me that."

"Ah." Edward smiled. "So you were worried about me."

"This is not a joke." Sylvia's tone was clipped.

"I didn't say it was."

"What do you mean you left the office with a friend? You knew I was heading back there to pick you up."

"I know, but it was a chance meeting with someone I haven't seen in years.

I stepped outside for a breath of fresh air and there she was. I decided to spend the day with her."

"*Her?*"

"Someone I knew a lifetime ago. One of my late wife's friends."

"You couldn't call?"

"I called the house a few times. You didn't answer."

"And what about my cell phone? You couldn't leave me a message?"

"I'm sorry, I forgot the number."

Exactly who was this woman who had Edward acting so out of character? Sylvia wanted to throttle him. "I thought maybe you had gotten disoriented. That you were hurt somewhere. I called the hospitals. The police, even. And all this time, you were out on a date?"

"Is that against the law?"

Sylvia's eyes bulged. "I don't appreciate that, Edward. I expect more from you. Better."

"I'm sorry for the inconvenience, but I did call. And this *was* my day off."

"What did you and this woman do?"

"We had a very nice day."

"Damn it, Edward. Tell me where you were."

His eyes narrowed with disapproval. "Excuse me?"

"After you had me worried out of my mind, the least you can do is give me answers."

"Don't I have any right to privacy?"

"Privacy? It's after ten o'clock at night, and the last I saw you was at your doctor's office around eleven this morning."

"Was I supposed to check in with you?"

Sylvia glared at him. What didn't he want to tell her? "What are you hiding?"

"Hiding is a strong word."

"You've never been like this before, Edward. Staying out at all hours—"

"I have a curfew now, do I? Last I checked, I was a grown man. And what I do off the clock is strictly my business."

"I can't believe you're speaking to me this way."

"You're blowing everything out of proportion."

What had happened to her trusted houseman? He never argued with her like this. And he never simply disappeared, especially with some woman.

"You make it sound like it's a crime I was worried about you."

"I went to the Riverfront." Edward sounded exasperated. "Enjoyed a nice dinner and listened to some wonderful jazz. It was something Philomena was happy to do with me."

His comment was like a slap in the face. "So this is about last week, about me turning down your invitation."

"It's about two old friends who did something enjoyable to pass the day. Lord knows any day could be my last."

"Don't say that, Edward." Sylvia hated when he talked about his inevitable passing.

"I don't fear death. My family took its passage into the arms of our ancestors long before me, but I feel their light around me always. Because of my faith, I know that what awaits is positive. Death is merely a time when we are nourished by the Master so that we can be reborn."

"Yes, I know." Sylvia didn't want to argue the point. She knew that Edward believed in reincarnation, but she did not. "Let's not digress, please."

"I thought we were finished."

"I wasn't."

"Are you planning to let me go because I haven't answered your questions well enough?"

"Let you go? Why on earth would you say that?"

"You seem pretty angry over this misunderstanding, as if you've never done anything wrong in your life."

"I didn't say that."

"Are you firing me?"

"Of course not! We've had our tiffs over the years. This time is no different."

"Good. Then I'll see you in the morning."

As Edward turned and walked away, Sylvia realized what he'd said. *As if you've never done anything wrong in your life.*

That was a strange thing to say, given the situation.

Her annoyance dissipated. It was replaced with wariness.

What had made those words come to his lips?

———

Belinda, what are you doing now?" Olivia could hardly contain her excitement as she spoke into the phone.

"Nothing, really."

"Good. I'm coming over."

"Right now?"

"Yes. We need to talk."

"Is everything okay?"

"Girl, everything is more than okay."

"All right, then. I'll see you soon."

Not more than twenty minutes later, Olivia was at Belinda's door. She grabbed her friend's hands and squeezed them hard.

"You're free to talk?"

"Uh-huh. Bernie's taken the kids to a matinee."

"Good." Olivia rushed into the house. "The living room?"

"Lead the way," Belinda said, giggling.

Olivia held Belinda's hand as she hurried to the living room. There, she plopped herself down on the plush sofa, taking Belinda with her.

"I swear, girl, your excitement is contagious. What did you do, win the lottery or something?"

Olivia released a gush of air. "You could say that."

"You did!"

"Not money, but something *so* much better." She paused, gripped Belinda's hands tighter. "Harvey showed up at my door yesterday."

"Harvey?" Belinda's eyes nearly bulged out of her head. "Come again?"

"Harvey from 1975. Harvey who I thought was dead."

"No!"

"Yes!" Olivia squealed with delight. "I swear, Belinda, I nearly fainted dead away when I saw him. At first I didn't know whether or not I was seeing a ghost."

"He's alive?"

"My mother lied to me," Olivia said with bitterness. She filled Belinda in on every last detail of her mother's manipulation. "I still can't believe it, but it doesn't matter. What matters is that he's alive, and he's back, and we're both still in love."

"After all this time."

"After all this time."

"I guess true love does exist."

"It does!" Olivia threw her hands in the air in a sign of victory. She felt as giddy as she had when she'd first told Belinda about Harvey when they were teenagers.

As she laughed her way down from her high, she slapped Belinda's arm. "You already know true love exists, you dolt. You married the man of your dreams right out of college."

Belinda's lips twisted in a pseudo-scowl. "Yeah."

Olivia narrowed her eyes with speculation. Something was going on with her friend. "What is it, Belinda?"

"I guess you won't want to go on our trip anymore."

Their trip. So that was what Belinda was worried about. Olivia moaned softly, thinking of what she should do.

"Look, hon," she said after a moment. "We already spoke about this. If you want to go to Miami, we'll go." She had lasted twenty-eight years without Harvey. A few more days wouldn't kill her.

"You don't have to. You and Harvey have just found each other again."

"And you're still my best friend. I'm not going to start ignoring you simply because Harvey's back in my life."

Olivia's gaze wandered to the wood coffee table. "Are these the brochures?"

"Uh-huh."

Olivia scooped them up. A stretch of white, sandy beach was pictured on the front cover of the top brochure. Dolphins, a ship, and turquoise blue water were featured on the second one.

"This looks amazing," Olivia said. "When do you want to go?"

"You're sure?"

"Of course I'm sure."

Belinda smiled faintly. "It doesn't have to be right away. We could plan it for next month. That'll give me enough time to book the days off work. Then again, maybe November would be a better option. Hurricane season should be over by then."

"Good point."

Olivia and Belinda both looked up as the sound of the front door opened. Feet pounded on the hardwood floor as Alex ran into the living room. Bernie and Allette followed him in.

"Baby." Belinda jumped up and ran to her son, drawing him into her arms.

"Hi, Mama."

"How was the movie?"

"Awesome!" he exclaimed. "Hello, Mrs. Harding."

"Hey there, Alex." Olivia stood. "Hello, Allette."

Allette dropped her purse onto the floor. "Hi," she said, but she was frowning.

"Sweetheart, what's the matter?" Belinda asked.

"She's upset with me because I didn't leave her at the mall to do some shopping," Bernie answered. "She knows I don't like leaving her out in the city. There're too many vultures out there."

"We can go out later, if you like," Belinda told Allette.

"It doesn't matter."

Bernie ventured further into the room. He picked up the brochures. "What's this?"

"Oh." Belinda placed her hands on her hips. "Um, some travel magazines."

"You're going somewhere?"

"Well, Olivia and I were throwing around some ideas."

Bernie's gaze moved from Belinda to Olivia, then back to Belinda. "I see."

"Maybe in a couple of months," Olivia told him.

Bernie nodded. "Hey, Alex. You want to head out to the park with the football?"

"Yeah, Dad."

"Great. I'll go change. You get the football."

"See ya later, Mrs. Harding," Alex said before leaving the room.

"Bye, Alex."

"I'll see you again, Olivia."

"Sure, Bernie."

When both Bernie and Alex were gone, Olivia turned back to Belinda. "You know, if you're planning to go to the mall, I can talk to Rachelle and maybe we could all go." Her daughter was here in New Orleans, not away at some school out of state, and she ought to take advantage of her time here.

"I've got studying to do," Allette said, dismissing the idea.

"Oh." Olivia swallowed her disappointment. "Okay, then."

"Maybe another time," Belinda suggested.

"Of course," Olivia replied. She crossed her arms over her chest. "Well, Belinda, your family's home. I won't take up any more of your time. Allette, I love those hip-hugger jeans. Reminds me of what was popular when your mother and I were teenagers."

Allette didn't even meet her eyes as she uttered, "Hmm."

Was Olivia mistaken, or was Allette being short with her?

Belinda linked arms with her daughter. "She doesn't want to believe that her mama once had it going on. But I could tell you some stories, girl."

Allette released an exaggerated groan. "Mama, you know I don't want to hear it!"

Perhaps Olivia was simply being sensitive where Allette was concerned. After all, there was no reason for the girl to be upset with her. She was probably a little peeved with her father and therefore in a poor mood.

"All right, Miss Miserable," Belinda said to Allette. To Olivia she said, "Liv, we'll talk about the Miami trip later. In the meantime, you go have fun." She winked at her.

Olivia's lips curled in a smile. "You know I will."

She hoped Harvey was ready for her.

CHAPTER FORTY-FOUR

Hey, Allette." Rachelle looked up at her friend from her table in the library. "You're late. I thought you were coming here right after church."

Allette dropped her books on the desk and slumped into the chair beside her. Rachelle's stomach took a little nosedive when she saw the serious expression on her friend's face.

"Something happen?" Rachelle asked.

"I'm just gonna say this. I've thought about it over the past several days, debating what I should do, and I think you need to know."

"Uh-oh." This *was* serious.

"I know you've been wondering how you didn't get accepted at Spelman, or any of the other colleges you applied to. I've always wondered, too."

Rachelle sat up straight. It was the question that had plagued her, ever since she learned she'd have to settle on going to Dillard. She didn't have the highest grade point average, but she was certain she'd had good enough marks to get accepted at the school of her choice.

"Why are you bringing that up?" Rachelle asked.

"Because . . ." Allette leaned forward, folding her arms on the desk. "Your mother was over last week. She was talking to mine and I overheard part of their conversation. Rachelle, she said . . . she said she tore up the acceptance letters you got from the other colleges."

Rachelle's stomach bottomed out. "What did you say?"

"She tore up the letters. Something about how it would have been culture shock for you to go to Washington. I'm sorry."

Rachelle's entire body trembled. She couldn't speak as she processed what Allette had just told her.

"I wouldn't have mentioned anything if I thought I'd possibly heard wrong, but I didn't."

"She tore up the letters?"

"I know this has to hurt, but I figured you ought to know."

Anger swirled inside Rachelle like a gale force wind picking up speed. She felt the brunt of the storm in her head, which almost seemed like it could explode from the pressure.

Anything but this, God.

"You're absolutely certain?"

"Yes," Allette said without hesitation.

Damn her mother! She had single-handedly destroyed her dream. Her dream to escape their dysfunctional family and go somewhere she was free to be herself.

"Was she drunk?"

"I'm not sure. I know she was drinking with my mom the night before." Allette placed a hand on Rachelle's arm. "As much as I love having you at Dillard with me, I really am sorry."

"Why would she do this to me?" Rachelle asked, but it was a rhetorical question. Allette would have no answers to that question.

"I wish I knew, hon."

"How could you know?" Rachelle's words were laced with bitterness. "How could anybody? This is beyond the realm of what normal people do."

"I can't be sure, but I kinda got the impression that she was going to miss you if you went away. I don't know."

"Oh, yeah. I believe that." Rachelle snorted. "She did this to make me miserable. She barely knows I exist. She'd never even miss me if I was gone!"

The intensity of Rachelle's voice startled even her. She looked around and saw that the students nearby were giving her curious glances.

Allette glanced around too, then asked, "You want to go somewhere else? Where we can talk about this?"

Rachelle flipped open her biology textbook. "No. I have to study for this quiz."

"You're sure?"

"Uh-huh."

Rachelle looked down, trying to concentrate on the words on the page. Because if she pondered the reason why her mother resented her so much, she would surely break down and cry.

Was that some sort of commotion?

Olivia lowered the notepad on which she'd been jotting ideas for her father's story and listened.

Hearing a blur of angry voices, her heart kicked into overdrive. Harvey! Had he shown up to see her and gotten into an argument with her mother?

Good Lord, the two would kill each other. Tossing the notepad onto the window ledge, Olivia jumped out of her chair and dashed to the door. Caution got the better of her and she opened it a crack instead of barging into the hallway.

"Right away. Yes. Three hours? That is much too long to wait. I have urgent business to attend to." Sylvia paused. "Of course I'll be here. I can't very well drive with four slashed tires!"

Olivia slipped back into her room and put on a terry cloth housecoat. She loved her silk one, but it needed mending after her episode with Harvey. Heading into the hallway, she padded barefoot down the stairs. Her mother stood with one hand on her hip, the other holding the cordless phone, and a frown on her face.

"Mother? What's going on?"

"Someone vandalized my car, that's what's going on. Slashed all four tires."

"My God." Olivia hurried to the front door and peered out the nearby window. Her mother's Lexus rested on four deflated tires in the driveway.

"It was fine this morning when I went to church. Now this. No, I'm not talking to you."

Turning, Olivia saw that her mother was now speaking into the phone. "How long do you expect me to wait, anyway? That is not my problem. Put your damn supervisor on the phone, young man."

Sylvia was definitely irate. She rarely cursed. Olivia waited, realizing it would be futile to ask her questions until she came off the line.

"Half an hour and not a second longer." Sylvia clicked the cordless phone off as if she hoped to crush it in her hands.

"Someone's coming to replace the tires?" Olivia asked.

"Apparently. And they had better. I'm having a meeting with the subcommittees regarding Outreach Day in a few hours."

"You can always take my car," Olivia suggested.

"With all due respect, I'd rather not."

"Oh?" Olivia's eyebrows shot up.

"Don't give me that look. You know damn well why I'm angry with you."

One step forward, three steps back. Olivia had come down here to offer assistance to her mother, and for that she had received a slap in the face. Why did she even bother?

She said, "I'm not even going to ask."

"I find my tires slashed not more than two hours since you came home."

"What's that supposed to mean?"

"I know you've got issues with me—"

"You're actually accusing me of this?" Olivia asked incredulously.

"I got both your notes, Olivia. Lord knows you're always angry with me. And when you've been drinking—"

"I haven't been drinking. And I can't believe you'd think I would do something like this, regardless."

Sylvia stepped toward her and shoved a crumpled piece of paper in her hand. Olivia opened it and read aloud, "You're not a mother. You're a whore." Her eyes flew to Sylvia's. "I didn't write this."

"You have a computer."

"So do a lot of people!"

Sylvia turned away, grunting her frustration. "Where the hell is that tow truck?"

Olivia breathed in deeply as she watched her mother make another phone call. She wanted to scream. Her mother needed to discuss this with her, not dismiss her as she was so prone to do.

As Sylvia disconnected the call, Olivia said, "I didn't write that note. And I can't imagine who did. Probably some idiot in the neighborhood trying to make someone's day miserable, thinking it's a joke."

"I'm sure that's what you'd want me to believe."

"Honestly, Mother." Olivia tried to reach her with a softer tone. "You can't really believe I would want to hurt you like this?"

"There's no one el—" Sylvia stopped abruptly as her eyes nearly leaped out of her head.

"Mother?"

"I . . ." She wobbled.

Olivia scrambled to her side, quickly taking hold of her mother's arm to hold her up. "Is it your heart?"

"I . . . I need to sit down."

"Of course." Olivia walked with her to the living room. She sat with her mother on the sofa. "You need some water? Edward?"

"He's at the temple."

That's right. It was Sunday, and Edward spent the entire day at a voodoo temple for some kind of religious service. "All right. I'll get you water."

"No, tea, please."

"Darjeeling?"

"Yes."

Olivia's heart beat frantically as she hustled to the kitchen. *Lord, please don't let my mother be dying. I know we don't get along. But don't take her now. Not like this.*

Olivia filled the kettle with water and plugged it in. Frustrated and scared, she dug her fingers into her hair. Surely her mother had some pills she needed to take. But damned if she knew what.

Edward! He would know. And he'd be a better source of comfort for Sylvia, so it was a good idea that he come home. He could catch a taxi and Olivia would pay for it.

She made her way to the wall phone. As she lifted it, she searched for the number to Edward's temple written on the small directory beside the phone's base. She punched in the digits and held the receiver to her ear.

The phone was answered on the sixth ring. "South Square Voodoo Temple."

"Oh, hello," Olivia said, relieved that a woman had answered. "I'm trying to reach one of your parishioners." That was the wrong word, she was sure, but she didn't know how else to describe him. "Edward Haughton."

"Ah, yes. Edward."

"Great. You know him. Can you please have him come to the phone?"

"I'm not sure I've seen him recently, but I'll take a look for him."

Olivia waited while the woman went in search of Edward. It seemed like hours before she returned, saying, "Sorry. Edward isn't here."

"Not there? He has to be."

"He was earlier. But he left a couple hours ago."

"You're positive? Edward Haughton?"

"I know exactly who he is, and yes, I was told he left quite some time ago."

"All right, then. Thanks, anyway."

Olivia frowned. If Edward had left the temple, why wasn't he home? What was she going to do now?

She needed to check on her mother. The water wasn't boiling yet, so she had some time.

Olivia rushed back to the living room. She drew up short when she saw her mother standing. Sylvia no longer looked flushed. In fact, she was wearing a hole in the floor in front of the sofa.

"The tea's not ready?"

"No, not yet."

Turning, Sylvia walked briskly to the window. She stared outside expectantly. Olivia watched her, a multitude of emotions churning inside her, but Sylvia didn't look her way.

The tension between them was palpable. Alone in a room, they couldn't figure out what to say to each other. Unless they were fighting.

"Maybe you should sit," Olivia suggested.

"I'm fine."

"You're sure?"

"Yes."

"All right. I guess I'll head back upstairs."

Sylvia turned then. "To bed?" Her tone held sarcasm. "Honestly, Olivia. Is it your goal to do everything in your power to shame me?"

Twice in the span of minutes, Olivia had extended herself to her mother. She'd felt true fear when she thought she could be dying. And here her mother was, attacking her.

She wasn't sick. She wasn't about to have a heart attack. It was all an orchestrated act.

The great Sylvia Grayson would probably live forever.

"Who were you out with last night?"

"I'm an adult. What I do is my business."

"And you have the nerve to call me a whore."

Olivia's breath left her in a rush. It was one of the worst things her mother had ever said to her. "The last thing I need is a lecture from you. You pretend to be a paragon of morality, but you're far from it."

"Oh, I know how you feel about me. You've made it clear in your nasty notes. Not to mention that bottle of wine."

"What wine?"

"Just admit it and stop these games."

"Are you losing it in your old age? Because you're sounding pretty insane right now."

Sylvia steeled her jaw. "I can't believe you want to hurt me like this."

"*Me* hurt *you*? How funny, considering you're the one who tried to destroy her own daughter's life."

"You did a fine job of that yourself."

"No, Mother. *You* did that. And you paid a pretty penny to do it. Fifteen thousand dollars. Isn't that right?"

There was a flicker of confusion in Sylvia's eyes, but then there was understanding.

"That's right. I know." Olivia chortled without mirth. "Aren't you curious as to how?"

Sylvia only stared, not saying a word, but the horror on her face was unmistakable.

Olivia couldn't hold back a victorious smile. It had taken nearly thirty years, but she had won. "It appears some people do come back from the dead. Harvey Jackson did."

Sylvia's already pale skin lightened by several shades. The piercing whistle from the boiling kettle punctuated her distress.

"That's right, Mother. You remember Harvey. The carpenter you'd hired in 1975, the summer Liza was murdered."

Olivia hadn't planned to tell her mother about Harvey's return for as long as possible, until she'd figured out when she would move out and into Harvey's home. But she was a grown woman. She didn't have to hide the truth. She didn't need to secretly plot how she and Harvey would be together for fear her mother would destroy her plans this time around.

"You failed, Mother. Because he's back."

"Harvey . . ." Sylvia swallowed. "He's not dead?"

"Oh, cut the bullshit! You knew he wasn't dead. You knew he didn't steal a car. Yet you lied to me with such calculating coldness. You didn't care that that news would destroy my life."

Sylvia whimpered. Clutched her chest.

Olivia wouldn't buy the act this time. "Fifteen grand was a lot of money, but did you expect it to last him for the rest of his life?"

Now more than ever, Olivia was happy that she'd ensured Rachelle's attendance at Dillard. If Harvey hadn't seen her in his classroom, he may never have thought to seek her out.

"And guess what?" Olivia continued in the face of her mother's silence. "He's still in love with me. We're in love with each other. We've messed around right in this living room and screwed in my bedroom upstairs. So what are you gonna do now, Mother?"

Sylvia's knees buckled. She swayed. This time, Olivia didn't stop her from falling to the floor.

CHAPTER FORTY-FIVE

t was time for a change. A drastic one.

All her life, she had been the good girl, hoping for approval from her mother. But where had that gotten her? Absolutely nowhere.

Yes, she had her grandmother's approval, and she was grateful for that. She'd had her father's love when he had been alive. It didn't matter how much time he spent in the courtroom, he always took time out for her.

But her mother? Rachelle may as well have been part of the furniture for all the attention her mother gave her. Yet it was her love and approval that she wanted the most.

Needed.

Had needed. Rachelle had hardened her heart since Allette's bombshell about why she'd only gotten accepted at Dillard. Her mother obviously didn't care about her. Rachelle couldn't even imagine why she was out to ruin her life.

Her mother wanted her around for some unknown reason—and fine, she was here. But her mother wouldn't like it.

No, Rachelle would make sure her mother lived to regret ever meddling in her life.

You ready?"

As ready as I'll ever be. Rachelle said, "Yes."

"All right." The hairdresser beamed. "Here you go."

The hairdresser slowly spun Rachelle's chair around so that she could see her reflection in the mirror. Rachelle sucked in a sharp breath at what she saw.

"You said you wanted different."

Rachelle eased off the chair and walked to the mirror. Her hair was not only drastically shorter, she now had blond highlights—and she had never *ever* colored her hair. The cut could only be described as severe, at least severe for her, even though the unkempt look was now in style.

Rachelle finally fingered some strands. "It's definitely different."

"Do you like it?"

Rachelle hesitated. It would take some getting used to. Hell, a lot of getting used to.

But her mother would absolutely hate it. "Yeah," she responded. "I *love* it."

Rachelle had the strange feeling that everyone was looking at her as she walked through the campus at Dillard. Looking and analyzing her new act of rebellion.

In reality, they probably weren't even noticing her. Why should they? She may have been a good girl her entire life, but most people weren't these days.

After leaving the hair salon, Rachelle had taken a bus to the mall. She had spent hours there, but still she wasn't ready to go home. Not yet. So she'd decided to swing by Claudia's dorm room and hang out for a while. They did entirely too much chatting when together, but Rachelle wasn't in the mood to study.

"My Lord." Claudia ground out her cigarette in the ashtray when Rachelle entered her room. "What happened to you?"

"I need your help." Rachelle walked to the bed and dropped her bags of recently purchased clothes onto it. "I'm going out with Grant tonight, and I need to wear a kick-ass outfit." Claudia was staring at her like she didn't know her. "Don't look at me like that. I didn't lose my mind."

"You took the words right out of my mouth."

"Aren't you the one who said I ought to change my image? That I was too conservative?"

"I didn't think you were gonna listen!" Claudia's eyes narrowed with suspicion. "Are you worried about Evoni?"

"No." Rachelle waved a hand dismissively. According to Claudia, Evoni had a thing for Grant—and bad—but she was the least of Rachelle's concerns. "It was time for an image change, that's all. Something more mature. Sexier."

"Sexy is right, girl. I love the cut." Claudia jumped up, squealing as she did. "Oooh, this is gonna be fun. Let me see what you bought." She dumped the contents of the bags onto the bed. "Love it, love it. Girl, what is *this*?" She held up the slinky black dress Rachelle had hemmed and hawed over purchasing. Suddenly it looked more like a dust cloth than any dress.

"It's a dress," Rachelle told her, snatching it from her hand.

"If you say so." She laughed. "Put it on."

"It's your typical form-fitting black dress. No big deal."

"C'mon. Put it on!"

"Okay. Just a second." She reached into the smaller plastic bag and pulled out a CD.

"What's that?" Claudia asked.

"A Barry White CD. I *love* his voice. I've always been into Barry, but even more so since he died last year."

"What a shame that was."

"I know. Can I put it on?"

"Of course. Shit, is this mood music for you and Grant?"

Rachelle shrugged nonchalantly as she inserted the CD into the stereo. "Maybe."

"What has gotten into you?"

Giggling, Rachelle peeled off her jeans and T-shirt. She kicked them aside, the way she was doing with her old life. She was becoming a different person. She was taking control of her life and it felt good.

"Damn, girl. That dress barely covers . . . barely covers anything."

"Can't get enough of your love, baby," Rachelle sang as she moved in front of the mirror to check herself out. The dress had spaghetti straps and a very low cut V-neck. Hell, a little lower and her belly button would be exposed. The lycra material hugged the top of her thighs. It was the kind of dress that she would have to keep pulling down, though she doubted the material would stay in place.

"You keep this up, and the Deltas will forget your family ties."

"That's what I'm hoping."

"You're really serious about not crossing over?"

Rachelle had confided in Claudia about her dilemma. She wasn't opposed to the idea of sisterhood, and perhaps if she hadn't been attached to the Etienne legacy, she would have wanted to become a Delta of her own free will. But everything in her life was thrust upon her, like she never had any choice in the matter. And no matter how good something was, if it was forced on you, you were bound to resist it in some way.

Besides, she also saw sorority life as a cover for her grandmother and mother. To the world, they were Hazel Etienne's legacy, boldly following in her footsteps to carve out a future of unity and promise for the Delta Gamma Psis. Yet behind closed doors, the two didn't practice what they preached. Family unity didn't have any meaning in their lives, and Rachelle hated hypocrisy. She didn't want to get caught up with sorority functions, working with her mother and grandmother, and pretending to the world that they were the epitome of strength and harmony.

"You didn't join a sorority," Rachelle pointed out to Claudia. "You're still having a great college experience. Maybe even better."

"Yeah, but my grandmother isn't Sylvia Grayson."

"I never wanted anything handed to me on a silver platter, anyway. Besides, I don't have the time or energy for that kind of thing." What would be next? Joining a grad chapter? Working with her mother and grandmother as a Delta for the next twenty years? Unless she fell in love, by next year she planned to be somewhere far, far away.

Claudia lit another cigarette and took a long drag. "You'll get no complaints from me about not becoming a Delta. You know how I feel about all those prissy girls. Stuck up bunch of heifers."

Rachelle couldn't agree with that, but she didn't make Claudia any wiser. It wasn't the Deltas she had a problem with. In fact, she liked the Deltas she met. She'd simply had doubts about becoming a sorority sister and being attached to her mother for years to come.

But after what her mother had done, the decision had been easy. She would not pledge. Her mother would be horrified, but too bad for her.

Rachelle focused on her reflection in the mirror. The outfit was definitely raunchy.

She smiled. She was off to a great start for her new life.

Hours later, Rachelle's stomach fluttered from a bout of nerves. She'd taken one last look at her appearance in the mirror before leaving to meet Grant and had almost suffered heart failure. Despite the secret thrill that had come earlier from knowing she was doing something her mother would despise, she now had second thoughts. She didn't care what her mother thought, but her grandmother?

This really wasn't her. The new hairstyle was drastic enough, but the whole hoochie-mama style of dress had her feeling completely out of her element.

And the high-heeled shoes with the clear plastic heels. Boy, she really did look like some type of whore.

But wasn't that what she wanted? A one-hundred-and-eighty-degree change?

In for a penny . . .

Rachelle drew in a deep breath and carefully exited the dorm's bathroom so as not to fall flat on her face. These heels were a killer. She yanked down on the hem of her skirt, but it slid back up to barely below her buttocks with every step she took.

"Shit, baby."

The sound of Grant's voice frightened her, and she whirled around. She barely managed to keep herself on her feet.

All apprehensions she had over her new image melted away when she saw the look on his face. His eyes were bulging, and his mouth hung open. Clearly, he approved.

"Grant." Rachelle spoke breathlessly. "I was just on my way out to meet you."

"Baby, baby, baby. What's gotten into you?" It was clear he hadn't heard what she said.

"Me?" Rachelle shrugged coyly. But she found herself standing taller, feeling instantly confident. Even the shoes no longer felt awkward. "Nothing."

"Nothing? A few weeks ago you were pulling the whole Virgin Mary act. Now . . . *mmm.*"

"I just needed to find myself."

"I like, girl. I definitely like." He curled an arm around her waist. "You ready? I don't want other guys lusting over my girl."

It was a pleasant surprise, but Grant's obvious appreciation of her feminine qualities made her feel powerful. She felt like a turtle coming out of its shell.

"I'm ready."

Grant whisked her outside and into his Mustang.

"Nice ride," Rachelle told him.

"Yeah, she's a pretty baby."

"So, where are we going?"

"One of the players is having a party at his place tonight. It's an apartment off campus."

As Grant started the car, he placed a hand on Rachelle's thigh. He trailed his fingers upward, nearly to the hem of her dress.

"Unless you don't want to go to the party," he suggested.

Rachelle swallowed, nervous. She was dressed like a tramp, heading off in a car with a jock. She couldn't pretend she didn't know what could happen.

"Sure I want to go. I'm looking forward to it, actually."

Grant bit down on his bottom lip, eyeing her with obvious lust. "Yeah, we'll go for a while. Then later . . ."

His statement hung in the air between them. Was she ready for what he was suggesting? She liked him, yes, but she didn't know him all that well.

She had never known any man all that well. What a joke for someone her age. And it was all because she had never been allowed to spread her wings and fly.

Tonight, whatever happened happened. She was tired of being the little girl who had always done the right thing. The little girl whose mother hated her for no good reason.

"You have any beer?" she asked. The words surprised her. She didn't advocate drinking.

"I was gonna go to one of those drive-through daiquiri shops on the way to Kevin's. Pick up a gallon of something."

"Great idea." A daiquiri was a stronger drink.

She had a feeling that tonight she would need it.

CHAPTER FORTY-SIX

Sylvia opened the door and screamed bloody murder.

Paralyzed to the spot, she screamed until her frantic screech became a terrified sob.

"Sylvia!"

Edward's voice jolted her into action. She twirled, collapsing right in Edward's arms.

"Oh, God," she bawled. "Edward, what is that?"

She felt his rapidly beating heart against her chest as he held her closer in order to look over her shoulder.

"I'm not sure. There's a lot of blood. It almost looks like a chicken's head."

Sylvia sniveled. "A what?"

Edward slowly pulled apart from her. "You stay in here. I'll . . ." He swallowed. "Take a better look."

Shaking from fear, Sylvia tried to suck in a steady breath but failed. She erupted in a fit of coughs.

God have mercy on her. What was going on? The image of whatever lay on her doorstep was committed to memory. A large, bloody mass that she knew was some dead creature.

"Yes, this most certainly was a chicken."

"Killed right on my doorstep?" she shrieked. She didn't dare turn around.

"I don't see a trail of blood anywhere else. I believe it was killed right here. And there are some other bones, some rocks."

"You think someone tortured that poor bird with rocks? Edward?"

"I'm looking at the placement . . . seems structured. Deliberate."

Sylvia's heart damn near imploded from rising panic. "Some kind of voodoo hex?"

When Edward didn't answer, she couldn't stop herself from spinning around. He looked up at her from beside the murdered bird.

"Answer me, Edward! What kind of thing is this?"

Rising slowly, he shrugged. "I can't say if it's voodoo, but like I've always maintained, voodoo is not normally used for ill."

"Then what do you call that?" Sylvia couldn't contain her hysteria.

"It could be black magic. Obeah. Or just some kids trying to get a rise out of you. If you want, I can call my high priestess and have her come inspect this."

"I want you to get rid of it!"

"But—"

"No, Edward. Get rid of it now!" Her body shuddered as she began to sob. "Please."

"Okay, okay. Just try to calm down."

Calm down? Was he serious? Someone had put some sort of curse on her and he expected her to calm down?

"Go inside, Sylvia. I'll take care of this."

Sylvia covered her mouth to stifle her cries. Her insides were clenched so tight, she could barely breathe from the pain.

Her world was crumbling. Falling apart at the very seams. And she knew exactly why.

There had been only one other time in her life when her world had come undone this way. The summer of 1975.

And one time before that.

It all came back to that. She would never escape it.

Sylvia rested her back against the wall housing the staircase. She should have drowned that night. She had wanted to. As the murky waters of the bayou had consumed her, she had welcomed the darkness and prayed for forgiveness for her sins.

But just before her head had submerged, hands had grabbed hold of her shoulders. Within moments her toes were no longer sinking into sludge; they were grazing the thick grass.

"Let me go," she had yelled. "Let me die!"

"Snap out of it," her mother had coldly said. "You've caused me enough trouble. I don't need you dying on top of it."

Sylvia struggled with whoever was holding her. Most likely the butch of a woman who had held her down earlier that evening. "Let me go!"

"Take her back to the house, Clara," her mother had said.

"No! Please, I can't go back there."

"He's there, Sylvia."

Her heart filled with hope. "He is?"

"Yes," her mother had replied. "We didn't take him away."

Sylvia cried harder at the memory. Her mother had lied to get her back to the carriage house. Then she had ordered her to go on with her life and forget what had happened, put it behind her, because no good would ever come of remembering.

Little did her mother know that the past would find her one day.

As the years went on, Sylvia had immersed herself in college. Activity in the sorority kept her busy enough to forget. She confided her secret in only one person, her best friend, Della, and Della had reiterated what her own mother had said.

"Forget it, Sylvia. It's in the past."

Sylvia had gone on to do just that. She had married, had a child. With the exception of losing her husband and her father, life had been reasonably good.

Until the summer of 1975.

Until Harvey.

He had come into her life at a time when she was least prepared for him, a time when the past had been buried so long that she didn't want to dig it up. She had achieved too much to let one indiscretion ruin everything she had worked so hard for.

But Harvey wouldn't stay away. He had taunted her by wooing Olivia, which was when Sylvia had known she had to get rid of him. She had given him thousands of dollars, praying she would never see him again.

Yet he was here again, working at Dillard.

It was all part of his sick plan for revenge.

Sylvia felt a little guilty for having thought Olivia responsible for the notes, the wine, slashing her tires. Harvey was sick. He was vengeful. Olivia was merely a pawn in his twisted game.

"Mother!"

Sylvia jumped from fear. She looked up to see Olivia, her eyes wide with frenzy.

Lord help her, did Olivia *know*?

"Have you seen Rachelle?" Olivia asked.

Sylvia felt a modicum of relief. "Not this morning, no."

"Oh, my God." Olivia threw her hands to her face. "She isn't here. She didn't come home last night."

"She didn't?"

"No! And she hasn't called. If something has happened to my baby . . ."

For the first time in a long time, Olivia actually looked vulnerable. Afraid. And Sylvia had the surprising urge to comfort her.

Yet she couldn't. At least not the way she once would have done so naturally. Perhaps this had been part of Harvey's plan all along. To drive them apart.

"You've called her cell?" Sylvia asked. Her back still hugged the wall. She was afraid to move for fear she'd crumple on the floor. One crisis was bad enough. She couldn't bear it if anything had happened to her granddaughter.

"Of course. She's never done anything like this before. Oh, Mama. What if she's hurt somewhere?"

Had Harvey gotten to her? The thought gave Sylvia the strength to move off the wall. She could not let fear cripple her.

Stepping toward Olivia, she took hold of her arm. "You call the hospitals. I'll take a drive and search for her."

"You will?"

"Why wouldn't I?" She looked her daughter square in the eye. "Try not to worry, Olivia. If something's happened to her, we'll find her."

Olivia was on her feet the moment she heard the door open. She ran from the nearby living room, asking, "Mother, did you find her?"

She stopped dead in her tracks when she saw her daughter. Relief flooded her. "Oh, my Lord." Olivia started moving again, practically pouncing on Rachelle. "Baby, are you okay?"

"Why wouldn't I be okay?"

Rachelle moved toward the stairs. Olivia was fast on her heels. "I was so worried."

"Really?"

"Of course." For the first time, Olivia took a good look at her daughter. Her previously shoulder-length hair was chopped off, but it looked like a two-year-old had done it. And the blond colored highlights?

Olivia fingered the strands. "What did you do to your hair?"

"What does it look like?"

"Sweetheart, what's wrong with you?"

Rachelle bit back the emotion that threatened to spill forth. There was a vulnerable note in her mother's voice, as if she really cared. And part of Rachelle wanted nothing more than to break down and tell her mother what had happened, then melt in her arms and let her soothe her pain. Instead, Rachelle kept the wall up—the wall her mother had built—because she didn't know how to break it down.

"I wanted to cut my hair. What's the big deal?"

"You stayed out all night."

Rachelle looked her mother dead in the eye, squared her jaw, and replied, "Yeah. I had to sleep off the hangover. Now I see why you drink so much, Ma. It's a great stress reliever."

"You were drinking?"

"Everyone does."

"You're too young to drink."

"It went down smooth just the same." Rachelle was shocked at her own bravado.

"You were with that Claudia girl, weren't you? Didn't I tell you she's not the type of girl I want you—"

"I wasn't with Claudia."

Rachelle took immense satisfaction in seeing horror flash in her mother's eyes. Finally, some sort of reaction from the Ice Queen.

"Who were you with?"

"None of your business." She started up the stairs.

"Don't walk away from me while I'm talking to you."

"I am not a child. No matter how much you think you're still entitled to control me."

"I'm not trying to control you. I'm trying to find out what's bothering you."

Rachelle reached the top of the stairs. "Like you'd care."

She felt her mother's fingers on her upper arm. "Why are you lashing out at me?"

Rachelle shook free of her mother's grip. "I just want to live my life. Why can't you let me do that? Why can't you let me be who I want to be?"

Not waiting for an answer, Rachelle turned and ran.

"Rachelle!"

She didn't stop. She slipped into her bedroom, slamming the door behind her. She turned the lock, just in case.

Her heart was pounding. She had never spoken to her mother with such disrespect before.

But she had already started the change. She wasn't going to back out now.

Seconds later, her mother was outside the bedroom door. "Rachelle, why are you acting like this? Will you open the door and tell me what's wrong? Please."

Again Rachelle felt a strange twinge in her soul. She almost wanted to open the door. But she didn't. Instead she marched to her stereo and turned it on. She put the volume way up to drown out her mother's voice.

Then she went to her closet. She withdrew a suitcase and started to pack.

CHAPTER FORTY-SEVEN

No, no, Margery. That won't do," Sylvia said into the phone. "See if you can persuade them to double their donation."

"The man I spoke with told me that was the best they could do."

"Did you speak with Gabriel Rice?"

"No."

"Call back and ask for him. Tell him you're calling on behalf of me and L.G.B. Enterprises, and I'm sure he'll be happy to give more of the company's money. I really want to raise at least fifty thousand this year. If anyone needs the money for college, it's the inner-city children of New Orleans."

"I couldn't agree more."

"Sometimes you just have to be pushier—in a polite way, of course." She would never have had to tell Della that. Her late friend knew exactly how to lay on the charm to get the most out of a company's checkbook.

Margery had only been volunteering with her organization for the past year and a half, though. Sylvia was certain she would get better with time.

The doorbell rang. "Oh, hold a second, please." Sylvia placed her hand over the mouthpiece. "Edward?"

Edward didn't reply. He was probably outside somewhere.

"Margery, I'm going to have to go." She was expecting a couriered package from her sorority's national office and couldn't risk not getting to the door in time.

"Okay. I'll see you at the meeting on Monday. Hopefully with better news."

"Yes, hopefully."

Sylvia hung up and hurried from the sunroom to the front of the house. She slowed to a stop when she saw that Olivia stood in the foyer, one hand resting on the open door.

Having heard her, Olivia turned. "Mother, there's an officer here to see you."

Sylvia's stomach dropped. It did every time she saw a police officer at her door. She drew in a sharp breath before continuing to the entrance.

Dressed in a suit, he was clearly a detective. He was tall, dark-skinned, and bald. He wore reflective sunglasses, so Sylvia couldn't see his eyes.

She said, "Yes?"

"Mrs. Grayson?"

She nodded.

"I'm Detective Brodin." He removed his sunglasses. "May I come in for a moment?"

The man would be considered attractive if he didn't look so serious. "What's this about?"

"I'd prefer to discuss this inside."

"Certainly. Come in."

A quick glance at Olivia told Sylvia that she was worried about the officer's visit, too. Rachelle had disappeared yesterday, leaving a note to say she was staying with friends for a few days. It was so unlike her. Could she have been in an accident?

"Has someone been hurt?" Sylvia asked, not able to bear another moment of suspense.

"Please don't tell me something's happened to my baby," Olivia said. Her voice quivered.

"I'm not here with bad news," Detective Brodin replied. He withdrew a handkerchief from his blazer and wiped the sweat from his forehead.

"I don't understand."

"I'm here about a murder that happened twenty-eight years ago. Liza Monroe."

"Oh, my," Sylvia exclaimed.

"So you remember the case."

"One never forgets a murder like that," Sylvia answered.

"Then you probably know that Miss Monroe's murder remains unsolved."

"Yes. And I for one never felt quite as safe in the neighborhood after that."

"Understandably." The detective gave her an odd look. "I'm here following up on some new information."

"A detective took our statements eons ago," Sylvia pointed out. "I can't see how we can be of any additional help now."

"Actually." The officer glanced away, clearly uncomfortable. "I know of your reputation in the community, Mrs. Grayson," he said as he met her eyes. "I admire you. That makes this hard."

"I don't understand."

"A tip has led to you."

Sylvia gasped. "Me?"

"Apparently when Liza was murdered, a ring was stolen from her. The department received an anonymous tip this morning that you have that ring."

"That's absurd."

"I'm sure it is. But I'm following up on every lead, and I'd like to rule it out one way or another. If you'd be so kind as to let me take a look in your room . . . ?"

Sylvia looked at Olivia. Olivia shrugged, as if to say she was as baffled as Sylvia was.

She turned back to the officer. "You're serious?"

"Afraid so."

"I should make you get a warrant," Sylvia told him. "But I have nothing to hide. I'll bring my jewelry box down."

"Why don't I go upstairs with you?" he suggested.

Sylvia was speechless. The best she could do was summon a look of distaste. If he actually thought she was going to take the ring out of the box before bringing it down for him to examine, he was crazy! She had a mind to send him out of her house and make him get a warrant.

But she said, "Fine. Let's go."

Sylvia led the way up the stairs, followed by the detective and Olivia. In her bedroom, she went straight for the jewelry box.

She handed it to him, saying, "Here you go. Though I should force you to get a warrant. I won't, however, as I have nothing to hide."

The detective carried the jewelry box to a nearby table. He slipped on latex gloves and then began to empty the contents of the box one by one. Sylvia stood over his shoulder, watching his every move, her arms crossed over her chest.

"Why would anyone say you have the ring, Mother?"

Sylvia turned toward Olivia, remembering that she was in the room. "I have no idea."

"Damn."

The detective's curse got Sylvia and Olivia's attention. Their eyes went to him expectantly.

Detective Brodin slowly raised a ring.

It was a ring Sylvia had seen twenty-eight years ago in a photo the original detective working on the case had shown her.

A ring that belonged to Liza Monroe.

The day after packing a suitcase and leaving her mother's home, Rachelle blew out a long, weary breath when Allette opened the front door. Allette, her anchor to sanity.

And in that moment, it seemed like the weight of the world crashed down on her shoulders.

What had she been thinking? Had she made a mistake she could never repair?

"What is it?" Allette asked without preamble.

Her friend knew her so well. "I . . . Allette, I messed up."

Rachelle pulled off her hat and raked her fingers through her new short do.

"Damn, what did you do to your hair?"

Started something I couldn't stop, she said silently. To Allette she said, "I wish this hair were the worst of my problems."

"Start from the beginning. And where were you Friday night? You were supposed to meet us at the soup kitchen. All the Deltas were looking forward to meeting you."

Rachelle had skipped the charity event to begin her osmosis. "I went out with Grant."

"Grant?" Allette looked at her as if she had sprouted a beard. "After he was such a jerk to you?"

"I know, but I didn't tell you—we continued to talk. He seemed like he cared about me."

"Let's go sit down." Allette took Rachelle's hand in hers and led her into the kitchen. At the small table Allette said, "Tell me what happened."

The memory of what had happened that night suddenly overwhelmed her, and Rachelle started to cry. "I had sex with him."

"Why are you crying? Did he force himself on you?"

Rachelle met Allette's eyes. Allette looked at her with not only concern but anger. Rachelle loved her friend for getting enraged on her behalf, and she was so ashamed of what she'd done that she wished she could say he had raped her. But he hadn't. She had willingly let him use her body as an instrument for his own pleasure.

Rachelle lowered her head in disgrace. "No. I don't know. Maybe I'm just upset because it wasn't what I thought it would be. I thought it would be magical and romantic." Not rough and painful. The things he had done to her . . .

"I told you Grant was bad news."

"I'm moving in with him," Rachelle blurted.

"What?"

They'd already been intimate. And she needed a place to stay now that she'd moved out of her family's home. "We can be happy together. I know it."

"Wait a second. You tell me you had sex with him and you start to cry, yet you're gonna move in with him?"

"I don't expect you to understand."

"You're damn right I don't! This isn't the kind of decision you make overnight. And for goodness sake, what's your mother going to say?"

"My mother certainly could care less."

"You don't believe that, do you?"

Rachelle shook her head as she stared at her friend. "You of all people know better than that."

"So that's what this is about. Lashing out at your mother? Seems to me you're only going to hurt yourself."

"It's a big step, I know, and maybe I have some regrets about how fast we ended up in bed, but we're a real couple now. I know moving in with him is the right thing."

"Daddy."

"What?" Rachelle asked, confused. Then she realized that Bernie had walked into the room. Sure enough, as she followed Allette's line of sight over her shoulder, she saw him standing at the entrance to the kitchen. Rachelle dragged a hand over her face and looked away.

"We were having a private conversation," Allette pointed out.

Bernie leveled a scolding look on Allette as he sauntered into the room. "What's this about you moving out?"

"Daddy, you can't just—"

"I don't want to hear any more lip from you."

Allette rolled her eyes.

Bernie turned to Rachelle. "I didn't mean to eavesdrop, but I can't pretend I didn't hear what you said. It may not be my business, Rachelle, but your mother and grandmother are friends of my family. Anything that happens to them affects us. Affects me. Moving in with a man is a serious step. Especially when you don't know him that well."

"Oh, God." He must have heard their entire conversation.

"I'm not judging you, Rachelle. Just trying to offer some advice." Bernie bent down before her, resting a hand on her knee. "Look, if you're having problems at home, you can always stay here for a little while. But don't go putting yourself in a bad situation."

Rachelle got to her feet. "I have to go."

"Rachelle—"

"Mr. Rousseaux, please." Rachelle hustled to the front door. "I just can't talk about this."

Allette scrambled after her. "Where are you going?"

"The library."

"What about later? Are you still gonna meet me?"

"Yeah. How about seven o'clock, at the fountain?"

"Okay. And Rachelle?"

Rachelle's hand was on the door, but she turned to face Allette. Bernie stood behind her.

"Whatever you're going through," Allette began, "hang in there."

"Thanks."

Rachelle was digging for her car keys inside her purse when she felt someone was watching her. Her head shot up.

Bernie smiled at her.

"Mr. Rousseaux."

"I hope I didn't scare you."

"N-no."

"Good. Listen, I wanted to catch you before you left. Maybe I can drive you to your campus and we can talk?"

"I'm driving, but thanks anyway."

Bernie slowly moved toward her. "Your father died years ago, but that doesn't mean you don't need one. Dealing with men and dating . . . you might find it helpful to talk to a man. I wanted to let you know I'd be happy to talk to you anytime."

"Oh. Well, thanks."

"I mean it. Anything you want to discuss with me. I won't judge you. But I will try to offer objective advice."

"I appreciate that."

Bernie placed his hand on her shoulder. Rachelle glanced at his fingers, then back up at him. She felt . . . she wasn't sure what she felt. Not good, not bad. Just weird.

"Take care."

She stepped away from him, away from his touch. "I have to go now."

"Of course. Enjoy your day. And remember what I said. Anytime."

"Thank you, Bernie."

Rachelle headed off in the direction of her car. When she looked over her shoulder, Bernie was still watching her.

For the last time, I have no idea how that ring got there," Sylvia said. "I did not put it in my jewelry box."

Olivia watched her mother, her heart still pounding. It hadn't stopped pounding since the detective had held up the ring that had once belonged to Liza Monroe.

"You're not helping me," the detective stated.

"You keep asking me the same questions over and over again," Sylvia retorted. "My answers aren't going to change. Clearly, someone is trying to set me up."

"You have an alarm system."

"People bypass alarm systems all the time."

The detective's gaze wandered to Olivia. "Of course, you're not the only one who lives here."

"I certainly didn't kill Liza," Olivia blurted out. "And for what it's worth, I doubt my mother did, either." But she suddenly remembered Cynthia Monroe's words that day at Liza's funeral, and she stared at her mother with more assessing eyes. There was so much her mother had kept from her. How well did she truly know her?

"Mrs. Grayson." The detective's tone was matter-of-fact. "Are you telling me there is no reason at all that you would have wanted that ring?"

"That is exactly what I'm telling you."

The detective sighed. "I know you're lying."

"Excuse me, young man?"

He placed both hands firmly on his hips. "I know why you'd want that ring, Mrs. Grayson. And worse, I know why you would have wanted Liza dead."

"You're crazy."

"You hated her. Didn't you?" The detective was getting more and more aggressive. He sounded like a prosecutor in a courtroom.

"I had no reason to hate her. I barely knew her."

"Really?"

"Yes, really."

"Are you saying that you didn't know Liza was your husband's illegitimate child?"

Olivia's eyes flew to her mother's. As her mother's face crumbled, Olivia's heart stopped beating.

"Mrs. Grayson?"

Sylvia closed her eyes for several moments. She didn't deny the detective's words.

"This . . ." Sylvia swallowed. Her eyes fluttered open. She wouldn't meet the detective's gaze. "This is all a big, big misunderstanding."

"What are you saying?" Olivia asked the detective. "Liza was my father's child?"

"Mrs. Grayson?" the detective prompted, clearly hoping she would answer Olivia's question.

"Mama?" Olivia reverted to her childhood name for her mother. "This isn't true, right? I mean, how could it be? If Liza was my sister . . . she wasn't, was she? Mama!"

When Sylvia finally faced her, Olivia saw tears brimming in her eyes. "I did not kill that girl," she said. "I swear."

"Oh, my God." Olivia clamped a hand over her mouth. Liza *had* been her sister? How could this be true? "Liza . . ."

"Cynthia Monroe was a whore!" Gone was Sylvia's stoic composure. "A filthy, dirty whore who tried to trap your father with a pregnancy! She didn't even love him. She wanted his money. He gave her plenty, but still she wouldn't let him see the child she claimed was his. Not unless he left me, which he refused to do."

"And that's why you killed her daughter," the detective proclaimed as though it were fact. "Because it was the one way you knew to hurt her."

"That's not true."

"And with Liza's death, the payments stopped. You didn't have to pay another dime to her from your husband's estate. Sounds like a pretty damning motive for murder."

Sylvia was on her feet, slapping her hands onto the table. "I hated that woman, but I didn't kill Liza. I would never kill anyone!"

"Wow. That's quite the temper, Mrs. Grayson."

"How the hell do you expect me to react? You came over here pretending to be nice, all so that you could accuse me of murder."

"Why do you have this ring? A ring your husband had given to his illegitimate daughter?"

A tear streamed down Sylvia's face.

"I think we should continue this discussion at the station."

"There's nothing to discuss."

"Seems there's plenty to discuss."

Sylvia caught a shaky breath as she brushed at loose hairs hanging in her face. "Is this mandatory?"

The detective didn't answer right away. Instead he turned and walked to the nearby window, then retraced his steps. "If you've got nothing to hide, you'll come in."

"And if you have anything on me, you'll have to arrest me."

Sylvia and Detective Brodin stared each other down. He was the first to back down, nodding his understanding.

"Don't leave town, Mrs. Grayson. In the meantime, I need to take this ring in for evidence. Cynthia Monroe will confirm if this is indeed the one her daughter was wearing before her disappearance."

"Maybe she's the one who put it in here," Sylvia suggested. "That woman has always had it out for me."

"I'll see myself out."

Detective Brodin breezed out of the room. Olivia waited until she could no longer hear his footfalls before turning to her mother. There were more tears. Mascara darkened Sylvia's eyes, making her look like a clown.

She could very well have been one, for how well Olivia knew her.

"Liza was my sister?"

Sylvia covered her face and turned away.

"No." Olivia marched across the room and stood in front of her mother. She yanked her hands from her face, forcing her to look at her. "Don't you do this."

"This isn't the time, Olivia."

"It's never the time with you."

"This is a setup. The strange letters I've gotten, my tires being slashed—the same person must have put the ring in here."

"You think I give a crap about the damn ring? You owe me answers about Liza!"

"Your father owes you answers. He's the one who had an affair."

"Something you knew plenty about. You knew about Liza. You knew, yet you never said a word. Hell, you were *paying* her."

"What exactly did you want me to tell you? That that whore was probably your sister?"

"If it was the truth!"

"I didn't want you embracing her. Wanting to be like her."

"You had no right!"

"I had every right. I'm your mother."

"No." Olivia shook her head. "I don't even know you. I don't think I ever did. What else is there? What else are you hiding in hopes of pretending you're the picture of morality?"

"Close the door on your way out."

"Did you kill Liza?"

"Go be with Harvey. I don't care anymore. This whole family's falling apart."

"Now I know why you never moved downtown. You walk around with your nose in the air, acting like you're better than everyone else, yet you don't live in a more affluent neighborhood with the rest of the snobs. Here, you can be the queen of the hood. Everyone looks up to you. But there . . . you'd be afraid that someone would find you out, learn that you're a fraud."

"That's not true. This is my home. Mine and your father's. He loved it here, felt more comfortable here than anywhere else."

"And where you could keep an eye on Liza, right?"

"Get out, Olivia." When Olivia didn't move, her mother said, "*Now!*"

Olivia flinched from the harshness of her mother's tone. God help her, she wanted to grab her and shake the truth out of her.

"You're gonna have to talk to me sometime," Olivia told her.

Sylvia didn't answer.

Olivia marched out of the room and slammed the door hard. A family picture gracing the wall in the hallway fell to the ground. The glass broke, marring the smiling faces of Olivia, Sylvia, and Rachelle.

CHAPTER FORTY-EIGHT

It seems the whole world around my family is falling apart." Sighing, Olivia rolled over, resting her head against Harvey's shoulder. "My mother a suspect in Liza's murder? Two weeks ago, I never would have believed it. Now I'm not so sure. I look at my mother and can honestly say I don't know her."

"I'm sorry," Harvey said.

"She mentioned something about it being a setup, but when I think back, she didn't say anything about the letters or her car being vandalized to the detective. Why wouldn't she, if she had nothing to hide?"

"Even twenty-eight years ago, it was obvious your mother had secrets. But I never would have thought her capable of killing Liza."

"I have no clue what to think anymore." Olivia moaned. "As if that wasn't bad enough, I have no clue what's going on with Rachelle. She's staying out all hours, not coming home for days. I'm thankful she wasn't home when the detective came around, but she still hasn't been home since and doesn't even know what's going on. She called and said she's spending more time on campus sleeping in a friend's room because it's easier, but I have the feeling she's mad at me. Or maybe something else is going on in her life. I don't know. She keeps slipping away, and there's nothing I can do to stop it."

"You want my opinion?"

"Of course."

"My guess is that she's going through something," Harvey said. "I've noticed the changes with her in the classroom. She seems more withdrawn, despite the drastic external changes." He exhaled sharply. "Maybe this is my fault."

Olivia jerked her head up to look into his eyes. "Why would you say that?"

"Because of our relationship. We've both jumped headlong into it again."

"She doesn't know that."

"But she knows something is up. I asked her about you, and she had to wonder why. Since then, she's pretty much kept her distance from me. As for you, you haven't been home much these days. Maybe that's why she hasn't turned to you with whatever she's going through."

"I'm still her mother. Whatever's going on in her life, she ought to know she can come to me. I couldn't talk to my own mother because she was always so rigid. So controlling. She refused to let me date. She was always on my back. Questioning my every move. Keeping me in shackles, practically. She kept things from me, outright lied. Look what she did to make sure you were out of my life. And after all that, what did she gain? I pulled away emotionally, and even now we don't get along the way we should. I don't want to make the same mistake with my daughter."

Harvey didn't say anything.

"What?" Olivia asked, knowing his silence meant something.

"I don't know."

Olivia eased herself up on one elbow. "I'm not going to stop spending time with you, if that's what you're insinuating."

"No, I'm suggesting that you tell her what's going on."

"Between us?"

"Yeah. You barely got finished saying that your mother kept secrets from you and that was part of the problem."

"I know. And I am planning to tell Rachelle. I'm just waiting for the right time."

"Is that the only issue?"

"Meaning?"

"Meaning Rachelle isn't your mother. She won't necessarily disapprove of our relationship."

"I know, but—" Olivia stopped, her words surprising her. Harvey was right. How had he figured out her reservations when she hadn't?

"And even if she does have problems with us seeing each other, she still ought to hear about us from you."

Olivia ran a finger along Harvey's shoulder. "I remember the past and all my mother did to keep us apart. And I so desperately want everything to be right. Some children never accept a parent's new partner. I want Rachelle to accept you."

"She can't accept me if she doesn't know about me."

"I know."

"And she's an adult. Not an immature child who'll have trouble seeing her mother move on."

"She shouldn't, but there were other men after Arthur." Olivia's voice softened. She felt shame over her affairs with most of those men. She hadn't loved any of them. "She wasn't happy about them. It made things much more difficult."

Harvey sat up. "So what are you saying?"

Olivia placed a hand on Harvey's naked chest. "Sweetheart, please. Don't get angry. You know I want our relationship out in the open. More than ever."

"Good. Because I've waited a long time to be with you again. I won't be your dirty little secret."

"You could never be that."

Olivia took Harvey's hand in hers and kissed it. He was right, and she was tired of hiding, anyway. Come what may, she would inform Rachelle of their relationship. "As soon as I see her again, I'll tell her all about us."

Rachelle drove through the Garden District, her mind deep in thought. After talking with Allette and Bernie, she had decided against going to Grant's place last night. She had opted to hang with Claudia instead, but this morning she regretted the decision. Claudia had practically forgotten all about her the moment Dion had shown up. Dion was her thug boyfriend, and the way the two had behaved last night with her in the room . . . Rachelle still couldn't believe it.

She wasn't that much of a prude. She knew that men and women should carry on their intimate relations in private.

Not with another person in the room who they thought was sleeping. Or maybe they hadn't even cared.

Worse than listening to their grunting and moaning and kissing and slapping, Rachelle had had to sleep on the floor so that Dion could share Claudia's bed.

All to avoid seeing Grant. And why? Because she hadn't been able to face him after all the sexual things he had done to her. But maybe that was one area where she *was* a prude. Because hearing the way Claudia and Dion had carried on made it obvious that lovemaking wasn't all sweet and romantic the way it was portrayed in the movies and on soap operas.

There really was no point in avoiding Grant any longer. She couldn't go back home. And she couldn't stay with Allette. Oh, she could try, but Belinda would call her mother, and in an instant her mother would be there, taking her back to the house.

Rachelle watched a trolley make its way along the tree-lined street as she slowly drove. She pulled into the parking lot of a restaurant and turned off her car.

She got out and stretched. Overhead, she heard the loud chirping of the green palm parrots that lived in the area. She glanced up, spotting the birds.

And suddenly she wanted to cry.

Her father had shown her her first parrot. She remembered the time with fondness. She remembered everything about her father. His salt-and-pepper hair. The wrinkles around his eyes when he smiled. His soft voice and gentle nature. She missed him so much. When he was around, her life had been normal.

It was stupid, childish even, to wish she could go back in time. Because it could never happen. But that's what she wanted.

She wanted to start over. She wanted to relive her past, but this time with a mother who cared for her. One who would take her on walks in the park, take her by the lake with a loaf of bread to feed the ducks. Was that too much to ask for? She had had that with her father and to some degree with her mother when her father had still been alive.

But since his death, all Rachelle had gotten was chaos and dysfunction.

There was no way she wanted to go back to that. Not now. Not ever. And that's what would happen if she returned home.

The memory of her father's death made Rachelle remember something Claudia had said yesterday. "Hey, you know what people are saying? They're saying that your family has the black widow curse."

"The black widow curse?"

"Yeah. Every man who marries into your family dies." Claudia laughed.

"That's not funny," Rachelle had told her. She had never known her grand-father, and her father had died well before she was ready to lose him.

"Hey, sorry. I heard it and I thought . . . well, I thought you'd get a kick out of it."

"Not hardly. Who said that?" And who knew so much about her family?

"I just heard it around," Claudia had answered. "Probably one of those sorority girls started it. You gotta watch your back where they're concerned."

"Yeah, it seems like it," Rachelle had replied. She had been deeply disap-pointed by the rumor. Were people trying to make fun of her, or were they clueless about how such words could hurt a person?

Her mind went back to Grant. What if he heard the rumor? Would he want to stay away from her?

"That's just too silly," Rachelle said aloud. She shouldn't even let it bother her.

The issue now was how they felt about each other. Was she rushing her feelings for him? Not until this moment did she realize how much she wanted a man who could sweep her away from all her problems, save her from her wretched life.

Did Grant really care for her? That was the question that was driving her nuts. They'd had sex, he seemed to like her . . . could she now consider him her boyfriend?

Rachelle sighed. What did she know about men? She'd lived her adolescent years in a household of women. Except for Edward, but he didn't count.

If only she knew what to expect. She didn't want to jump to conclusions.

Bernie had suggested she talk to him. She had never gotten to know him well, but maybe she should.

But not yet.

Rachelle headed back to her car. Claudia said that Grant was only mean when he was drinking, and from what she knew of him, that was true. Perhaps she could get him not to drink so much. He would do that if he cared for her, wouldn't he?

As for her, she was through with alcohol. That had been an attempt to hide from her pain, but she was now ready to move on with her life in a positive direction.

With a man she could be happy with.

Rachelle settled behind the steering wheel. She felt better. She would go with her gut and head to Grant's place. Her gut said that Grant cared for her. And if he cared for her, he wouldn't turn her away in her time of need.

CHAPTER FORTY-NINE

Trying to work was futile.

Sylvia slammed the day planner shut, then pushed it off the table. Loose papers went flying—important papers that had to do with the scholarship drive—but she could care less. She didn't care if she never stepped foot outside this room again.

She was alone. Rachelle hadn't returned home. Olivia had left after their argument and had been gone for the night. Sylvia had pushed her away, not sure how to break down the wall she had erected around herself. Not sure how to simply talk to her daughter.

And right now she wanted to talk to her. Desperately. She wanted to turn to someone with all that weighed on her soul. Della was the one friend she had told everything growing up, but Della had passed away nearly three years ago.

Sylvia felt more alone than ever, and the sad thing was, she had only herself to blame. She wasn't getting any younger. The last thing she wanted was to die an old, lonely woman.

Was it too late for her and Olivia to repair their relationship? Sylvia was a God-fearing woman. It was important that she had faith. Anything was possible through Christ.

And something as crucial as this . . . she had to try.

It was the only way she could get through to her about Harvey.

She hadn't even seen the man again, yet he had sent her world into a tailspin. His threat to bring her secrets to light in that first letter had become a reality. He was responsible for the ring, she was sure, which meant it was even more important for Olivia to stay away from him.

Harvey *was* a murderer.

Back in 1975, she had tossed the idea around but hadn't really believed it. Now she knew without a doubt that it was true. She didn't know what had happened to him in his life, but Harvey was one sick man.

Sick enough to try to get to her through her daughter.

He knew she couldn't possibly stand by and ignore his affair with Olivia. He was forcing her hand, making sure she admitted to her sin.

So many years she had kept this secret, how could she bring it to light now? Yet she had to, for the sake of her daughter and her family.

Sylvia clasped her hands together where she sat and closed her eyes. "Lord, please guide me. This is probably the hardest thing I will ever have to do, but I can't be afraid. I can't worry about myself, not anymore. Give me the strength to do what I have to do. I know that Olivia may never forgive me, and help me to deal with that reality should it come to that. But my heart's desire, dear Lord, is that we can repair our relationship. It has been far too long since we have been a true family. I want to leave the dark days behind me. With Your direction I know all things are possible."

Sylvia finished her prayer. A feeling of determination came over her as she opened her eyes and stood.

There was only one thing she could do. And she would do it.

Feeling somewhat better, she went downstairs. A walk in the backyard, perhaps near Rosa's grave, would be nice right about now.

She rounded the corner from the staircase toward the back of the house. That's when she saw the dead crow on her floor.

She fainted dead away.

When Rachelle walked into Grant's dorm building and saw him sitting in the common area with Evoni, her stomach dropped.

Damn the woman. It didn't matter what Grant told her, Rachelle knew she was trouble. The way she was laughing and staring at Grant made it clear that she wanted him.

Rachelle's chest tightened. What if she'd already had him? Of course. Last night, when Rachelle had told Grant that she was studying and couldn't see him.

He hadn't wasted a bloody minute.

Feeling like a fool, Rachelle quickly spun around. She was almost at the door when she heard her name.

She stopped. Turned.

"Hey, baby. What are you doing here?"

"Weren't expecting me, I see." She hated that she sounded upset. Grant didn't deserve any reaction from her.

"What does that mean?"

"This is the second time I've seen you with Evoni."

"She hangs out here a lot."

"But not with her man. Why's she always with you?"

"Look, don't start anything. If you're with me, you have to trust me."

Rachelle looked past him to the woman. Every time she saw her, she felt uneasy. Evoni was any man's dream girl.

She was staring at her and Grant with interest. Rachelle's gut said that Evoni wanted him. Was Grant blind, or did he know it, too?

"She's just . . . she's very pretty."

Grant lightly touched her cheek. "She's not you."

Such a simple response, but Rachelle's mood instantly changed. She couldn't help feeling giddy and high inside. No one had ever said anything so nice to her.

Grant looked down. For the first time, he noticed her large duffel bag. "Hey. What's this?"

Rachelle blew out a gush of air. "Can I stay with you? I don't know if they allow that in the frat house, but I need a place to chill for a while. I can't go home."

"What happened?"

"Nothing. I just . . . I just needed to leave. So, can I?"

"Sure, baby."

"Great." She dropped the bag and put her arms around him. "Thank you."

"No need to thank me. You're my girl."

Evoni strolled by leisurely, heading toward the dorm's exit. Her eyes met

Rachelle's. She didn't look away. Then her lips lifted in a grin before she slipped out the door.

O livia, thank God."
       Olivia dropped her keys to the floor as her hand went to her heart. "Mother. You scared the life out of me. What are you doing here sitting in the dark?"

Sylvia gripped a banister railing and slowly rose from her seat on the step. "I called your cell phone. It was off."

"Oh, God. It's Rachelle. Something's happened."

"No." Sylvia shook her head. "I need to speak with you about something. Something important."

A cold chill swept over Olivia. "You're sick." It was a statement.

"No. That's not what this is about. You told me not too long ago that I owed you answers, and you're right. What I'm going to tell you is something I should have told you a long time ago."

Olivia bent to retrieve her keys, then placed both her keys and her purse on the nearby hall table. "About Liza?"

"Let's talk in the sunroom."

"Where's Edward?" Olivia asked as she followed her mother. "And why are most of the lights off in here?"

Sylvia didn't answer. She continued to walk with determined strides to the back of the house.

In the sunroom, the shadows of the leaves from the backyard trees danced against the windows. The contrast of darkness and moonlight made the hanging moss resemble human heads and other body parts.

Sylvia quickly turned on one of the lamps, hoping to dispel the eerie atmosphere. The artificial light blocked the images from outside.

Facing her daughter, Sylvia said, "I know I asked if you were responsible for sending me those letters—"

"Mother," Olivia interjected.

"No, hear me out. It's not a mystery that you've been angry with me for a very long time. That's why it was easy for me to want to accuse you of being the one trying to hurt me. But in my heart, I know you wouldn't set out to destroy me. I want to apologize for ever thinking, even for a moment, that you could."

"Wow." A slow breath oozed out of Olivia. "I'm surprised. Apology accepted."

"Please sit. There's a lot I have to say."

Olivia did as she was told. Sylvia, however, stayed on her feet.

"I suppose Rachelle's going to have to hear this, too. But I haven't seen her for the past couple nights. Do you know where she's staying?"

"I believe she's with a friend on campus." Olivia couldn't bring herself to admit that she had no clue where her daughter was.

"I guess it's just as well. Even though she should, I'm not sure I want her to hear this."

"Hear what?"

"Please bear with me, Olivia. I don't know how to start. This is painful." Sylvia clasped her hands together and held them under her chin. She moaned softly, then said, "But I can't . . . I can't keep this a secret any longer."

Be sure your sins will find you out.

This was her day of reckoning. All those years of trying to keep the past buried had only made this moment that much more painful.

"Someone wants to destroy this family. Destroy me. I could have ignored the letters and even my vandalized car. Even the dead chicken outside. But not Liza's ring. And not . . . not the crow."

"The crow? I'm not following you."

"There was a dead crow in the house today." With each word, Sylvia's voice grew in pitch. "Same as when my auntie Nora took ill and died when I was a child. I knew then that a bird in the house meant death. And that's what someone wants now. For one of us to die. Me, I'm sure."

Olivia tried to process everything her mother was saying. "What do you mean there was a dead crow in here? Someone put it in here, or you think it flew in before? And what chicken are you talking about?"

"There is no doubt that someone put that crow in here." Sylvia closed her eyes, then slowly reopened them. "I didn't tell you about the chicken because I thought you knew. I thought you were behind it, no matter how crazy that seems now. Edward wanted to call in some voodoo priestess to check it out."

"You think it was some kind of voodoo?"

"I didn't want to know. It was easier that way. But now—yes, I do. At least it was meant to look like voodoo or black magic and scare me."

"This all sounds crazy."

"Of course it does. It *is* crazy. But now I know that whoever killed the chicken on our porch did so as a warning. But he didn't get what he wanted and that's why he went a step further and put a dead bird in the house."

Sylvia collapsed onto the loveseat. Olivia stared at her with increasing worry. It wasn't all the bird talk but the bizarre look in her mother's eyes. It was a look she had never seen before, somewhere between panic, shame, and downright fear.

Was this paranoia, dementia, or something worse?

"Why would someone want you dead?"

"Because of something that happened a long time ago. Something I did."

"So you know who this is."

"Yes." Sylvia waited a beat, then said, "Harvey."

Olivia drew up short. Then scowled. Once again, she'd fallen hook, line, and sinker for one of her mother's stories. But this was another ploy to get her away from Harvey.

Her sense of disappointment was profound. To think she'd actually started feeling sorry for her mother!

"You're wasting your breath if you start bashing Harvey. I love him, and there's nothing you can do now to keep us apart. No more lies, no more manipulation. I'm an adult, completely entitled to make my own decisions."

The pained expression on her mother's face made Olivia shut up.

"Oh, Olivia. You don't understand. That's what I'm trying to do now. Make you understand. You think I didn't like Harvey . . . it wasn't that. But I have every reason to believe that he is the one out to destroy this family."

Olivia shot to her feet, not in the mood to listen to another smear campaign.

"Sit. Unless you truly hate me enough to not care what happens to me."

There was something in her mother's tone, a note of helplessness, that made Olivia do what she commanded.

"That's not fair, Mama. I . . . I don't hate you. Of course I don't want anyone to hurt you."

"I don't hate you either." Sylvia's eyes met and held Olivia's. "No matter what you think about what I did all those years ago. And I need you to listen to me, Olivia. Just listen."

Olivia honored her mother's request and stayed silent. Several beats passed before Sylvia spoke. "As I was saying, I liked Harvey. If I didn't, I wouldn't have hired him. But some things happened that led me to believe he was out to blackmail me back then. Or even worse."

"Blackmail?" Olivia looked at her mother as if she'd just turned green. "Do you hear yourself? I don't know what's going on with the birds and the letters, but where Harvey is concerned, you are completely paranoid. Why the hell—"

"Because I'm his mother!"

Sylvia's body shook now that she'd blurted out her life's burden, but she didn't feel any better. She was hurting Olivia all over again, when all along she'd only wanted to protect her. Olivia had been sleeping with Harvey, her half-brother, and there was nothing that could change the horror of that truth.

The eerie silence ended when Olivia's laughter filled the air. She laughed until she was almost breathless.

"Oh, Mama." Olivia placed a hand on her chest as she began to calm down. "That is the craziest thing I've ever heard."

Sylvia felt a spurt of anger. "You—you think I would make something like this up? Do you think so lowly of your own mother, the woman who brought you into this world?

"I had *two* children, Olivia," Sylvia continued. "You weren't my first. Five years before you, I had a son. A son my mother made me give away."

Olivia looked at her mother, really looked at her, and seemed at last to finally hear her. "You had a son?"

"I was a teenager."

"*You* had a son?"

"I wasn't a wild and crazy teenager; it just happened. I thought Clinton loved me. But he didn't stand by me once I told him I was pregnant." Sylvia waved a dismissive hand. "I'm sure that didn't make a lick of sense. But it's really not the issue. The issue is, I had a son. And when Harvey showed up all those years ago, some things started to click, started to make me realize that he could be my child. Maybe he didn't know it; I suspected he was looking for his parents. And when you started to fall for him . . . Olivia, can't you see that I had to do anything I could to prevent that? *Anything?*"

"No." Olivia slowly stood. Her stomach was roiling. She wanted to wretch. "This . . . this can't be true."

"You must know him well enough to know his age. Is there a five-year difference between you two?"

Olivia thought a minute, then her face crumbled.

"Do you see now, Olivia? Do you see that I'm not crazy?"

Olivia paced back and forth like a caged lion, and Sylvia could only imagine what was going through her mind. What she was feeling. If it was a fraction of what she was experiencing right now, her daughter would wish she could simply disappear.

Olivia faced her, saying, "But you can't be sure. Fine, you had a son. But it could be anyone."

"I saw a clairvoyant. Years before Harvey ever came to town. And she told me that my son would show up in my life when I least expected it. When I was least prepared for it."

The room was spinning. Olivia thought she might faint. "That's not proof of anything."

"Just after Harvey started working for me, my son's father called my mother out of the blue, trying to reach me. He apparently had something important to tell me. At that time, I couldn't imagine what he could want, considering how he had left my life. Then it made sense. He must have been calling to warn me that Harvey was coming to town to find me."

"You didn't talk to him?" Olivia asked incredulously.

"I tried. When I finally got around to calling him back, he'd been killed in a car accident days earlier."

"That's a bizarre coincidence." Olivia started to pace again. But she remembered Harvey's words, his admission that he was in town to find his mother.

Lord help her.

Olivia asked, "Did he tell you? Tell you that he was in town to find his mother? Is that why you made sure you got rid of him?"

"No," Sylvia responded, her voice a frightened whisper. "My God, Olivia. Is that what he told you?"

Olivia didn't answer. She shouldn't have said anything. Shouldn't have given her mother any more reason to believe that Harvey could actually be her child.

Because it couldn't be true.

"Good Lord. He *did* tell you he was in town looking for his mother. Do you see now?" Sylvia asked. "Now do you believe me?"

"It doesn't make sense," Olivia told her. "If Harvey is—is your son—and came looking for you—then he'd know I was his . . ."

Olivia's voice trailed off. She couldn't say the word.

"His sister."

"Don't say that! Damn, I need a drink."

"Alcohol won't save you from this awful truth. If it could, I'd get you some myself. And you know how much I hate your drinking."

For the first time, Olivia reacted to the news. She pressed her back to the wall and slid down until her butt hit the floor.

"Harvey couldn't have known. No, this can't be true."

"If he knew, Olivia, that would make him sick. Maybe that was his way of torturing me."

"He didn't know." Olivia sobbed softly. "He couldn't have known. If you saw him with me . . . he was so sweet. He's not sick. If you are in fact his mother, it is a complete coincidence that he ended up working for you."

"It's a possibility." But Sylvia said the words simply to make things a little better for Olivia. "All I know is that Harvey is back in town, and now I'm getting these veiled threats from someone who clearly knows about my past."

Olivia dragged a hand over her face and stared ahead of her. Stared but didn't see anything.

She would give anything to undo her mother's revelation.

But she couldn't.

There was only one thing she could do.

Talk to Harvey.

And find out if there was any possible way that she'd fallen in love with her brother.

CHAPTER FIFTY

Rachelle giggled as Grant kissed her neck. "Not here, Grant."

"Why not?" He sounded completely serious.

Rachelle looked around but couldn't see anything in the darkness. They had been on their way back from the cafeteria when Grant had stopped and swept her into his arms. "Because we have a room to go to."

"Trey's probably up there."

"We can ask him to leave."

Grant squeezed her ass. "I don't want an audience, baby. After last night, you know how loud the dorm can be. I wouldn't put it past those guys to stand outside my door and listen."

Grant had said the same thing last night. In fact, because of his concerns, they hadn't made love. While Trey had taken a shower, they had kissed and fondled each other, but they hadn't had time to have sex. Rachelle hadn't minded one bit.

"I don't know . . ." Rachelle looked around again. "I sort of feel like someone is watching us. Don't you?"

"You're just shy about making love out in the open. Under the stars."

Making love. The words made her cringe. What she and Grant had done days ago could not be described that way.

He took her hand. "Come on. Let's go somewhere a little more private."

Despite her reservations, she let him lead her along the cobblestone path away from the dining hall and onto the grass that led to a more private area among the sprawling magnolia trees.

When he slipped his arms around her and pulled her close, this time he was gentler than he had been the first time. Rachelle was pleasantly surprised.

It was the alcohol, she told herself, that thought making her feel better.

Grant kissed her cheek, then moved his lips to her neck. "You smell good, baby." He glided his hands down her back and cupped her backside. "I've been dreaming about this magnificent body of yours ever since Friday night." He edged her dress up and caressed her bare butt. "You have no clue how crazy it made me to have you sleeping in my bed last night, but not being able to have you the way I wanted."

Rachelle slowly looped her hands around Grant's neck. The apprehension she had over their second sexual encounter drained from her body. He was so much better at seducing her when he wasn't drunk.

He pulled her down onto the grass with him. Pushing her skirt up around her waist, he said, "Let me please you."

"Grant—what are you doing?"

"Just lie back and enjoy."

"Wait. Did you hear that?"

"Relax, baby. I'm gonna make you feel like you've never felt before."

She strained to listen but suddenly didn't hear anything else. Her senses were tuned to what Grant was doing.

Rachelle tried to stay perfectly still, but when she felt his head between her legs, her body flinched.

"Relax."

She squeezed her eyes shut, certain she would die of embarrassment. No man had ever done anything like this to her before.

"How's that feel, baby?"

"Mmm . . . I . . ."

He used a finger to play with her, and Rachelle moaned her sudden pleasure. "Oh, yeah. That's it."

Rachelle dug her hands into the grass as his mouth covered her. A few deep breaths and she finally let her reservations go. Opened herself up to this new experience.

His tongue was making her feel new and wonderful sensations. Every inch of her being was more alive than it had ever been.

She was on fire. This felt delicious.

Oh, yeah, she could get used to this.

Sweetheart. What are you doing here so early?" A grin as wide as Texas spread across Harvey's face when he saw Olivia. But the grin went flat when she marched past him into his home.

"What's the matter?" Harvey asked. He walked toward her, placing his hands on her shoulders.

She shrugged away from him and turned. She couldn't meet his eyes.

"I did something." It was a statement, but there was confusion in his voice.

Olivia had barely made it through the night, her mind replaying her mother's revelation. She had been afraid to see Harvey. Afraid to find out if the worst could be true. But by the morning she had known that she couldn't go on without being certain. Thankfully, Harvey didn't have a class until the afternoon. That would give them a chance to talk.

"When you . . . when you came to New Orleans all those years ago." Olivia exhaled loudly, sadly. "I think about it now, and you were so secretive about everything." She whirled to face him. "My mother told me something last night . . . something too horrible to believe."

"About me?"

Olivia nodded.

"You know she's never liked me, Olivia."

"This is beyond liking and not liking." And, God help her, it was too appalling to think, much less say. She didn't want to say it, because saying it would make it real. And what if Harvey's answers made her worst nightmares come true?

"My mother's been getting some nasty letters. Threatening letters. Would you know anything about that?"

Harvey looked at her with surprise. "Of course not. How could you even ask me that?"

"Because you've said a couple things . . . talked about people like her getting what's coming to them. I know you're angry with her, and maybe your anger goes deeper than I ever imagined."

She studied Harvey and felt sick with the prospect of the truth. She quickly looked away. "You came back to town out of the blue . . ."

"It wasn't out of the blue. I got a job here."

"Because you wanted to punish my mother?"

"Because in my crazy fantasies, I thought that maybe I would find you again. And I did."

Olivia whimpered, and she shot a hand over her mouth to stifle the cry.

"Olivia, what is it?" He reached for her, but again she stepped away from him. "Whatever it is, you need to tell me."

"Mama says . . . she says . . . she thinks . . . oh, God."

"What, damn it?"

Meeting his gaze, Olivia replied, "She thinks she's your mother! And I remember, that time I asked why you'd come to New Orleans, you said you were looking for your mother whom you'd never known."

Harvey gaped at her. "That's what this is about?"

"I need to know if it's true? If you knew all along . . ."

This time, Olivia didn't move away when Harvey touched her. Oh, how she wanted to fall against his chest and know that it was right.

"Calm down."

"How the hell can you tell me to calm down?"

"Because you're not my sister, Olivia." Harvey spoke calmly and clearly. Matter-of-factly. "My God, do you think that if I even thought you could be my sister, that I'd get involved with you the way I have?"

He spoke with such confidence that Olivia allowed a smidgen of hope to burn in her heart. But there were still so many questions.

"But my mother had a son. She's certain you're him."

"I'm not."

"You're sure?"

"Yes, I'm sure. I knew who my mother was, Olivia. I was raised by my father and he told me all about her. My mother couldn't raise me on her own, so she relinquished her rights to me. She and my father lost contact over the years, but he knew where her family was. After my father went to jail and I got into trouble with my cousin, I decided to head to New Orleans to find my mother. I hoped she would take me in."

"Did you find her?"

Harvey shook his head. "No. I didn't find out until later, because my father hadn't wanted to tell me. But my mother . . . she died. She was working the streets as a prostitute."

"Oh, Harvey." Olivia placed a palm on his cheek. "I'm sorry."

"Listen, I'm not even concerned about that right now."

"You don't know how bad I felt. Because I love you so much. If you were my half-brother . . ."

"I'm not."

"My mother said that if you were and you knew back then, then getting involved with me would be some sick form of payback."

"Olivia, if you want me to get you proof, I will. I am not out to get your mother, despite what she did to us. And I am most definitely not your brother. You want to take a DNA test, let's do it."

Hope burned within her like a roaring fire. It could not be squelched. The man she loved was not her brother.

"No. We don't need a DNA test to tell me what I already know. You're the man I love, Harvey. I believe you. And I trust you. I always have."

He kissed her. She kissed him back without hesitation, not giving her mother's words another thought.

When Grant headed off for a biology class the next morning, Rachelle decided to get up and check her voice mail. Not wanting to be reached, she had kept her cell phone off.

Trey was out cold in the bed on the opposite wall. He didn't stir as Rachelle rummaged around in her tote bag until she found her cell.

She dialed her number and punched in her access code. An automated voice told her that she had seven new messages.

"Rachelle, sweetheart, it's your mother. Please call me. Let me know you're okay."

Rachelle scowled at the sound of her mother's voice. As if she cared whether or not she was okay. She deleted the message.

"Rachelle, it's Nadine. We missed seeing you on Sunday. Give me a call when you get a chance."

Rachelle skipped that message and went on to the next one. "It's Allette. Wondering where you are. You never showed for the volunteer drive at the soup kitchen. Your mother doesn't know where you are either and she's concerned. Call me."

Rachelle deleted the message.

The next four messages were from her mother, each new one sounding more urgent than the previous. In the final one, her mother said that she needed her to come home right away because she had something important to tell her.

Another ploy?

"I hope you're going crazy, Ma," Rachelle said smugly. "You never should have done the unthinkable."

But Rachelle's satisfaction was short-lived. She couldn't very well stay away forever. And now that she knew she could stay with Grant indefinitely, there was no reason for her not to head home and get more of her things. She wouldn't let her mother or grandmother bully her into not leaving once she got there.

She glanced at the digital clock on Grant's night table. Her first class wasn't until the afternoon. That would give her time to quickly head to the house, then come back and grab a bite to eat in the cafeteria.

Maybe Grant would join her for lunch.

She smiled like an idiot as she remembered their night together. Unlike the first time, their lovemaking had been incredible. Grant had done everything in his power to please her, to make her go totally wild with lust, and he had succeeded.

Living with him was right, as she had known it would be.

Rachelle glanced at Trey. A pillow over his face, he hadn't moved. She doubted she would wake him if she made a call.

Hopefully Allette hadn't left the house yet. She dialed her friend's number. "Hello?"

Rachelle sat up straight. The voice was quaking, as though she had been crying. "Allette?"

There was sniveling. "No, dear."

"Mrs. Rousseaux?"

"That you, Rachelle?"

"Yes, ma'am."

"Girl, your mama is so worried about you." She no longer sounded like she'd been crying. "Where are you?"

"At school. I'm fine. Tell her not to worry."

"You know you have to tell her that yourself."

"I know. And I will." Rachelle paused. "But I was hoping Allette is there."

"Yes, she is. One moment. But please do call your mama."

"Okay."

Rachelle heard the receiver being placed on a hard surface. It took Allette a couple minutes to pick up. "Hey," she said, sounding out of breath. "What's up with you? I've been so worried. So have your mama and grandma."

"Nothing's up. Just returning your call."

"What happened to you Sunday night?"

"I couldn't make it."

"Couldn't make it? Let me guess. You were with Grant."

"And if I was?"

"You actually moved in with him?"

"Don't sound so shocked. I told you I needed a place to stay."

Allette sighed, then said, "I know you're frustrated living at home, but to move in with Grant? I thought you said you were gonna think things over."

"I did."

"In what? A day?"

"You're not my mother."

"I know that. But I am your friend. And I don't want to see you hurt. Weren't you the same one who was concerned about Evoni? Well, I've heard rumors that she *is* involved with Grant."

"A guy has an attractive friend and he has to be screwing her?" Rachelle's words sounded crass to her own ears. She never spoke like this.

"No. No, I didn't say that."

"I'll bet these are the same people who've been saying my family has a 'black widow' curse."

"A what curse?"

"I'm sure you've heard the rumors. But you know what, I really don't care what anyone has to say about me."

There was a long pause before Allette spoke. "You've changed."

"You've just figured it out?"

"Rachelle, I'm not the enemy here."

Trey stirred. Rachelle glanced at him. He didn't wake.

Drawing in a deep breath, Rachelle counted to ten. What was she doing, pushing Allette away? She had no clue. She only knew that she felt frustrated and lost.

"Look, Allette," she continued in a quieter voice. "I'm just stressed. Whatever I'm doing, I need to figure it out on my own. You questioning my relationship with Grant isn't gonna help me."

Allette didn't say a word.

Rachelle shook her head, discouraged. "I've gotta run. I'm gonna head by the house and pick up some stuff."

"Wait."

"Why? You're obviously upset with me."

"I'm concerned. There's a difference." Allette exhaled harshly. "Look, I want to say one thing before you go. Something for you to think about. You've missed a couple of the sorority charity drives you promised to attend, and yeah, I know—that's not the biggest thing in the world. But you're also not coming around the sorority house, and when I talk about pledging, you don't seem interested at all. Call me crazy, but I'm getting the vibe that you're having doubts about becoming a Delta."

You're finally getting it!

"Well, think about this," Allette went on. "Nadine asked me if you're okay. She's worried about you. So are a few other girls. They haven't known you that long, but they realize something's up with you. And they care. I guarantee you they care more than that one girl you've been hanging with so much. Remember this: ain't nobody gonna stick by you like your sorority sisters. They're like your family."

"Uh-huh." She didn't want to hear any more about sororities and how they were like family. She had lived with two members of the Delta Gamma Psi sorority and they were the farthest thing from family, even though they were related by blood.

"All right, I'll let you go. Talk to you later?" Allette sounded tentative.

"Of course. I'll probably see you on campus, too."

As soon as Rachelle ended the call, she got off the bed and walked the few steps to where her duffel bag lay. She was determined to put Allette's words out of her mind.

She picked up the bag and brought it to the bed with her. There, she sorted through it, looking for clean underwear and an outfit she could wear today.

What would Grant want to see her in? That's what she wanted to think about instead of all that crap Allette had rambled on about. Her man was most important.

Maybe Grant would go crazy if he saw her in a red thong? She dumped the contents of the duffel bag onto the bed and sifted through it, looking for all her panties. Deciding on one of the silky black thongs she had bought on her recent shopping trip, she scooped up the others. She was about to stuff them back in the duffel bag when she realized she ought to make room for them in Grant's drawer. After all, she was living with him now.

Trey knocked his second pillow onto the floor as he rolled onto his back. Rachelle jumped from fright. She watched him, waiting for him to open his eyes, but he started snoring instead. Stifling a giggle, she relaxed and made her way to Grant's drawer. She opened the top one.

Her giggle died as quickly as it had started.

Some type of women's lingerie was on top of the heap of briefs.

Rachelle's stomach contracted painfully as she lifted the items with her free hand. She thought her new clothes were pretty racy, but these were far worse. The black bra was held together by a few strips of material, capped off by balls of fuzz at the front. And the panty—what panty? This was one long piece of material barely wider than a piece of thread, held together with another fuzz ball. Rachelle couldn't even tell what was the front and what was the back.

She dropped the items in disgust. Whose were they? An ex-girlfriend's?

Or Evoni's?

She dropped her armful of panties on top of the dresser and started sifting through the drawer. She found stockings. Another thong. Then, finally, a picture.

She stared at it long and hard, her hand shaking as a wave of nausea made her want to puke.

It was a Polaroid shot of a naked Evoni. She was touching herself in a lewd manner while smiling for the camera.

CHAPTER FIFTY-ONE

Rachelle pounded on the door like she wanted to break it down. This was the one time she needed Allette. Where on earth was she?

Her first choice had been Claudia, but Claudia had opened her dorm room door a crack and told Rachelle that it wasn't a good time, not even after Rachelle told her how important it was.

Rachelle knocked Allette's door again and whispered, "Please."

It swung open moments later.

Bernie smiled. "Why, Miss Rachelle." His smile faded. "Sweetheart, what's happened to you?"

Shit, I must look like a mess. Rachelle wiped at her tears. "Hi. I, uh, was looking for Allette."

"She left not more than ten minutes ago."

Damn. Rachelle nodded jerkily. "Okay. Thanks."

She turned to leave, but Bernie took hold of her arm. "Wait a second. I can't let you leave in this state. Why don't you come in and we can talk about whatever's bothering you."

Rachelle glanced over his shoulder. Where was Belinda?

He must have read her mind, because he said, "Belinda's upstairs. She's not feeling well this morning. Actually, I'd just brought her some tea when you knocked on the door. That's why it took me a while to answer."

"I don't want to bother you."

"You're not bothering me. I offered an ear, remember? Seems you could use it right now."

Rachelle stared at Bernie. He wore a faint smile and a gentle expression. Maybe she should talk to him. Lord knew she needed to speak with someone.

Bernie stood back, holding the door open wide. "Come in."

Rachelle stepped into the house, saying, "Oh, Bernie. I'm so confused."

"What happened?"

"That guy Grant. I thought he cared about me. But I found out this morning that he was lying to me. I feel so stupid."

"Let's take a seat in the kitchen. I've got a pot of tea on. I suspect you could use some."

Rachelle didn't argue. Minutes later, she was at the kitchen table seated across from Bernie, a warm mug of tea in between both hands.

"Okay," Bernie said. "Tell me everything."

So she did. She told him about Grant and Evoni and how she had wondered about their relationship from the beginning. She told him about the picture she had found.

"I know I've only been dating him a short while. Evoni could be an ex. But if that was the case, why didn't he tell me about her before? I rushed everything with him, all because I wanted a place to stay."

"Hold up," Bernie said. "You have a home. I know good and well no one kicked you out."

"No, but . . . I found out something . . . and I don't want to be there anymore. At least not right now."

Bernie eyed her with curiosity. "What could be so bad?"

"I . . . I don't want to talk about it." She paused. "You're a man. Please give me advice about Grant. Am I jumping to conclusions?"

"You may not want to hear this, but from the first time I heard you talk about Grant, I knew he was trouble. He's a player, sweetheart. I don't want to judge him too harshly, because he's young. But it doesn't matter how young he is. He shouldn't lead you on."

Rachelle whimpered. "You don't think this is all a misunderstanding?"

"I don't. He sounds like a womanizer to me. Who knows how long it would have lasted now that you've already given him the milk for free?"

Rachelle glanced away, embarrassed. Never in her wildest dreams would she have imagined regretting her first sexual encounter the way she did now. Especially since she hadn't been a promiscuous type of girl.

"I can't believe I was so stupid." Rachelle dragged a hand over her face. "I knew from the beginning that a popular basketball player like him wouldn't have a true interest in me. Yet I wanted to believe him so badly. I let that man take my virginity."

"I wish I could have spared you this pain. Now you've got a mark against your virtue."

Rachelle's eyes went to Bernie's at his comment. His expression said he was serious. She didn't bother telling him that she didn't think any guy would care if she was no longer a virgin. Bernie was from a different generation, and clearly old-fashioned.

"I'll be smarter next time."

"I know you will." Bernie reached across the table and covered Rachelle's hand with his. She looked at his hand, then at him. He smiled gently at her.

An odd feeling washed over her. Why was Bernie being so nice, so attentive? Could he be hitting on her?

"Rachelle."

At the sound of Belinda's voice, Rachelle jerked her hand backward. Bernie did the same. She glanced at Belinda, feeling as if she and Bernie had just been caught doing something bad.

Belinda marched into the kitchen. She wore sunglasses and a hat. "Young lady, what are you doing sitting here in my kitchen when you know your mama and grandma are worried sick about you?"

"I . . . I was heading over there. I just wanted to see Allette first."

"Good. I'm heading over there, too. I'll make sure you get there safely."

"That's not necessary."

"Oh, I think it is. And you ought to be ashamed of yourself, making your mama worry."

"I know, ma'am."

Bernie got to his feet. "You're going to Olivia's?"

"Someone needs to make sure this child gets home." Belinda took Rachelle's hand in hers and urged her to her feet. "I'll be back in a little while."

Belinda started out of the kitchen, still holding Rachelle's hand.

"Belinda."

Bernie's voice stopped Belinda cold in her tracks. She slowly turned.

"You're not gonna give me a kiss?"

Belinda stood still as Bernie made his way toward her. Rachelle watched them. When Bernie planted his lips on Belinda's, she stiffened. Clearly, Belinda hadn't wanted to kiss him.

Oh, no. She *did* suspect something had been happening between her and Bernie. She was probably going to blast Rachelle once they got out of the house.

"How long will you be?" Bernie asked.

"Maybe an hour," Belinda replied. "I'll call if something changes."

Bernie nodded.

Belinda gripped Rachelle's hand tighter and walked with her out of the house.

Well, thank the Lord!" Olivia exclaimed when she opened the door and found Belinda and Rachelle standing on the step.

"She came by to see Allette," Belinda explained, walking into the house. "I figured I'd bring her straight over."

"You don't need to talk about me like I'm not here," Rachelle complained.

Olivia cut her eyes at her daughter. "You watch your tongue. You've already let your grandmother and me nearly worry ourselves into our graves."

"You ought to be thankful that you have people who care about you," Belinda added. "I lost my mother and I still miss her every day."

Rachelle bit down on her inner cheek to avoid a feisty retort. If there was one thing people in her tight-knit community were good at, it was mothering other people's children. She had been raised to respect her elders the same way she respected her parents.

Olivia faced Belinda. "You're hanging around for a while, right?"

"Yes."

"Will you give me a few minutes? I need to speak with Rachelle."

"Take care of your business," Belinda told her, then headed off in the direction of the sunroom.

As soon as Belinda was out of view, Olivia scowled at Rachelle. Her new haircut truly looked awful. But at least today her body was covered up in jeans and an oversized T-shirt.

"Upstairs," Olivia demanded.

"Ma—"

"*Now.*"

Rachelle huffed, but she started up the stairs nonetheless. Olivia followed her. When they were in Rachelle's bedroom, Olivia tore into her.

"What on earth are you thinking? Going out and not coming home for days? Do you know how worried we all were? Your grandmother has a bad heart. Are you trying to kill her?"

"Of course not. I just needed space."

"Space?" Olivia gaped at Rachelle. "I promised myself I wouldn't get upset with you when you came home, but your actions were entirely selfish. The least you could have done was call and let us know you were all right."

"And you would have told me to come home."

"You're damn right I would have!"

Rachelle tramped to the window. She exhaled a gush of air before facing her mother again. "With all the *worry* you did, did you even ask yourself why I would leave? Did you even notice my duffel bag was missing from the closet? Did you notice anything other than your own needs?"

Olivia's eyebrows shot up in surprise.

"I wasn't planning on coming back, Ma. So when I left, I didn't particularly care how you would feel." She paused. "No, that's a lie. I wanted you to be hurt."

Olivia's mouth nearly hit the floor. "I can't believe the words that are coming out of your mouth."

"Of course you can't. Because until now, you've tried to control everything I say. Everything I do."

"That is not true," Olivia protested.

"Really?"

Olivia marched toward Rachelle, wagging a finger at her. "Don't make excuses for your bad behavior. I needed you and you couldn't be found."

"Oh, that's precious. *You* needed me? Ma, you've never needed me. All you've ever needed is the bottle. Scotch, bourbon, vodka. Whatever could get you drunk enough to forget about the real world. Well, I was in that real world, and I needed you. So many times I needed you, and you were never there." Rachelle croaked but pressed on. "So spare me the crap about needing me now."

Olivia now looked at her daughter with concern as opposed to anger. She reached for her. "Rachelle."

Rachelle stepped away from her. "Don't touch me."

"Honey, what is it?" Olivia spoke in a softer tone. "Something more must be going on. Please talk to me about it."

"I know about the letters."

"So you *do* know. I thought your grandmother said she didn't tell you."

"Oh, God. She knew, too?"

"Of course she did. She's the one who received them."

A small cry escaped Rachelle's mouth. "So she was part of this?"

Olivia's eyes narrowed. A moment passed before she said, "Honey, I'm not following you."

For the first time, Rachelle wondered if they were talking about the same thing. "I'm talking about the acceptance letters. The ones I got to the other colleges I applied to. I know you tore them up! You forced me to go to Dillard, even though you knew how badly I wanted to go to another school."

Olivia's face blanched.

Finally, her mother understood. "That's right. I know, Ma. Did you really believe something like that would never come out?"

Olivia clamped a hand over her mouth and turned away.

Her mother's silence was the last thing Rachelle wanted, the last thing she was prepared for. She wanted denial, even if it was a lie. She didn't want her mother to admit she cared so little for her that she would do anything to ruin her life.

Slowly, Olivia faced her again. "How did you find out?"

"Is that what you think matters?"

"Oh, honey."

"You hate me," Rachelle went on. Her throat was clogged. She could barely speak.

"No. Oh, honey. Of course I don't hate you. That's why I did it."

"That's why you tried to ruin my life?" Rachelle asked, bowled over.

"I couldn't bear to live without you. I wasn't thinking of what you wanted. Only what I needed. After losing your father . . ."

"That's the problem. You never think of what anyone else needs."

To Rachelle's surprise, a tear fell down her mother's cheek. "Rachelle, I know I've been a bad mother. I've been far from perfect. I was lost in my own world of pain about things you don't yet understand. That's no excuse, and I'm sorry. But I'm willing to do whatever it takes, right now, to make things better."

"It's too late."

"Please don't say that."

"It's the truth. I'll never trust you again. Never."

Olivia began to cry. "Sweetheart."

Rachelle couldn't bear to see her crying. She didn't know how to deal with it. So she ran out of the bedroom and down the stairs.

"Please, let's talk about this."

Rachelle opened the front door and ran outside. Olivia hurried after her, pausing in the foyer to face Belinda, who had seemingly appeared out of nowhere.

"She knows, Belinda. And she hates me."

Olivia started off again, but Belinda grabbed her by the wrist, stopping her. "Let her go, Liv."

"But I want to resolve this."

"I know you do. But give her time. She'll be back."

Olivia glanced outside. Rachelle was nowhere in sight. Moaning, she turned back to Belinda.

Her friend squeezed her hand in support. Then she slipped off her sunglasses.

Olivia gasped in horror when she saw her bruised eye.

CHAPTER FIFTY-TWO

O h, Belinda. No."

Belinda's brave smile crumbled.

Olivia opened her arms to her and Belinda walked into her embrace.

"Belinda, what on earth—"

Belinda sobbed softly.

"Who did this to you? You have to tell me!"

"He's just not the same, Olivia. He's changed so much over the years."

"Who's not the same? Oh, no. You can't be talking about . . . about *Bernie*?"

Belinda nodded through her tears.

"Oh my God." Olivia released Belinda to close the front door. Her heart was beating out of control as she led her friend to the nearby living room.

Bernie had beat her like this? The man who loved her more than life itself? It wasn't possible.

"What happened? What kind of argument could get out of control to this extent?"

"I only wish we were arguing. Bernie came home last night, told me I couldn't go to Miami, then slapped me upside the head."

"What?"

"The thing is, that day you came over, we talked about it. He didn't say I couldn't go, but I could tell he wasn't happy. He's so damn jealous these days. Every time I leave the house he thinks I'm heading off to see another man."

"But why?"

"I don't know." Belinda's voice cracked.

Olivia reached for the box of Kleenex on the nearby end table. She offered it to Belinda, who withdrew several.

"So you're saying he just hit you?"

Belinda blew her nose. "This isn't the first time."

Olivia's hand flew to her mouth.

"It's worse when he's drinking, and that's what he's been doing a lot of. And he lost his job again. Said his manager's an asshole who had it out for him."

"How long has he been hitting you?" Never in a million years would Olivia have imagined this. Belinda and Bernie were the perfect couple. At least that's what she had believed.

"Ever since Alex came along."

"Son of a bitch!" Olivia shot to her feet.

"That's the first year I threatened to leave him. He was out of work, hanging around the house like a bum and not giving me any help."

"Alex is thirteen."

"I know. Bernie beat the shit out of me. He said if I ever tried to leave him, he would kill me. I didn't know what to do. I had two young children. My mother was dead. And my father wasn't a part of my life."

"You could have turned to me."

"I was too ashamed. I didn't even know if you'd believe me."

Olivia sank onto the sofa beside Belinda. "How can you say that?"

"You thought he was such a great guy."

"But I've known you all my life. I absolutely would have believed you."

Belinda glanced down in shame. "He apologized. He always did after he hit me. And it wasn't like he was beating me every day. I figured I could make it work."

"Oh, Belinda. I can't believe you went through this alone."

"I didn't know what else to do."

Olivia stood again. Paced the floor. "Have you called the police?"

"The police! God, no. If I called the police and he ever found out . . . and who knows? I'm so stubborn sometimes, maybe this is all my fault."

Olivia dropped to her knees before Belinda. She took Belinda's hands in hers. "Don't you say that. No man should ever hit you, no matter what."

"I know, but—" Belinda sniveled.

"Don't go making excuses for that son of a bitch."

"He apologized this morning. Said he was depressed because he'd lost his job. And I know money is tight sometimes."

"He needs to leave. You hear me? You said yourself he's done this for years. He'll never stop, not until he kills you. And God knows I can't sit around and watch that happen."

Belinda nodded.

"I know you're afraid, but you have to call the police."

"No. I can't! And you can't, either. Promise me you won't."

"Don't you want to put an end to this?"

Belinda quickly stood. "I do, but . . . you don't understand."

"Yes, I do. And you're not alone—"

"No, you don't understand," Belinda insisted.

She charged out of the living room. Olivia followed her. "Belinda, wait a second."

"I'm sorry." Belinda hurried out of the house, leaving Olivia standing in the foyer in shock.

Rachelle sat at a corner desk in the library, her head down on the open textbook on her desk. She was supposed to be researching the life of Frederick Douglass, but she couldn't bring herself to think about schoolwork.

She felt more depressed than she had ever felt in her life. And so confused she wasn't sure she'd ever find the answers to the questions that were nagging at her.

Her mother had actually wept in front of her, and it was an image Rachelle couldn't put out of her mind. Had her mother been crying because she actually cared, or because she had been found out?

And why, considering Rachelle had hoped to hurt her mother the way she had hurt her, did the tears make her feel so damn bad?

The Lord said you should forgive those who had hurt you, but Rachelle still had so much anger inside her. Anger that she had no control of her crazy life. She wanted to make her own way, do her own thing. Going to a university out of state would have been the first step toward accomplishing that. But her mother had stolen that opportunity from her.

How could she forgive something like that?

"Hey."

The soft voice made Rachelle look up. Nadine smiled down at her.

"Oh, hi," Rachelle said, sounding flustered. "I didn't hear you."

Nadine's smile morphed into a concerned expression. "You all right?"

"Yeah." But the word sounded like a soft moan.

"You're not." Nadine grabbed a chair from a nearby table and dragged it to her desk. "Wanna talk about it?"

Rachelle exhaled loudly. "It won't do any good. I've made a mess of my life and I don't know how to fix it."

"Hey." Nadine spoke softly. "Nothing's that bad. Except death."

"Easy for you to say."

"Not really. I do speak from experience."

"Oh?"

"The day I met you at the dorm, I wasn't even supposed to be there. I hadn't been feeling well and was supposed to go to the doctor. I'd had bad cramps for a day and a half, but that morning I woke up feeling better. Then when I saw you . . . something about you made me feel compelled to seek you out. I think the Lord wanted me to reach out to you."

Great. The last thing Rachelle needed was a religious freak.

"I know what you're thinking. That I'm trying to win your soul." She grinned. "That's not the case. But I think I can help you."

"All right. I'll bite. How can you help me?"

"You're upset about a guy, aren't you?"

"How'd you hear?"

"I didn't. I just knew. Maybe because I've been there." Nadine paused. "Last year, I got involved with someone I met here. I fell pretty hard for him. He seemed real nice. I thought he cared about me. And I was so happy to have someone who cared for me because I had left a home where it seemed no one cared. Sound familiar?"

"Surprisingly, yes."

Nadine nodded before continuing. "This guy ended up raping me."

"Oh, God."

"It's okay. I mean, it wasn't at the time, but I've dealt with it." Nadine paused, then said in a hushed voice, "Girl, he even gave me a sexually transmitted disease. Now, please don't tell a word of this to anyone."

"I won't."

"I thought my life was over. In fact, I wanted to die. Then the Lord sent someone into my life. A Delta. I met her when I was real down about everything. She reached out to me, told me about sisterhood and how sorors are like family. She took me under her wing for whatever reason. We started hanging out. I started doing volunteer work with her. And you know what? I learned that as bad as my situation was, there were people worse off. People who were homeless, or who had been badly burned in a fire. I know I'm rambling, but I just want to say that the Lord doesn't give you more to deal with than you can handle. And He sends people into your life who can help you when you need it. Rachelle, I'm here for you."

Nadine gave Rachelle's hand a gentle squeeze before pushing her chair back and rising to her feet.

"Nadine, wait."

"Uh-huh?"

Rachelle had always believed in God, but almost in an unreal way. As far as she was concerned, God had put the world in motion but left people to fend for themselves.

Now she knew that wasn't true. Nadine was right about Him sending people into your life at a time when you needed them. Nadine's words had profoundly touched her.

"There is something I need."

"Anything."

"I could use a place to stay. Probably just for tonight. But I promise—"

"As long as you need."

Rachelle finally smiled. "Thank you."

"You want to head to my room now? I was gonna go there before my evening class."

Rachelle sighed her relief. "That would be great."

"Let's go."

———

Now, Sylvia. Admit it. You're glad I dragged you out of the house, aren't you?"

Sylvia glanced up at the clear blue sky, inhaled the floral-scented air, and listened to the sounds of the various birds chirping as they went about their day. Her lips curled in a wry smile as she faced Edward. "Yes, Edward. I am."

He grinned his satisfaction. "Here in New Orleans we have great weather all year round. Yet so many of us take the simple things for granted. Like a walk in the park."

City Park this late afternoon was lovely. Sylvia and Edward were near a beautiful flower garden, away from the picnickers and most of the strollers. It was quieter, more private. A place to get in touch with nature and forget about one's problems.

"You know what I want to do before we leave? Take you to the swings."

"Edward . . ."

"I'm serious."

"I'm much too old for that."

"You're never too old to do the simple things that gave us pleasure as children."

The mention of swinging and childhood immediately brought to Sylvia's mind the memory of the swing her daddy had built for her in their backyard, and the numerous hours he had spent pushing her to her heart's content. She conceded, "Perhaps you're right."

They strolled a while longer in silence. Rounding a curve, a wooden bench shaded by a large oak came into view. Edward headed straight toward it and took a seat.

Sylvia did the same. As she sat, she let out a sigh of contentment. Reaching for Edward's arm, she gave it a gentle squeeze. It was one of his better days, thank the Lord. Clearly his arthritis wasn't bothering him.

He said, "We're away from the house. It's peaceful here. We won't have any interruptions. Maybe now we can talk?"

Sylvia met Edward's eyes. "About?"

"What's going on. The fact that someone is out to make your life miserable, at the very least."

Sylvia groaned softly. "I'd rather not spoil the mood."

"You sure it's not that you'd rather not discuss it with me?"

"Oh, Edward, no. It's·not that—"

"Good. Then there's no reason not to have this talk. I think keeping all this inside is what led you to these problems in the first place. You can only hide for so long."

Hide?

Edward's gaze was steady as he regarded her. "I know what you're dealing with, Sylvia. I know what happened in 1953."

All the blood drained from Sylvia's head. The world around her began spinning out of control. Surely she had heard Edward wrong.

"What did you say?" she whispered in horror.

"Exactly what you think I said. Sylvia, I know about your son."

CHAPTER FIFTY-THREE

E*dward knew.*

Sylvia's breath came in and out in rapid spurts. Her heart beat like a locomotive out of control. Good God Almighty, Edward *knew.*

He simply stared at her as though waiting for her to speak. But she couldn't form a single word. She felt faint. She felt ill.

She felt fear.

According to Olivia, Harvey was not her long-lost son. Harvey had convinced Olivia of that, but Sylvia had doubted it. But what if Harvey had been telling the truth? What if he wasn't the one out to hurt her, but someone much closer to her than she had ever expected?

"Guess I shouldn't have just dropped that on you," Edward said after a moment. "But I figured it was best to simply get it out in the open."

She didn't say a word.

"Sylvia, why are you looking at me like that? Oh, damn. What—do you think? No, you couldn't possibly. Let me explain myself. I overheard you talking to Della once, years and years ago. It wasn't intentional, but I heard it nonetheless. This was after Harvey was gone, and you confided in Della that you thought he was your son."

All these years Edward had known and he'd never told her!

"You knew?"

"Yes."

"Yet you never said a word?"

"I didn't figure I should. I knew you'd be embarrassed."

"All this time . . ." Sylvia would have bet money that the time would never come when she thought she couldn't trust Edward. But now that time had arrived.

"What should I have done, Sylvia?"

"You shouldn't have let me—" Sylvia stopped short. Let her what? Keep her dignity?

"I didn't want to cause you any more pain."

She swallowed hard. "Why are you bringing this up now, Edward?"

"Because I want to help. If Harvey is trying to hurt you, I can't stand by and watch that happen."

"You didn't simply mention that I had a son. You mentioned 1953." Same as the person had typed on the wine label. "Why?"

"I saw parts of the bottle that had broken on the porch. You cleaned up the mess but I sifted through the garbage. I wanted to know why you were so afraid. I put two and two together, given the conversation I'd overheard between you and Della."

Sylvia's heart slowed its frantic pace. Edward's words rang true. She remembered the conversation with Della, so she knew he wasn't lying. Still, she was wary.

"You're upset because I know."

"I'm . . . in shock."

"Of course you are. Believe me, I was waiting, hoping, you would bring this up to me. But you didn't. And in light of everything going on now, that's why I decided to."

Syliva covered her face with both hands. "Maybe I should have told you. But it wasn't exactly an easy thing to talk about."

"Not even with me?"

"Especially not with you."

A flash of pain streaked across Edward's face. "It hurts to hear you say that, Sylvia."

"That's not what I—"

He didn't let her finish. "We've been together how many decades? I thought you'd know by now that you could come to me with any problem. *Anything.*"

His eyes held Sylvia captive. There was a mix of emotions in their depths.

Disappointment, sadness. And something else. Something Sylvia had seen on occasion before but hadn't dared to read more into.

"I'm not a young man anymore. We have to grab moments when we can, make the most of them. That's why I wanted to talk to you. Make sure you know that there's nothing I wouldn't do for you."

They were no longer talking about Harvey and his quest to make her life miserable. Sylvia could play dumb, run from this conversation as she had so many times before. But she was tired of running from everything. And tired of hiding behind facades—at least with Edward.

"Maybe if we'd met in a different way," she said softly.

"In a different life, you mean?"

"No, no, I don't mean that." She shrugged. "I don't know. I was so in love with Samuel."

"I know. But I loved you even then."

Sylvia's mouth fell open in surprise. It was shocking to hear Edward confess his feelings, regardless of the truth she knew in her heart.

"I knew how unhappy you were, even before Samuel died. Of course, I would never have done anything to compromise your marriage. And I didn't expect you to love me soon after he was gone. I suppose I never expected it, period. But there was a time I started to hope. When I'd look at you and see something in your eyes . . . something that made me wonder . . ."

"Wonder what?" Sylvia was shocked at how breathless she sounded.

"It was fanciful thinking, I know. Hoping that we could be together, even if you did have feelings for me. I was your hired help. To the world, it wouldn't look right."

"Edward, please. Don't say that." Because hearing the words out of his mouth, she suddenly seemed shallow. Shallow enough to let a lifetime of love pass her by because of class differences.

But wasn't that exactly what she had done? Because she had known a very long time ago that Edward was attracted to her. She had also known that he was probably the best damn thing for her. And Olivia had loved him like a father.

It could have been so easy . . .

"When did you know?" Sylvia asked.

Edward's soft chuckle floated on the warm air. "Remember that crazy night when we went to see the voodoo priestess?"

"How could I forget it?" The memory was like yesterday. All the good it had done her, considering Harvey had ultimately returned.

"I saw something in your eyes that night. The way you leaned on me for support. It felt nice. And though I wanted more, that was enough."

"Oh, Edward."

"I always knew it wasn't meant to be. At least not in this lifetime," Edward added wistfully. "But it didn't stop me from pretending in my mind. Wishing things were different."

She should have been surprised by the sudden tears in her eyes, but she wasn't. Nor was she surprised to find herself reaching for Edward's hand.

He squeezed it, held on to her fingers as though he wanted to make up for the last thirty years.

As a breeze moved gently around them, Sylvia and Edward did not speak. Words were inadequate.

Finally, Sylvia broke the silence. "You shouldn't have wasted your time dreaming about me. I'm sorry. That came out wrong. I'm not putting you down. It was me, Edward. You deserved better."

"I've had the best, even if it was from a distance."

Sylvia tried her damndest to hold it together. If that wasn't the sweetest thing anyone had ever said to her.

"Given what you know about me, how can you say that?"

"And you think when you found me inebriated on the street that there weren't any skeletons in my closet? Yet you took me into your home, gave my pitiful life a new start. How could I ever think any less of you?"

"I'm so ashamed of what I did."

"I'm ashamed of a lot of things I did."

"It's not the same."

"Why don't you tell me? Tell me what happened in 1953?"

Sylvia looked into the depth of Edward's eyes, looking to see even the slightest hint of scorn. She found none.

The next thing she knew, words were spilling out of her mouth. She told him everything about that very dark time in her life. And felt the weight of her burden lift from her shoulders.

G rant wouldn't stop calling.

"C'mon, Rachelle. When are you gonna call me back?" went his latest message. "I know I should have told you about Evoni, but the truth is, we're just friends. We haven't been more than that for a long time. I'm tired of talking to your voice mail. Call me. Better yet, come see me."

Rachelle deleted the message.

"Grant again?" Nadine asked her. She sat cross-legged on her bed.

"Yeah."

"You gonna call him?"

"No."

Sooner or later, Grant would stop calling. He would figure out that she wanted nothing more to do with him.

I didn't tell her."

Harvey frowned at her. Clearly, he wasn't pleased. "You said you would."

"I know what I said. But it wasn't the time. She found out that I'd intercepted her acceptance letters and we argued. She ran out of the house and I haven't seen her since."

Harvey got up from the sofa. He lifted the remote from the coffee table and turned on the television.

Olivia was on her feet in a flash. She snatched the remote from him and turned the television off.

"Give me the remote."

He reached for it, but Olivia held it behind her back. "No."

"I don't have time for games."

"Don't you shut me out, too. I can't deal with that, not from you."

Harvey placed his hands on his hips and met her eyes with a level gaze. "Seems to me you're the one shutting me out."

"You know all I'm going through, damn it. What my mother is going through. I need your support and understanding right now."

"And I want to give that to you. But not from the sidelines. You sneak around to see me, like I'm some guy you met at a bar you're ashamed of screwing."

"Oh, that was low." He had thrown her past in her face, and he knew how much she had regretted her actions at moments of weakness in her life.

"Is it? I keep hearing the same story from you. That this isn't the right time to openly have me in your life."

"My mother thinks you're out to destroy our family! I told her that we're not related, but you know what she said? She said that if you're not her son, then you know who is. That you're still the one out to blackmail her."

"And you believe that?"

Olivia hesitated only a moment, but that was apparently too long. Harvey looked at her with acute disappointment. "You need to leave, Olivia."

"Harvey, I didn't say—"

"Go. Now."

Olivia groaned into her hands. When she looked up, Harvey was still staring at her with determination.

And a harshness she had never seen in his eyes before.

Sighing with resignation, Olivia snatched her purse from the sofa and walked out of his place.

When Rachelle walked into the cafeteria the next morning, she had the powerful sense that something was wrong. A group of women she had seen around the frat house looked up at her from a table near the door. Two of them glared at her.

Or was it her imagination? Was she being paranoid?

Rachelle ignored them and strolled to the front of the room. The delicious scent of bacon, eggs, and hash browns filled the air. Maybe she would skip her normal breakfast of cereal and a banana and load up on the calories instead. Bacon and eggs right about now sounded heavenly.

As Rachelle went for a tray, she spotted Claudia in the line. *Great*, she thought. At least there was someone here she could eat with.

Smiling, she hurried to her friend. "Hey, Claudia. What's up?"

Claudia turned, saw her, and glowered. "I don't believe you."

Rachelle drew up short. "What?"

"Look, bitch. Even if he did cheat on you, he didn't deserve what you did."

Claudia's harsh words were like a punch in the gut. They were friends. How could she talk to her this way? "Excuse me?"

"You better mind I don't knock you upside the head. And I'm tempted, but I'm heading to the hospital soon, so I don't have time to waste on you."

"The hospital?"

Claudia moved forward. Rachelle stepped with her. "You heard what I said," Claudia warned.

Damn, the girl was serious. She really did want to hurt her. Rachelle said, "For whatever reason you're angry, but I have no clue why. What'd I do to piss you off?"

Claudia's eyes were hard as she stared Rachelle down. She finally said, "Grant."

"Are you saying Grant's in the hospital?" Rachelle asked, her voice rising in pitch.

"Yeah, he is. He was beat up real bad."

"Oh my God! Here on campus?"

"For your sake, you better not be playing dumb."

"How could you say that, Claudia? You know me better than that." At least she should have.

"Grant told me you found the picture of Evoni. I know you were pissed with him."

"Yeah, but . . . you think *I* beat him up?"

"Not you personally, but you could have had someone do it."

"I didn't!"

Claudia's expression softened only slightly. "I hope to hell not."

Even though Rachelle had been angry with Grant, she suddenly wanted to see him. "Where is he?"

"Charity Hospital. But only family is allowed to see him. It's pretty serious, Rachelle," Claudia added, finally sounding like the woman Rachelle had gotten to know. "He might not make it."

Rachelle stared at Claudia in disbelief.

"Yeah, it's that bad." Her expression hardened once again. "I swear, if I find out that you had anything to do with this . . ." Claudia let her threat hang in the air.

Rachelle stared at Claudia in disbelief. She was supposed to be a friend, yet she was thinking the worst of her. "I didn't."

"You know, I thought that whole black widow curse shit was just that—bullshit. But something's up with your family. Any man who gets involved with any of you has to do so at his own risk."

Rachelle opened her mouth to respond, but what could she say? Until now, the black widow curse had sounded ridiculous. But could it be that there was actually merit to that rumor? This was New Orleans, and some people believed in voodoo and whatnot, including Edward. Rachelle never had, but was it possible someone had put a curse on their family years ago, a curse that still lived today?

No longer was Rachelle hungry. She knew she had to see Grant.

She turned and fled the cafeteria.

CHAPTER FIFTY-FOUR

Belinda ground out her finished cigarette and promptly lit another one. Nerves. It was the only time she chain-smoked.

". . . go away for the weekend. Get away from Alex and Allette and have some time to ourselves."

At Belinda's silence, Bernie looked over his shoulder at her. He stood at the stove, frying eggs. "You said that's what you needed. A vacation. And I realize now that you're right. We haven't gone away in years. It's more than time we do that. Go somewhere we can concentrate on us."

Belinda inhaled deeply. She held the cigarette smoke as long as she could, until her lungs burned, before exhaling. Watching Bernie cook breakfast was making her ill.

He was pretending they were a happy couple. But they weren't. They hadn't been in years.

"Hmm?" Bernie pressed.

"I don't think so."

"Why not?"

"One of the stylists quit. I've got to help take over her clients until we find someone new. Which could take a while, since you know how picky Sandy is. So I won't be able to get the time off."

Several seconds passed. Belinda hardly dared to breathe as she eyed Bernie. He removed the eggs with a spatula and placed them on a plate.

"So you don't want to go away with me?"

"I just told you—"

"You sure that's it?"

" 'Course I'm sure."

Bernie cracked two new eggs and emptied them into the skillet. They sizzled in the hot oil.

"I never liked you working at the damn salon, anyway. Sandy's one stupid bitch."

"Don't start this again. I'm not quitting. One of us has to have a steady job."

"You want me to call her? Because I will. Any time someone quits, she has you working extra hours like a dog. I'm gonna call her and tell her that this time I won't put up with it."

"No, I don't want you calling Sandy."

He whirled to face her. "Why not?"

Belinda lurched backward at the murderous look on Bernie's face. She inwardly cringed.

He can't hit me again.

"You're getting so angry, Bernie. Please try to calm down."

"Don't tell me how to feel."

"God, I can't take this anymore." Belinda pounded a fist on the table. "We need some time apart." The words came out hastily, unexpectedly.

Bernie stepped toward her. "What did you say?"

She uttered a silent prayer. Thank God Alex had slept over at a friend's and Allette had left early for some sorority function.

Belinda forged ahead. "We're not getting along. Taking some time apart . . . a lot of couples do it."

A cry made its way up her throat when two hands grabbed her and threw her back against a wall. Anger blazed in Bernie's eyes.

"Bernie—please—"

"Who is he?"

"No one," Belinda cried.

"Don't lie to me!"

"Bernie, stop."

"You won't leave me. Not after everything we've been through together. After all I've done for you. You owe me. Or have you forgotten?"

How could she forget? Till the day she died, she would never forget. Bernie had made sure of that.

"You can't kick me out of your life. You hear me?"

Oh, God. What had she gotten herself into?

Bernie pulled her off the wall, then slammed her hard against it. "Do you understand?"

"Yes." She winced as pain shot through her body. "I understand."

"Good." He relaxed his hold on her, but only slightly. "Where would you be if it wasn't for me?"

"Nowhere," she said softly, knowing that was what he wanted to hear.

"Living a shit life, that's where. Maybe even dead. But I saved you from that. I was the best damn thing that ever happened to you!"

"I know, Bernie."

"Everything I did—it was because I loved you—yet you have the nerve to treat me this way?"

"I . . ." Belinda fought the tears. "I'm sorry."

Bernie was still. So was she. Their hot breaths mingled, that's how close his mouth was to hers. "You think you deserved my love?"

Pause, then, "No. I was never worthy of your love."

"That's right. You weren't nothing but a whore."

He flattened his body against her. Belinda could feel his erection.

"Sometimes a man is weak. I was weak for you all those years ago." He paused. Grinned. "And for that tramp, Liza Monroe."

Belinda's body began to tremble.

"But you know that already, don't you, sweetheart?"

Belinda didn't dare close her eyes, even though fear threatened to swallow her whole.

"It's high time you showed me some gratitude for loving a whore like you." He stroked her cheek. "There's something you're gonna do for me."

God, no. Not sex. Bernie had often gotten amorous after being rough with her. And Belinda had cringed every time.

He smiled, but it didn't reach his eyes. "Something . . . *special*. And make no mistake, Belinda. You *will* do it."

CHAPTER FIFTY-FIVE

The attack on Grant Wilson, one of Dillard's star basketball players, was big news. Merely hours after it had happened, everyone on campus had heard.

Rachelle hadn't known that so many people knew of her relationship with him, but clearly they did. At least a few people in each of her classes had asked her questions.

Did she have any idea who would want to hurt Grant? Why wasn't she at his bedside? And the worst question of all: Where was she last night? Rachelle had had no answers for anyone.

Now, as she sat on a plastic deck chair in Nadine's room, she thought of the women in the cafeteria who had given her dirty looks. They thought her guilty. Others obviously did as well. How long before everyone thought she'd had someone hurt her ex-boyfriend?

"Why'd you have to get yourself beat up, Grant?" Rachelle asked. The four walls gave her no answer.

She should have called him back last night. She should have gone to see him. If she had, maybe he wouldn't be lying in a hospital bed right now.

She wanted to see him, to know that he was all right, but Claudia had made it clear that she should stay away. But it was killing her just sitting here. Grant needed to know she cared, that she could never in a million years be responsible for something like this. She hoped against hope that he didn't believe what people were starting to suspect.

Her thoughts were interrupted by the sound of the doorknob turning. As she looked up, Nadine swiftly entered the room. Allette followed her in.

Rachelle held her breath, knowing what would come next. Nadine was here to kick her out. Allette was here to give her a verbal lashing. She couldn't blame either of them.

"Thank God you're here," Nadine said.

"Oh, hon." Allette's mouth twisted in a sad smile.

Rachelle's gaze narrowed with speculation. Neither Nadine nor Allette looked or sounded angry, or even in the least disillusioned with her. What Rachelle saw between them was enough concern to fill Lake Pontchartrain.

Allette opened her arms to her.

Tears sprang to Rachelle's eyes. "Allette," she sobbed as she went into her friend's embrace. "Please tell me this is a nightmare."

Allette held her tight. "Hon, I wish it was."

"People are talking behind my back and giving me dirty looks," Rachelle went on, relieved to have someone to talk to. "They actually believe I could have had Grant hurt!"

Allette held her while she cried. "No one believes you had anything to do with this."

"That's not true. Even Claudia thinks I was behind this. I thought she was a friend!"

"Rachelle, I'm really sorry about all this."

At the sound of Nadine's voice, Rachelle pulled away from Allette and wiped at her tears. Just yesterday, Nadine had offered her a place to stay. Today, there was talk of her possible responsibility in having a man nearly beaten to death. Nadine didn't need this.

"I'm sorry, too," Rachelle said. "I'll get my stuff and be out of here."

Her forehead wrinkled with confusion. "Why?"

"Because. You're still pledging. I know how important that is to you. If people think I had something to do with this assault, and you're hanging with me—that won't be good for you and your hopes of crossing over."

And I can kiss any chance of crossing over good-bye.

To Rachelle's utter surprise, the thought brought with it a heavy sense of distress. All of a sudden, the reality that the very thing she hadn't wanted could be taken away from her bothered her—more than she ever thought it could.

"Anyone who knows you knows you had nothing to do with this," Nadine said. "No matter what bad-minded people might say."

"Still, this is a bad situation that might get even worse. I can't put you in a negative position."

"After I was raped, many people said really awful things. That I was lying. Or that I'd led Steven on. That I was some kind of slut. If people had abandoned me simply because of those rumors, God only knows where I'd be now." Nadine put a hand on Rachelle's shoulder. "You're my friend, Rachelle. And I stick by my friends. If that costs me sisterhood in the Delta Gamma Psi sorority, so be it."

"I feel the same way," Allette chimed in.

Rachelle could only stare at Nadine and Allette, dumbfounded. "How can you say that?"

"Easily," Nadine replied with a grin. "But judging from what the other Deltas are saying, they've all got your back."

"Why are you being so nice to me?" Rachelle asked.

Nadine replied, "I told you. I know what it's like to deal with the kind of challenges you think you'll never get through. But you can. And you will."

"Especially with friends you can rely on," Allette added.

Warmth filled Rachelle's heart. If Allette and Nadine were representative of the rest of the Deltas, then the sorority was full of wonderful women, indeed.

Rachelle hadn't wanted to become a sorority sister simply because her mother and grandmother and great-grandmother before her had been. But she remembered Allette's comment about the sorority being true family.

"Ain't nobody gonna stick by you like your sorority sisters. They're like your family."

Allette was right.

Claudia certainly hadn't stood by her.

Rachelle felt even more the fool for having pushed Allette away and for avoiding the various charitable events put on by the Deltas. She had robbed herself of a chance to get to know the women who had embraced her with open arms the first time they had met her.

Not because of her family's ties to the sorority, but because they truly cared for her.

When she thought of all she'd been through . . . There was no point thinking about it. It was over and she couldn't change it. And maybe she'd had to go through that wild ride in order to return to a place of sanity—a place where she could see what she wanted with clearer eyes.

Suddenly she embraced the idea of becoming a soror—and not because of any family pressure. She wanted to be a Delta because it felt right in her soul.

Olivia sucked in a sharp breath when she opened the door and Belinda breezed past her. Not wearing any makeup, Belinda's bruised eye was obvious. It looked horrible, but that wasn't the worst thing. It was the red, swollen eyes that told a tale much more sinister than the external signs of abuse.

"This can't go on," Olivia said before Belinda could utter a word. "You're leaving him. Today."

"I know, it can't," Belinda said bravely. "That's why I'm here."

"Thank God." Olivia's shoulders drooped with relief. "I'm so glad you're ready to do this."

Belinda's face contorted in pain. "I'm afraid."

"I know you are. But it's gonna be okay. I promise." She draped a hand around Belinda's shoulder. "My mother and I were heading to the police station, anyway. For a different matter. That whole ugly business about Liza Monroe," she added in a whisper so that her mother wouldn't hear. She didn't want her to know that she'd told Belinda about it.

"You're heading to see the police now?"

"Yes, and you're gonna come with us. Come with us and we'll report the bastard. No, don't be afraid," Olivia told her when Belinda's eyes widened in alarm. "The police will listen to you. My God, all they have to do is look at your face."

Belinda moved away from Olivia.

"I'm sorry," Olivia said. "I'm not being sensitive at all, am I? I know you love him. This can't be easy—"

"Olivia, I—" Belinda exhaled a frazzled breath. "There's something I've got to tell you."

"Of course. You want to sit down?"

Belinda turned away and buried her face in her hands.

"Belinda? Hey, look at me." Olivia took Belinda by the shoulders and circled her back around. "It's okay," she said, looking directly in her eyes. "Are you having second thoughts? Is that it? Because—"

The door flew open and slammed against the hall table. "Oh, God," Olivia exclaimed, a hand flying to her heart with fright. An icy chill snaked down her spine when she saw Bernie in the entrance.

Belinda jumped backward a foot.

"Bernie." Olivia moved in front of her friend, blocking her. "Bernie, you get the hell outta my house."

He advanced instead of retreating, his eyes hard. Cold. Olivia swallowed her fear.

"Did she tell you yet?" Bernie asked.

"Yeah, I know all about your sick ways," Olivia answered. "And it's gonna stop. I thought you were a man, Bernie. But you ain't shit."

Bernie glowered at her. Olivia's knees wobbled, but she stood her ground. She wasn't going to let this jerk come into her house and intimidate her.

"Where's your mother?" he asked.

"None of your damn business. You better leave before I call the cops."

"Go ahead. Call them." His lips curled in a sadistic grin as he eyed Belinda. "That's what you want, isn't it, sweetheart?"

"Bernie, don't. This isn't gonna make anything better."

Sylvia appeared at the top of the landing. She halted when she saw everyone in the foyer.

"Excellent," Bernie exclaimed. "The gang's all here."

"What's going on?" Sylvia asked, slowly descending the stairs.

"Belinda has something that's been weighing on her mind," Bernie replied. "Don't you, Belinda? Something you want to tell everybody."

"Go home, Bernie. I only came over to spend some time with Olivia. I'll be back right quick."

"I don't believe you."

"Mother," Olivia said, "get the phone."

"No!" Bernie's command stopped Sylvia mid-pivot. "Believe me, you'll want to call the cops in a moment. Once you hear what Belinda has to say."

"Bernie, please," Belinda protested. Tears ran down her face.

Bernie's eyes danced with sick excitement. "It's never gonna be easy, Belinda.

You may as well just say it. These people are your friends. Do you really want to see Sylvia pay for a crime you committed?"

Olivia quickly swept Belinda into her arms, pulling her further away from Bernie. "Okay, Bernie. We won't call the cops," she lied. His ass was going straight to jail the moment she had the chance to get him arrested. "But you have to promise to stay away from Belinda. Your marriage is over. Let her go peacefully."

Bernie ignored Olivia. His attention was solely on Belinda. "You are gonna tell them the truth, aren't you, baby? Isn't that why you came over here?"

Olivia's gaze bounced from Bernie to Belinda to her mother—and stopped. Something about her mother's expression made her stomach flutter with an odd sensation.

Sylvia wouldn't take her eyes off Belinda. She stared at her with a mix of disbelief and horror.

Why? Olivia whipped her gaze to Bernie. He was entirely too smug for a guy who would be facing assault charges.

What had he said? Something about Belinda not letting Sylvia pay for a crime she had committed?

Olivia's gut wrenched, as if someone had struck her.

Oh, God.

"Tell them, baby. You have five seconds."

Olivia gripped Belinda by the shoulders. The thought running through her mind was inconceivable. Impossible. Completely out of the question.

"Belinda, I don't know what's going on here," Olivia said. "But I know that whatever Bernie is implying is a lie. It's sick. It's a friggin' ploy to make you stay with him. But you don't need to be afraid of him anymore."

Belinda didn't respond. She wouldn't stop crying.

"Belinda." Sylvia spoke calmly. "Belinda, look at me." Belinda raised her head only slightly. "Tell me. Was it you? All these years?"

"Don't fall for what Bernie's saying," Olivia told her mother. "The man is clearly insane. Look what he's done to Belinda!"

"Answer me, Belinda." Sylvia's tone was gentle, but it had an eerie undertone. "Please."

Belinda slapped her hands against her head and wailed. "It was an accident. I never meant for it to happen. Damn it, Bernie. You know that!"

"No!" Olivia's stomach heaved, forcing a trace of warm vomit into her mouth. "Bernie's lying. He's beat her so badly she'll say anything to get away from him."

"That's not true, Liv," Belinda said.

"You killed Liza." Sylvia spoke in a deadpan voice.

" 'Course she didn't! Don't let Bernie get you caught up in this lie."

Sylvia came alive. She marched toward Belinda, her eyes wide and angry. "You tell me. Tell me!"

"It was an accident." Belinda covered her face as deep sobs shook her body.

Lord, no. Please not this.

Olivia looked at the woman she'd called a friend for most of her life and realized she was a stranger.

Sniveling, Belinda wiped her face. "I didn't murder her. She just . . . she died. We were fighting . . . because of Bernie," she added with disgust. "She'd been hitting on him, and I was angry. I didn't want her taking my man. It seems so foolish now, so senseless, but I was young, and in love for the first time. She followed me out of the club and kept arguing with me, getting up in my face. Next thing I know, we're in an all-out brawl. I managed to get away, but somehow she fell. She hit her head on the edge of the sidewalk. And then she wasn't moving. Wasn't breathing. I was so scared."

This was too incredible to believe. Too awful. Belinda wasn't capable of this.

"Bernie's the one who said I should hide the body, that no one would understand it was an accident."

Somehow, Olivia found a voice to ask the question, "You killed Liza?"

"It was an accident."

"Don't tell me that." Olivia's head shook. Her whole body shook. "I need to hear you say it."

Belinda looked Olivia dead in the eye. "I killed her, Liv. It was me. All this time, it was me."

CHAPTER FIFTY-SIX

Bernie's smile was victorious. "See, Belinda. That wasn't so hard."

"No," Olivia moaned. Her eyes flitted between Bernie and Belinda. "Why are you saying this? You couldn't kill Liza. You know you couldn't."

"I didn't want to. I didn't mean to. But, God forgive me, I did. And it was the one thing Bernie had over me all these years, his trump card. He could beat me, and I couldn't leave him. Because if I did, he'd have me arrested and thrown in jail. That's what he told me time and time again."

Belinda sobbed softly. "I have kids, Liv. How could I go to jail? So I stayed. Put up with it. But then . . ." Belinda's eyes went to Sylvia, then back to Olivia. Finally, her gaze fell on Bernie. "I couldn't do it, Bernie. I just couldn't."

Bernie moved forward with lightning speed and punched Belinda in the face. She cried out and flew backward.

Olivia screamed. "Mother! Get the phone!"

"Go for the phone, and you die."

When Sylvia didn't move, Olivia spun around and began to run. The sound of a gun cocking stopped her dead in her tracks.

"Turn around," Bernie instructed her. "Nice and slow."

Though she knew what she'd heard, seeing the gun leveled on her made her whole body tingle with dread.

"No more games," Bernie said. "All of you. In the living room. Now."

Belinda didn't move. Bernie nudged her body with his foot. She didn't budge. Then he kicked her. Still she didn't flinch.

"Seems Belinda's no longer with us."

"No!" Olivia burst into tears.

"You take the body," Bernie told Olivia. "Drag her into the living room. I'm not taking any chances."

Olivia's nerves were stinging so bad it felt like her body had short-circuited. She couldn't tell her hand from her foot.

"*Now.*"

She tried to get her brain to work. Then almost lost it when she looked down at Belinda's still body.

Bernie placed the gun against her temple. "In case you haven't figured it out, I'm pretty fucked up. Don't give me a reason to use this."

Olivia jolted into action. She bent and took Belinda's hands in hers, then struggled to drag her body into the living room.

While Olivia bawled, Sylvia didn't say a word. But her mother looked like she might pass out any minute.

"Mama, sit," Olivia told her through her tears. "You have a bad heart."

The alarm system beeped as the front door opened. Bernie whirled around. Edward drew up short as he appeared at the entrance to the living room.

Bernie aimed the gun at him and fired.

This time, Sylvia joined Olivia in screaming as the two women watched Edward topple backward, then fall into a heap on the floor.

Professor Jackson said good-bye to the last of the students who had been lingering around, then turned to Rachelle. "Rachelle." He grinned. "What can I do you for?"

Rachelle blew out a frazzled breath. "I really hate to do this, but I need an extension on my paper."

He stared at her with concern. "Is there a problem?"

"Yes." Rachelle sighed. "It's personal," she added quickly. "I know that may seem like a flimsy excuse, but I really can't say more than that. I'm hoping you'll trust me."

Professor Jackson glanced around. When the last of the chatting stragglers exited the lecture hall, he faced Rachelle once more. "Can we sit down?"

"Uh . . ." Rachelle really wasn't in the mood for a sermon on why she should be punctual in meeting her deadlines. "If you don't mind, I'd kinda like your answer without any speeches."

Surprising her, the professor laughed softly. "Is my reputation that bad?"

Rachelle smiled sheepishly.

"Don't worry, I'll spare you the speech. And yes, you can have two more weeks to finish your paper. Is that enough time?"

"Plenty. Thank you."

"Great. Now if you have a minute, I need to speak with you about something else."

Rachelle shrugged. "Okay."

Professor Jackson gestured to the first row of seats. Rachelle sat, and he sat beside her.

He began without preamble. "Your mother hasn't told you about me, has she?"

Rachelle flashed him an odd look. "No. She was supposed to?"

"Yeah." The professor sighed his disappointment. "Well, I was hoping, anyway."

His jaw hardened, and it was clear to Rachelle that he was upset. She went on carefully. "What, Professor Jackson? What were you hoping she would tell me?"

"We're lovers, Rachelle."

Rachelle gaped at him. "You and my mother?"

"At least we were," he added, frowning.

"*What?*"

"Our relationship started a long time ago. Nearly thirty years. Another lifetime. Your grandmother hired me to do some work at her house. That's when I met Olivia and fell in love with her."

God, how could she have been so naive? He had asked about her mother weeks ago. How could she have not realized why? "You're telling me that you and my mother are seeing each other now?"

"We got involved again, yes. But we're having a disagreement about something. Namely, her telling you about us."

"Whoa." Rachelle didn't know how to process what she'd just been told.

"Your grandmother never approved of our relationship. She doesn't want us seeing each other now. That's why your mother's been hesitant to tell you. When I say your grandmother didn't approve . . . she went to extreme lengths to make sure I was out of the picture.

"That's all a story your mother can tell you when she's ready. The bigger issue is that I love her. And I don't feel comfortable doing so from a distance. That's why I wanted to let you know what was going on. If I'm going to be part of her life, I want you to know about it."

Professor Jackson and her mother were lovers. Rachelle tried to digest the information.

"Your mother's probably going to be mad at me for telling you this . . . oh, well. I couldn't deal with the secrecy any longer."

"I . . . I don't know what to say."

"Your mother's concerned that our dating will be an issue for you, but I'm hoping it won't be."

"Professor Jackson—"

"No, let me finish. Given what I've just told you, I understand you may have reservations about staying in this class. That's another reason I wanted to let you know what's going on. I'm sure you can switch to another class if you want, but I wanted to assure you that I can and will remain objective where you're concerned—no matter how my relationship with your mother goes."

Rachelle liked him. He had wise eyes and a gentle spirit. Much like her father, she realized.

More important, she believed him. "I don't think that's necessary."

His audible exhalation told her how nervous he had been. "Thank you."

"And for what it's worth, you seem like a nice guy. Much better than most of the guys my mother has dated in the past."

"Really, now?" Professor Jackson laughed, and his eyes lit up. In his eyes, Rachelle could see his love for her mother.

"Yeah."

His laughter faded. "That's good to hear."

"I wish she'd told me."

"This has been hard for her."

"Not now," Rachelle explained. "Told me about you before. Maybe after my father had died. It would have helped me understand so much. Stuff that makes perfect sense now."

"Like?"

"Like why she couldn't give her heart to him."

"Ooh," the professor said softly.

"I always knew something was off in their relationship. My father was openly affectionate with her, but she wasn't with him. And it bothered me for so long. Maybe if I had known about the great love of her life, I would have been able to deal with it better."

"You sound . . . very mature."

"I appreciate you telling me."

Professor Jackson groaned. "Your mother probably won't appreciate it. In fact, we had a fight about it. She's already mad at me."

This man was good for her mother. Rachelle knew it in her soul. "We'll just have to change that, won't we?"

"Ha. If only it were that easy."

"If anyone knows how hard it is to get through to my mother, it's me." And if there was one thing Rachelle had learned, she was more like her mother than she ever would have imagined. She was hardheaded and stubborn, and she wasn't open with her emotions.

But she was ready for a new beginning. Nadine and Allette had reached out to her in her time of pain, accepting her despite her mistakes. Maybe it was time she do the same with her mother and work toward putting the past behind them.

"See?"

"But," Rachelle said, holding up a hand. "That doesn't mean it's impossible. And it sounds to me like she's got a soft spot where you're concerned."

"I'm open to suggestions."

"Well, I think you ought to go to her—say, tonight—and work out your differences."

"Tonight?"

"Yeah. I was on my way home now to have a chat with my mother and grandmother. Why don't you join me? We can all sit down and talk. If there's anything I've learned, it's that keeping things inside causes more problems in the long run."

"You're a bright girl, Rachelle. You'll do well in this class."

"But it doesn't hurt that my mom's dating my professor," she replied, smiling playfully.

"Smart and witty, too."

Rachelle savored the compliment. It felt like the dark cloud over her head was finally moving away. She was coming out of her shell and seeing the person she wanted to be.

And while she never would have imagined it, she was happy to be at Dillard.

Edward, no." Sylvia couldn't stop her tears. After all these years together, after all these years of loving her, Edward was gone.

"He was an old man," Olivia said, angry, though she was crying. "Why'd you have to kill him?"

"He had one foot in the grave, anyway."

Sylvia balled her hands into fists at her sides. She felt helpless. "You are an evil, evil man."

Bernie *tsk*ed. "Is that any way for you to greet your only son?"

Sylvia's next breath died in her throat. She gaped at Bernie, too stunned to say a thing.

One day, when you least expect it, he will come into your life.

Dear God, no.

"That's right, *Mama*." Bernie flashed an evil grin.

"Oh, my God."

Bernie slapped the gun against his palm in a steady, chilling rhythm. Sylvia was all too aware that at any minute it could go off, ending her life.

"All this time," Bernie began, "I'd hoped you would recognize me. I saw you often enough. But every time you looked at me, there was nothing in your eyes. Nothing."

Her son. This . . . this monster? She moaned as reality crashed down on her shoulders.

"You know, Mama, I was kind of hoping you'd have a lot more than that to say to me. Like why you gave me up."

Sylvia's head was swimming. This was her son. The baby she'd had in that dark carriage house. The one her mother had forced her to give up. What kind of life had he led? What had driven him to madness?

Bernie slowly walked toward her. "Tell me. That's all I want to know. Why'd you give me up like I was worthless?"

"I never thought you were worthless. Never, not even for a second." Sylvia cried softly. "I didn't give you up because I wanted to. But at that time . . . I was so young, and my mother . . . she took you right after you were born. She didn't let me see you."

"You didn't fight for me."

"I wanted to," Sylvia said, remembering that awful time. "But my mother wouldn't let me see you. There was nothing I could do."

Bernie continued the annoying gun-slapping against his palm. "Do you know what happened to me, Mama? Do you?" Bernie shouted.

"I . . . no. I never knew. But I wanted to. I prayed so many nights that you were okay."

"You did, huh?"

"Yes. Of course."

"Well, I wasn't okay!" Bernie shouted at the top of his lungs. His chest heaved with each labored breath. "Because you gave me up, I ended up in a foster home where the daddy's idea of fatherly love wasn't exactly what anyone would call conventional. He believed in coming into my room at night and making me do things to him . . ."

Sylvia threw a hand to her mouth. "Oh, God."

"Yeah, I called out to God so many times when I was in that house, and you know what? It was pointless. God didn't answer one of my prayers."

This was her fault. She was to blame for what he'd become.

"You have to believe me," Sylvia said. "If I ever, ever had any idea that anything like that would happen to you, I would have dealt with the shame—"

"The shame of being a whore?"

"I . . . it wasn't like that."

"I was a baby. A helpless baby. My mother was supposed to protect me from evil, but where were you? Pretending I never existed."

Sylvia sobbed. "My mother made me do it . . ." But she could have fought her. Or she could have run away. Run away from her mother's strict household so that she could raise the baby she had so deeply grown to love in her womb.

"But I dealt with all the shit. I dealt with not having a mother. I grew up knowing I had to depend on me." Bernie walked a few steps, closing the distance between them. "I grew up hating whores. Hating myself for what had been done to me. Do you know what that's like, to hate yourself for something someone else made you do?"

"Yes, I do know," Sylvia answered easily. "I was never proud of how I let my mother take you away. That first night you were gone, I wanted to die. I tried to kill myself. I went right into the bayou, wanting to drown. But they dragged me out."

"I tried to forgive you," Bernie went on, walking slowly toward the large window. He was lost in his own world. "I put you behind me. Then I finally met a woman who loved me, who needed me. I made a difference in her life. For once, I felt good about myself.

"Like me, she'd been in and out of foster homes. And she'd been molested, too. Her stepfather. Stepbrothers. Anyone who wanted to put their filthy hands on her. We understood each other. I thought we were gonna get married. But she was so messed up, so messed up because of the abuse, and in the end, she was too screwed up even to be happy. She broke up with me. Left me and ran right into the hands of a man who killed her."

Bernie peered outside, then spun around. He ignored Olivia, his eyes narrowing in on Sylvia. "I started looking for you right after that. I realized that you needed to die. People like you needed to die. You live your lives in boutiques and hair salons, driving fancy cars, not giving a shit about whose lives you've messed up. You thought your judgment day would never come, but you were wrong, *Mama*. You were wrong."

Bernie leveled the gun on her.

Olivia gasped in horror. Sylvia closed her eyes, awaiting her death. *Let it be quick, Lord.*

"Please," Olivia said. "You don't want to do this."

"I had nothing, Olivia. Nothing! While you had everything. A happy household with a mother who loved you, and I had *nothing.*"

Sylvia opened her eyes. She stifled a cry when she saw that Bernie was now standing before Olivia.

"You have no excuse for being a whore," he said to Olivia. "Not like my Celine. You grew up with privilege. Yet you turned into a dirty slut anyway."

He faced Sylvia. "Maybe she couldn't help it, having a mother like you."

Sylvia said a silent prayer. For atonement. She had ruined her son's life, and to some extent her daughter's. *Dear Lord, let there be peace once I'm gone. Forgive me for my weakness, but don't punish others for it any longer. And forgive Bernie. He's confused. And he's hurt.*

"Open your eyes."

Sylvia did as she was told.

"I want you looking at me when I kill you."

"No, Bernie," Olivia begged.

The alarm system beeped. Bernie spun in the direction of the door. *Rachelle!*

Olivia didn't think. She lunged on Bernie's back. She clawed at his eyes, and he roared in pain. But he fought her, wringing his body back and forth while moving backward, trying to get Olivia off him. Still, Olivia held on.

Bernie lifted the gun, blindly trying to aim for Olivia's head.

Sylvia grabbed his arm and clenched her teeth into his wrist.

"Grandma!"

The gun went off. Rachelle screamed as the bullet whizzed across the room and went into the wall. Continued screaming as her grandmother hit the floor.

Harvey took only a second to assess the situation. Then he dove into the melee. Olivia was wrapped around Bernie and not letting go, but he still had the gun.

His finger pulled the trigger.

"Get down, Rachelle!" Harvey yelled a moment before the shot went off.

Harvey grabbed Bernie's wrist. The son of a bitch wouldn't release his hold on the gun. Blood streamed down his face, and Harvey didn't even know if the man could see.

Gripping Bernie's arm with both hands, Harvey brought it down hard on his knee. Damn, it hurt, but Harvey ignored his own pain. He kneed him again. Another round went off, spewing drywall.

"Son of a—"

Harvey twisted Bernie's hand, but Bernie yanked his arm free. The effort threw him off balance, and Bernie fell backward. With Olivia still hanging on to him, his body slammed into the large window. The glass made a tremendous crashing sound as it broke.

Olivia screamed as she flew through the window.

"Olivia!" Harvey watched in helpless horror. He wanted to run to her, but one glance at Bernie told him that would be suicide.

Bernie still had the gun. Damn the man!

"You're all gonna die." Bernie wheezed from the effort to speak. He was winded, but he was still a danger.

Without the gun, Harvey could take him. With the gun . . .

Bernie swiped at the blood dripping in his eyes. He squinted as he opened them.

"Say your prayers, Mama," Bernie said, turning to her. "I'll allow you that."

From her spot on the floor, Sylvia clasped her hands together. Harvey watched her, feeling utterly useless.

The loud thud made him look up. Bernie's body wobbled, then he fell face forward. His head clipped the side of the marble coffee table, and a horrible cracking sound filled the room.

Bernie's body came to rest on the floor, his head at an unnatural angle.

Still, Harvey was almost afraid to take his eyes off the man. But he did. He glanced up once again. Belinda stood, her hands holding what looked to be a marble sculpture of the globe.

"It's over, you son of a bitch! It's over!"

Harvey dropped to his knees. He grabbed the gun first and shoved it aside. Holding Bernie's wrist, he checked for a pulse. He found none.

"Olivia."

He jumped to his feet and raced outside.

EPILOGUE

Olivia had broken her hip, but she would live. Harvey was going to make damn sure of that.

In the days since the awful event at the Grayson house, he had been with Olivia, Sylvia, and Rachelle every day. He was staying with them until he nursed Olivia back to good health. Then they were all moving.

The house had a lot of history for Sylvia, but she didn't want to live there anymore. Not after what had happened.

"I'll always look in that living room and see Edward's body," she had said. "See the life seeping out of him on the hardwood floor."

Harvey understood. They could only put the horrible incident behind them with a fresh start somewhere else.

Now, he looked down at the tray in his hands and wondered if he should enter the room. Olivia had been resting when he'd headed downstairs to prepare a snack for her, and she may have drifted into sleep.

He nudged the door with his shoulder.

"Hey, you."

Well, she was awake. He moved into the room, saying, "Hey, yourself."

Olivia strained to lean forward as he sat beside her on the bed. But she quickly fell backward, wincing in pain.

"Eh, eh. Don't move."

"I know." Olivia blew out a steady breath. "I keep forgetting. I can't wait till I'm out of this bed."

"In good time. When you're ready."

Her eyes danced as she regarded him. "What'd you bring for me?"

"A ham sandwich and some vegetable soup."

"You gonna feed me?"

He flashed her a lopsided grin. "I think you love having me wait on you hand and foot."

"You know it."

Harvey lifted half of the sandwich to Olivia's mouth. She took a bite.

"Mmm. This is so good."

"Thank you."

"Remember those days I would always make you lunch? Do you believe this is the same tray from back then?"

"Really?"

"Yeah," she said softly. "So much has changed, yet some things have stayed the same."

Silence fell between them. Harvey knew they were both thinking of all that had transpired three weeks ago.

"I still can't believe it. Bernie was my brother."

"I know. Truth is stranger than fiction."

"I want to hate him," Olivia went on. "For all he did. For killing Edward. But I can't. I think of all the things he said, the rough life he led, and I just feel sorry for him."

"Not everyone who has a hard life ends up like him. They don't use that as an excuse to hurt others."

"I know, but . . ." She sighed. "I think the only way I can really go on, make sense of any of this, is to forgive. There was so much anger with my mother. It was eating me up alive. But you know what? I understand why she kept all those secrets, even if in the end they came back to haunt her. She kept all that inside. I'm surprised she didn't have some kind of breakdown."

"Your mother's strong, Olivia."

"Yes, she is."

"And so are you. When you fell out that window, my heart stopped."

"So did mine." Olivia sighed. "It all seems like a dream, doesn't it?"

"I'm just glad it's over."

Olivia crossed her arms over her chest. "Rachelle and my mother left for church already?"

"Yeah."

"I wish I could have gone with them." And she meant it. She couldn't wait to step foot in church with her mother and daughter—as a family. If this experience had taught her one thing, it was that she needed to count her blessings.

"The church will be there when you get well."

"I know, but . . . it's funny how you can go to church for years but not really learn something till you live through something life-changing. I always heard people testifying, but it went through one ear and out the other. Talking about how when one window closed, God opened another one for them. But that's exactly what happened. The Lord opened a window. Out of this tragedy, we've gotten closer. We're a family again. I guess it's only natural, knowing what we almost lost. How could any of us remain angry after that?"

"There's nothing like a loss to make people start appreciating what they have."

"Poor Edward. God bless his soul. And poor Belinda."

"If you want my opinion, I don't think she'll do much time. Not if she gets a good lawyer, anyway. What happened years ago was a tragic accident, from what she described. Or self-defense. Had she come forward then, she probably would have gotten off."

"But she hid the body in the bayou."

"Because Bernie told her to do it. I'm betting he helped instigate that fight in the first place."

Harvey dipped the spoon into the soup, then brought it to Olivia's mouth. She sipped it.

"Promise me you'll never keep secrets from me," she said when she finished swallowing.

Lowering the spoon, Harvey stared at her. "You know I won't."

"Secrets never stay hidden. That's what I've learned from this. You're better off telling the truth."

"You think I want to confess something?"

Olivia's face grew serious as she looked at him. "Do you?"

"Now that you ask . . . I guess I do."

Olivia reached for Harvey's hand. She squeezed it hard. "What? Harvey, please tell me."

He paused. Sighed. Then he met her eyes and smiled. "I love you."

A beat, then, "Is that it?"

"Isn't that enough?"

Olivia laughed. "You are too silly."

"Yeah, well, get used to it. 'Cause I'm not going anywhere."

"You'd better not!"

He saluted her. "Okay, then."

"And you know what else?"

"What?"

Reaching for his shirt, Olivia pulled him toward her. The tray tilted, and the soup spilled onto her lap.

"Aw, sweetheart." Harvey pulled back, quickly grabbing up what he could.

"No. I'm okay." She pulled him toward her again. "Kiss me."

"Is that an order?"

"You're damn right it is."

"In that case . . ." Harvey's voice trailed off as Olivia planted her lips on his.

ABOUT THE AUTHOR

Kayla Perrin spends her time between Toronto and Miami. She has bachelor's degrees in English and sociology and a bachelor of education, having entertained the idea of becoming a teacher—but she always knew she wanted to be a writer.

In six years, she has had nineteen original releases published. An *Essence* bestselling author, she has received many awards for her writing, including twice winning the Romance Writers of America's Top Ten Favorite Books of the Year Award. She has also won a Career Achievement Award from *Romantic Times* magazine for multicultural romance.

You can visit Kayla's Web site at www.kaylaperrin.com.